THE TIME MUSEUM VOL. 2

Matthew Loux

First Second
NEW YORK

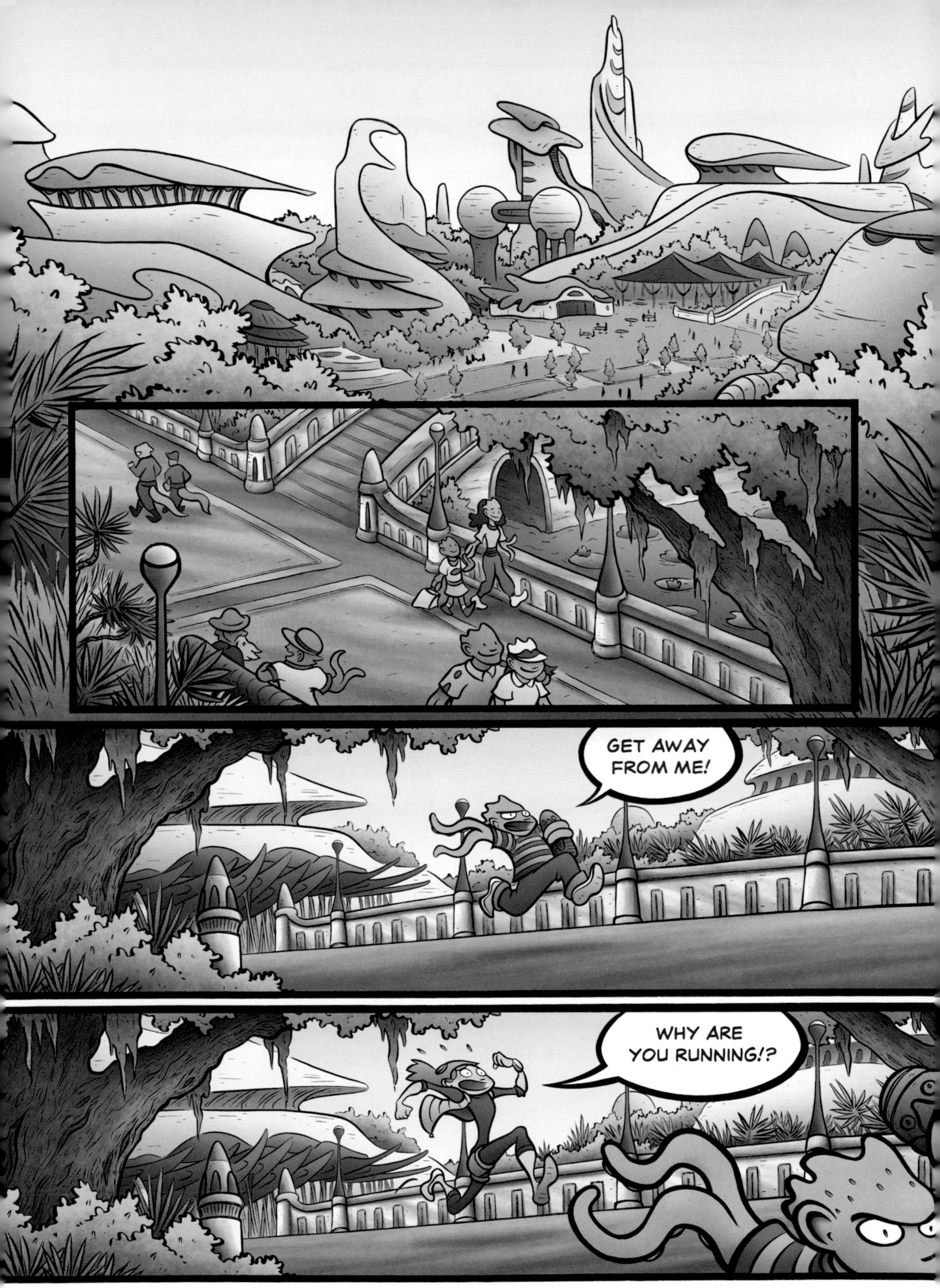
GET AWAY FROM ME!
WHY ARE YOU RUNNING!?

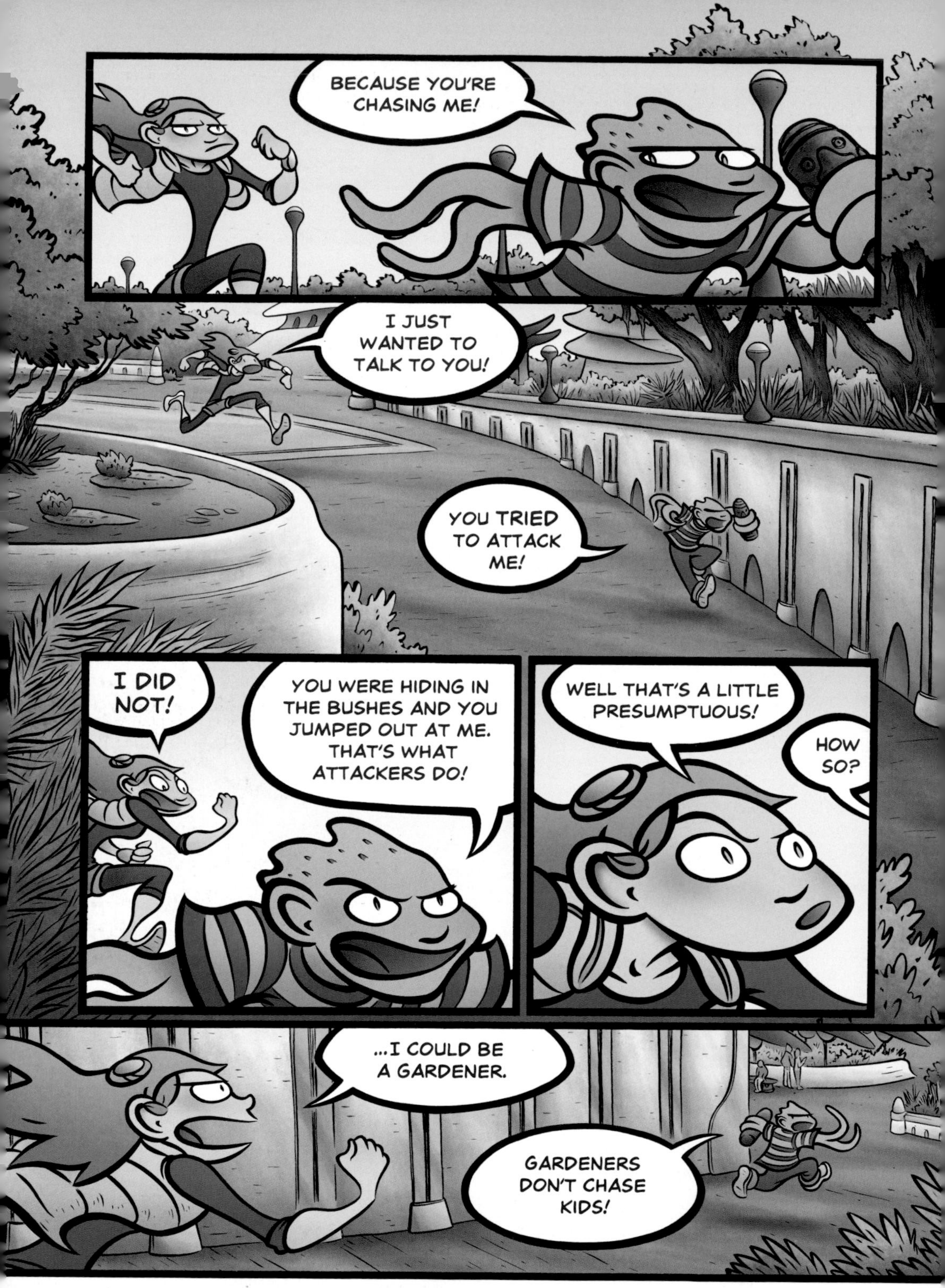
BECAUSE YOU'RE CHASING ME!
I JUST WANTED TO TALK TO YOU!
YOU TRIED TO ATTACK ME!
I DID NOT!
YOU WERE HIDING IN THE BUSHES AND YOU JUMPED OUT AT ME. THAT'S WHAT ATTACKERS DO!
WELL THAT'S A LITTLE PRESUMPTUOUS!
HOW SO?
...I COULD BE A GARDENER.
GARDENERS DON'T CHASE KIDS!

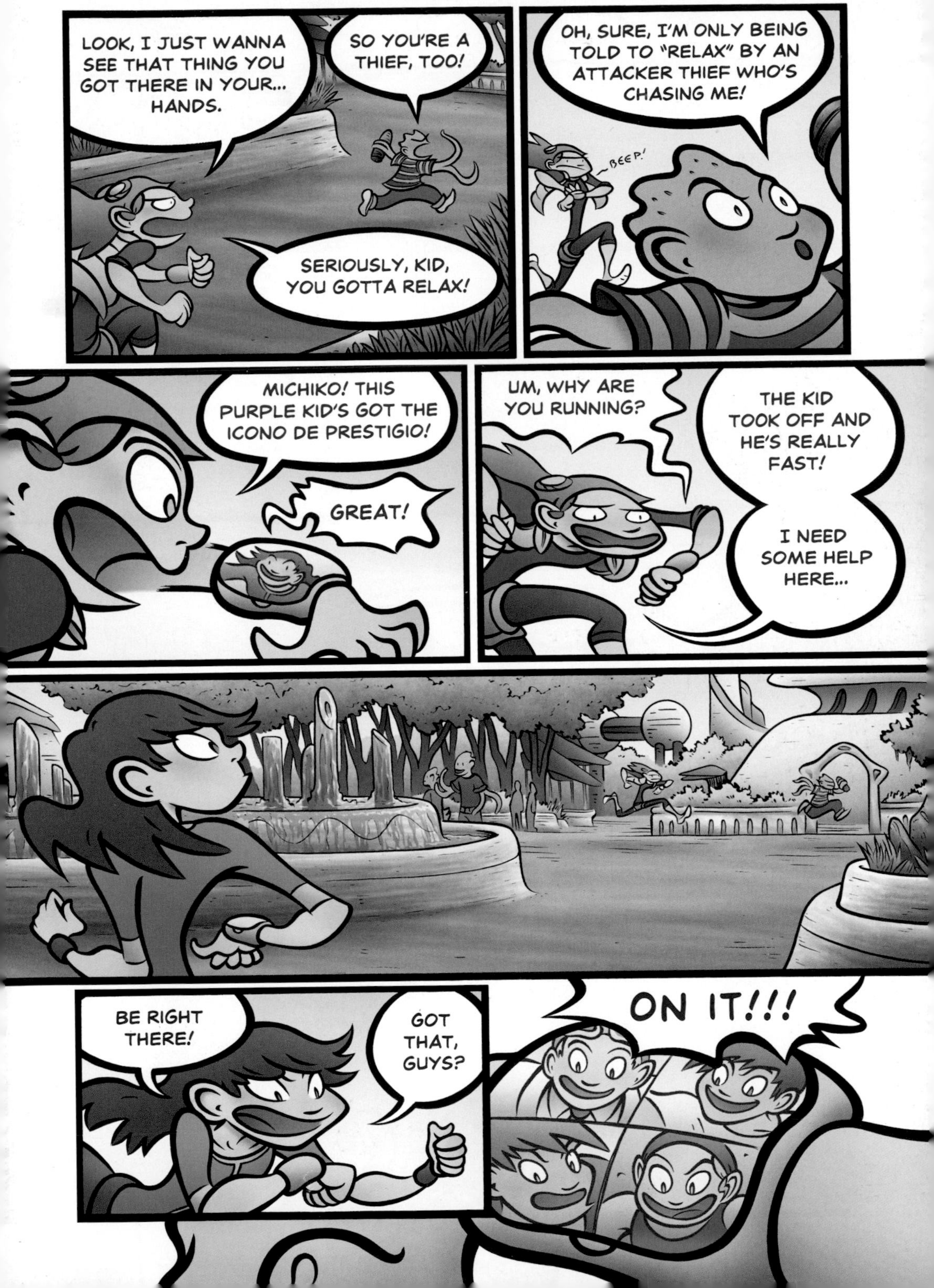
LOOK, I JUST WANNA SEE THAT THING YOU GOT THERE IN YOUR... HANDS.
SO YOU'RE A THIEF, TOO!
SERIOUSLY, KID, YOU GOTTA RELAX!
OH, SURE, I'M ONLY BEING TOLD TO "RELAX" BY AN ATTACKER THIEF WHO'S CHASING ME!
BEEP!
MICHIKO! THIS PURPLE KID'S GOT THE ICONO DE PRESTIGIO!
GREAT!
UM, WHY ARE YOU RUNNING?
THE KID TOOK OFF AND HE'S REALLY FAST!
I NEED SOME HELP HERE...
BE RIGHT THERE!
GOT THAT, GUYS?
ON IT!!!

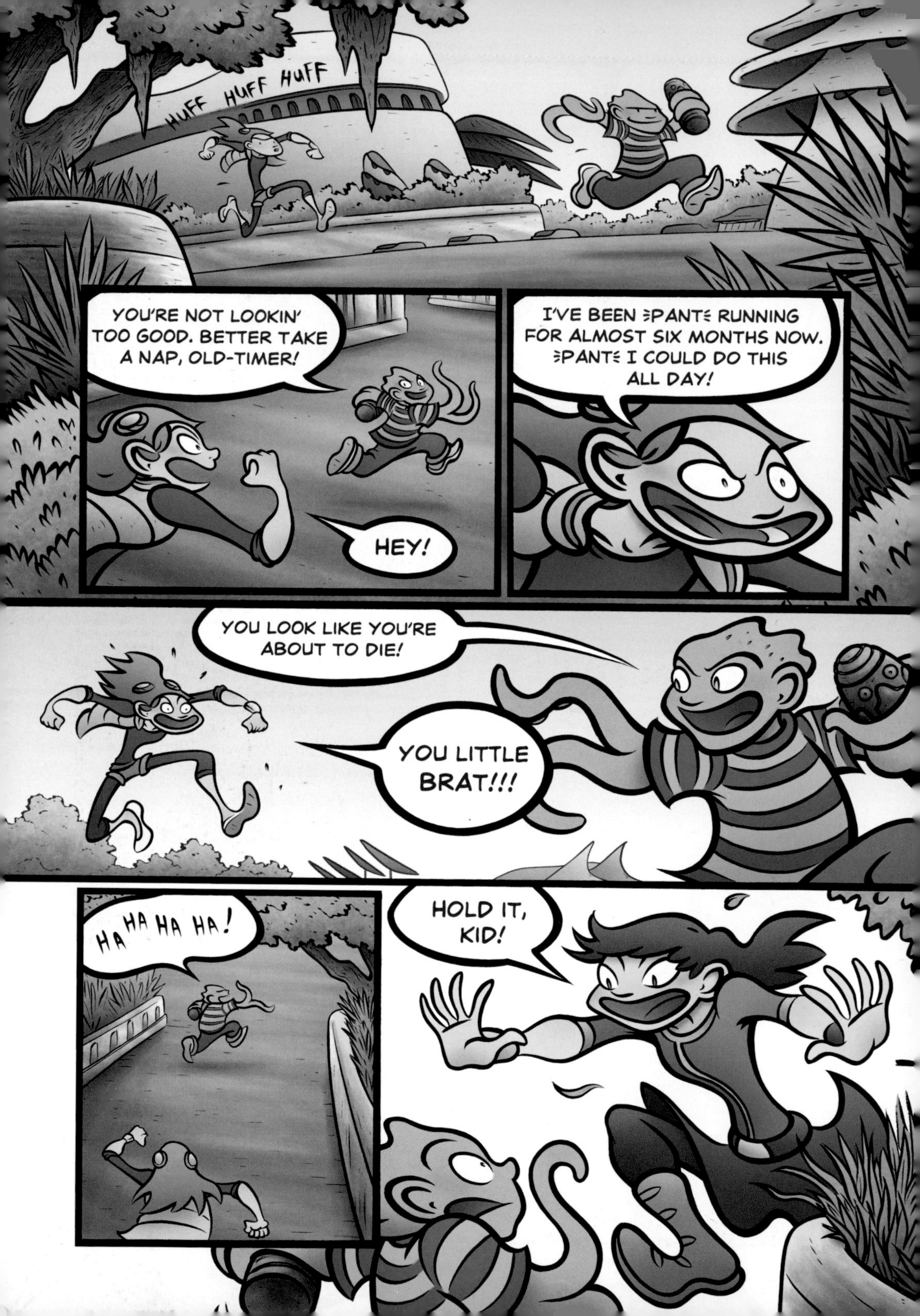
HUFF HUFF HUFF
YOU'RE NOT LOOKIN' TOO GOOD. BETTER TAKE A NAP, OLD-TIMER!
HEY!
I'VE BEEN ƎPANTƐ RUNNING FOR ALMOST SIX MONTHS NOW. ƎPANTƐ I COULD DO THIS ALL DAY!
YOU LOOK LIKE YOU'RE ABOUT TO DIE!
YOU LITTLE BRAT!!!
HA HA HA HA!
HOLD IT, KID!

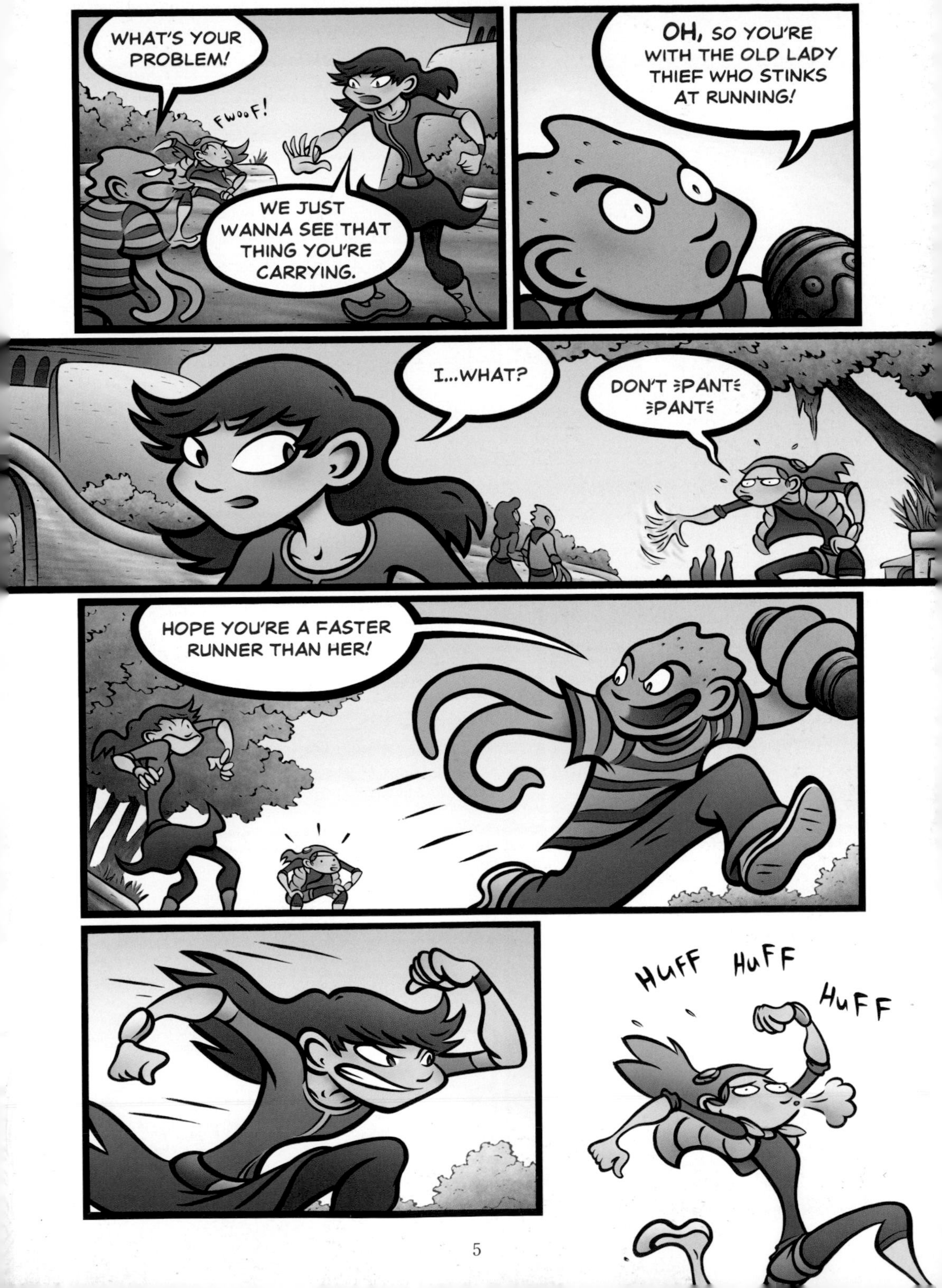
WHAT'S YOUR PROBLEM!
FWOOF!
WE JUST WANNA SEE THAT THING YOU'RE CARRYING.
OH, SO YOU'RE WITH THE OLD LADY THIEF WHO STINKS AT RUNNING!
I...WHAT?
DON'T ⋛PANT⋚ ⋛PANT⋚
HOPE YOU'RE A FASTER RUNNER THAN HER!
HUFF HUFF HUFF

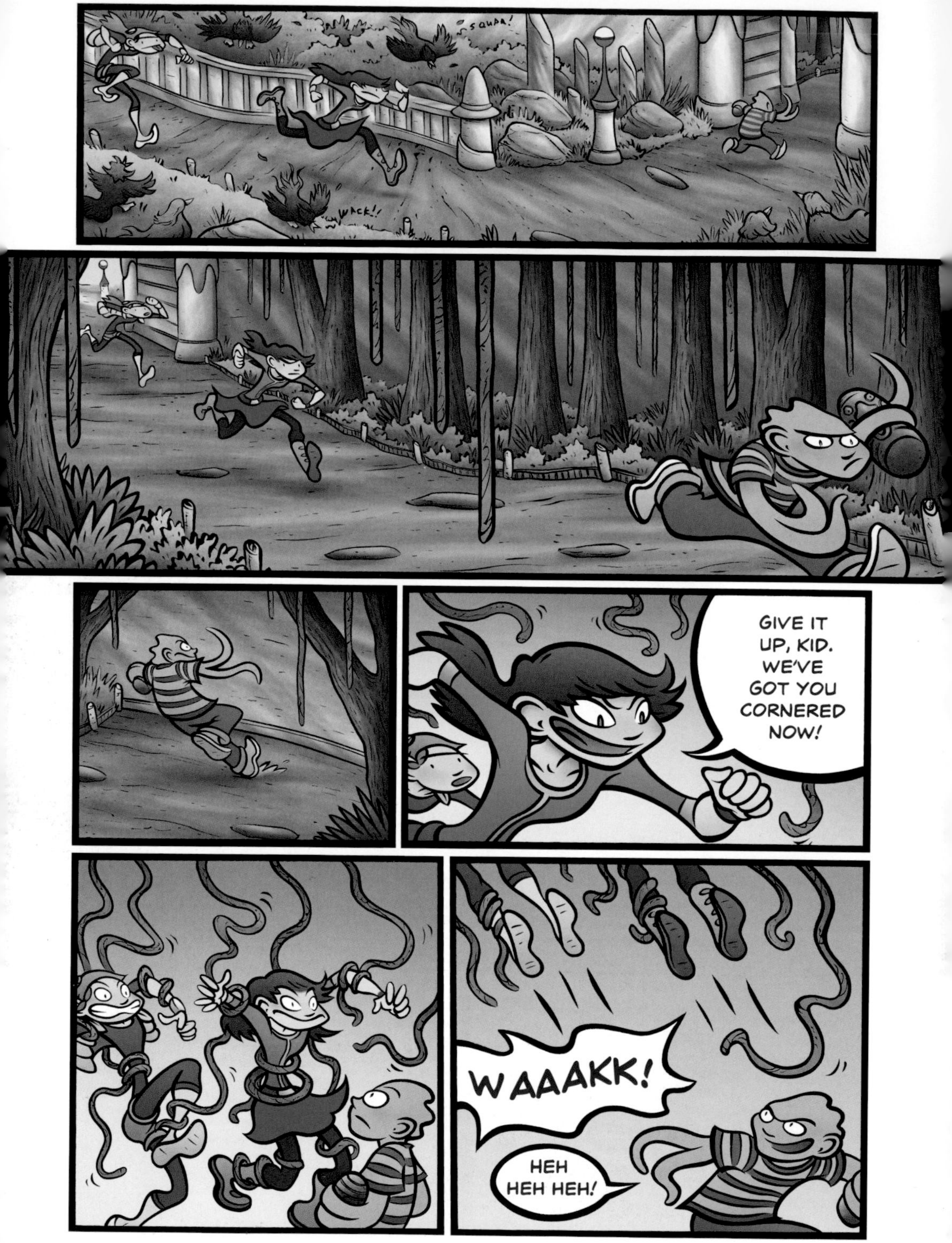
SQUAA!
WACK!!
GIVE IT UP, KID. WE'VE GOT YOU CORNERED NOW!
WAAAKK!
HEH HEH HEH!

WAIT, WHERE'D THEY GO?

I TRACKED THEM HERE, BUT NOW...

AH.

THE PURPLE KID WENT THAT WAY.

REGGIE, HELP UNTANGLE THEM. I'LL GET THE KID!

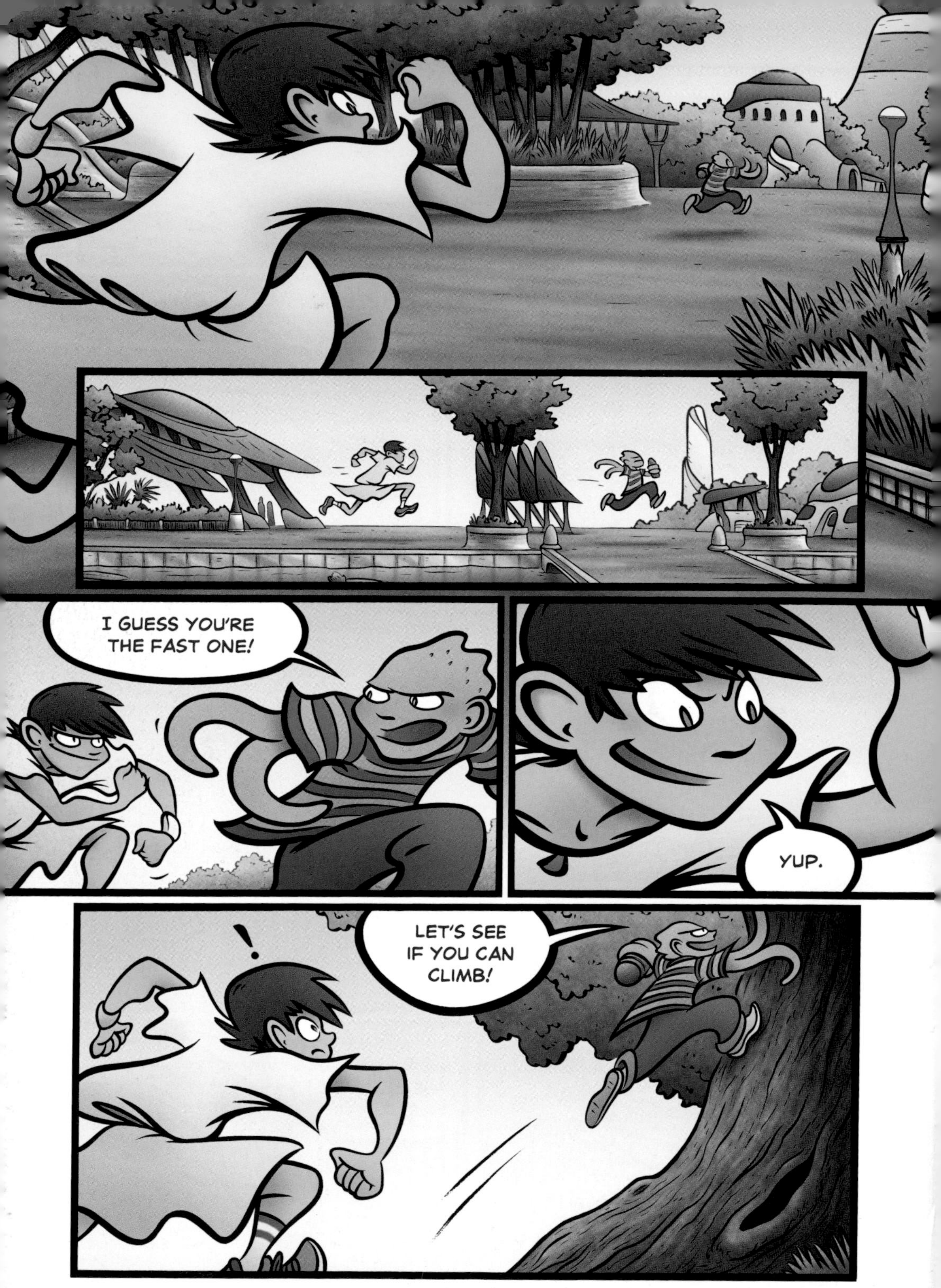
I GUESS YOU'RE THE FAST ONE!
YUP.
!
LET'S SEE IF YOU CAN CLIMB!

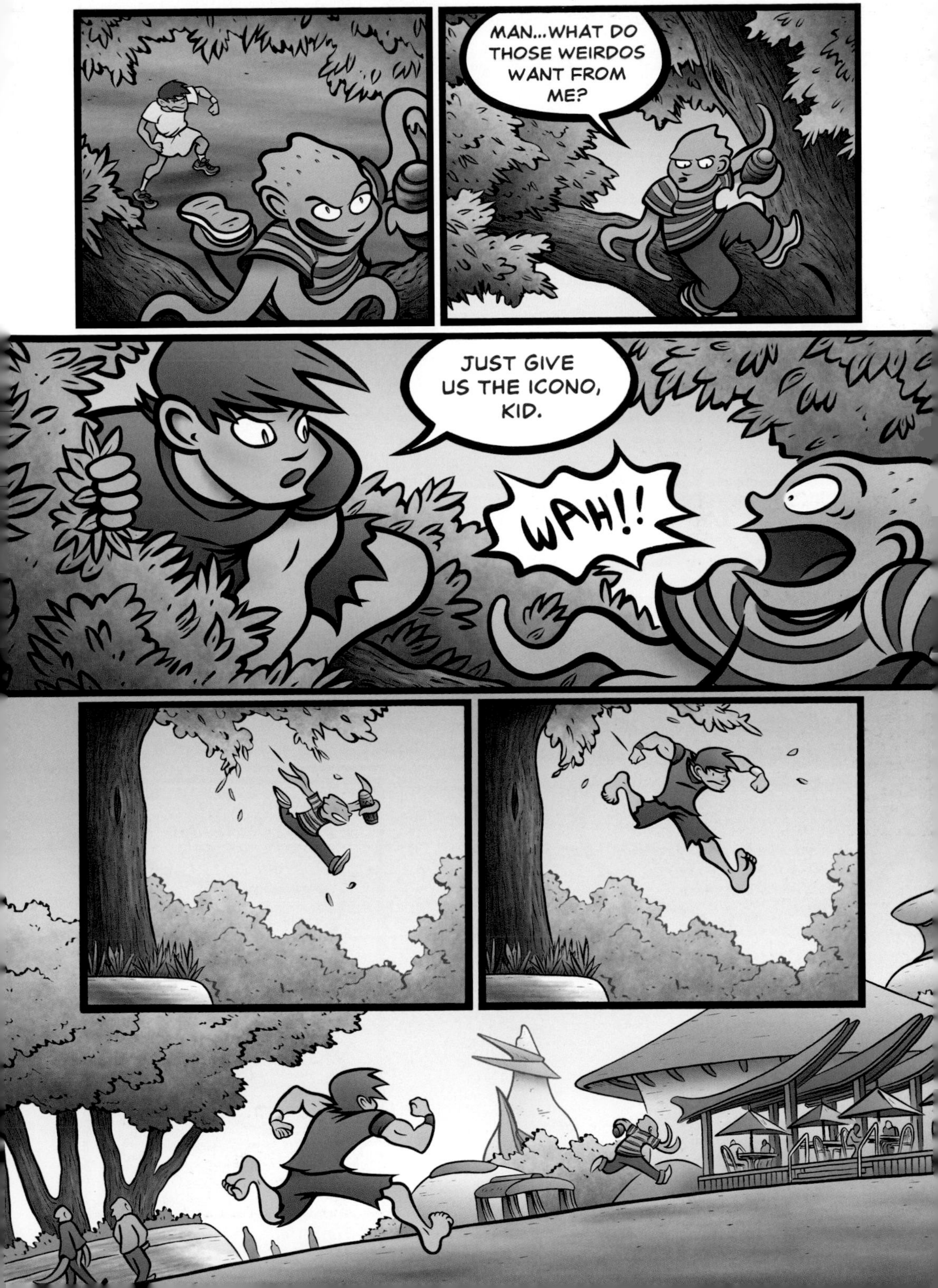
MAN...WHAT DO THOSE WEIRDOS WANT FROM ME?
JUST GIVE US THE ICONO, KID.
WAH!!

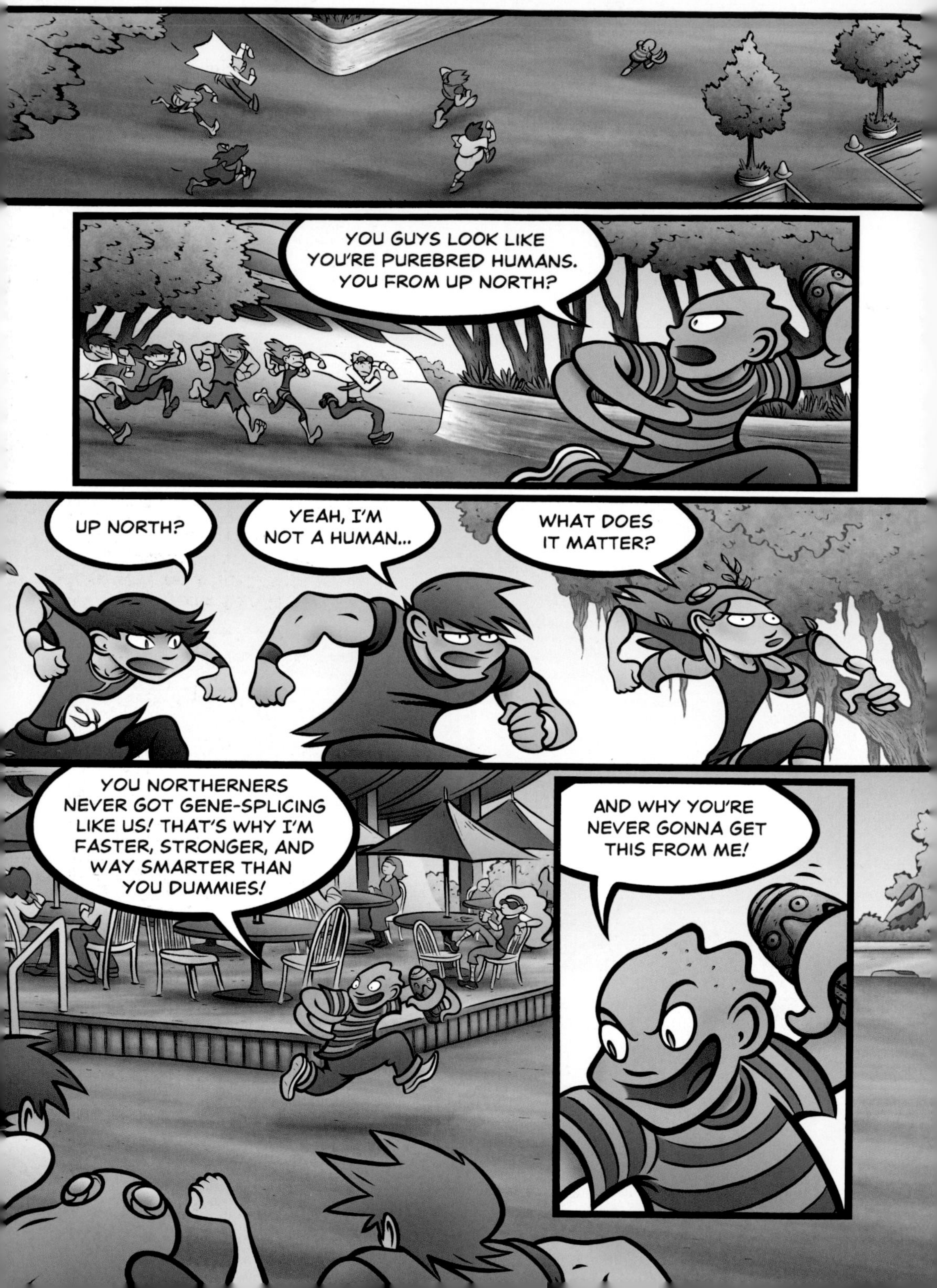
YOU GUYS LOOK LIKE YOU'RE PUREBRED HUMANS. YOU FROM UP NORTH?
UP NORTH?
YEAH, I'M NOT A HUMAN...
WHAT DOES IT MATTER?
YOU NORTHERNERS NEVER GOT GENE-SPLICING LIKE US! THAT'S WHY I'M FASTER, STRONGER, AND WAY SMARTER THAN YOU DUMMIES!
AND WHY YOU'RE NEVER GONNA GET THIS FROM ME!

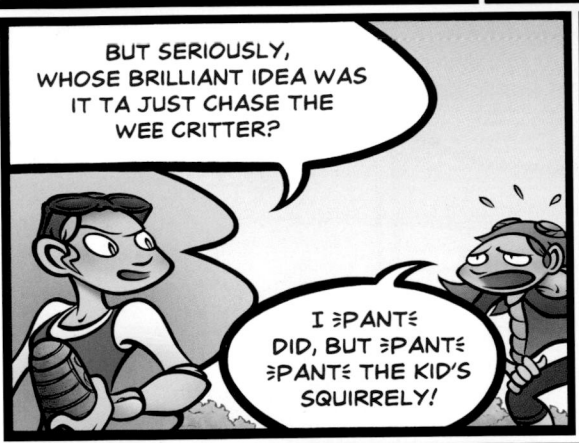

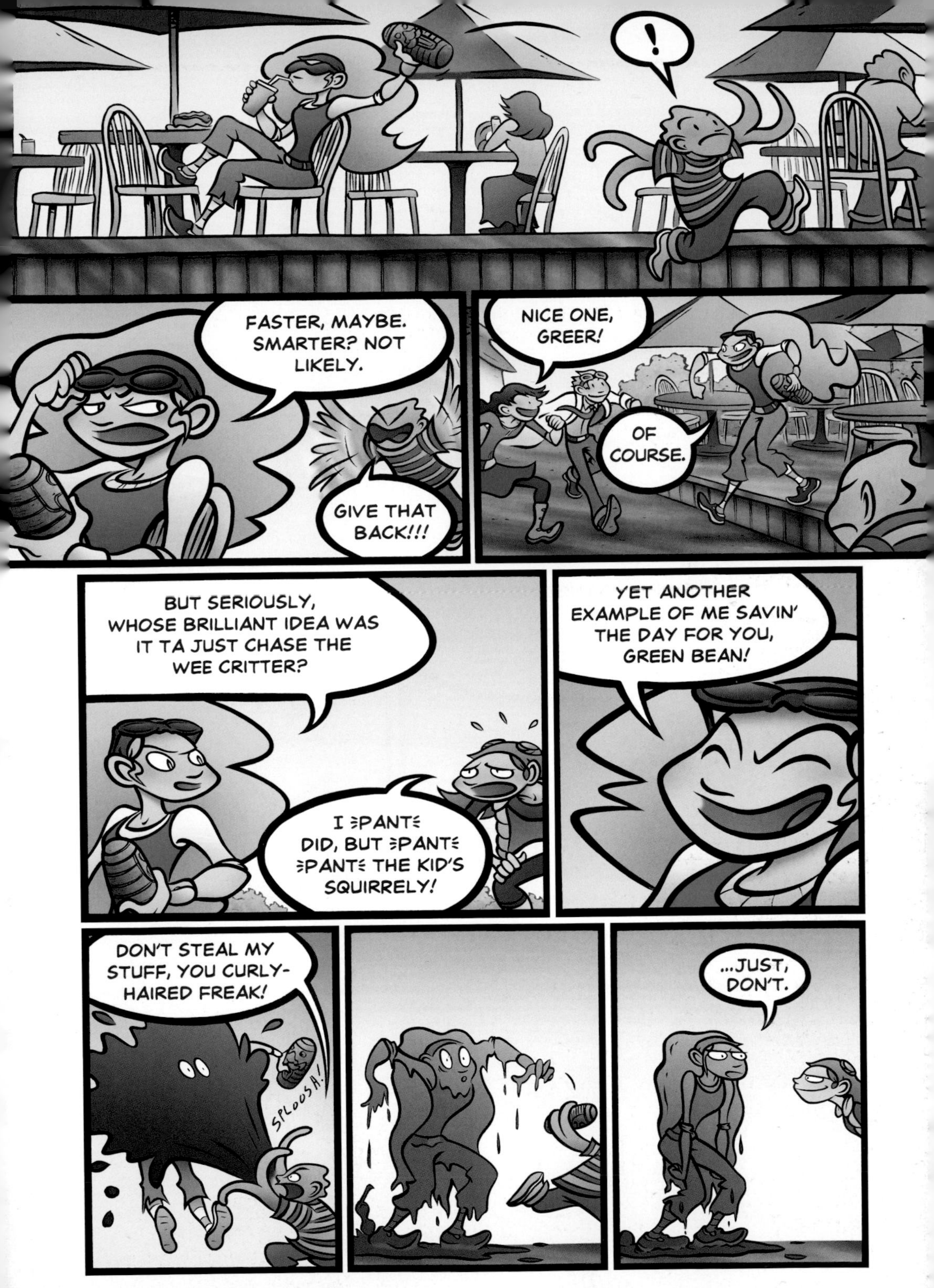
!
FASTER, MAYBE. SMARTER? NOT LIKELY.
GIVE THAT BACK!!!
NICE ONE, GREER!
OF COURSE.
BUT SERIOUSLY, WHOSE BRILLIANT IDEA WAS IT TA JUST CHASE THE WEE CRITTER?
I ≑PANT≑ DID, BUT ≑PANT≑ ≑PANT≑ THE KID'S SQUIRRELY!
YET ANOTHER EXAMPLE OF ME SAVIN' THE DAY FOR YOU, GREEN BEAN!
DON'T STEAL MY STUFF, YOU CURLY-HAIRED FREAK!
SPLOOSH!
...JUST, DON'T.

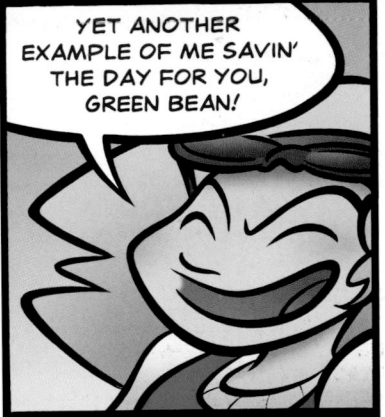

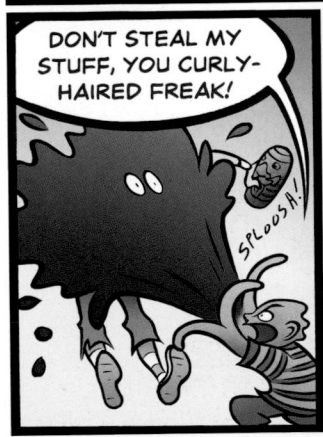

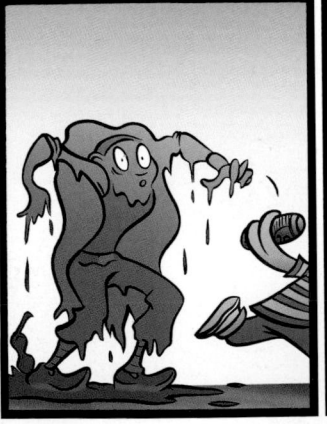

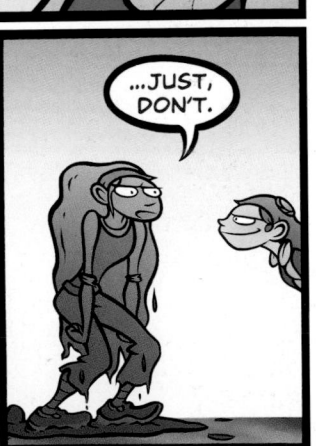

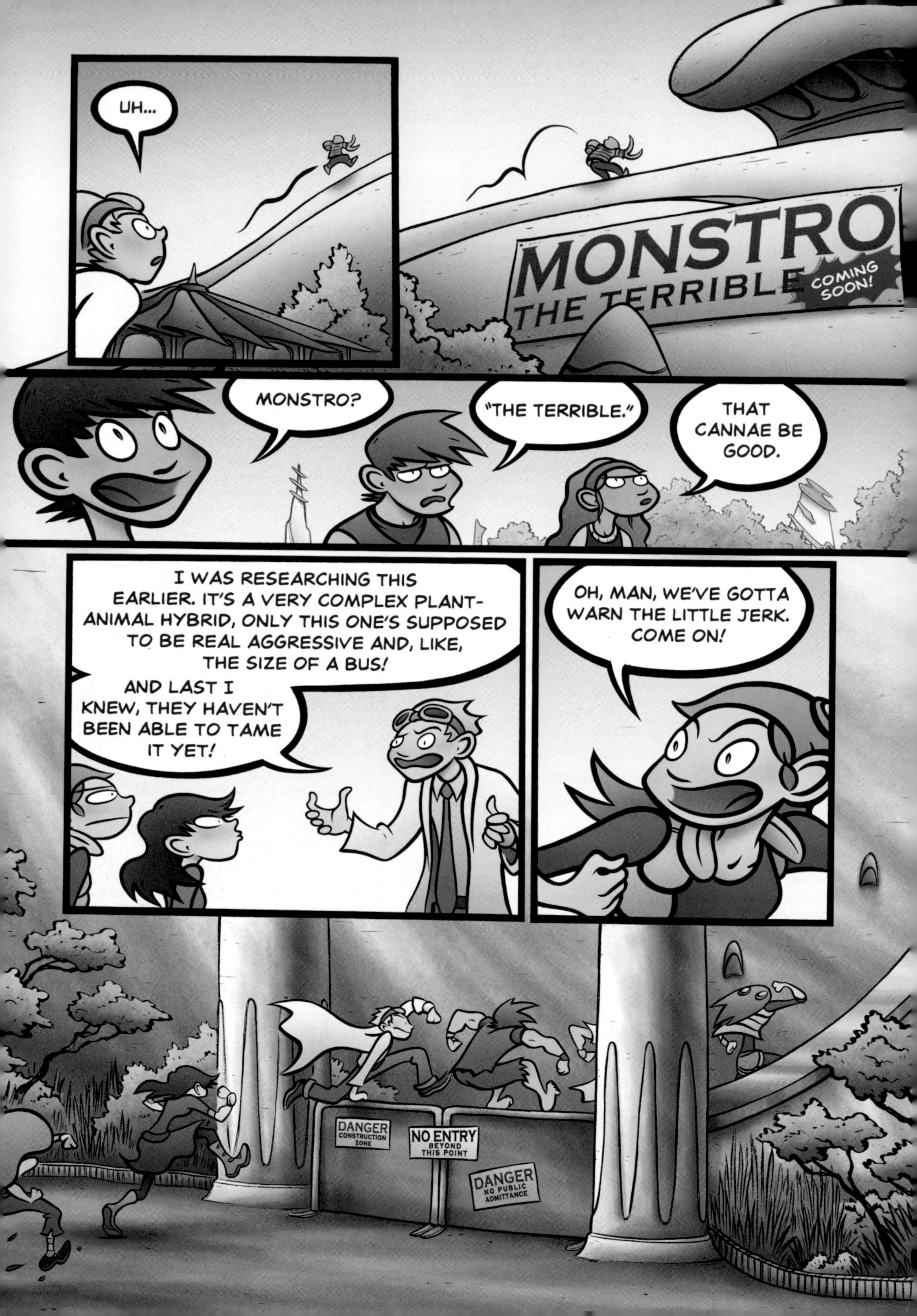
UH...
MONSTRO
THE TERRIBLE
COMING SOON!
MONSTRO?
"THE TERRIBLE."
THAT CANNAE BE GOOD.
I WAS RESEARCHING THIS EARLIER. IT'S A VERY COMPLEX PLANT-ANIMAL HYBRID, ONLY THIS ONE'S SUPPOSED TO BE REAL AGGRESSIVE AND, LIKE, THE SIZE OF A BUS!
AND LAST I KNEW, THEY HAVEN'T BEEN ABLE TO TAME IT YET!
OH, MAN, WE'VE GOTTA WARN THE LITTLE JERK. COME ON!
DANGER CONSTRUCTION ZONE
NO ENTRY BEYOND THIS POINT
DANGER NO PUBLIC ADMITTANCE

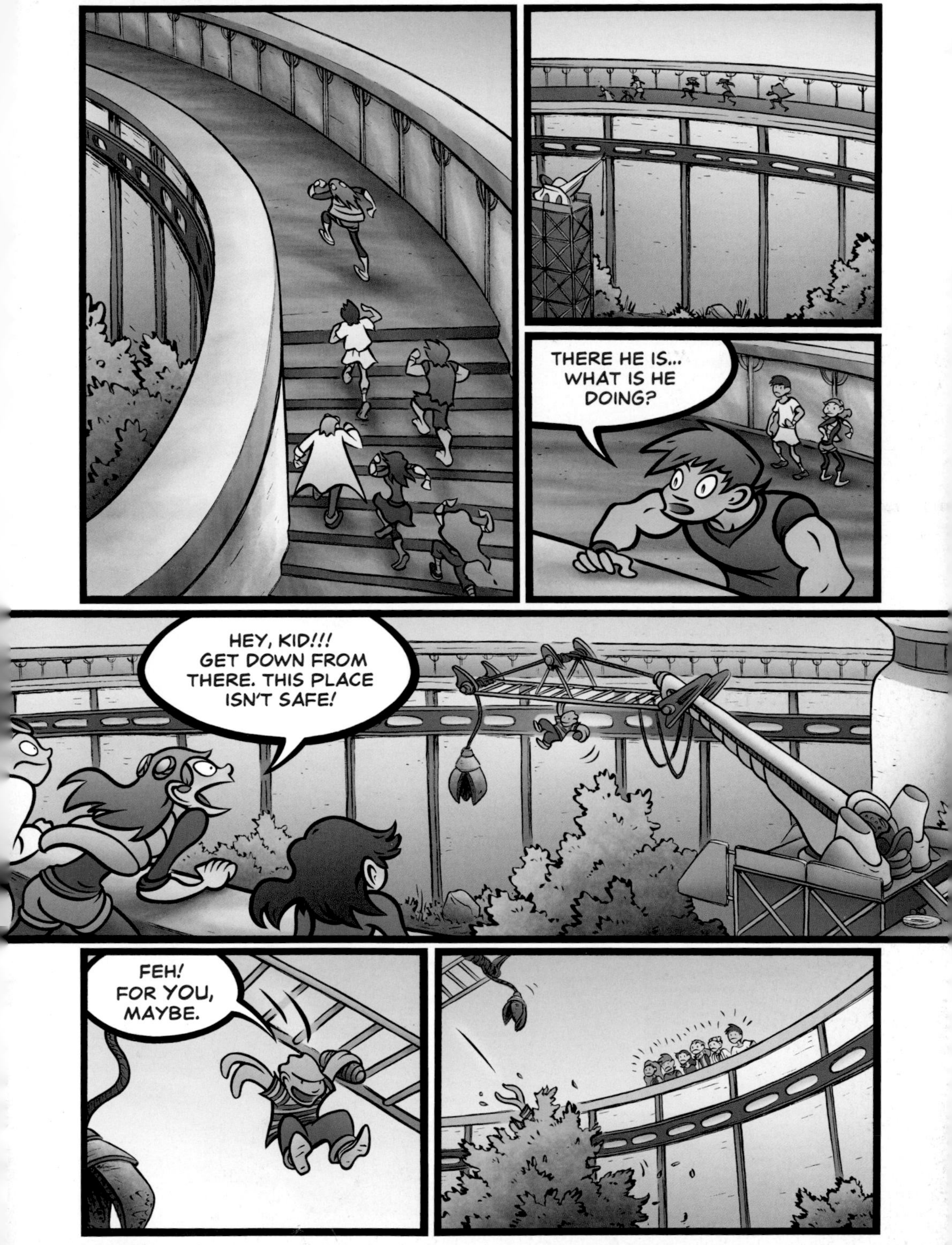
THERE HE IS... WHAT IS HE DOING?
HEY, KID!!! GET DOWN FROM THERE. THIS PLACE ISN'T SAFE!
FEH! FOR YOU, MAYBE.

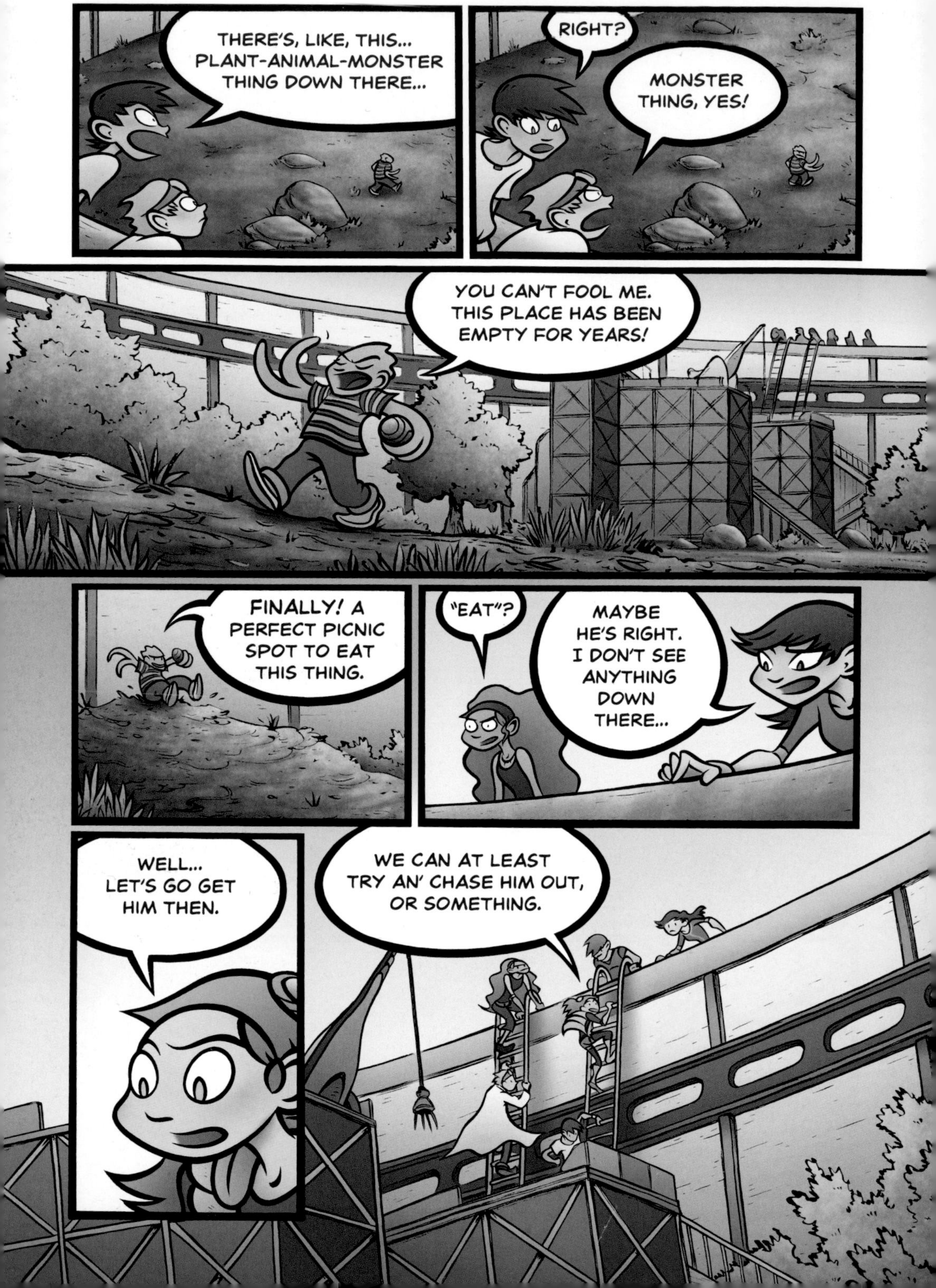
THERE'S, LIKE, THIS... PLANT-ANIMAL-MONSTER THING DOWN THERE...
RIGHT?
MONSTER THING, YES!
YOU CAN'T FOOL ME. THIS PLACE HAS BEEN EMPTY FOR YEARS!
FINALLY! A PERFECT PICNIC SPOT TO EAT THIS THING.
"EAT"?
MAYBE HE'S RIGHT. I DON'T SEE ANYTHING DOWN THERE...
WELL... LET'S GO GET HIM THEN.
WE CAN AT LEAST TRY AN' CHASE HIM OUT, OR SOMETHING.

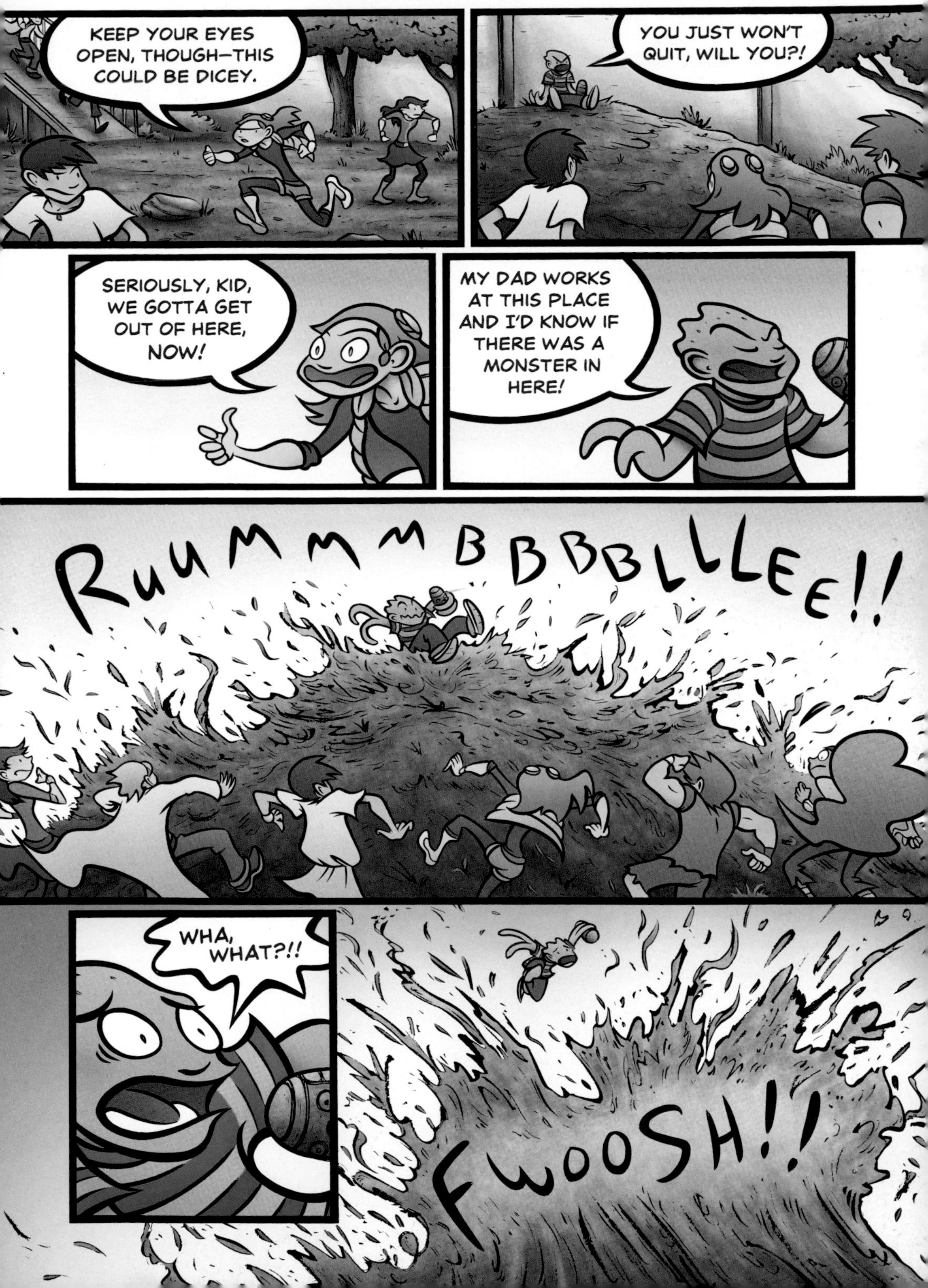
KEEP YOUR EYES OPEN, THOUGH—THIS COULD BE DICEY.
YOU JUST WON'T QUIT, WILL YOU?!
SERIOUSLY, KID, WE GOTTA GET OUT OF HERE, NOW!
MY DAD WORKS AT THIS PLACE AND I'D KNOW IF THERE WAS A MONSTER IN HERE!
RUUMMMMBBBBLLLEE!!
WHA, WHAT?!!
FWOOSH!!

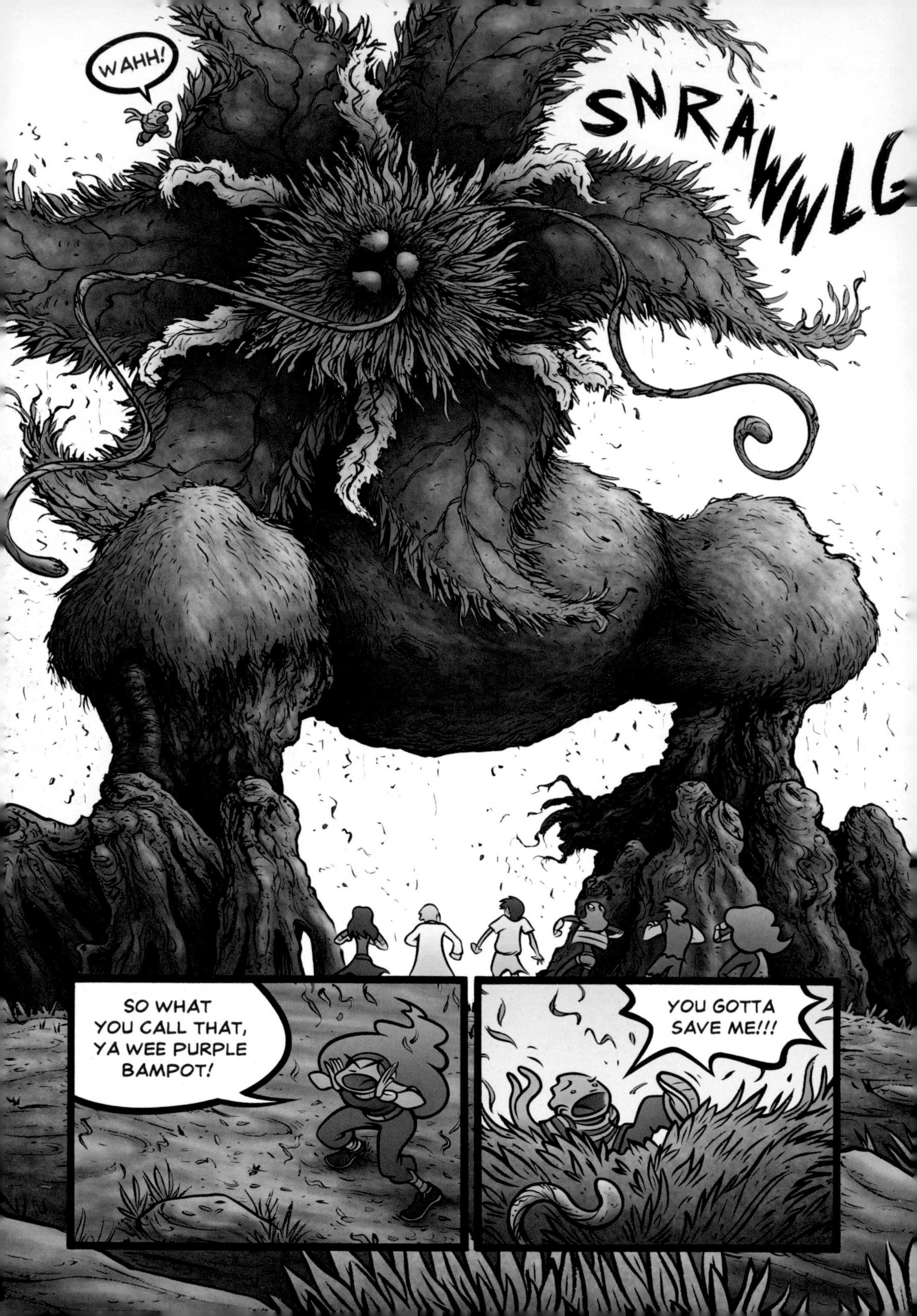
WAHH!
SNRAWWLG
SO WHAT YOU CALL THAT, YA WEE PURPLE BAMPOT!
YOU GOTTA SAVE ME!!!

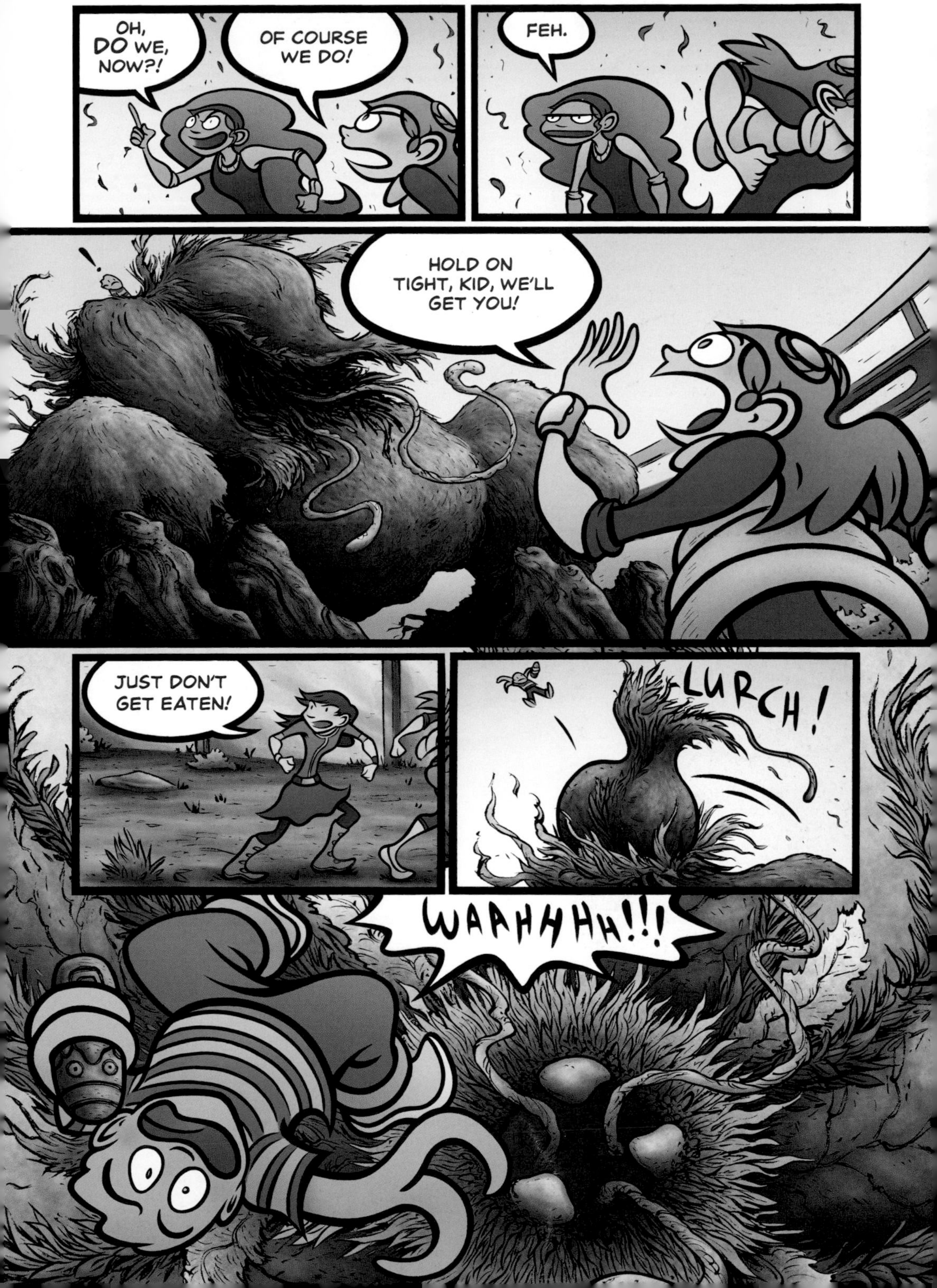
OH, DO WE, NOW?!
OF COURSE WE DO!
FEH.
!
HOLD ON TIGHT, KID, WE'LL GET YOU!
JUST DON'T GET EATEN!
LURCH!
WAAHHHH!!!

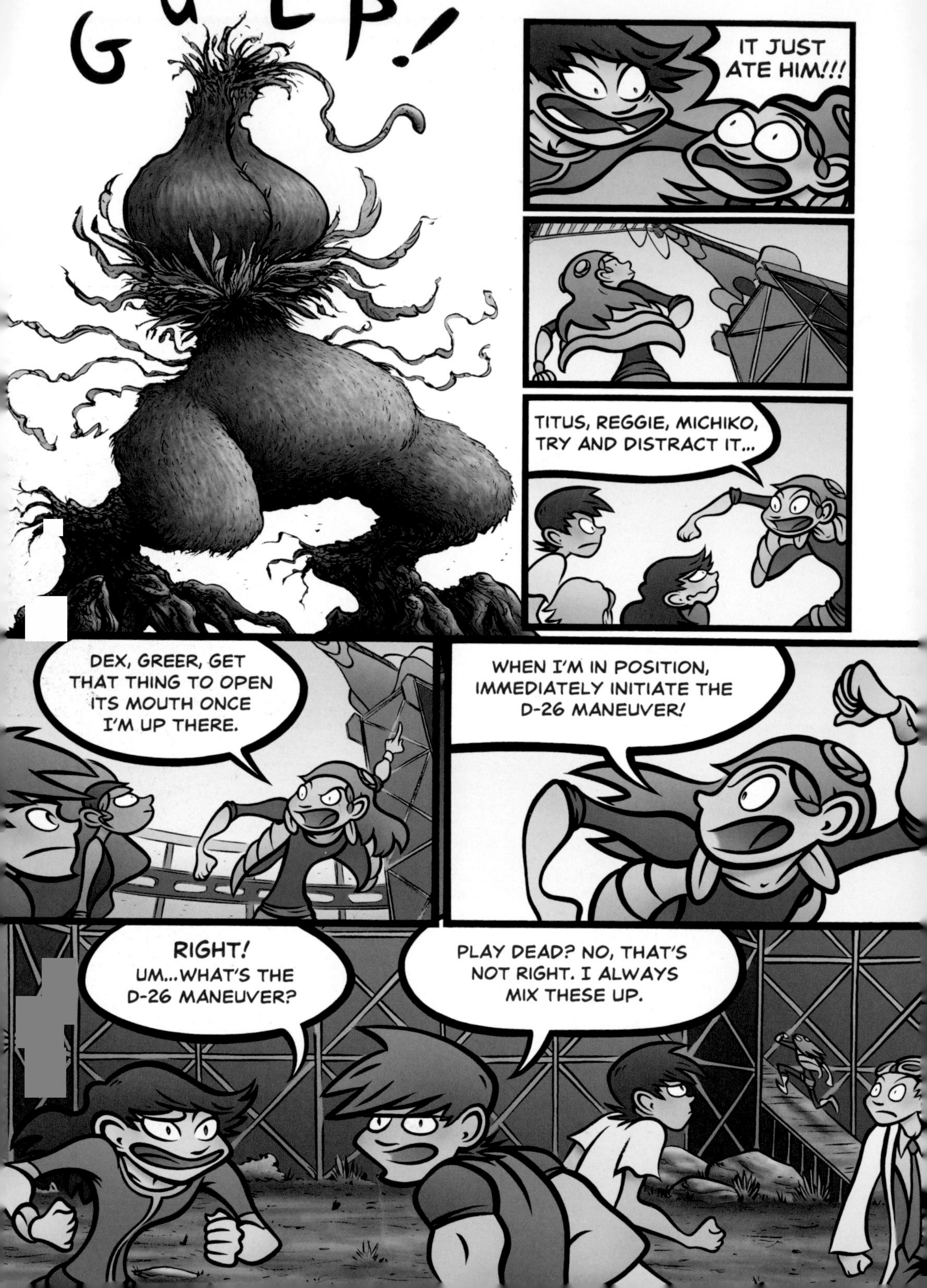
GULP!
IT JUST ATE HIM!!!
TITUS, REGGIE, MICHIKO, TRY AND DISTRACT IT...
DEX, GREER, GET THAT THING TO OPEN ITS MOUTH ONCE I'M UP THERE.
WHEN I'M IN POSITION, IMMEDIATELY INITIATE THE D-26 MANEUVER!
RIGHT! UM...WHAT'S THE D-26 MANEUVER?
PLAY DEAD? NO, THAT'S NOT RIGHT. I ALWAYS MIX THESE UP.

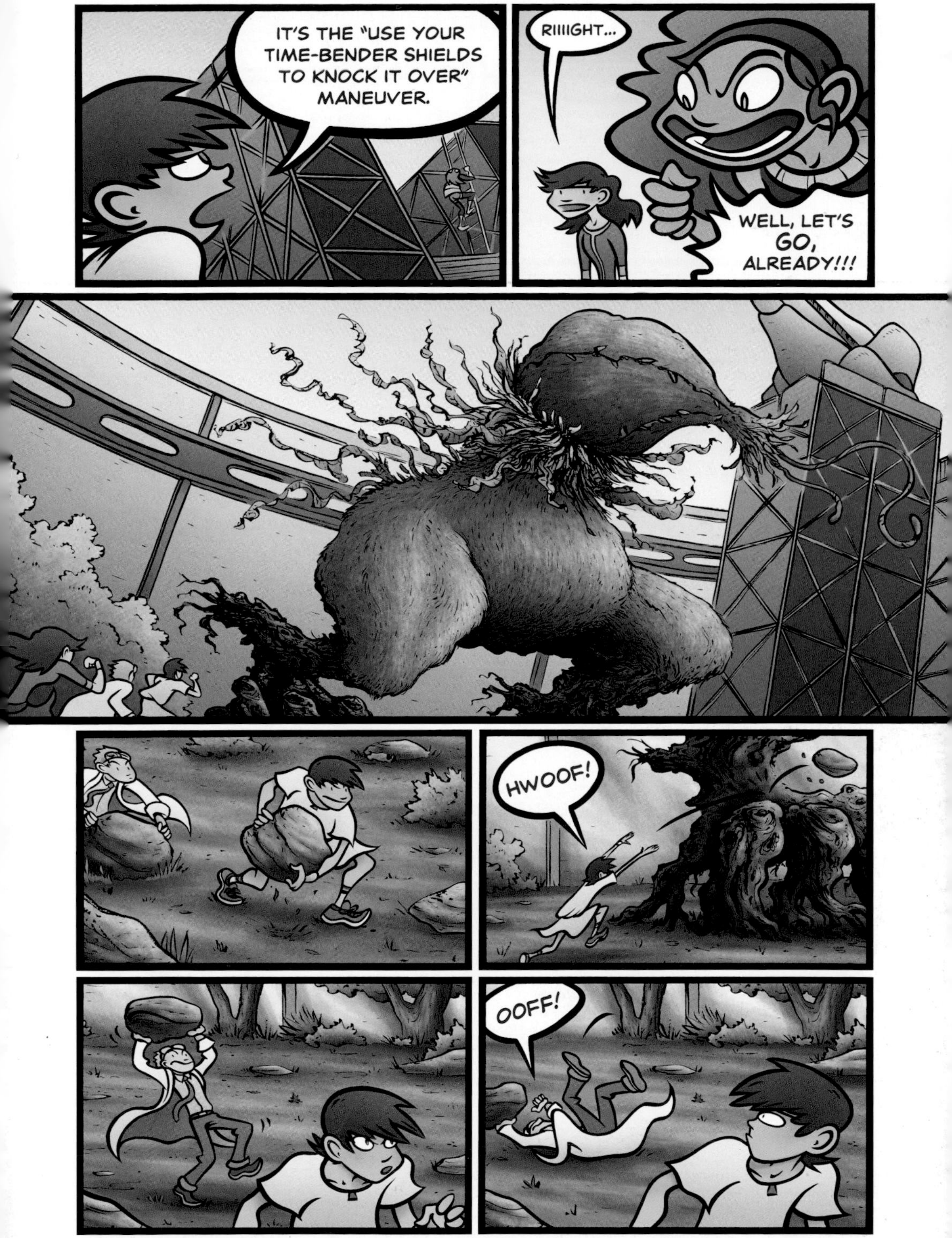
IT'S THE "USE YOUR TIME-BENDER SHIELDS TO KNOCK IT OVER" MANEUVER.
RIIIIGHT...
WELL, LET'S GO, ALREADY!!!
HWOOF!
OOFF!

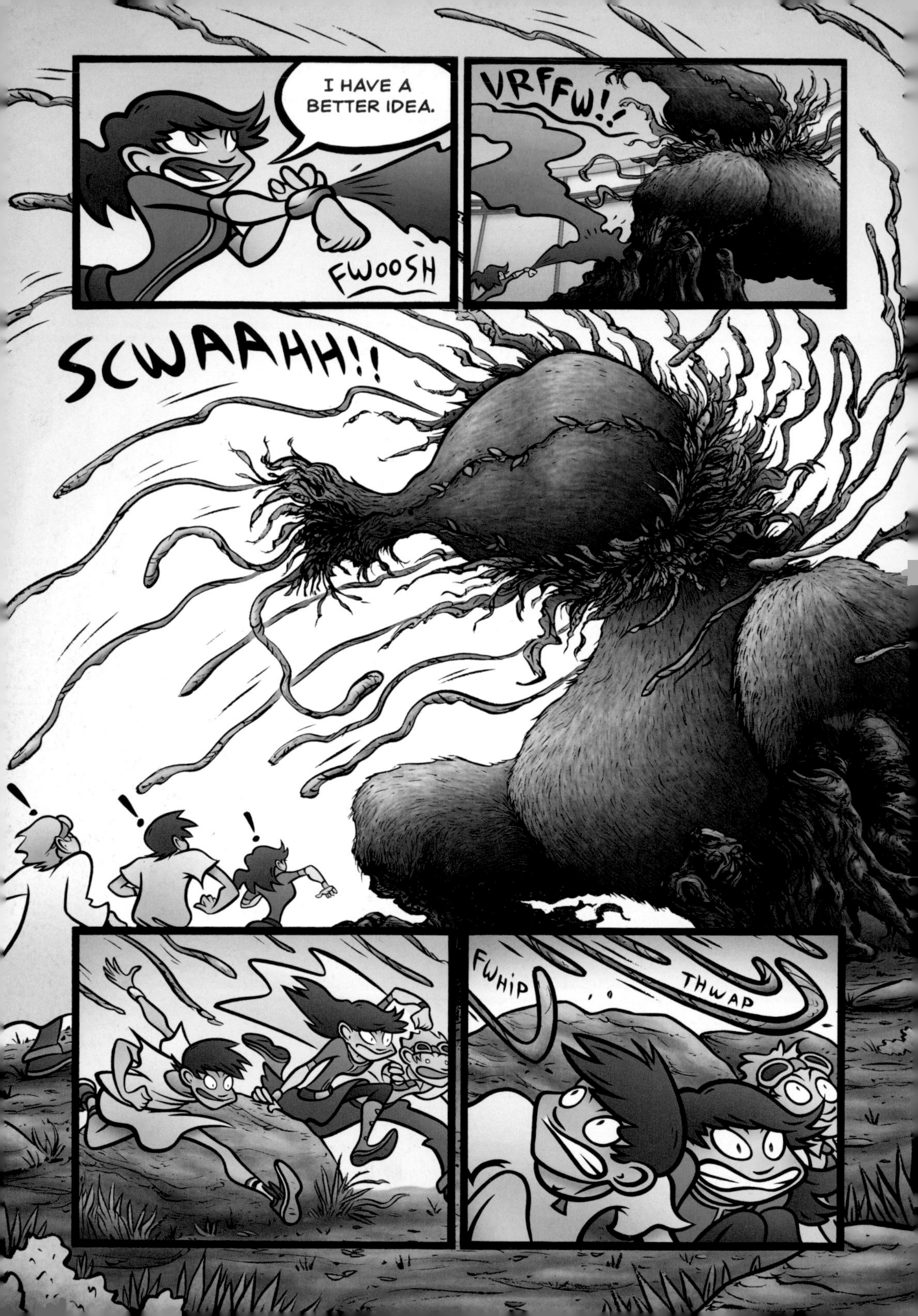
I HAVE A BETTER IDEA.
FWOOSH
VRFFW!!
SCWAAHH!!
!
!
!
FWHIP
THWAP

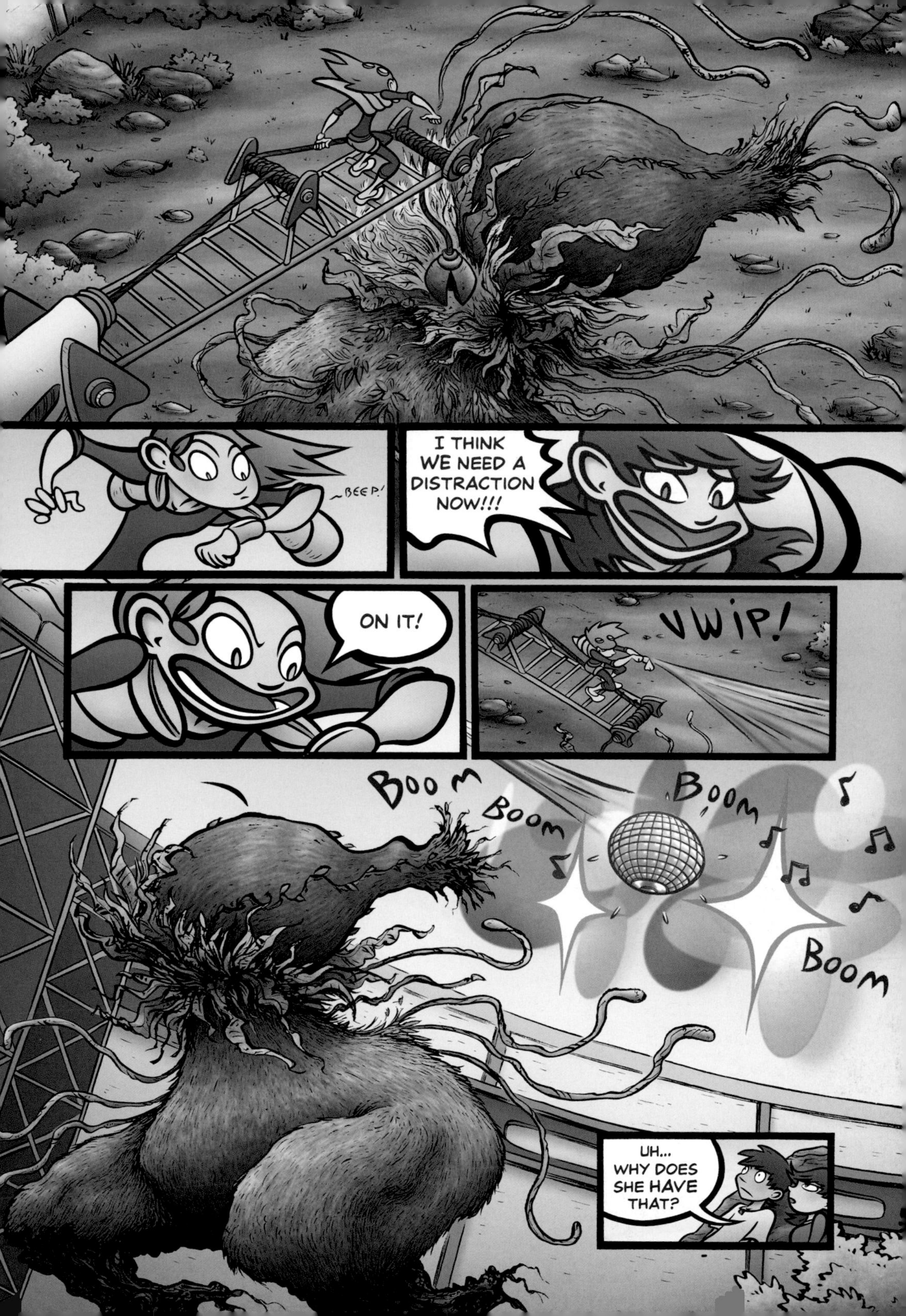
~BEEP!
I THINK WE NEED A DISTRACTION NOW!!!
ON IT!
VWIP!
Boom
Boom
Boom
Boom
UH... WHY DOES SHE HAVE THAT?

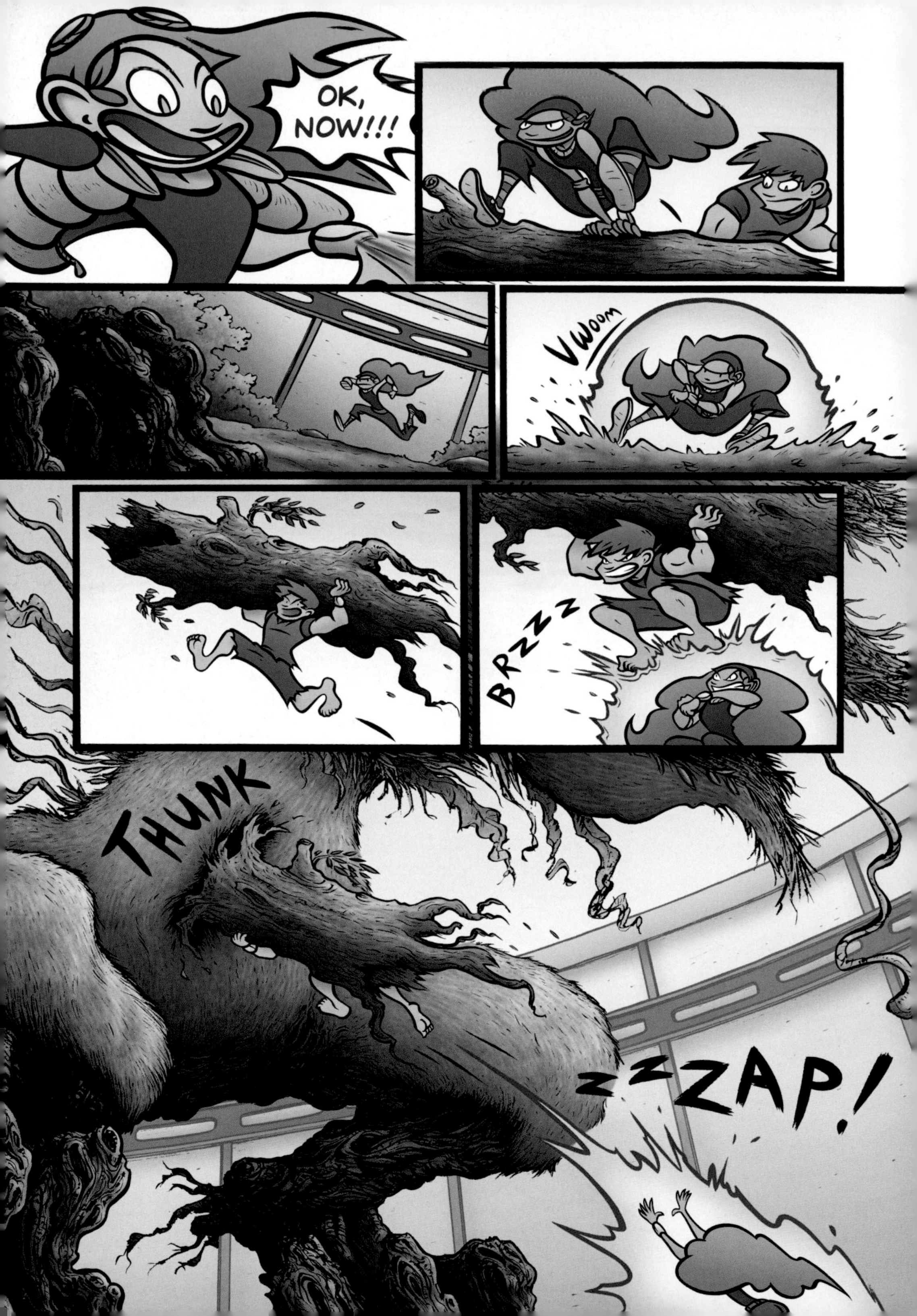
OK, NOW!!!
VWoom
BRZZZ
THUNK
ZZZAP!

RAAWWWWWW!!!

GULP

23

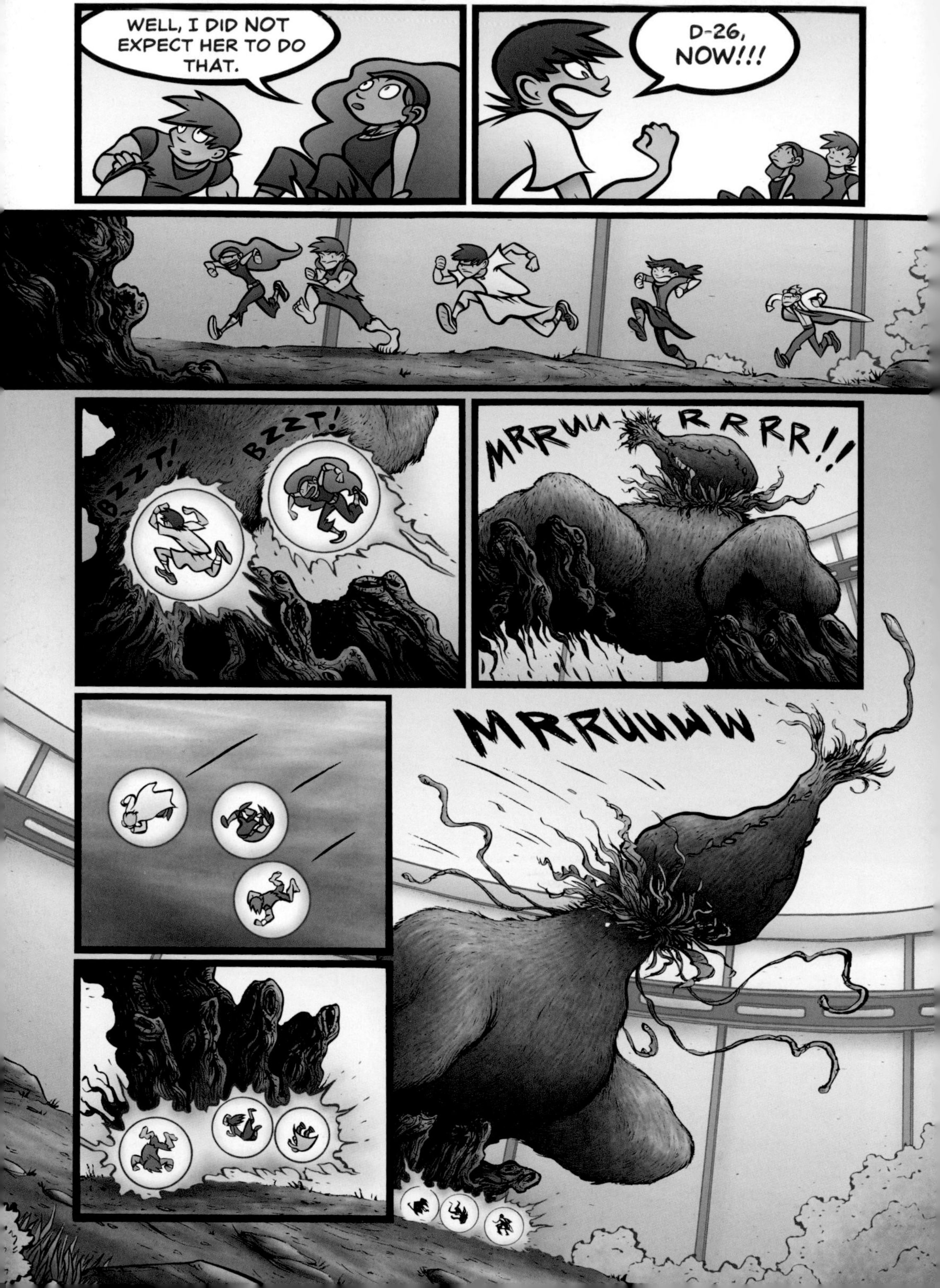
WELL, I DID NOT EXPECT HER TO DO THAT.
D-26, NOW!!!
BZZT!
BZZT!
MRRUU RRRRR!!!
MRRUUUW

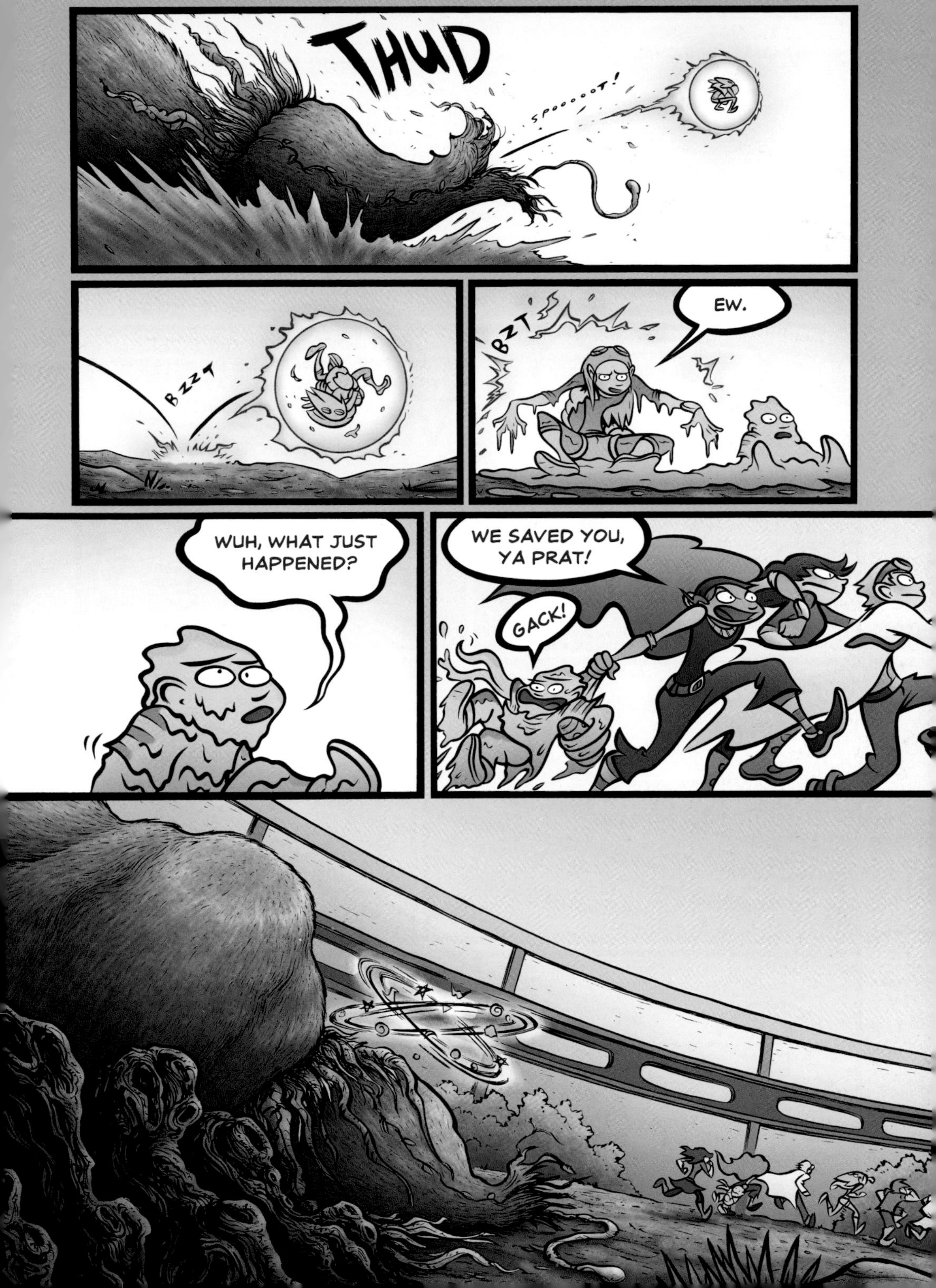
THUD
SPOOOOOT!
BZZT
BZT
EW.
WUH, WHAT JUST HAPPENED?
WE SAVED YOU, YA PRAT!
GACK!

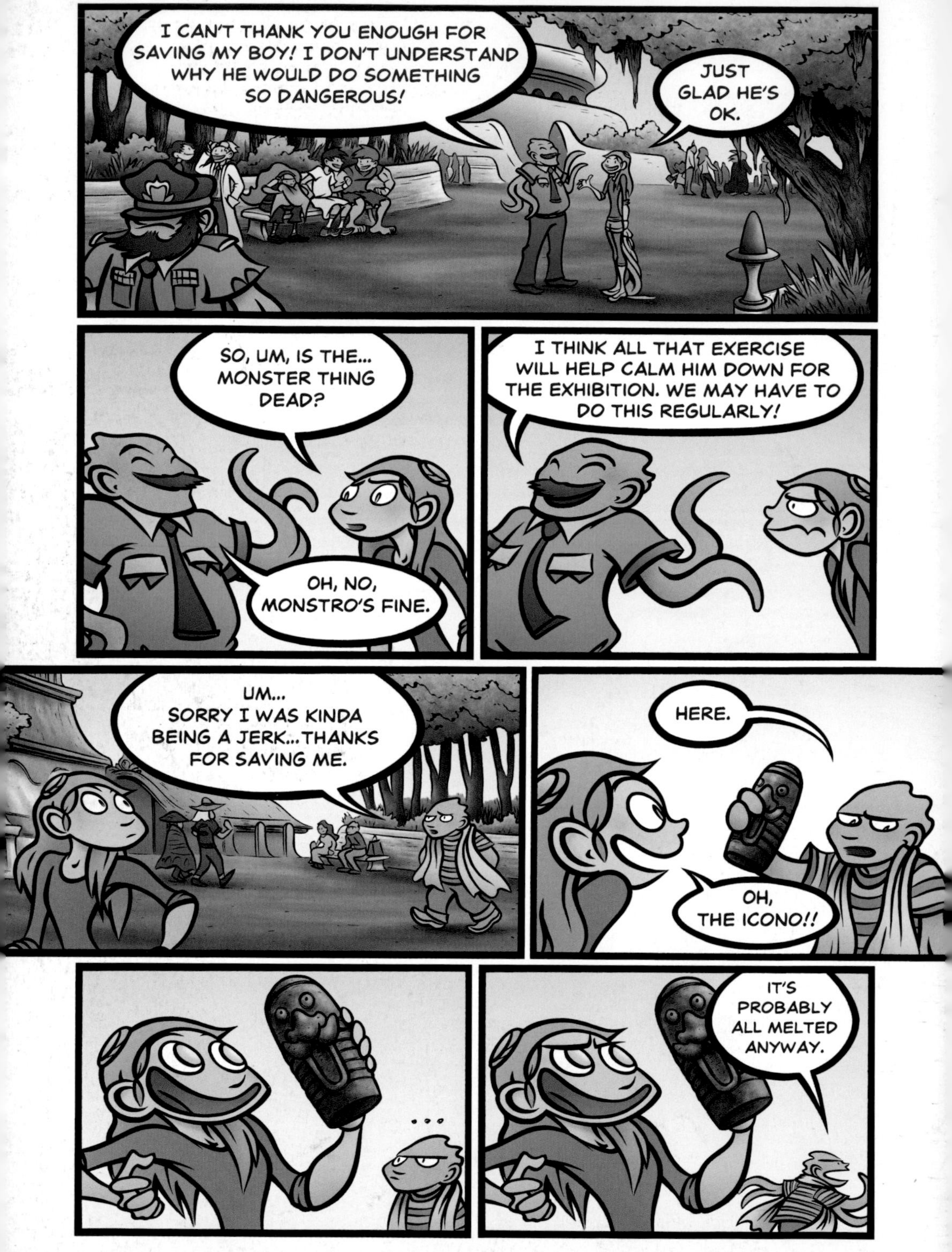
I CAN'T THANK YOU ENOUGH FOR SAVING MY BOY! I DON'T UNDERSTAND WHY HE WOULD DO SOMETHING SO DANGEROUS!
JUST GLAD HE'S OK.
SO, UM, IS THE... MONSTER THING DEAD?
OH, NO, MONSTRO'S FINE.
I THINK ALL THAT EXERCISE WILL HELP CALM HIM DOWN FOR THE EXHIBITION. WE MAY HAVE TO DO THIS REGULARLY!
UM... SORRY I WAS KINDA BEING A JERK...THANKS FOR SAVING ME.
HERE.
OH, THE ICONO!!
IT'S PROBABLY ALL MELTED ANYWAY.

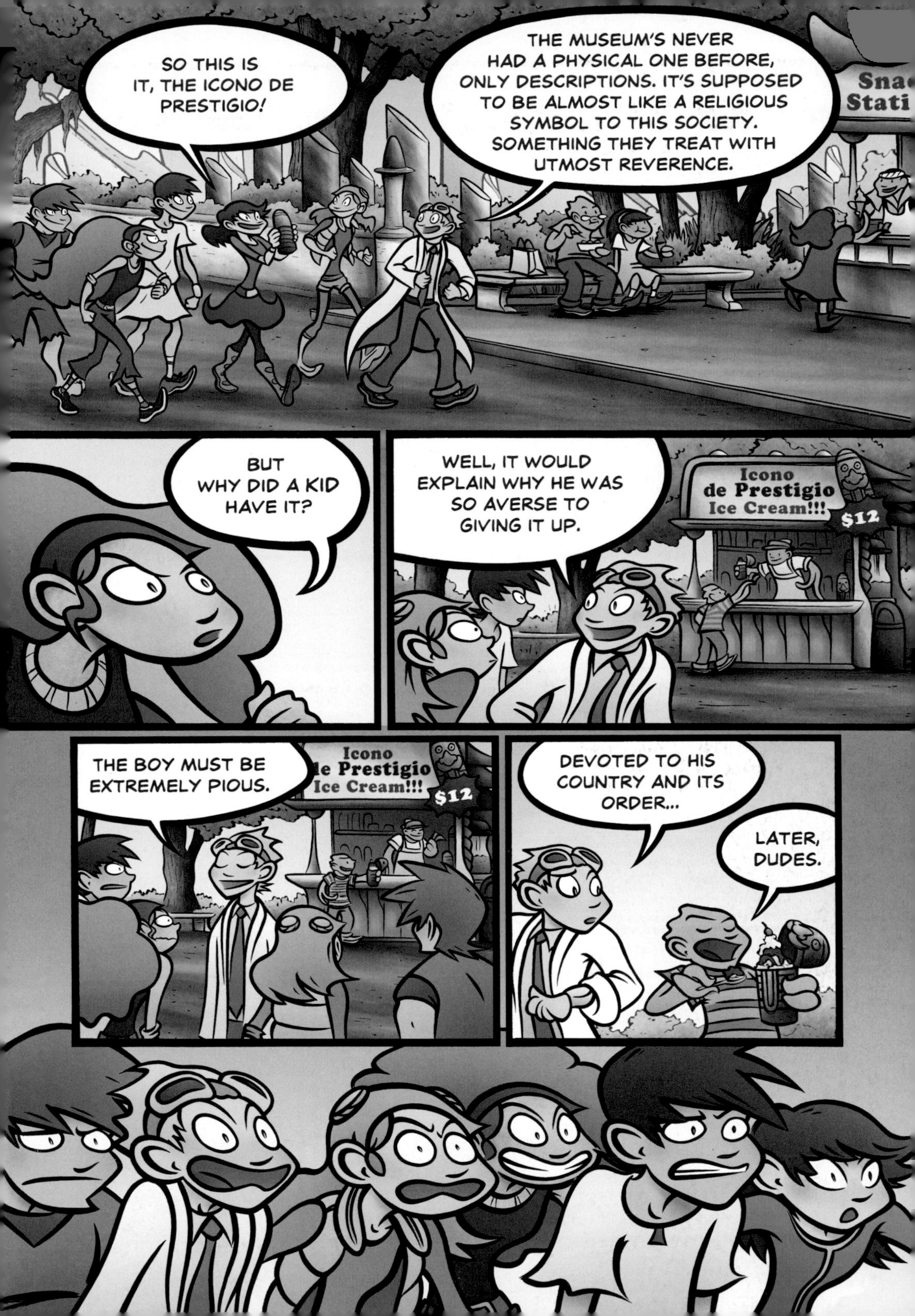
Snac
Stati
SO THIS IS IT, THE ICONO DE PRESTIGIO!
THE MUSEUM'S NEVER HAD A PHYSICAL ONE BEFORE, ONLY DESCRIPTIONS. IT'S SUPPOSED TO BE ALMOST LIKE A RELIGIOUS SYMBOL TO THIS SOCIETY. SOMETHING THEY TREAT WITH UTMOST REVERENCE.
BUT WHY DID A KID HAVE IT?
WELL, IT WOULD EXPLAIN WHY HE WAS SO AVERSE TO GIVING IT UP.
Icono de Prestigio Ice Cream!!!
$12
THE BOY MUST BE EXTREMELY PIOUS.
Icono de Prestigio Ice Cream!!!
$12
DEVOTED TO HIS COUNTRY AND ITS ORDER...
LATER, DUDES.

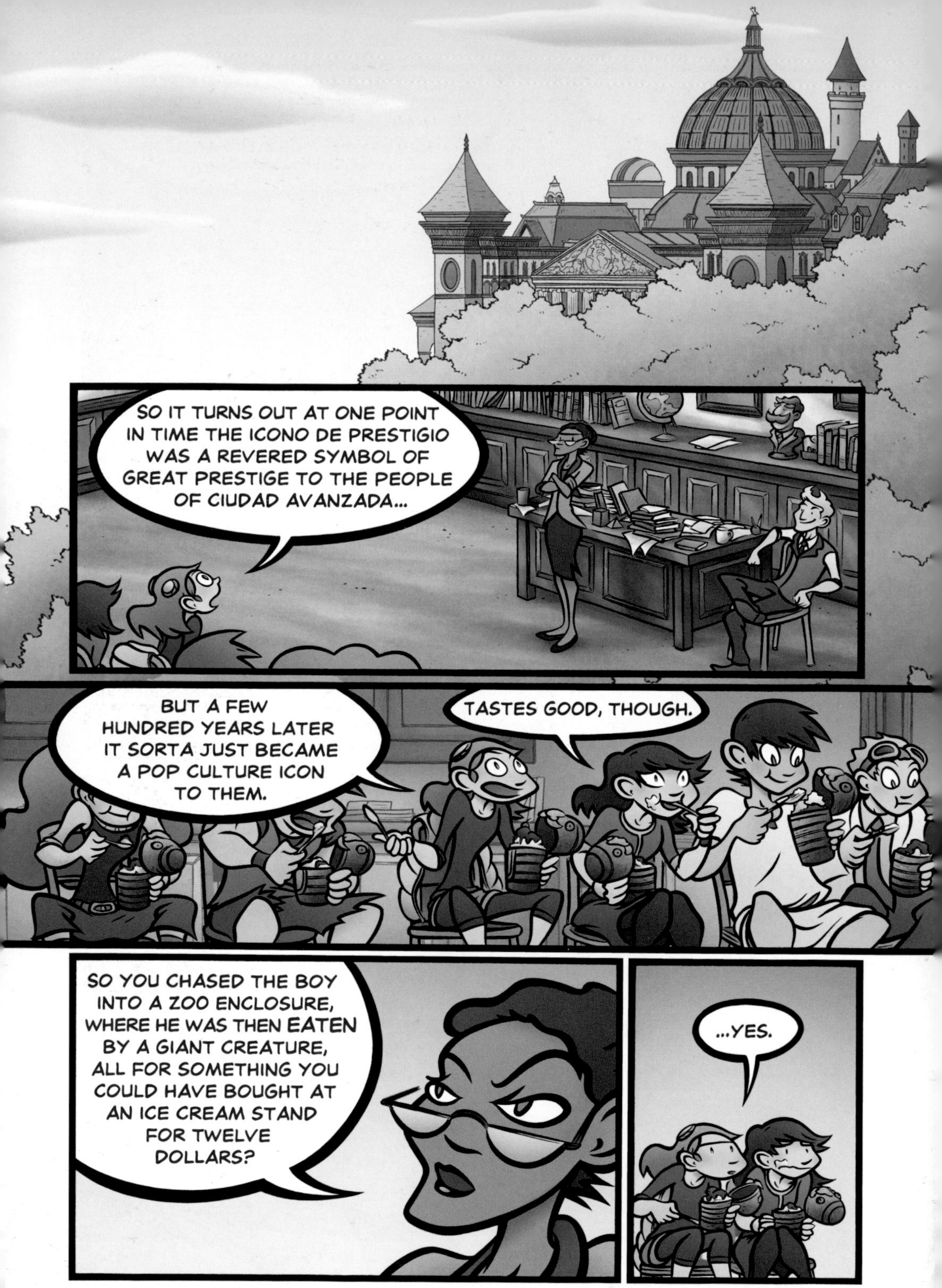
SO IT TURNS OUT AT ONE POINT IN TIME THE ICONO DE PRESTIGIO WAS A REVERED SYMBOL OF GREAT PRESTIGE TO THE PEOPLE OF CIUDAD AVANZADA...
BUT A FEW HUNDRED YEARS LATER IT SORTA JUST BECAME A POP CULTURE ICON TO THEM.
TASTES GOOD, THOUGH.
SO YOU CHASED THE BOY INTO A ZOO ENCLOSURE, WHERE HE WAS THEN EATEN BY A GIANT CREATURE, ALL FOR SOMETHING YOU COULD HAVE BOUGHT AT AN ICE CREAM STAND FOR TWELVE DOLLARS?
...YES.

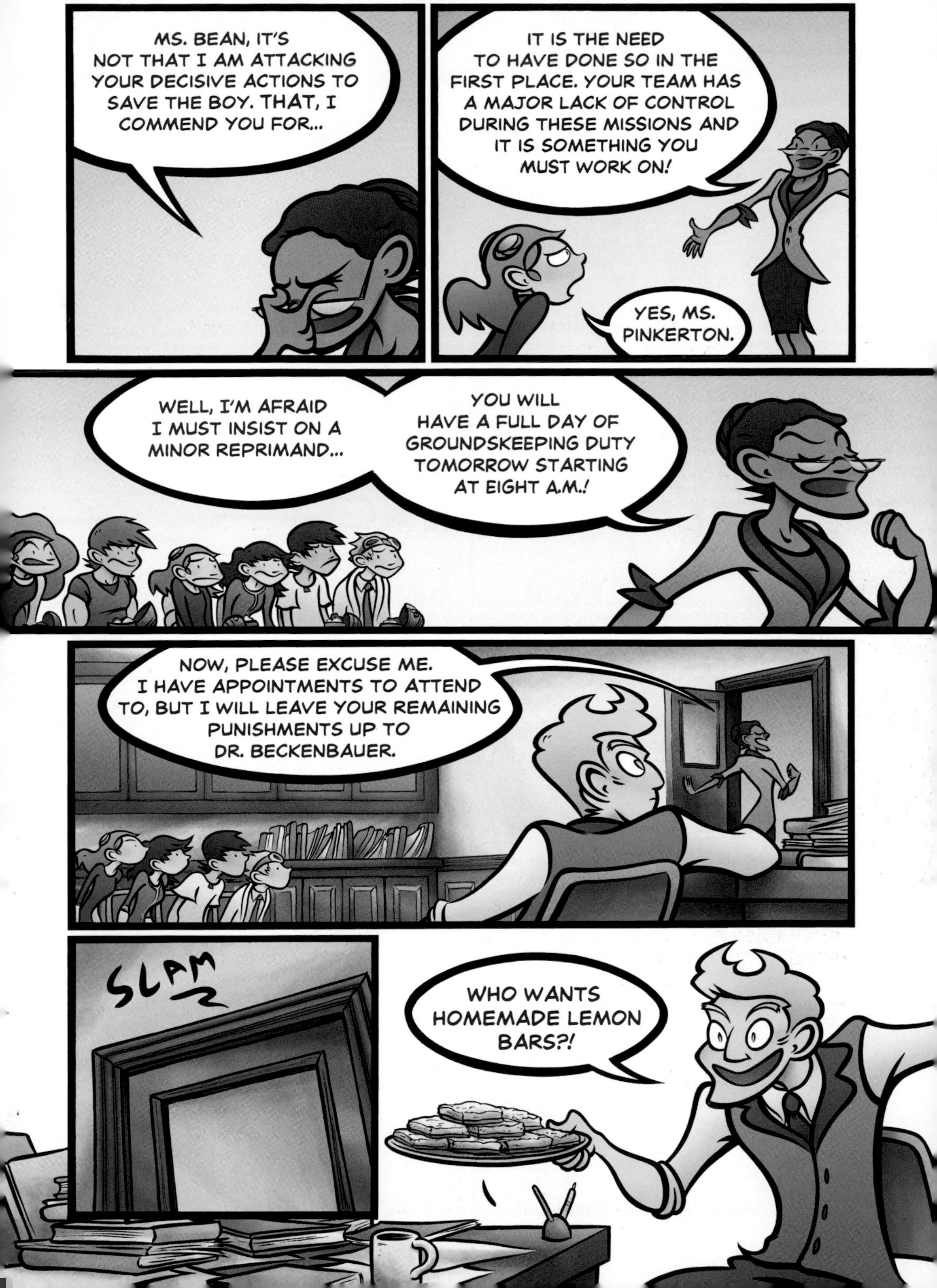
MS. BEAN, IT'S NOT THAT I AM ATTACKING YOUR DECISIVE ACTIONS TO SAVE THE BOY. THAT, I COMMEND YOU FOR...
IT IS THE NEED TO HAVE DONE SO IN THE FIRST PLACE. YOUR TEAM HAS A MAJOR LACK OF CONTROL DURING THESE MISSIONS AND IT IS SOMETHING YOU MUST WORK ON!
YES, MS. PINKERTON.
WELL, I'M AFRAID I MUST INSIST ON A MINOR REPRIMAND...
YOU WILL HAVE A FULL DAY OF GROUNDSKEEPING DUTY TOMORROW STARTING AT EIGHT A.M.!
NOW, PLEASE EXCUSE ME. I HAVE APPOINTMENTS TO ATTEND TO, BUT I WILL LEAVE YOUR REMAINING PUNISHMENTS UP TO DR. BECKENBAUER.
SLAM
WHO WANTS HOMEMADE LEMON BARS?!

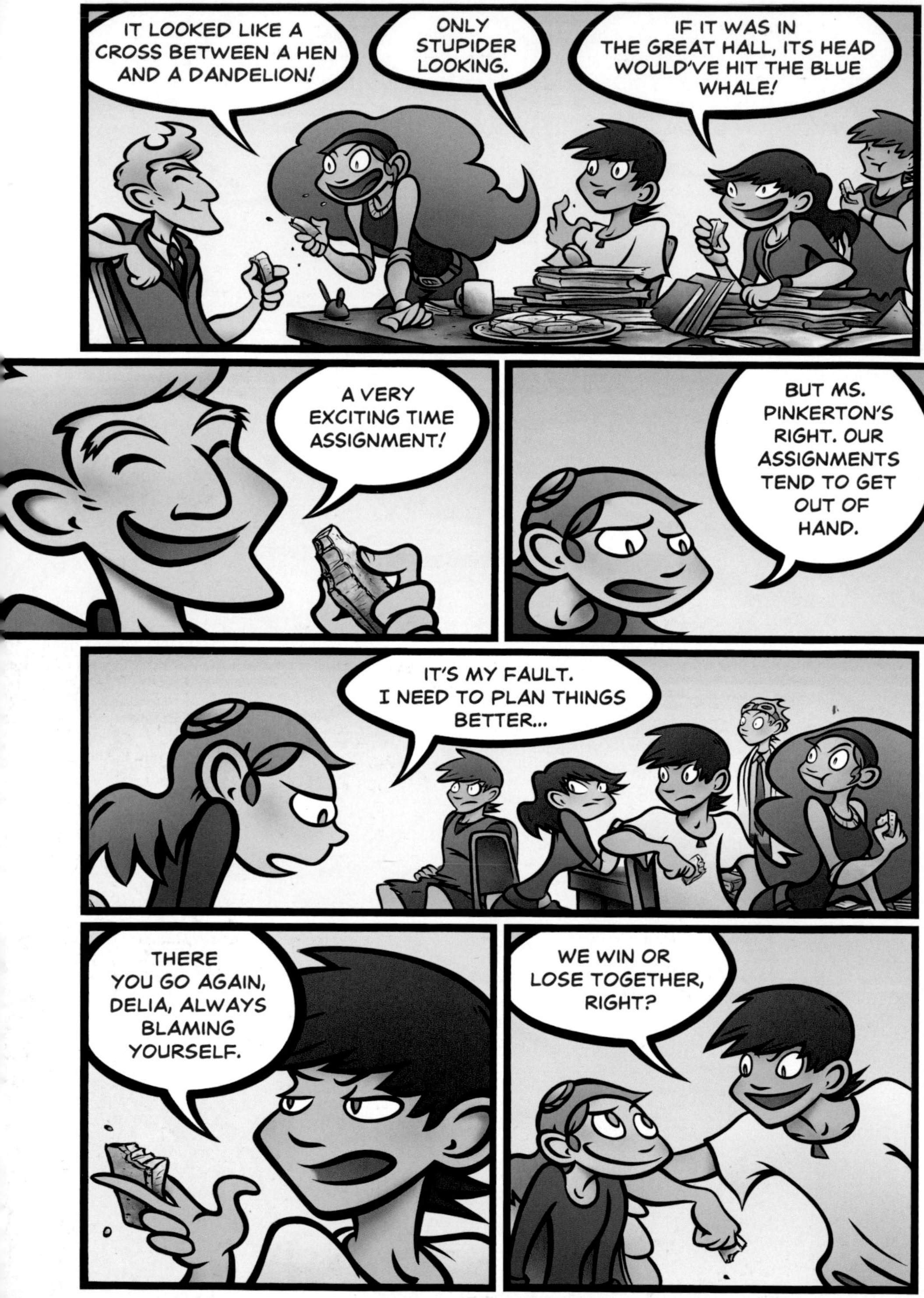
IT LOOKED LIKE A CROSS BETWEEN A HEN AND A DANDELION!
ONLY STUPIDER LOOKING.
IF IT WAS IN THE GREAT HALL, ITS HEAD WOULD'VE HIT THE BLUE WHALE!
A VERY EXCITING TIME ASSIGNMENT!
BUT MS. PINKERTON'S RIGHT. OUR ASSIGNMENTS TEND TO GET OUT OF HAND.
IT'S MY FAULT. I NEED TO PLAN THINGS BETTER...
THERE YOU GO AGAIN, DELIA, ALWAYS BLAMING YOURSELF.
WE WIN OR LOSE TOGETHER, RIGHT?

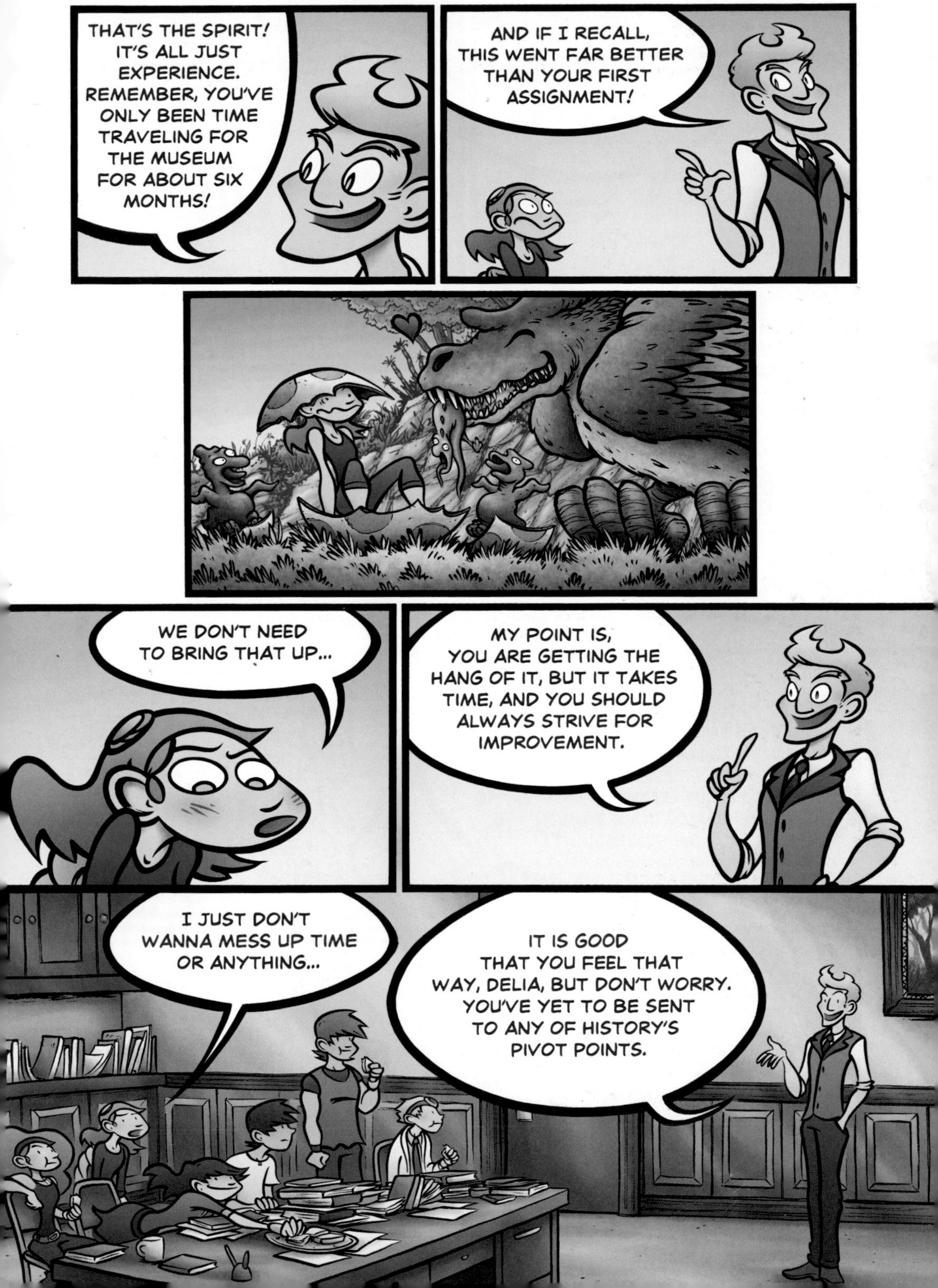
THAT'S THE SPIRIT! IT'S ALL JUST EXPERIENCE. REMEMBER, YOU'VE ONLY BEEN TIME TRAVELING FOR THE MUSEUM FOR ABOUT SIX MONTHS!
AND IF I RECALL, THIS WENT FAR BETTER THAN YOUR FIRST ASSIGNMENT!
WE DON'T NEED TO BRING THAT UP...
MY POINT IS, YOU ARE GETTING THE HANG OF IT, BUT IT TAKES TIME, AND YOU SHOULD ALWAYS STRIVE FOR IMPROVEMENT.
I JUST DON'T WANNA MESS UP TIME OR ANYTHING...
IT IS GOOD THAT YOU FEEL THAT WAY, DELIA, BUT DON'T WORRY. YOU'VE YET TO BE SENT TO ANY OF HISTORY'S PIVOT POINTS.

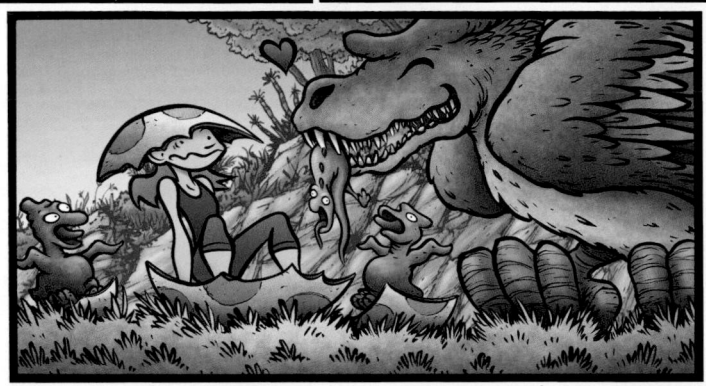

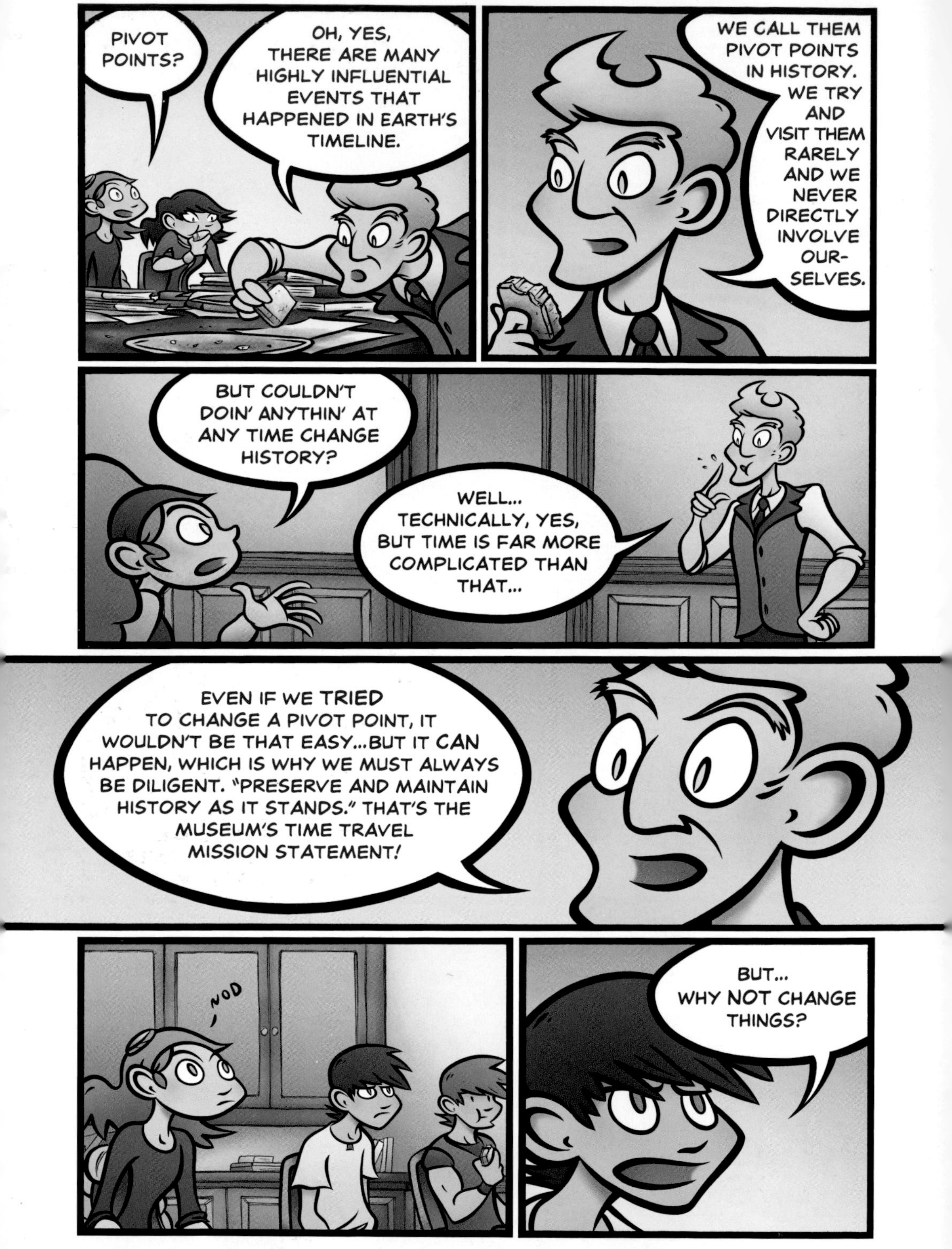

PIVOT POINTS?
OH, YES, THERE ARE MANY HIGHLY INFLUENTIAL EVENTS THAT HAPPENED IN EARTH'S TIMELINE.
WE CALL THEM PIVOT POINTS IN HISTORY. WE TRY AND VISIT THEM RARELY AND WE NEVER DIRECTLY INVOLVE OUR-SELVES.
BUT COULDN'T DOIN' ANYTHIN' AT ANY TIME CHANGE HISTORY?
WELL... TECHNICALLY, YES, BUT TIME IS FAR MORE COMPLICATED THAN THAT...
EVEN IF WE TRIED TO CHANGE A PIVOT POINT, IT WOULDN'T BE THAT EASY...BUT IT CAN HAPPEN, WHICH IS WHY WE MUST ALWAYS BE DILIGENT. "PRESERVE AND MAINTAIN HISTORY AS IT STANDS." THAT'S THE MUSEUM'S TIME TRAVEL MISSION STATEMENT!
NOD
BUT... WHY NOT CHANGE THINGS?

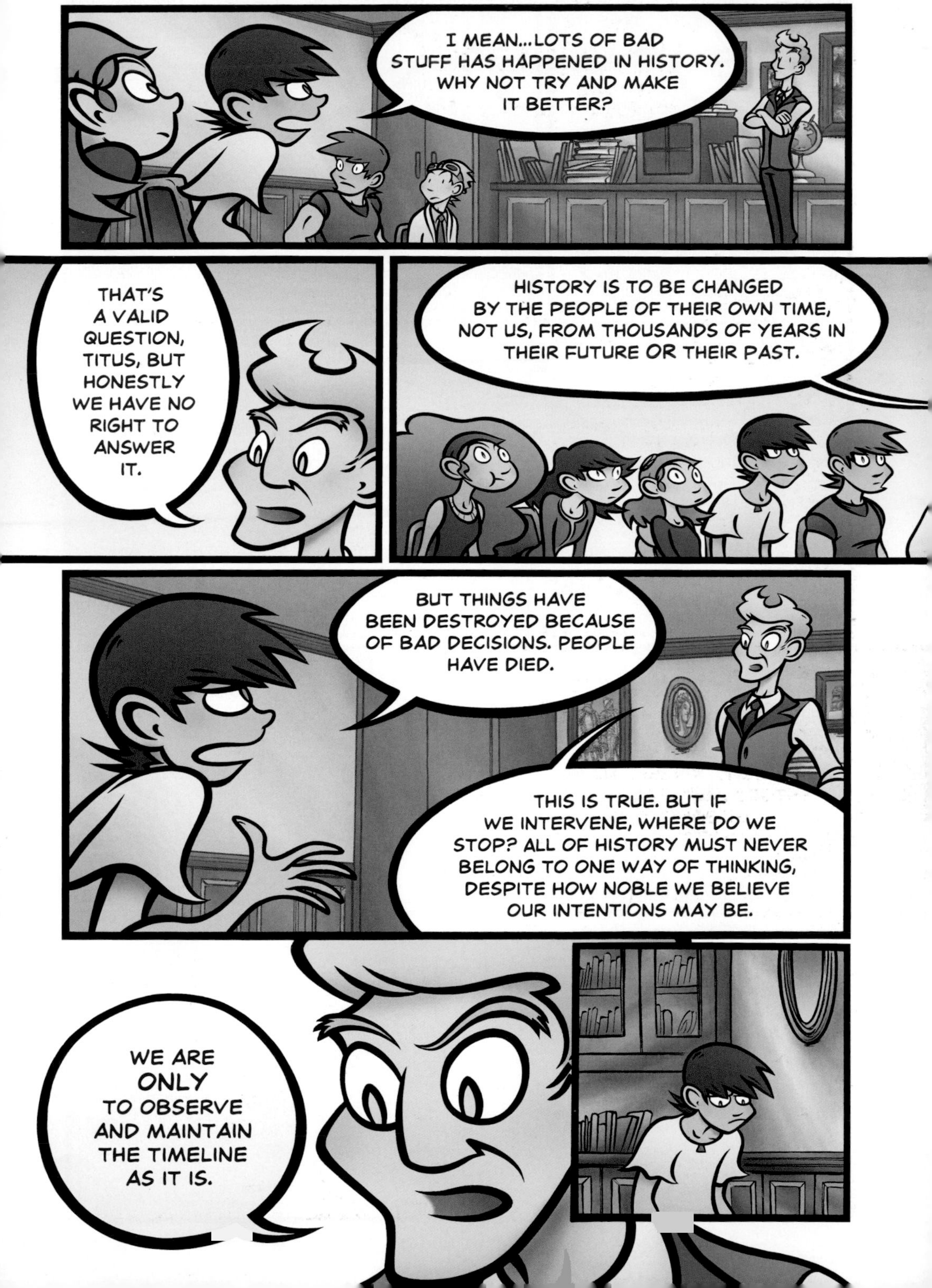
I MEAN...LOTS OF BAD STUFF HAS HAPPENED IN HISTORY. WHY NOT TRY AND MAKE IT BETTER?
THAT'S A VALID QUESTION, TITUS, BUT HONESTLY WE HAVE NO RIGHT TO ANSWER IT.
HISTORY IS TO BE CHANGED BY THE PEOPLE OF THEIR OWN TIME, NOT US, FROM THOUSANDS OF YEARS IN THEIR FUTURE OR THEIR PAST.
BUT THINGS HAVE BEEN DESTROYED BECAUSE OF BAD DECISIONS. PEOPLE HAVE DIED.
THIS IS TRUE. BUT IF WE INTERVENE, WHERE DO WE STOP? ALL OF HISTORY MUST NEVER BELONG TO ONE WAY OF THINKING, DESPITE HOW NOBLE WE BELIEVE OUR INTENTIONS MAY BE.
WE ARE ONLY TO OBSERVE AND MAINTAIN THE TIMELINE AS IT IS.

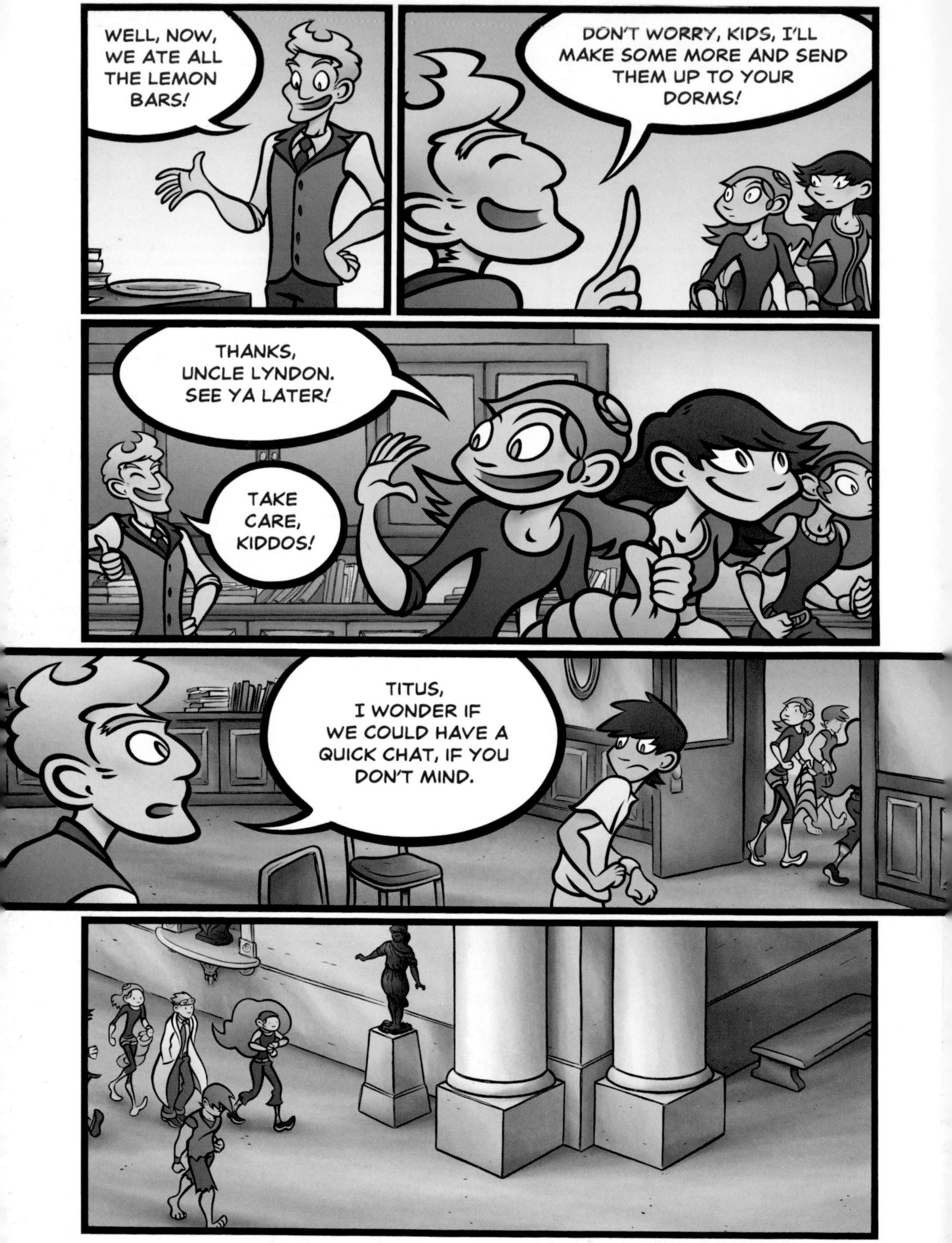
WELL, NOW, WE ATE ALL THE LEMON BARS!
DON'T WORRY, KIDS, I'LL MAKE SOME MORE AND SEND THEM UP TO YOUR DORMS!
THANKS, UNCLE LYNDON. SEE YA LATER!
TAKE CARE, KIDDOS!
TITUS, I WONDER IF WE COULD HAVE A QUICK CHAT, IF YOU DON'T MIND.

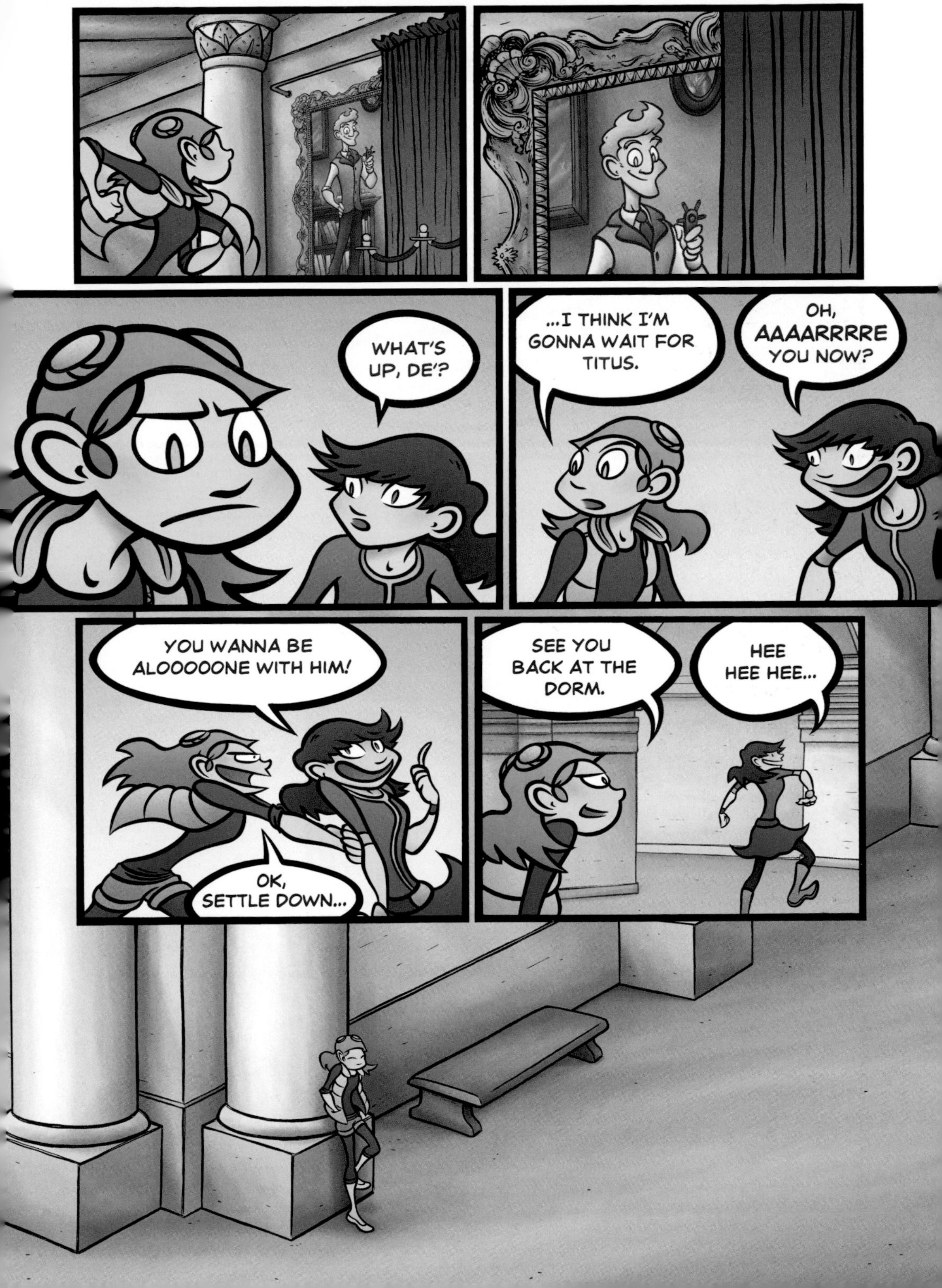
WHAT'S UP, DE'?
...I THINK I'M GONNA WAIT FOR TITUS.
OH, AAAARRRRE YOU NOW?
YOU WANNA BE ALOOOOONE WITH HIM!
OK, SETTLE DOWN...
SEE YOU BACK AT THE DORM.
HEE HEE HEE...

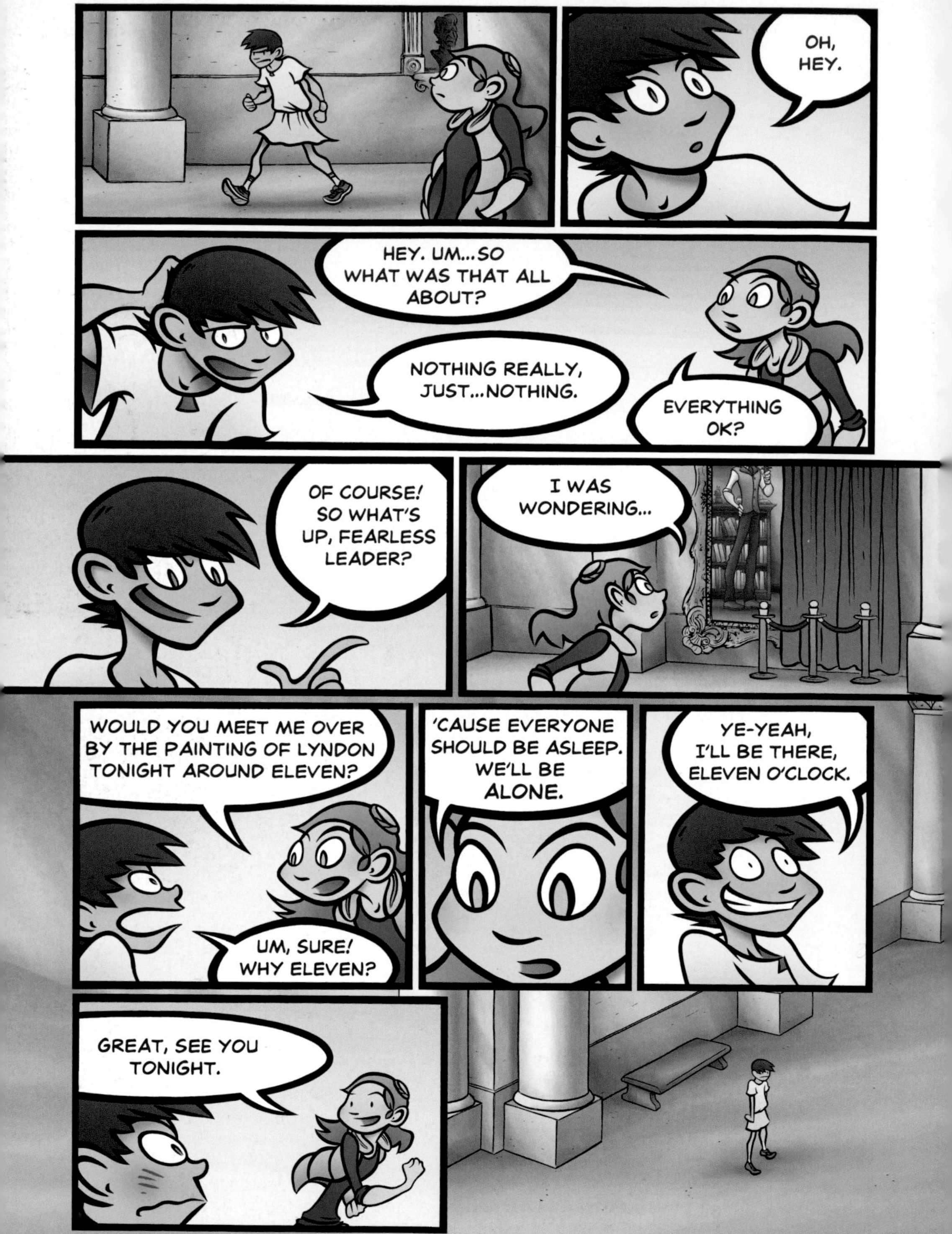
OH, HEY.
HEY. UM...SO WHAT WAS THAT ALL ABOUT?
NOTHING REALLY, JUST...NOTHING.
EVERYTHING OK?
OF COURSE! SO WHAT'S UP, FEARLESS LEADER?
I WAS WONDERING...
WOULD YOU MEET ME OVER BY THE PAINTING OF LYNDON TONIGHT AROUND ELEVEN?
UM, SURE! WHY ELEVEN?
'CAUSE EVERYONE SHOULD BE ASLEEP. WE'LL BE ALONE.
YE-YEAH, I'LL BE THERE, ELEVEN O'CLOCK.
GREAT, SEE YOU TONIGHT.

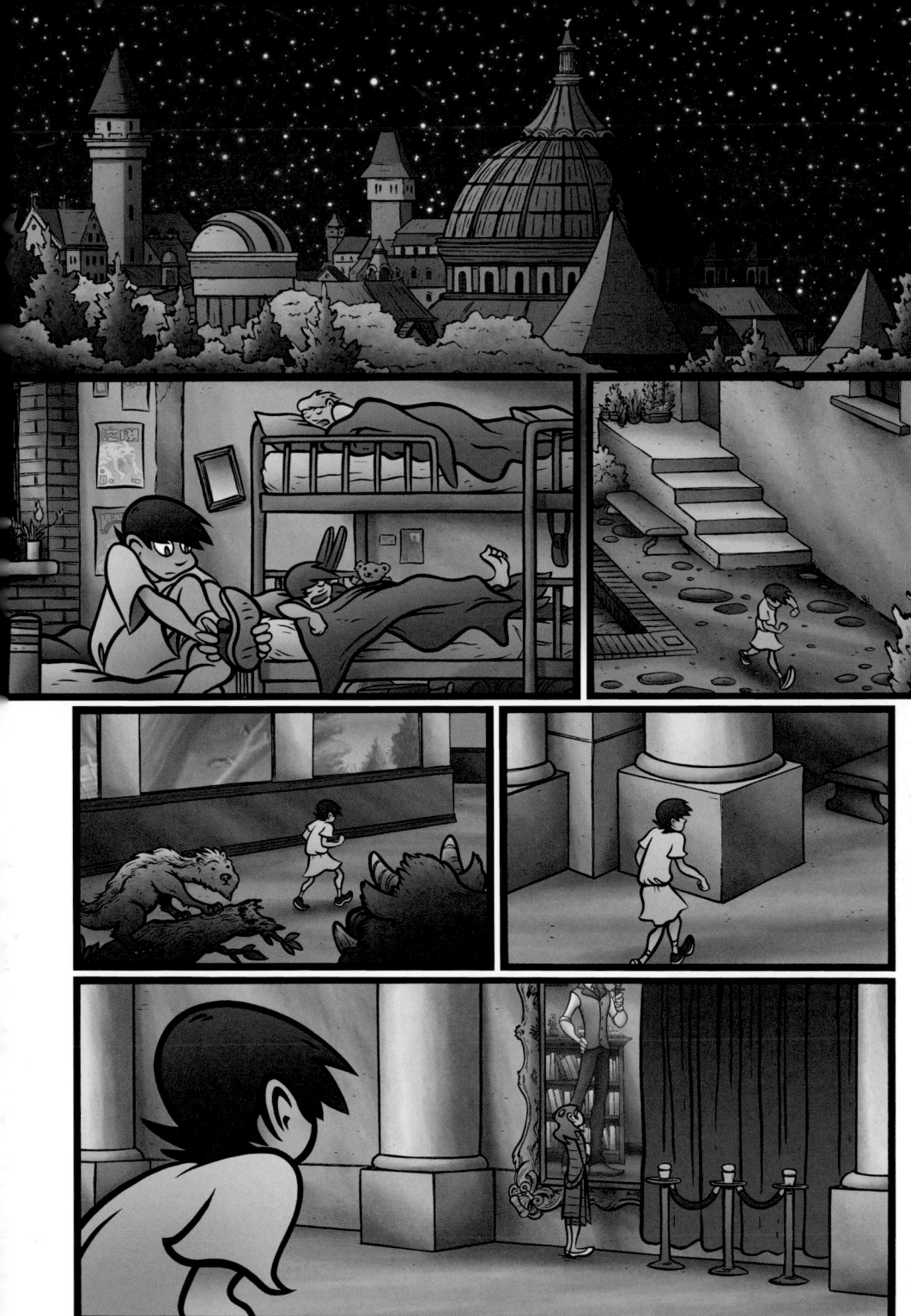

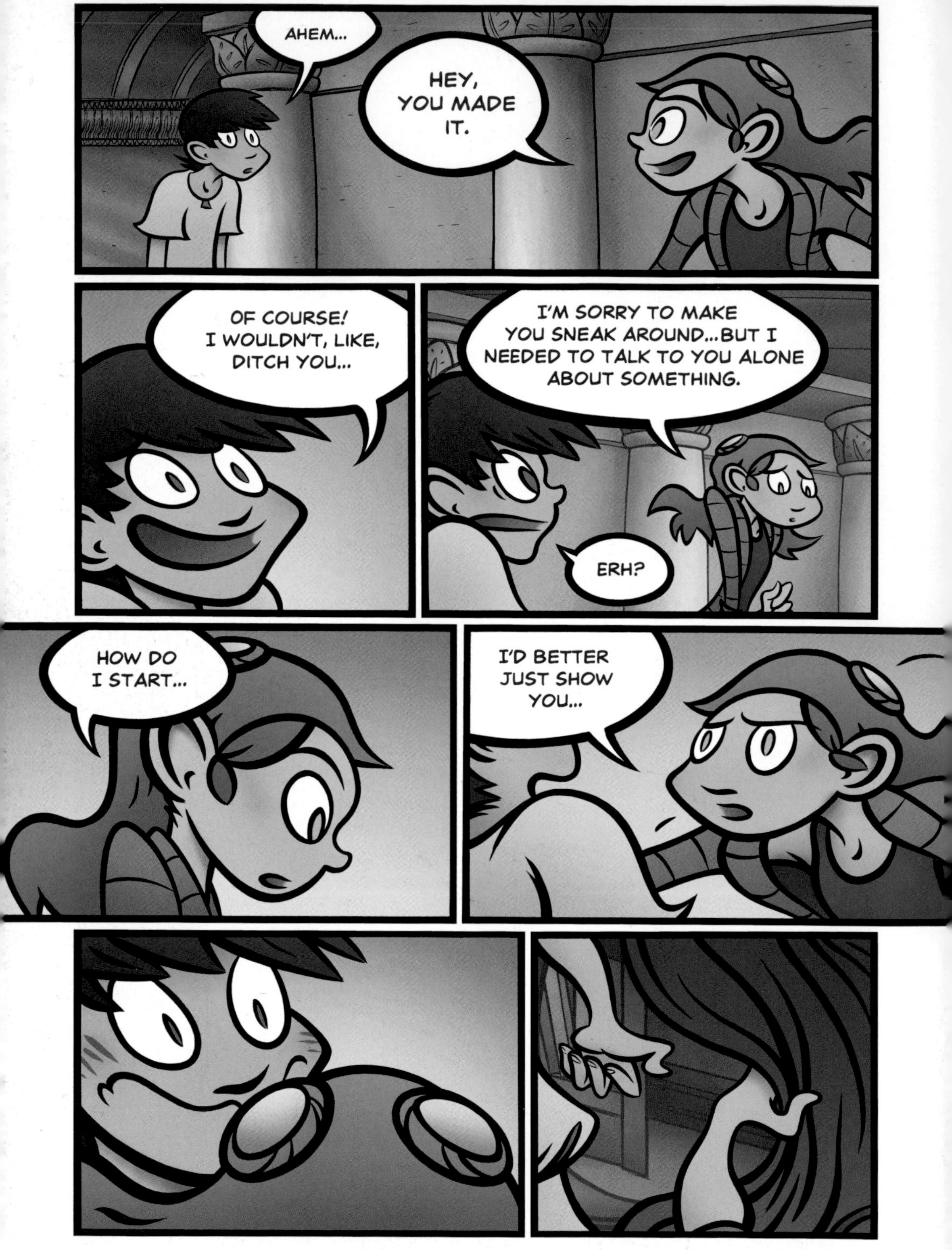
AHEM...
HEY, YOU MADE IT.
OF COURSE! I WOULDN'T, LIKE, DITCH YOU...
I'M SORRY TO MAKE YOU SNEAK AROUND...BUT I NEEDED TO TALK TO YOU ALONE ABOUT SOMETHING.
ERH?
HOW DO I START...
I'D BETTER JUST SHOW YOU...

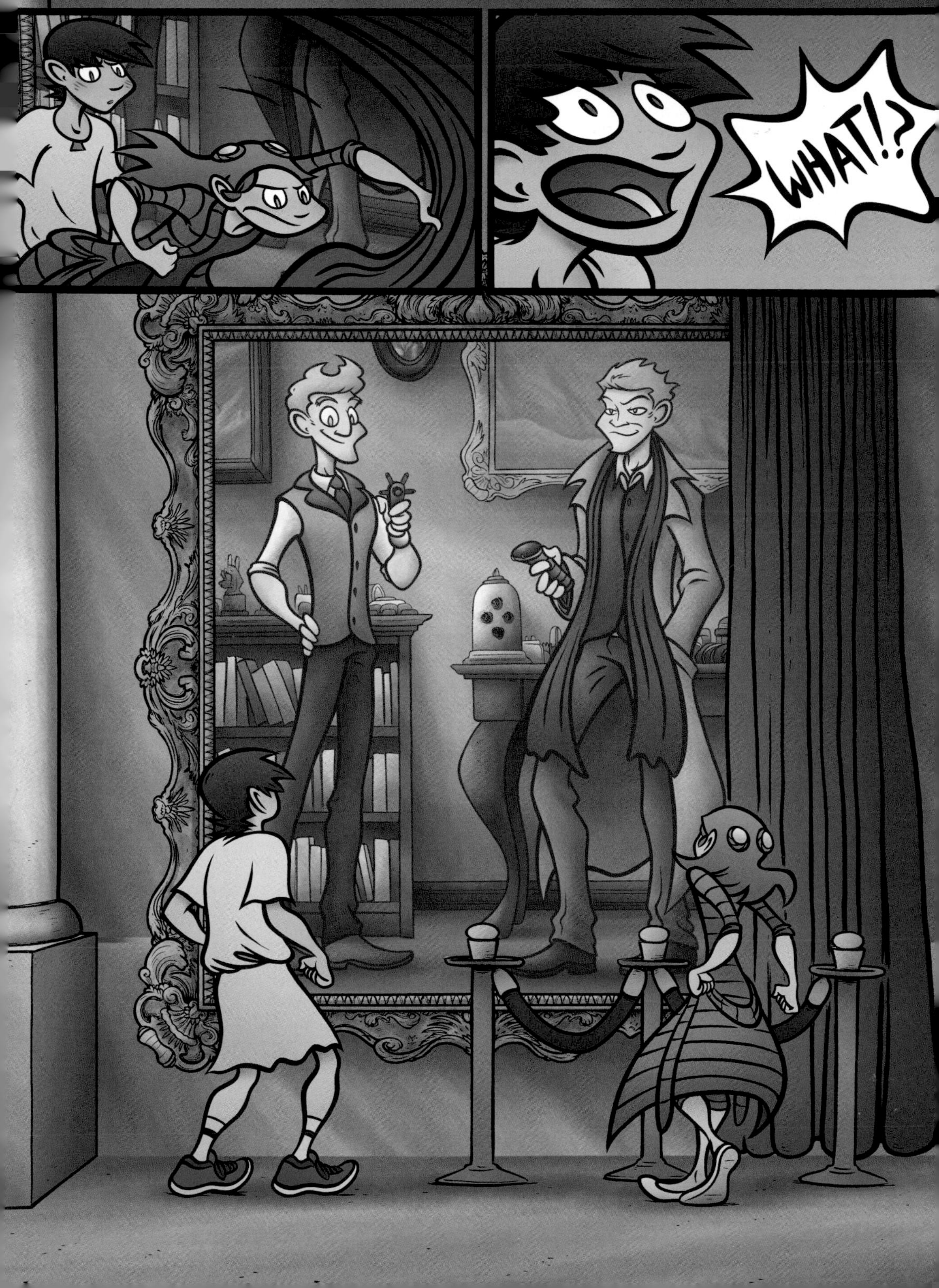
WHAT!?

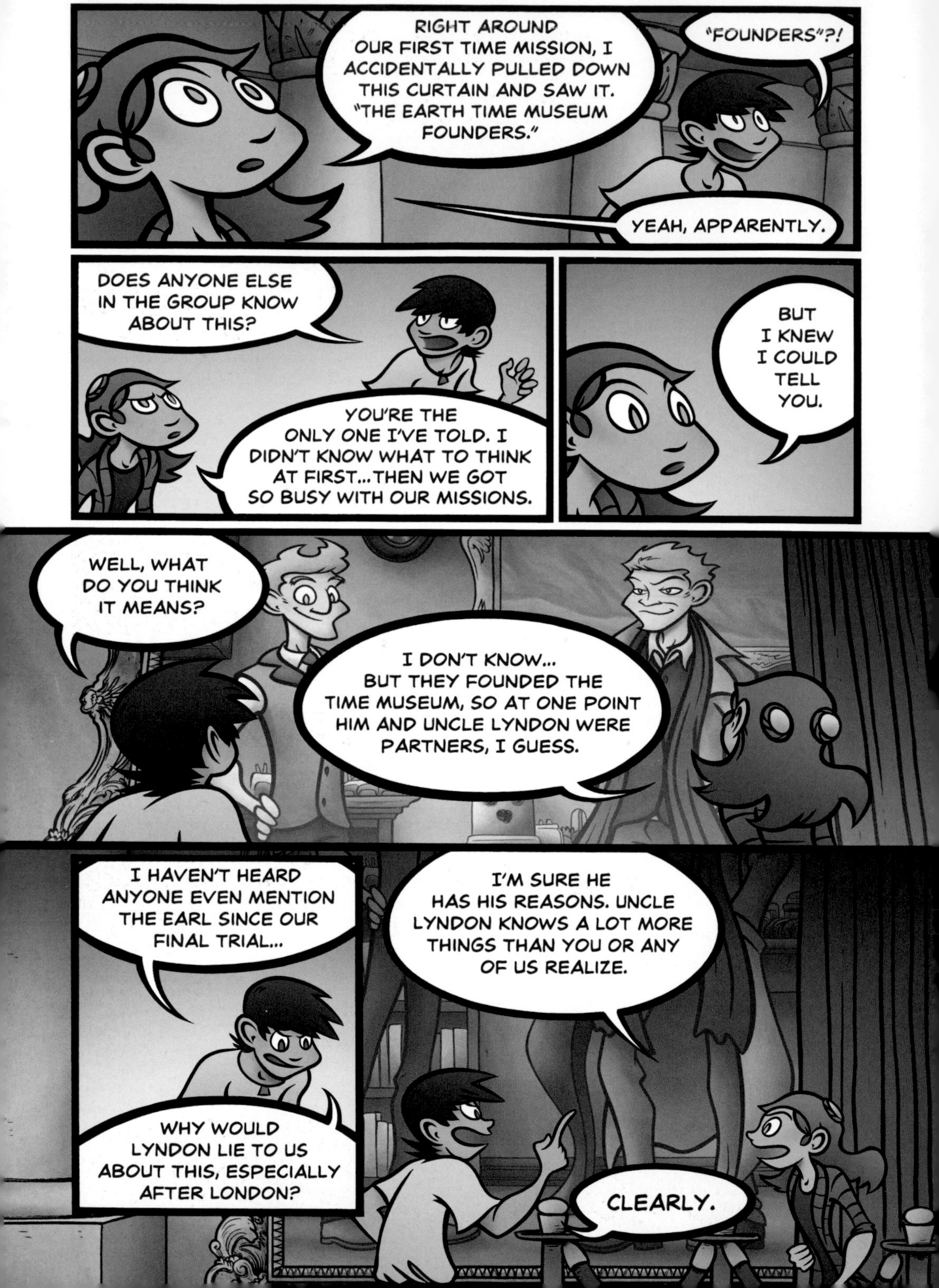
RIGHT AROUND OUR FIRST TIME MISSION, I ACCIDENTALLY PULLED DOWN THIS CURTAIN AND SAW IT. "THE EARTH TIME MUSEUM FOUNDERS."
"FOUNDERS"?!
YEAH, APPARENTLY.
DOES ANYONE ELSE IN THE GROUP KNOW ABOUT THIS?
YOU'RE THE ONLY ONE I'VE TOLD. I DIDN'T KNOW WHAT TO THINK AT FIRST...THEN WE GOT SO BUSY WITH OUR MISSIONS.
BUT I KNEW I COULD TELL YOU.
WELL, WHAT DO YOU THINK IT MEANS?
I DON'T KNOW... BUT THEY FOUNDED THE TIME MUSEUM, SO AT ONE POINT HIM AND UNCLE LYNDON WERE PARTNERS, I GUESS.
I HAVEN'T HEARD ANYONE EVEN MENTION THE EARL SINCE OUR FINAL TRIAL...
WHY WOULD LYNDON LIE TO US ABOUT THIS, ESPECIALLY AFTER LONDON?
I'M SURE HE HAS HIS REASONS. UNCLE LYNDON KNOWS A LOT MORE THINGS THAN YOU OR ANY OF US REALIZE.
CLEARLY.

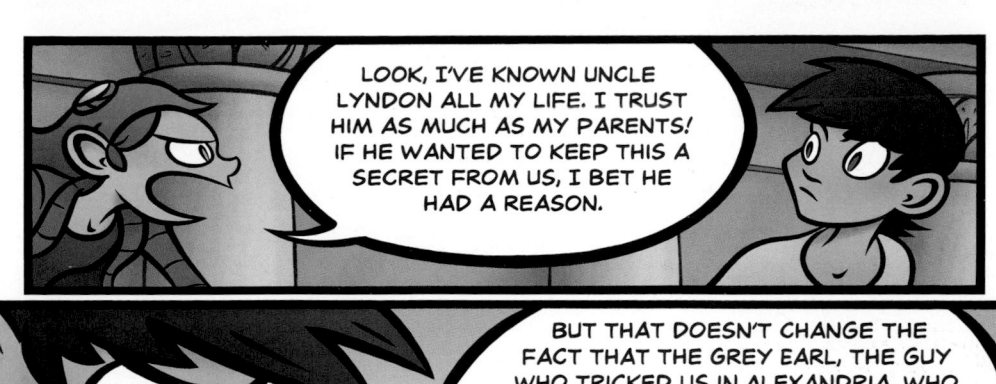

LOOK, I'VE KNOWN UNCLE LYNDON ALL MY LIFE. I TRUST HIM AS MUCH AS MY PARENTS! IF HE WANTED TO KEEP THIS A SECRET FROM US, I BET HE HAD A REASON.

BUT THAT DOESN'T CHANGE THE FACT THAT THE GREY EARL, THE GUY WHO TRICKED US IN ALEXANDRIA, WHO TRIED TO DESTROY FUTURE LONDON, THE GUY WHO CLEARLY HAS AN AGENDA AGAINST THE MUSEUM...WAS ONCE LYNDON'S PARTNER!

HAVE YOU BROUGHT THIS UP TO HIM?

NO! AND I'M NOT GOING TO, 'CAUSE I TRUST HIM...

AND I THOUGHT I COULD TRUST YOU!

YOU CAN, DE', YOU CAN... I'M SORRY, THIS IS JUST... KIND OF A BIG SHOCK.

NO, YOU'RE RIGHT, I FELT THE SAME WAY...

BUT I REALLY DO TRUST UNCLE LYNDON... AND YOU SHOULD, TOO.

I'D BETTER GET BACK. WE HAVE TO BE UP EARLY TOMORROW.

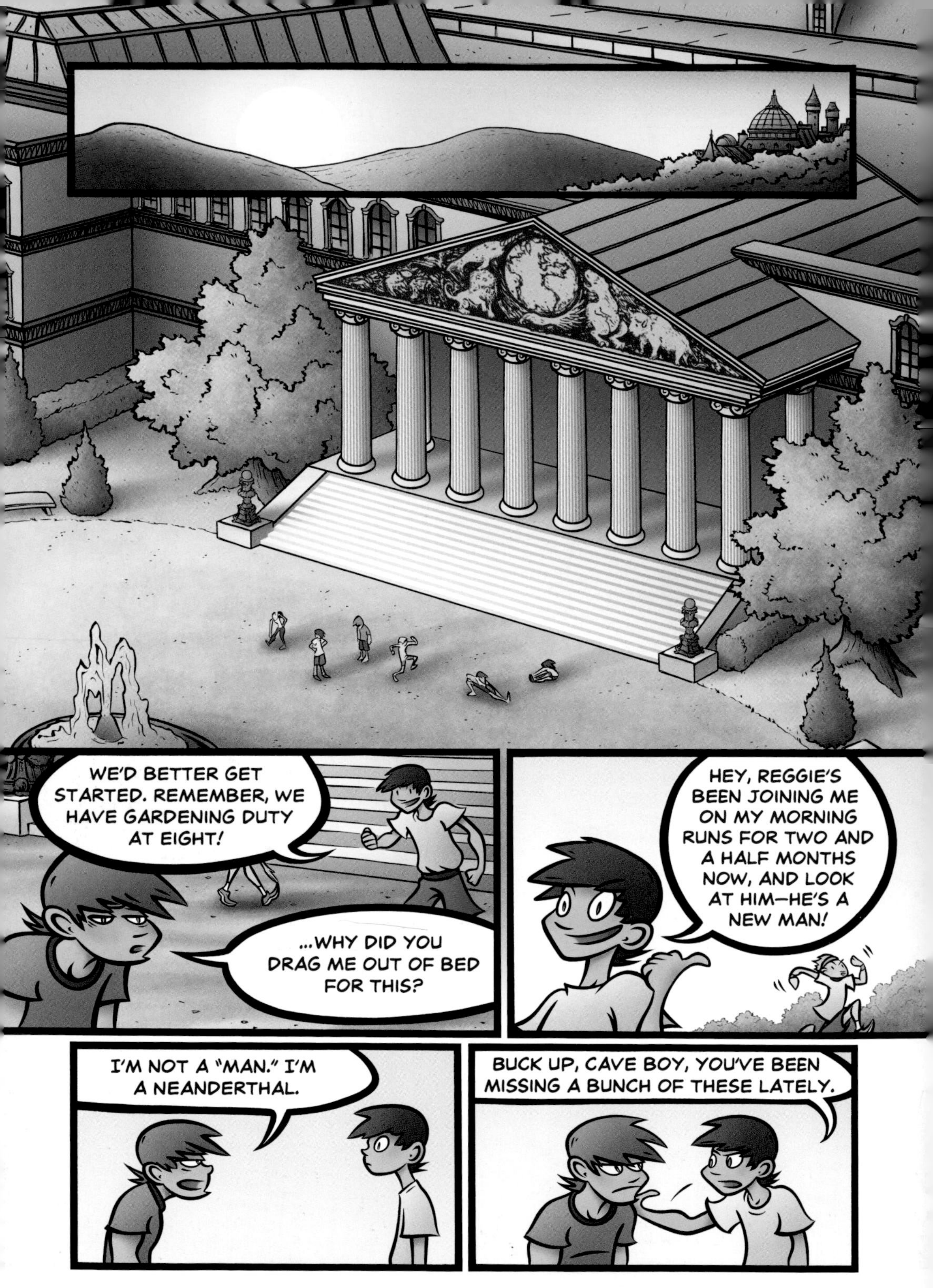
WE'D BETTER GET STARTED. REMEMBER, WE HAVE GARDENING DUTY AT EIGHT!
...WHY DID YOU DRAG ME OUT OF BED FOR THIS?
HEY, REGGIE'S BEEN JOINING ME ON MY MORNING RUNS FOR TWO AND A HALF MONTHS NOW, AND LOOK AT HIM—HE'S A NEW MAN!
I'M NOT A "MAN." I'M A NEANDERTHAL.
BUCK UP, CAVE BOY, YOU'VE BEEN MISSING A BUNCH OF THESE LATELY.

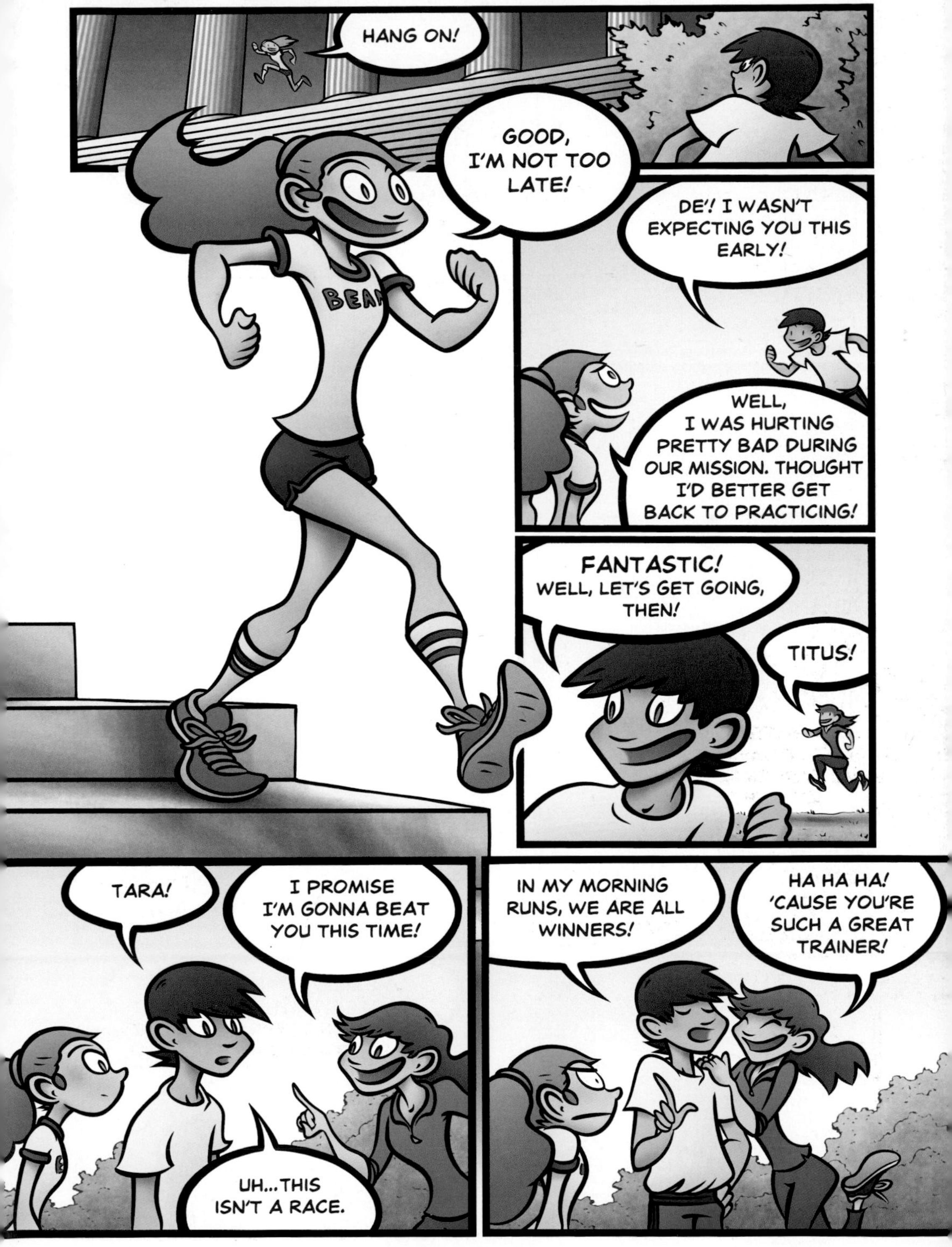
HANG ON!
GOOD, I'M NOT TOO LATE!
BEA
DE'! I WASN'T EXPECTING YOU THIS EARLY!
WELL, I WAS HURTING PRETTY BAD DURING OUR MISSION. THOUGHT I'D BETTER GET BACK TO PRACTICING!
FANTASTIC! WELL, LET'S GET GOING, THEN!
TITUS!
TARA!
I PROMISE I'M GONNA BEAT YOU THIS TIME!
UH...THIS ISN'T A RACE.
IN MY MORNING RUNS, WE ARE ALL WINNERS!
HA HA HA! 'CAUSE YOU'RE SUCH A GREAT TRAINER!

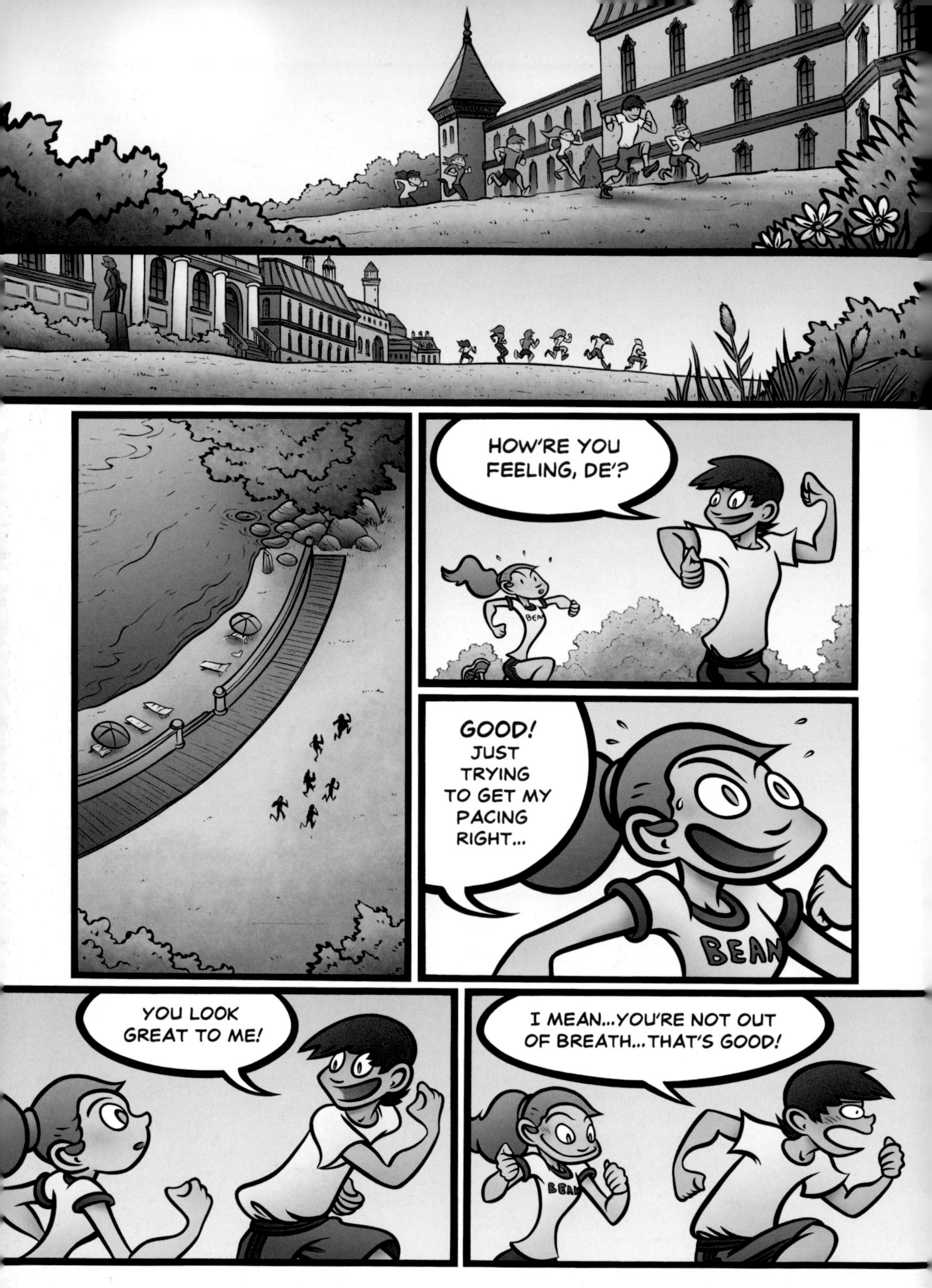
HOW'RE YOU FEELING, DE'?
BEAN
GOOD! JUST TRYING TO GET MY PACING RIGHT...
BEAN
YOU LOOK GREAT TO ME!
I MEAN...YOU'RE NOT OUT OF BREATH...THAT'S GOOD!
BEAN

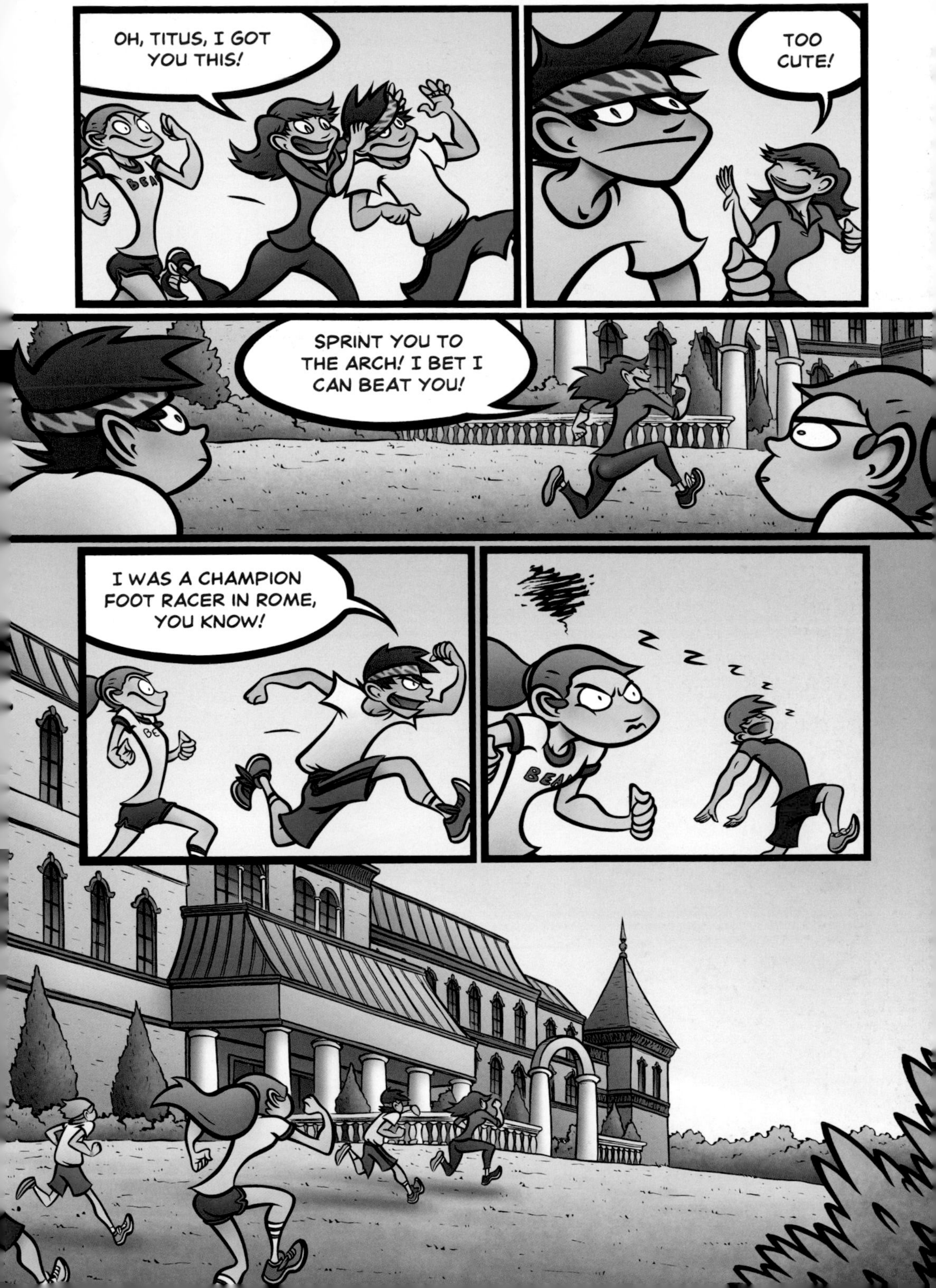

OH, TITUS, I GOT YOU THIS!
TOO CUTE!
SPRINT YOU TO THE ARCH! I BET I CAN BEAT YOU!
I WAS A CHAMPION FOOT RACER IN ROME, YOU KNOW!

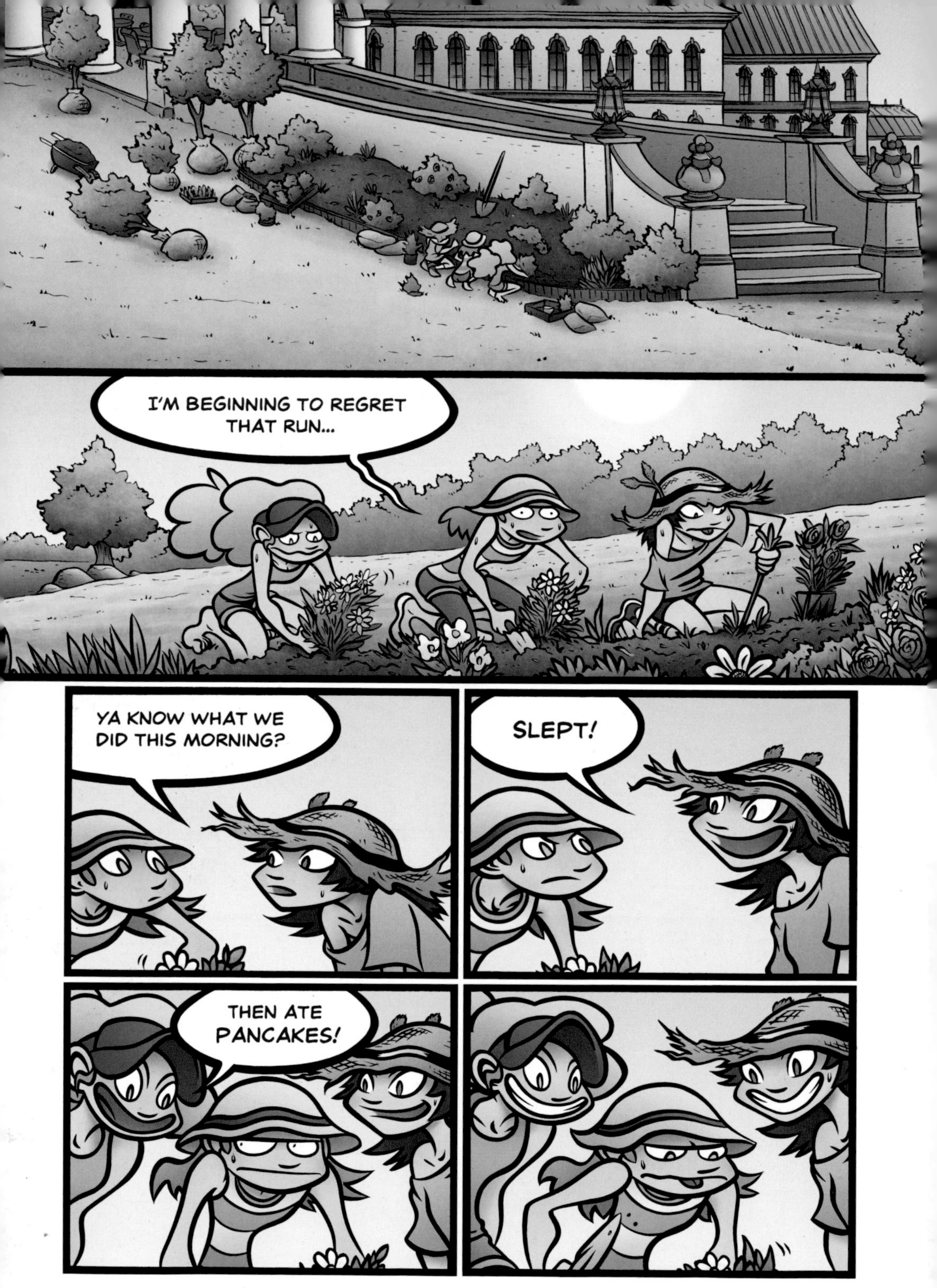
I'M BEGINNING TO REGRET THAT RUN...
YA KNOW WHAT WE DID THIS MORNING?
SLEPT!
THEN ATE PANCAKES!

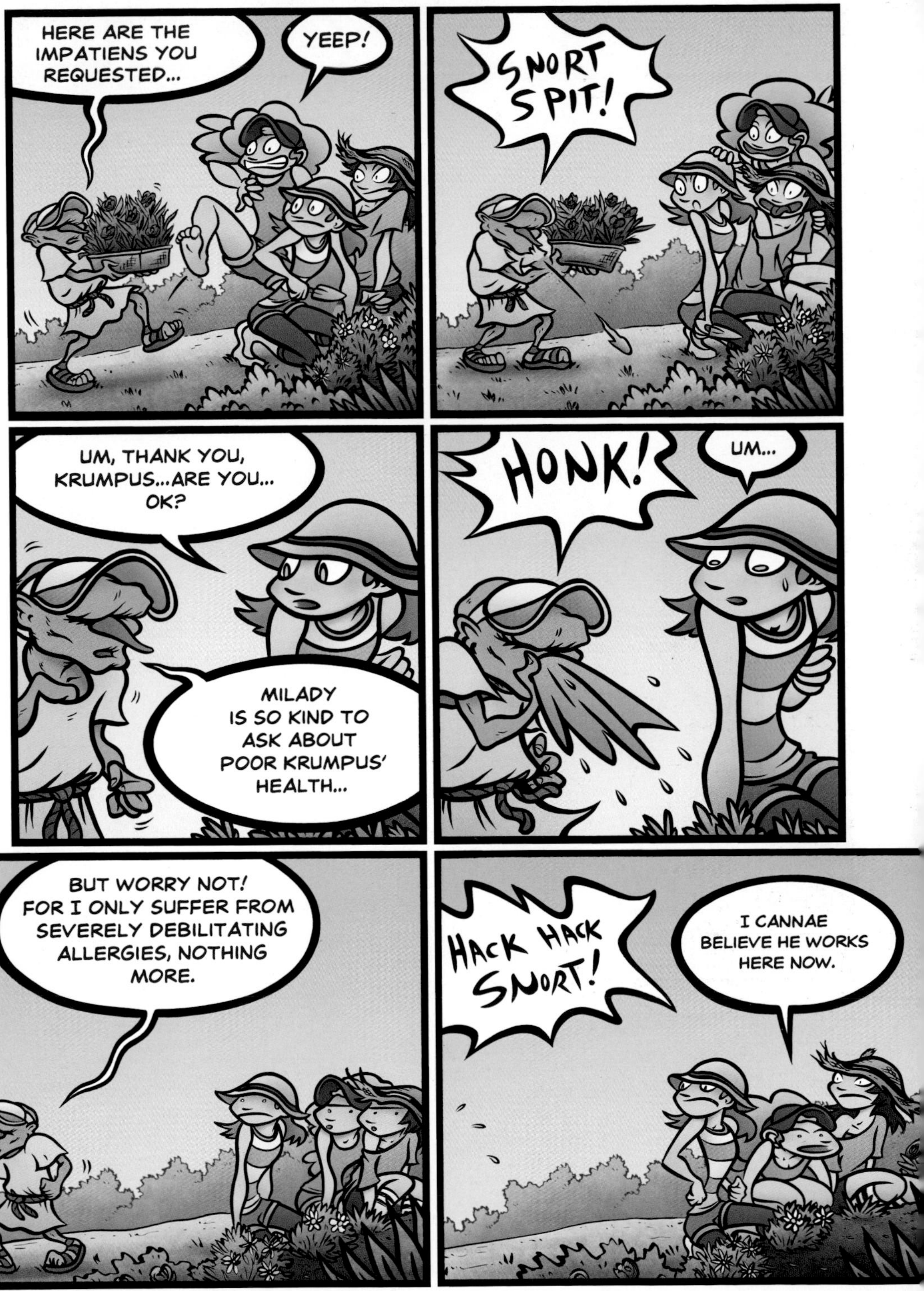
HERE ARE THE IMPATIENS YOU REQUESTED...
YEEP!
SNORT SPIT!
UM, THANK YOU, KRUMPUS...ARE YOU... OK?
MILADY IS SO KIND TO ASK ABOUT POOR KRUMPUS' HEALTH...
HONK!
UM...
BUT WORRY NOT! FOR I ONLY SUFFER FROM SEVERELY DEBILITATING ALLERGIES, NOTHING MORE.
HACK HACK SNORT!
I CANNAE BELIEVE HE WORKS HERE NOW.

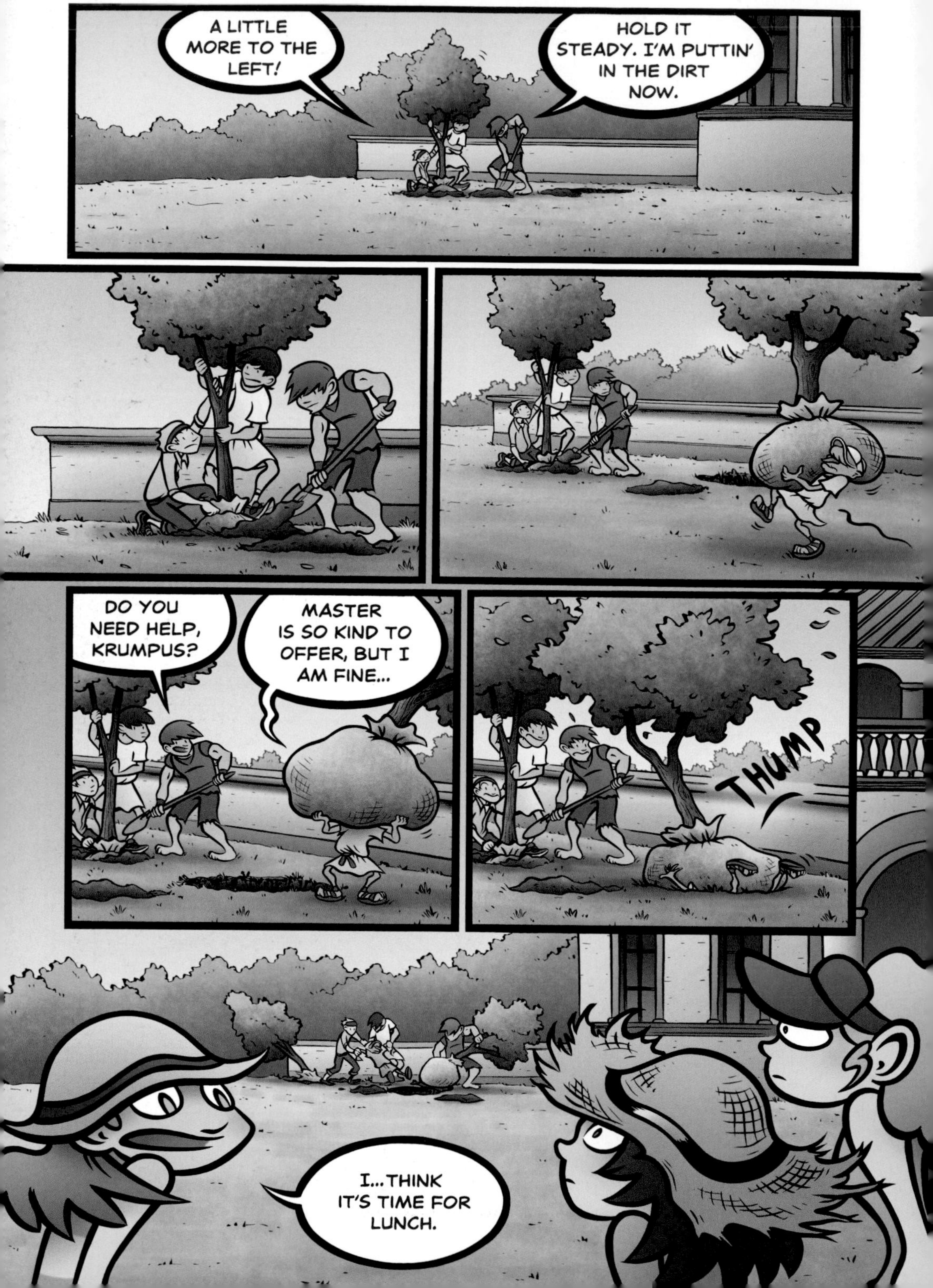
A LITTLE MORE TO THE LEFT!
HOLD IT STEADY. I'M PUTTIN' IN THE DIRT NOW.
DO YOU NEED HELP, KRUMPUS?
MASTER IS SO KIND TO OFFER, BUT I AM FINE...
THUMP
I...THINK IT'S TIME FOR LUNCH.

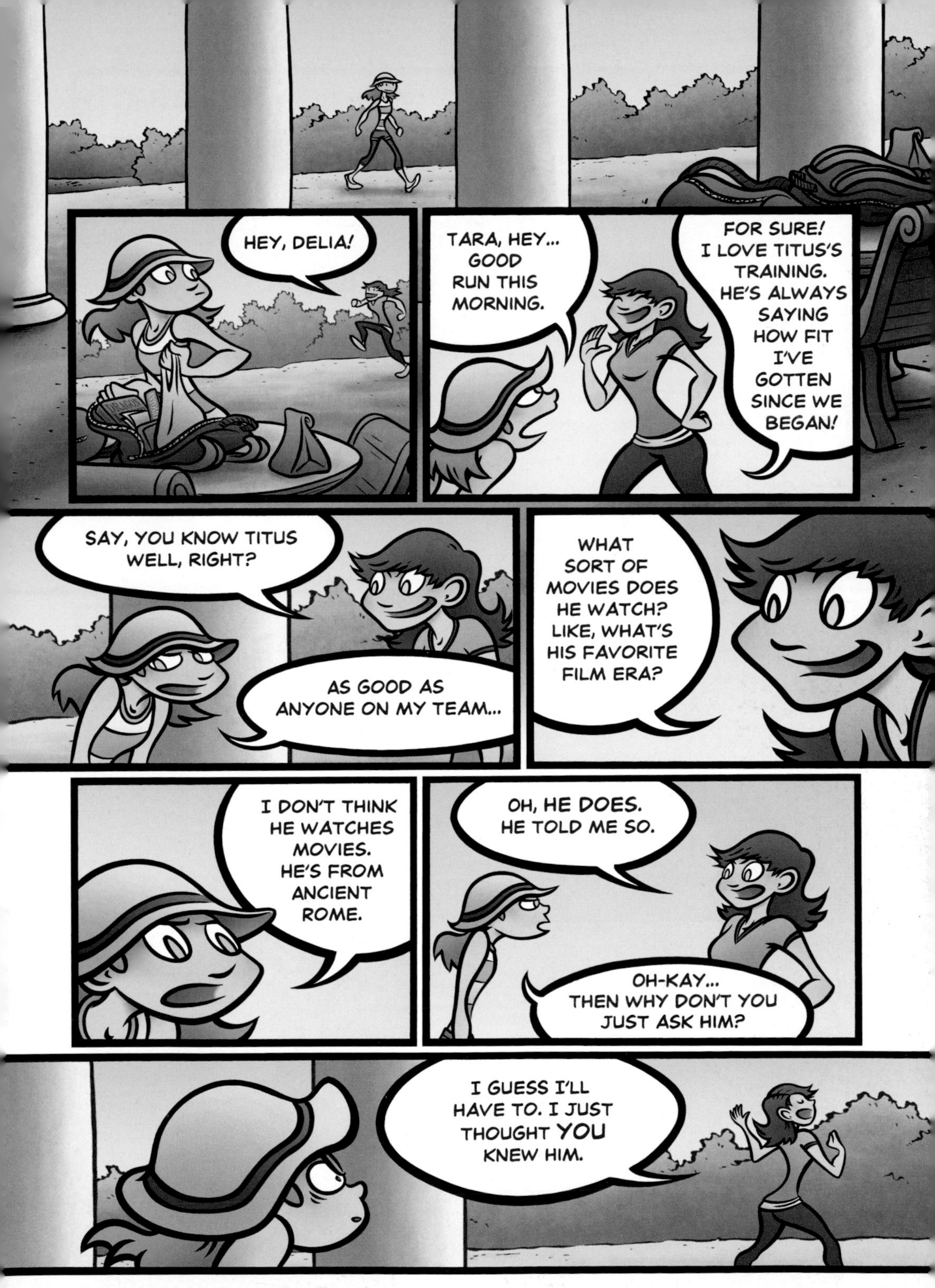
HEY, DELIA!
TARA, HEY... GOOD RUN THIS MORNING.
FOR SURE! I LOVE TITUS'S TRAINING. HE'S ALWAYS SAYING HOW FIT I'VE GOTTEN SINCE WE BEGAN!
SAY, YOU KNOW TITUS WELL, RIGHT?
AS GOOD AS ANYONE ON MY TEAM...
WHAT SORT OF MOVIES DOES HE WATCH? LIKE, WHAT'S HIS FAVORITE FILM ERA?
I DON'T THINK HE WATCHES MOVIES. HE'S FROM ANCIENT ROME.
OH, HE DOES. HE TOLD ME SO.
OH-KAY... THEN WHY DON'T YOU JUST ASK HIM?
I GUESS I'LL HAVE TO. I JUST THOUGHT YOU KNEW HIM.

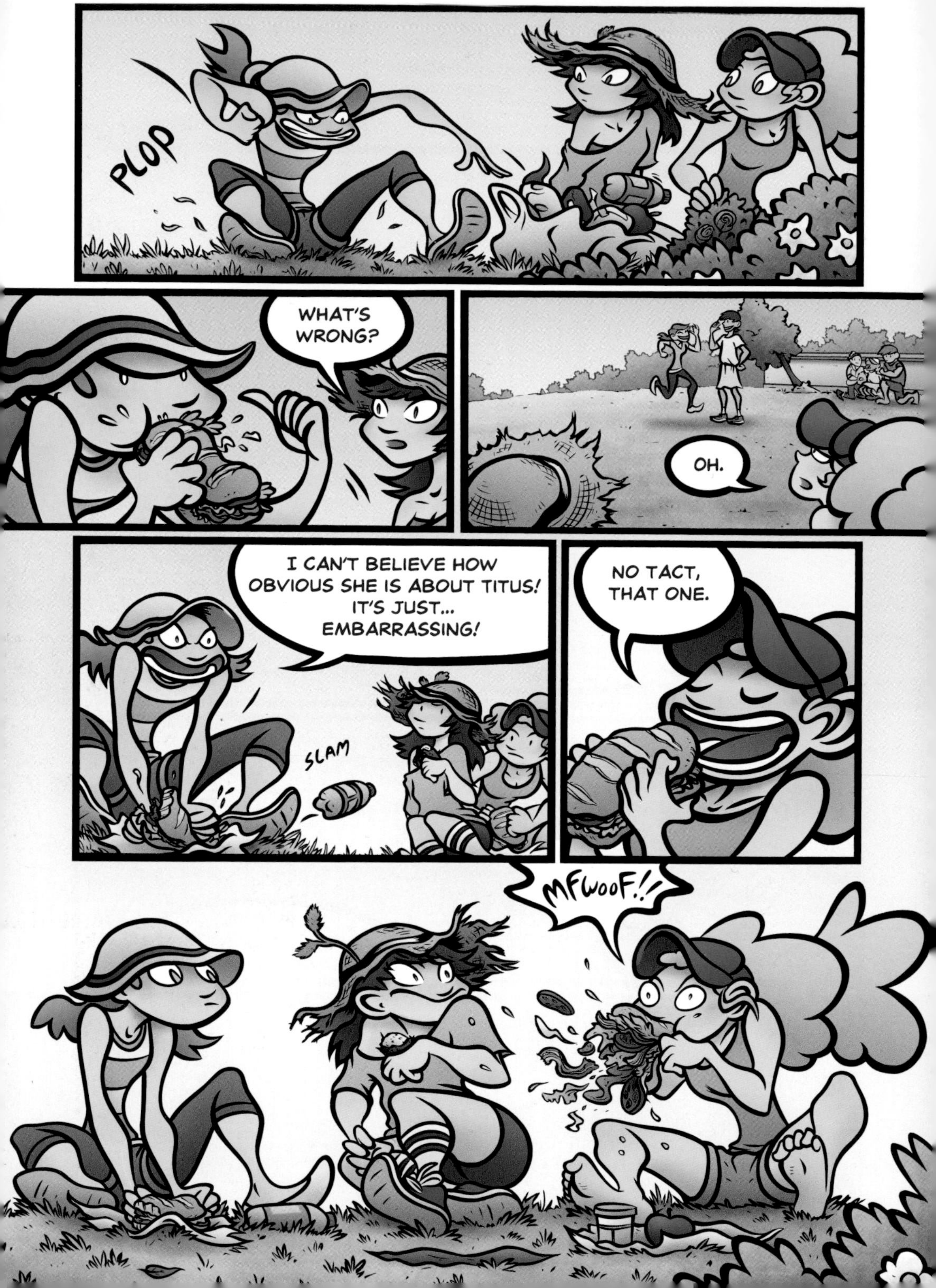
PLOP
WHAT'S WRONG?
OH.
I CAN'T BELIEVE HOW OBVIOUS SHE IS ABOUT TITUS! IT'S JUST... EMBARRASSING!
SLAM
NO TACT, THAT ONE.
MFWOOF!!!

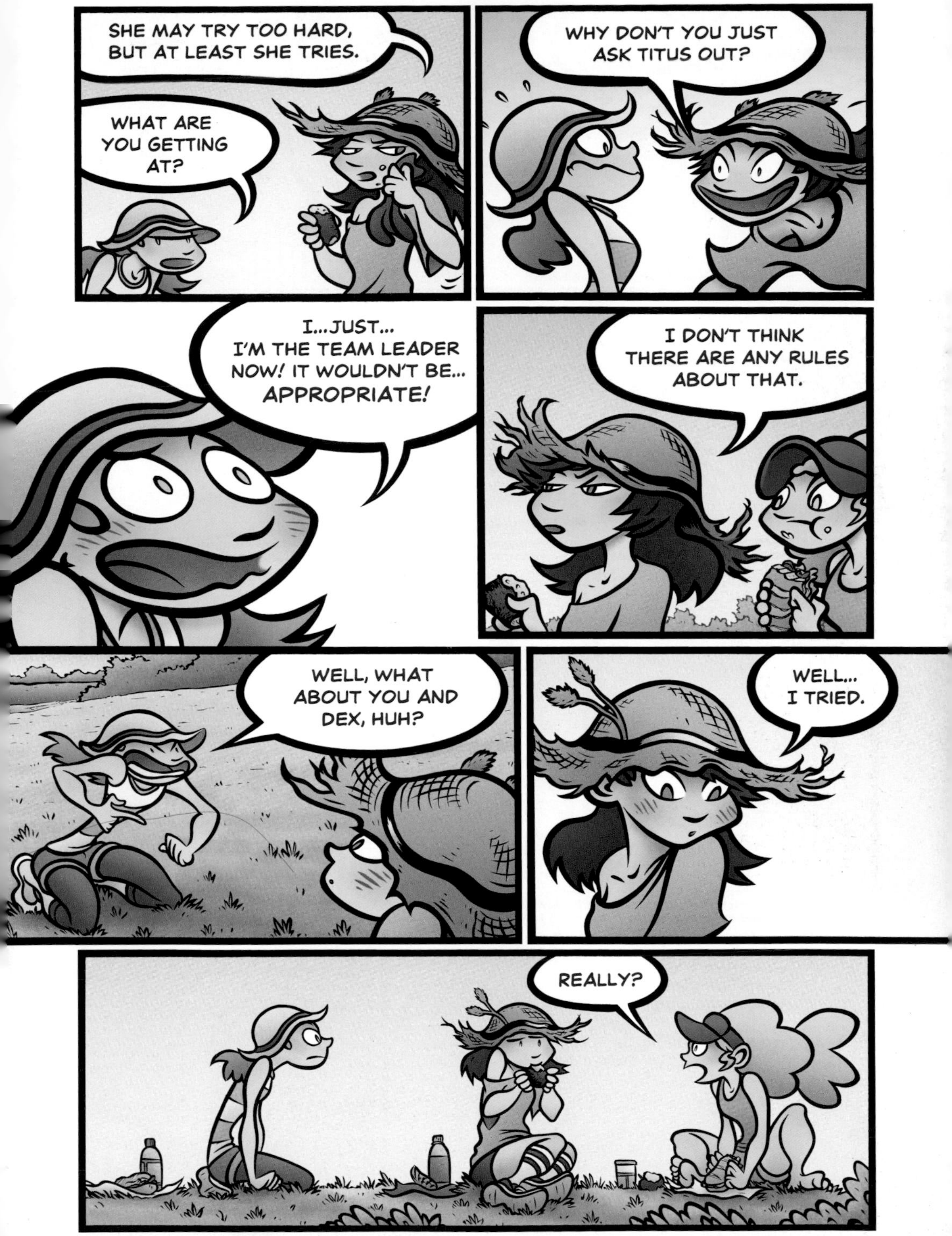
SHE MAY TRY TOO HARD, BUT AT LEAST SHE TRIES.
WHAT ARE YOU GETTING AT?
WHY DON'T YOU JUST ASK TITUS OUT?
I...JUST... I'M THE TEAM LEADER NOW! IT WOULDN'T BE... APPROPRIATE!
I DON'T THINK THERE ARE ANY RULES ABOUT THAT.
WELL, WHAT ABOUT YOU AND DEX, HUH?
WELL... I TRIED.
REALLY?

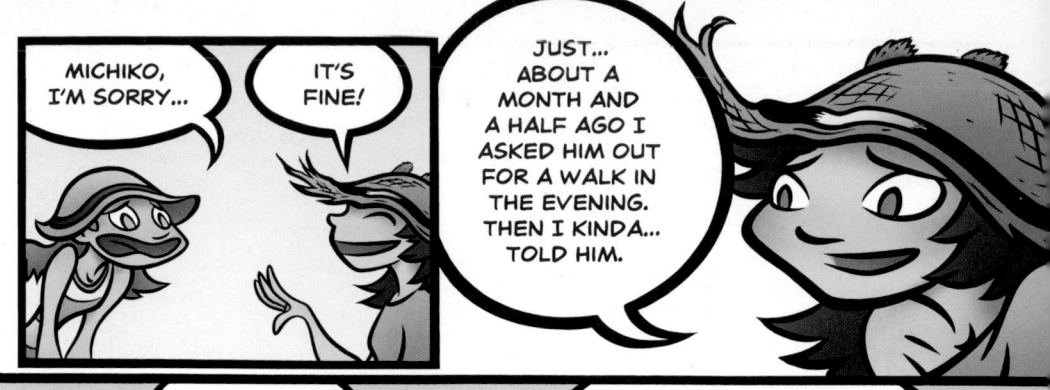

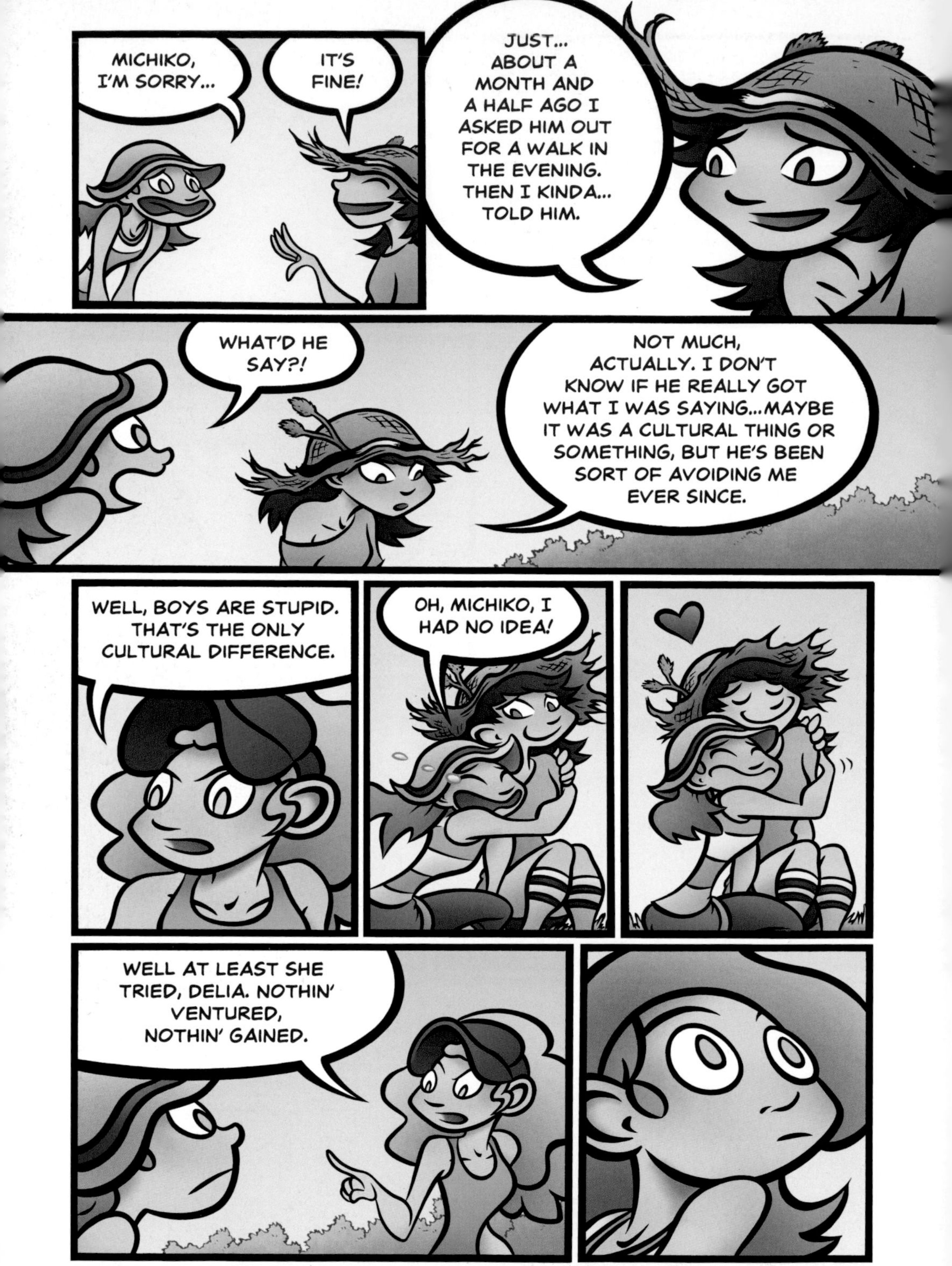
MICHIKO, I'M SORRY...
IT'S FINE!
JUST... ABOUT A MONTH AND A HALF AGO I ASKED HIM OUT FOR A WALK IN THE EVENING. THEN I KINDA... TOLD HIM.
WHAT'D HE SAY?!
NOT MUCH, ACTUALLY. I DON'T KNOW IF HE REALLY GOT WHAT I WAS SAYING...MAYBE IT WAS A CULTURAL THING OR SOMETHING, BUT HE'S BEEN SORT OF AVOIDING ME EVER SINCE.
WELL, BOYS ARE STUPID. THAT'S THE ONLY CULTURAL DIFFERENCE.
OH, MICHIKO, I HAD NO IDEA!
WELL AT LEAST SHE TRIED, DELIA. NOTHIN' VENTURED, NOTHIN' GAINED.

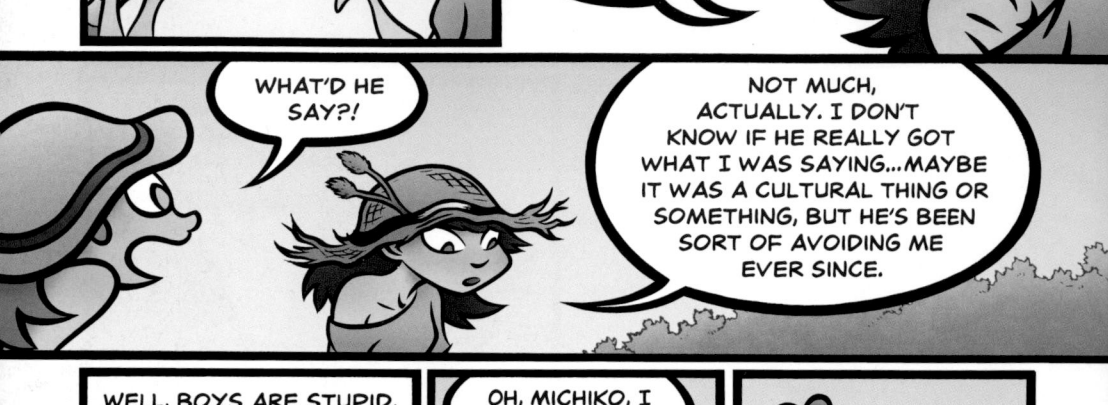

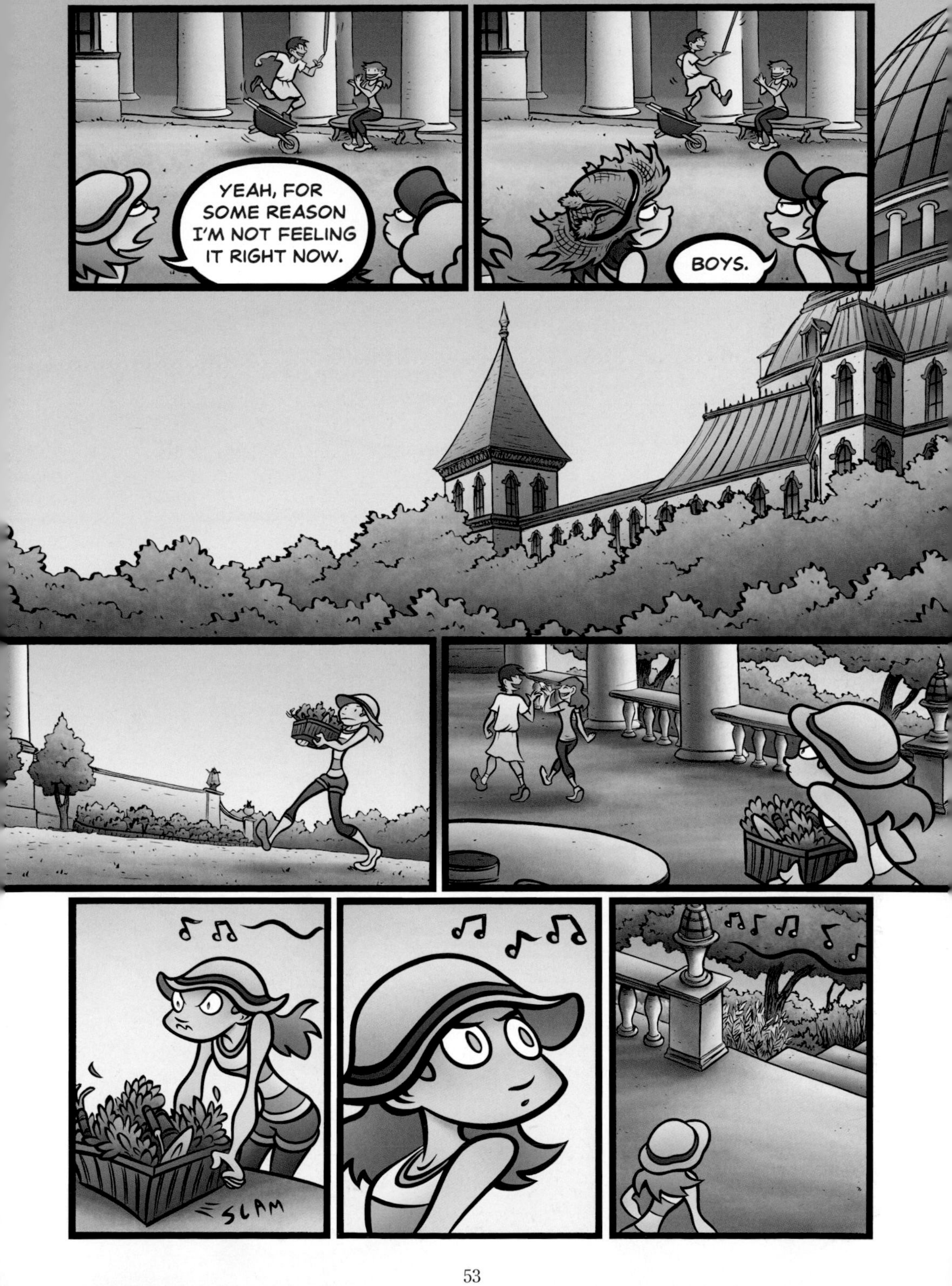
YEAH, FOR SOME REASON I'M NOT FEELING IT RIGHT NOW.
BOYS.
SLAM

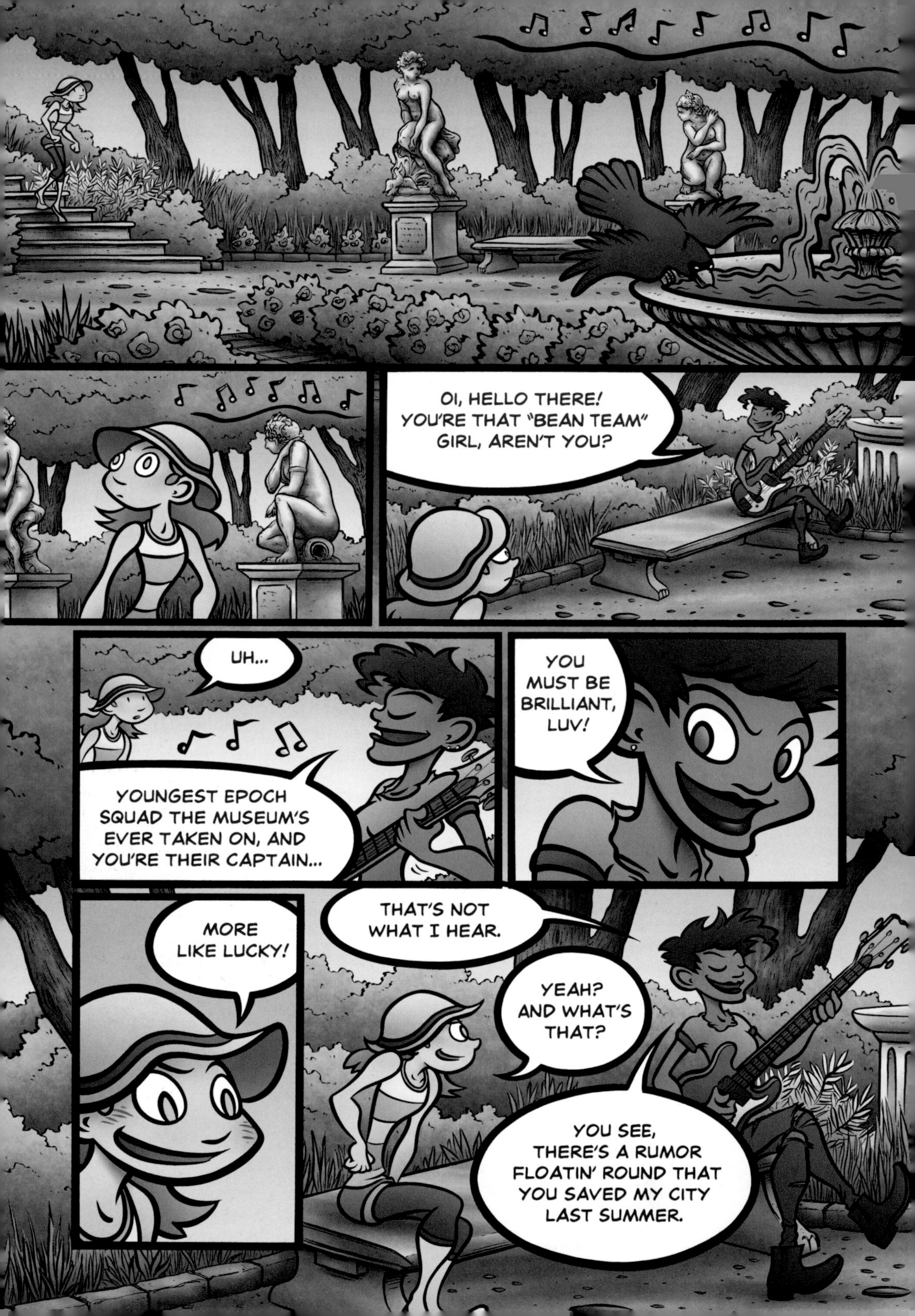

OI, HELLO THERE! YOU'RE THAT "BEAN TEAM" GIRL, AREN'T YOU?
UH...
YOUNGEST EPOCH SQUAD THE MUSEUM'S EVER TAKEN ON, AND YOU'RE THEIR CAPTAIN...
YOU MUST BE BRILLIANT, LUV!
MORE LIKE LUCKY!
THAT'S NOT WHAT I HEAR.
YEAH? AND WHAT'S THAT?
YOU SEE, THERE'S A RUMOR FLOATIN' ROUND THAT YOU SAVED MY CITY LAST SUMMER.

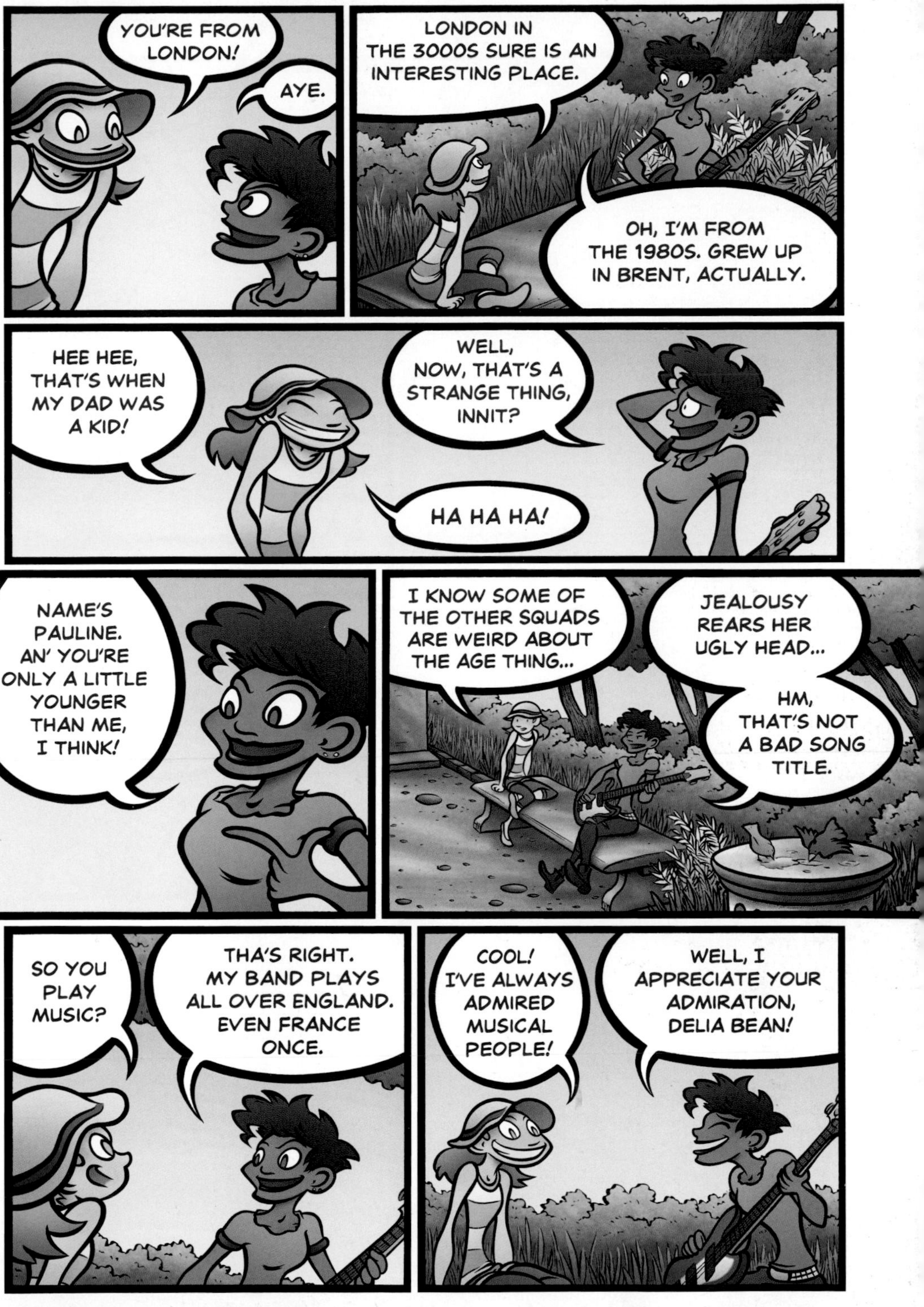
YOU'RE FROM LONDON!
AYE.
LONDON IN THE 3000S SURE IS AN INTERESTING PLACE.
OH, I'M FROM THE 1980S. GREW UP IN BRENT, ACTUALLY.
HEE HEE, THAT'S WHEN MY DAD WAS A KID!
WELL, NOW, THAT'S A STRANGE THING, INNIT?
HA HA HA!
NAME'S PAULINE. AN' YOU'RE ONLY A LITTLE YOUNGER THAN ME, I THINK!
I KNOW SOME OF THE OTHER SQUADS ARE WEIRD ABOUT THE AGE THING...
JEALOUSY REARS HER UGLY HEAD...
HM, THAT'S NOT A BAD SONG TITLE.
SO YOU PLAY MUSIC?
THA'S RIGHT. MY BAND PLAYS ALL OVER ENGLAND. EVEN FRANCE ONCE.
COOL! I'VE ALWAYS ADMIRED MUSICAL PEOPLE!
WELL, I APPRECIATE YOUR ADMIRATION, DELIA BEAN!

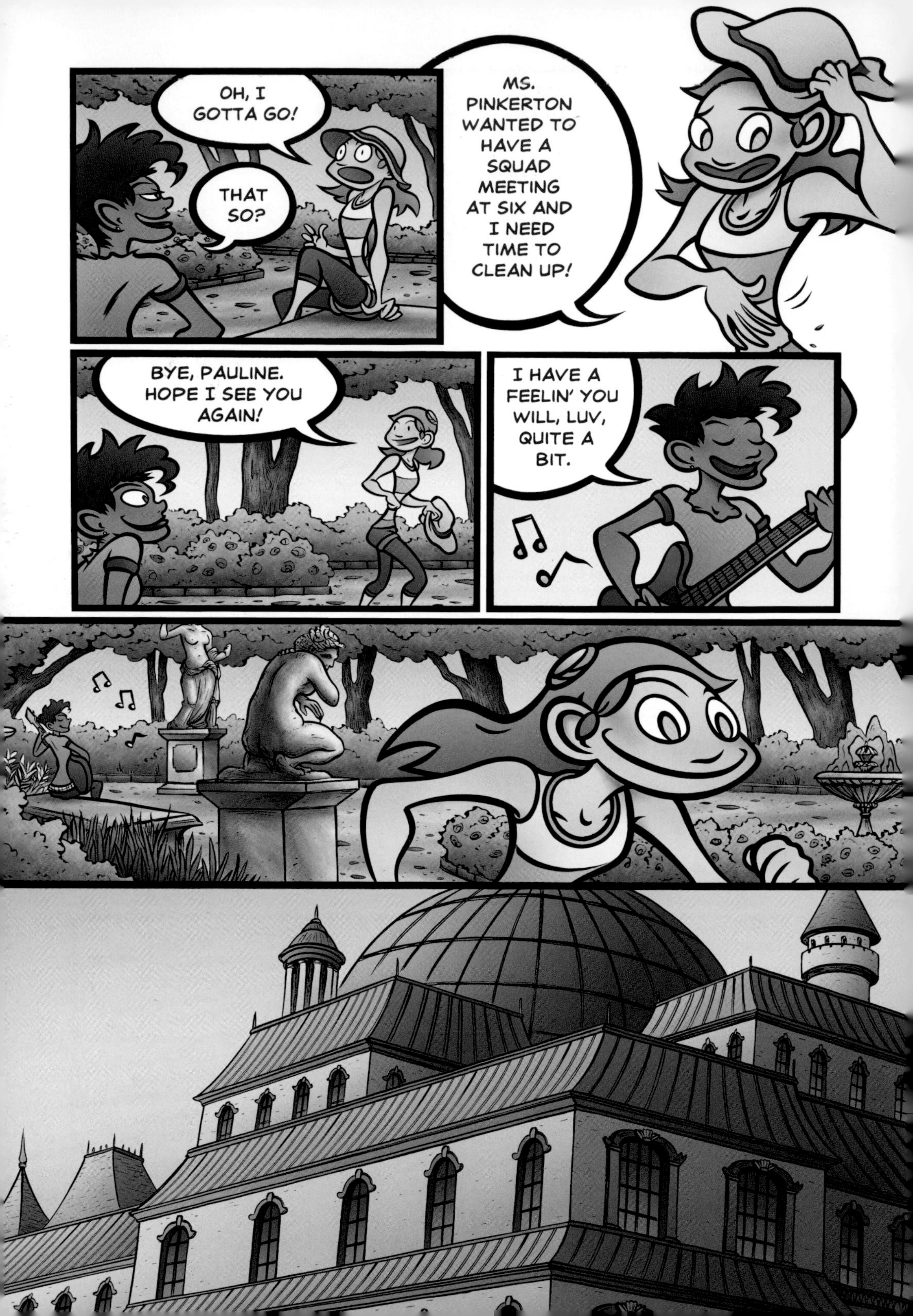
OH, I GOTTA GO!
THAT SO?
MS. PINKERTON WANTED TO HAVE A SQUAD MEETING AT SIX AND I NEED TIME TO CLEAN UP!
BYE, PAULINE. HOPE I SEE YOU AGAIN!
I HAVE A FEELIN' YOU WILL, LUV, QUITE A BIT.

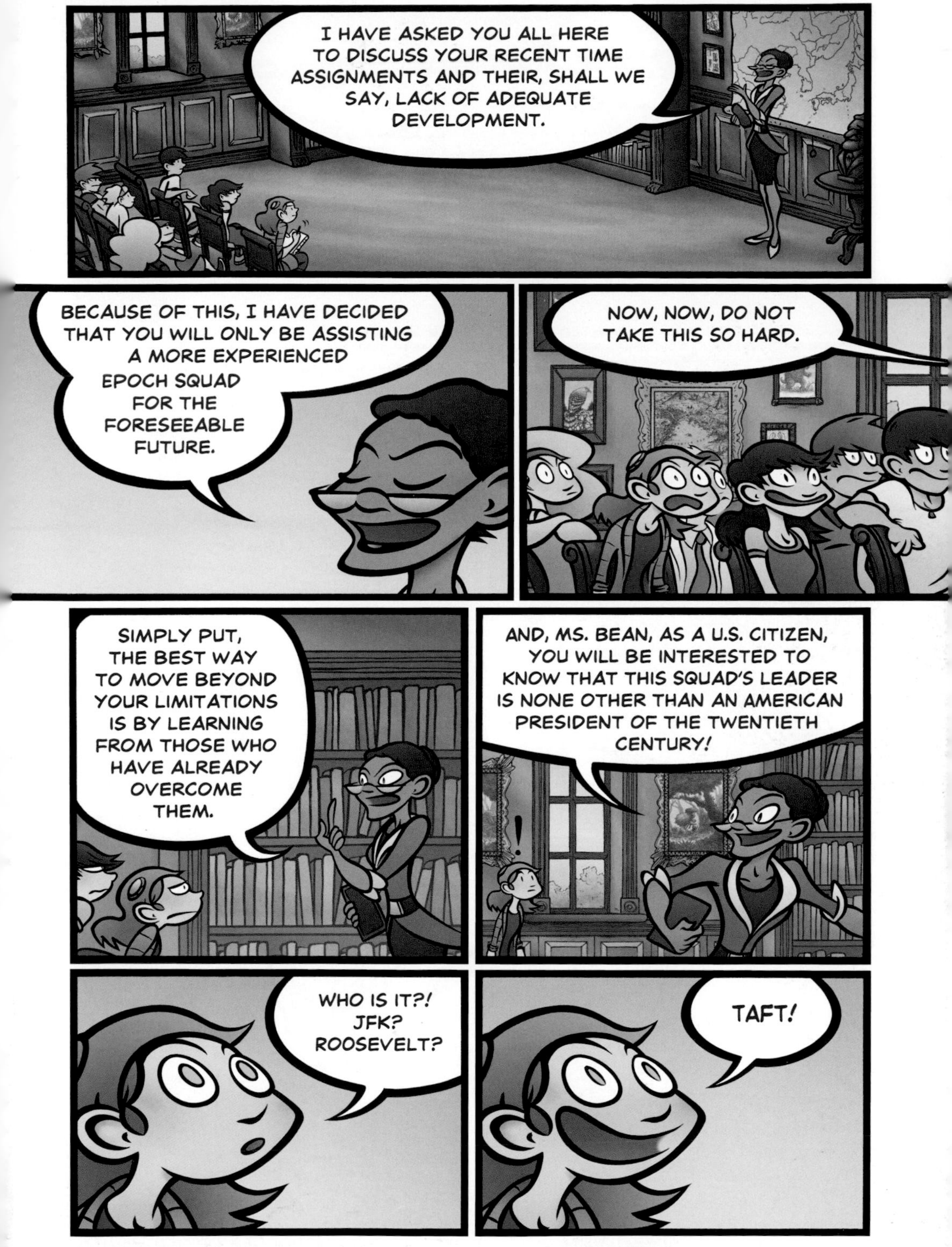
I HAVE ASKED YOU ALL HERE TO DISCUSS YOUR RECENT TIME ASSIGNMENTS AND THEIR, SHALL WE SAY, LACK OF ADEQUATE DEVELOPMENT.
BECAUSE OF THIS, I HAVE DECIDED THAT YOU WILL ONLY BE ASSISTING A MORE EXPERIENCED EPOCH SQUAD FOR THE FORESEEABLE FUTURE.
NOW, NOW, DO NOT TAKE THIS SO HARD.
SIMPLY PUT, THE BEST WAY TO MOVE BEYOND YOUR LIMITATIONS IS BY LEARNING FROM THOSE WHO HAVE ALREADY OVERCOME THEM.
AND, MS. BEAN, AS A U.S. CITIZEN, YOU WILL BE INTERESTED TO KNOW THAT THIS SQUAD'S LEADER IS NONE OTHER THAN AN AMERICAN PRESIDENT OF THE TWENTIETH CENTURY!
!
WHO IS IT?! JFK? ROOSEVELT?
TAFT!

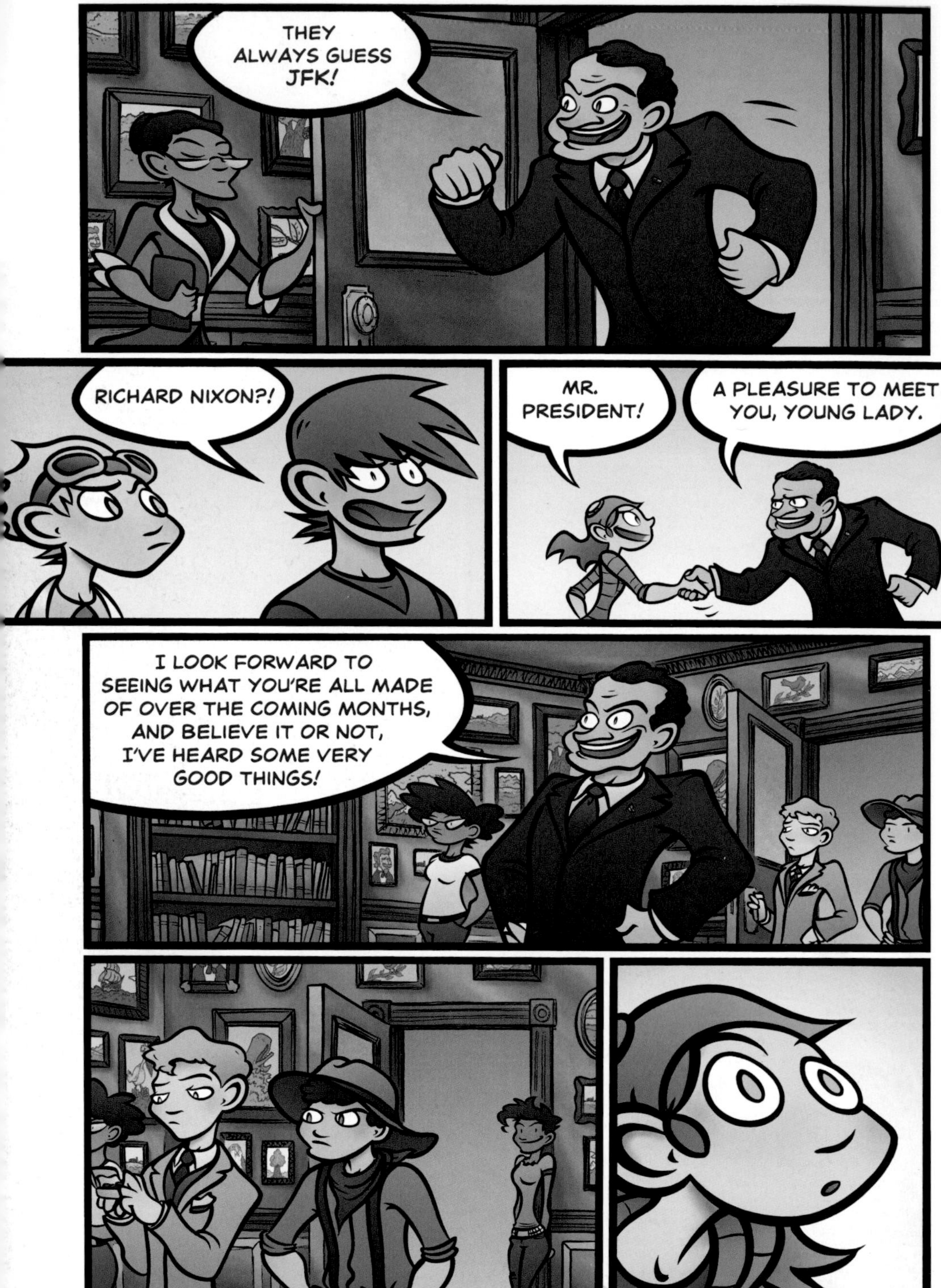
THEY ALWAYS GUESS JFK!
RICHARD NIXON?!
MR. PRESIDENT!
A PLEASURE TO MEET YOU, YOUNG LADY.
I LOOK FORWARD TO SEEING WHAT YOU'RE ALL MADE OF OVER THE COMING MONTHS, AND BELIEVE IT OR NOT, I'VE HEARD SOME VERY GOOD THINGS!

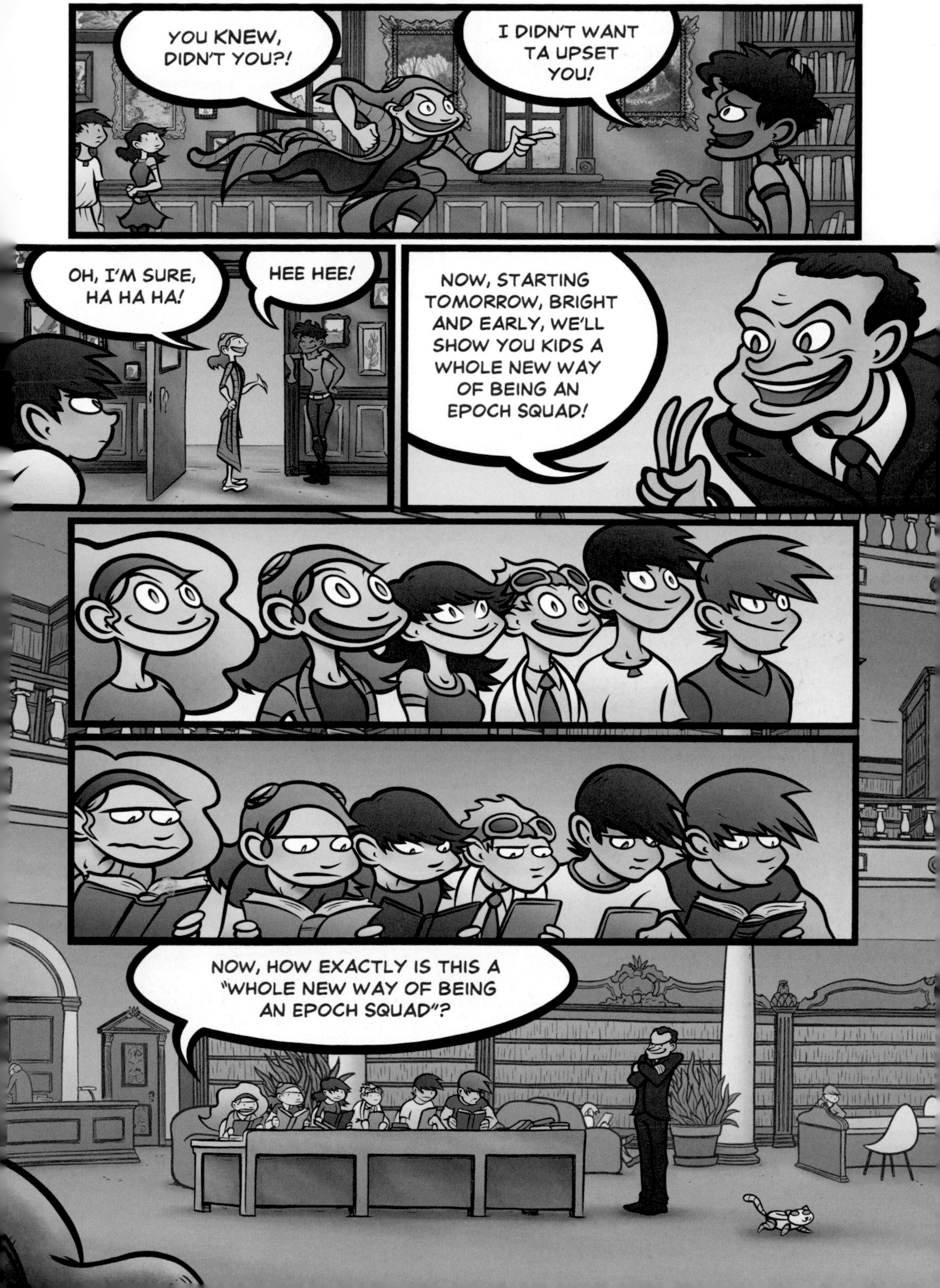
YOU KNEW, DIDN'T YOU?!
I DIDN'T WANT TA UPSET YOU!
OH, I'M SURE, HA HA HA!
HEE HEE!
NOW, STARTING TOMORROW, BRIGHT AND EARLY, WE'LL SHOW YOU KIDS A WHOLE NEW WAY OF BEING AN EPOCH SQUAD!
NOW, HOW EXACTLY IS THIS A "WHOLE NEW WAY OF BEING AN EPOCH SQUAD"?

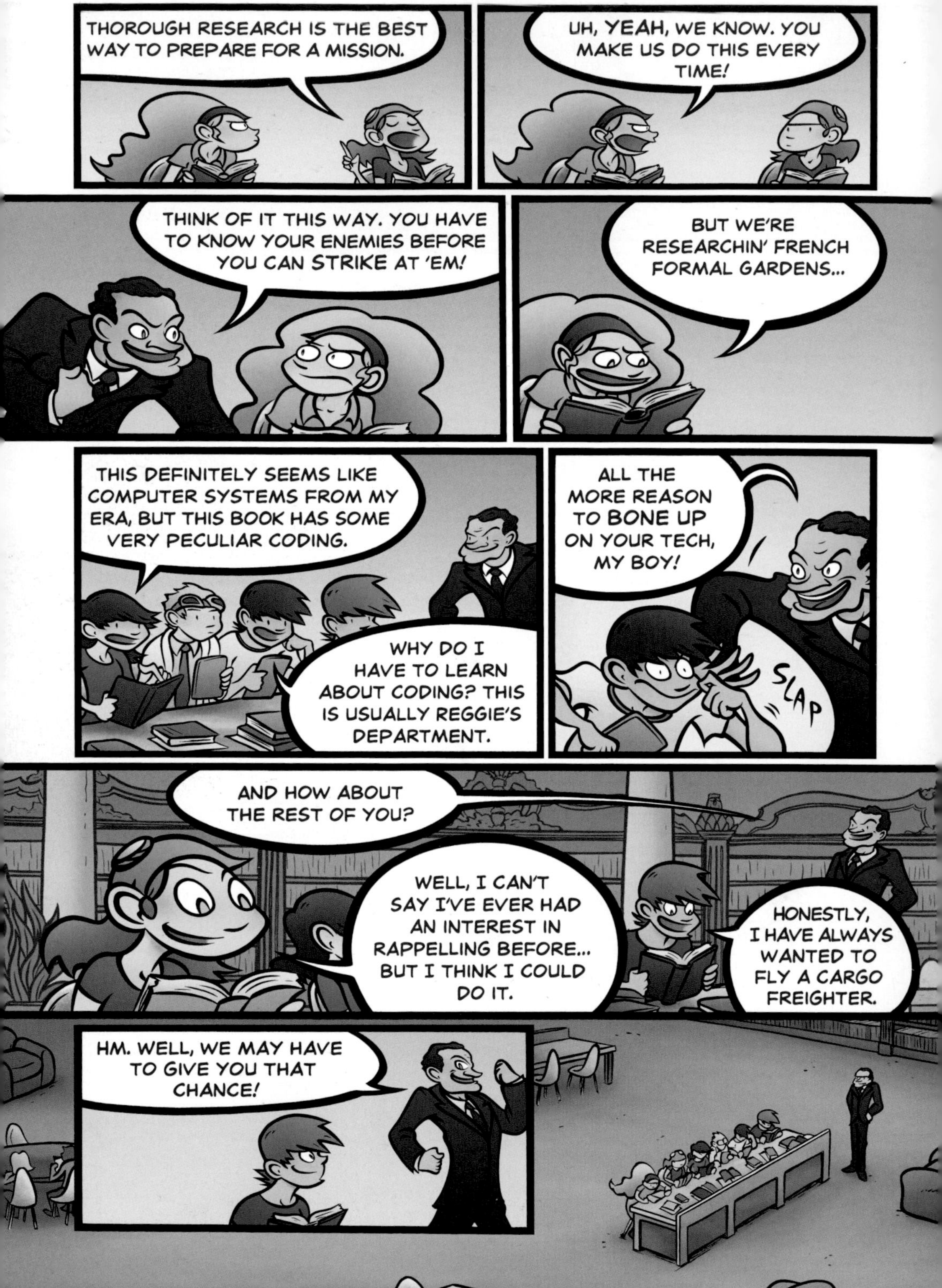

THOROUGH RESEARCH IS THE BEST WAY TO PREPARE FOR A MISSION.
UH, YEAH, WE KNOW. YOU MAKE US DO THIS EVERY TIME!
THINK OF IT THIS WAY. YOU HAVE TO KNOW YOUR ENEMIES BEFORE YOU CAN STRIKE AT 'EM!
BUT WE'RE RESEARCHIN' FRENCH FORMAL GARDENS...
THIS DEFINITELY SEEMS LIKE COMPUTER SYSTEMS FROM MY ERA, BUT THIS BOOK HAS SOME VERY PECULIAR CODING.
WHY DO I HAVE TO LEARN ABOUT CODING? THIS IS USUALLY REGGIE'S DEPARTMENT.
ALL THE MORE REASON TO BONE UP ON YOUR TECH, MY BOY!
SLAP
AND HOW ABOUT THE REST OF YOU?
WELL, I CAN'T SAY I'VE EVER HAD AN INTEREST IN RAPPELLING BEFORE... BUT I THINK I COULD DO IT.
HONESTLY, I HAVE ALWAYS WANTED TO FLY A CARGO FREIGHTER.
HM. WELL, WE MAY HAVE TO GIVE YOU THAT CHANCE!

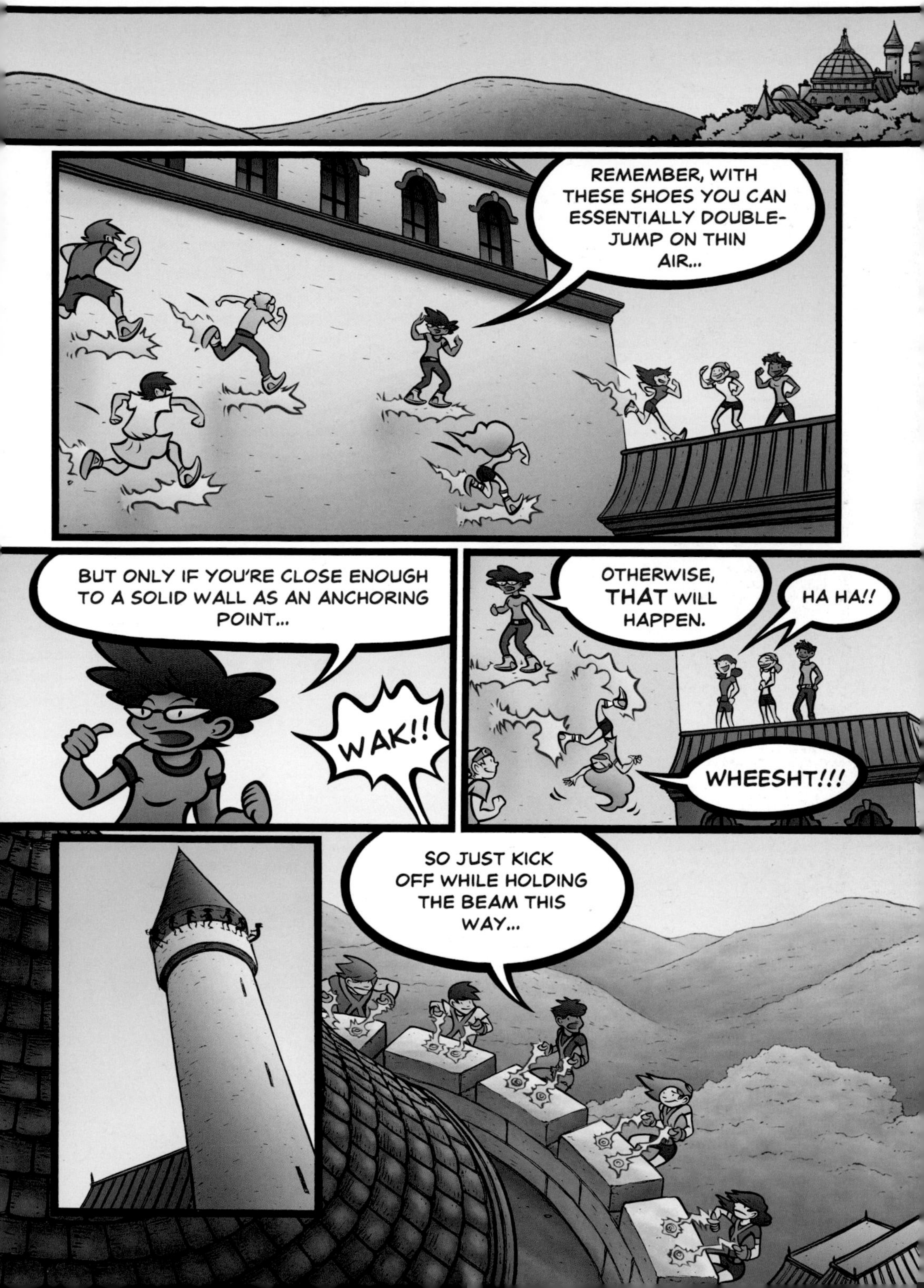
REMEMBER, WITH THESE SHOES YOU CAN ESSENTIALLY DOUBLE-JUMP ON THIN AIR...
BUT ONLY IF YOU'RE CLOSE ENOUGH TO A SOLID WALL AS AN ANCHORING POINT...
WAK!!
OTHERWISE, THAT WILL HAPPEN.
HA HA!!
WHEESHT!!!
SO JUST KICK OFF WHILE HOLDING THE BEAM THIS WAY...

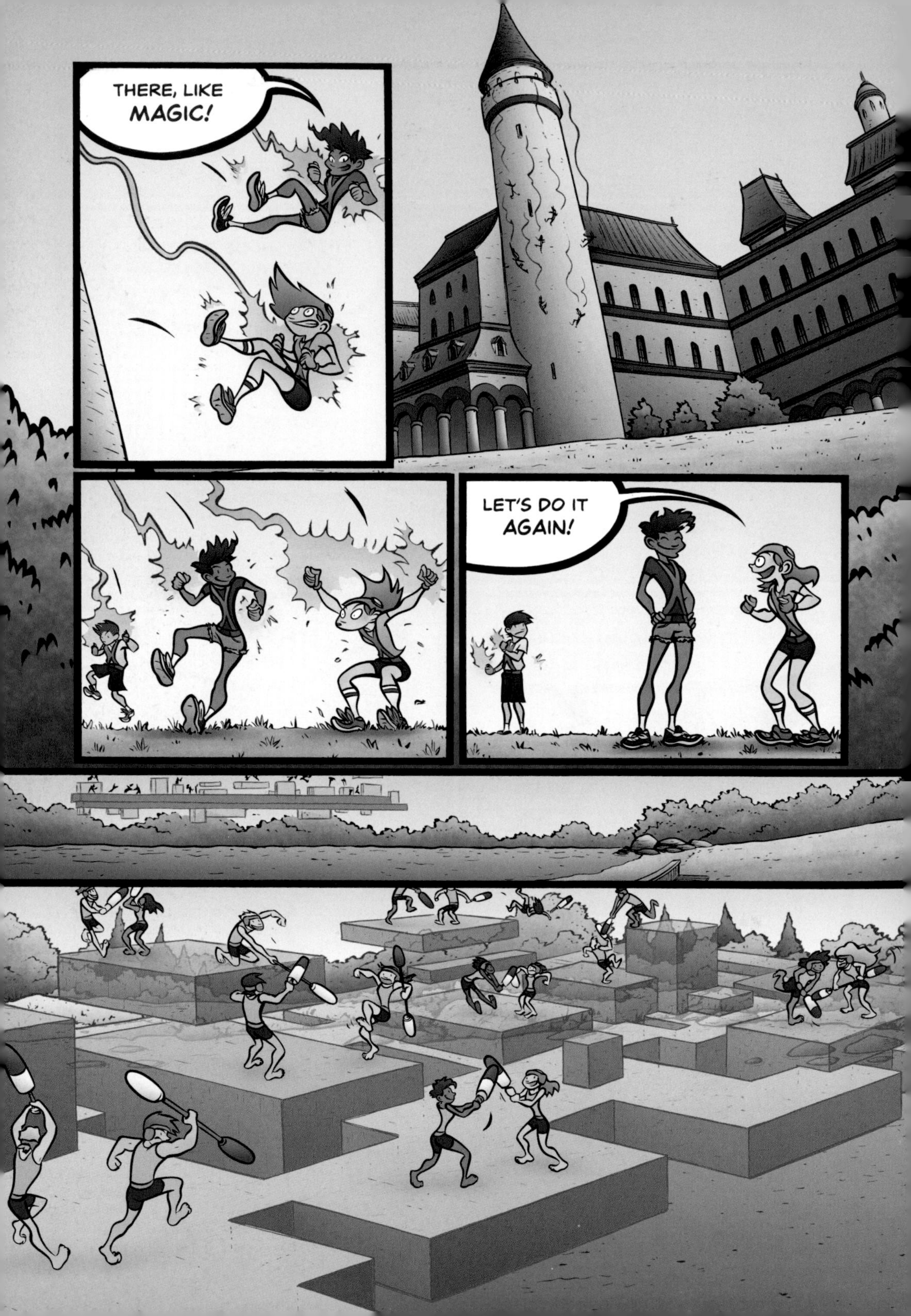
THERE, LIKE MAGIC!
LET'S DO IT AGAIN!

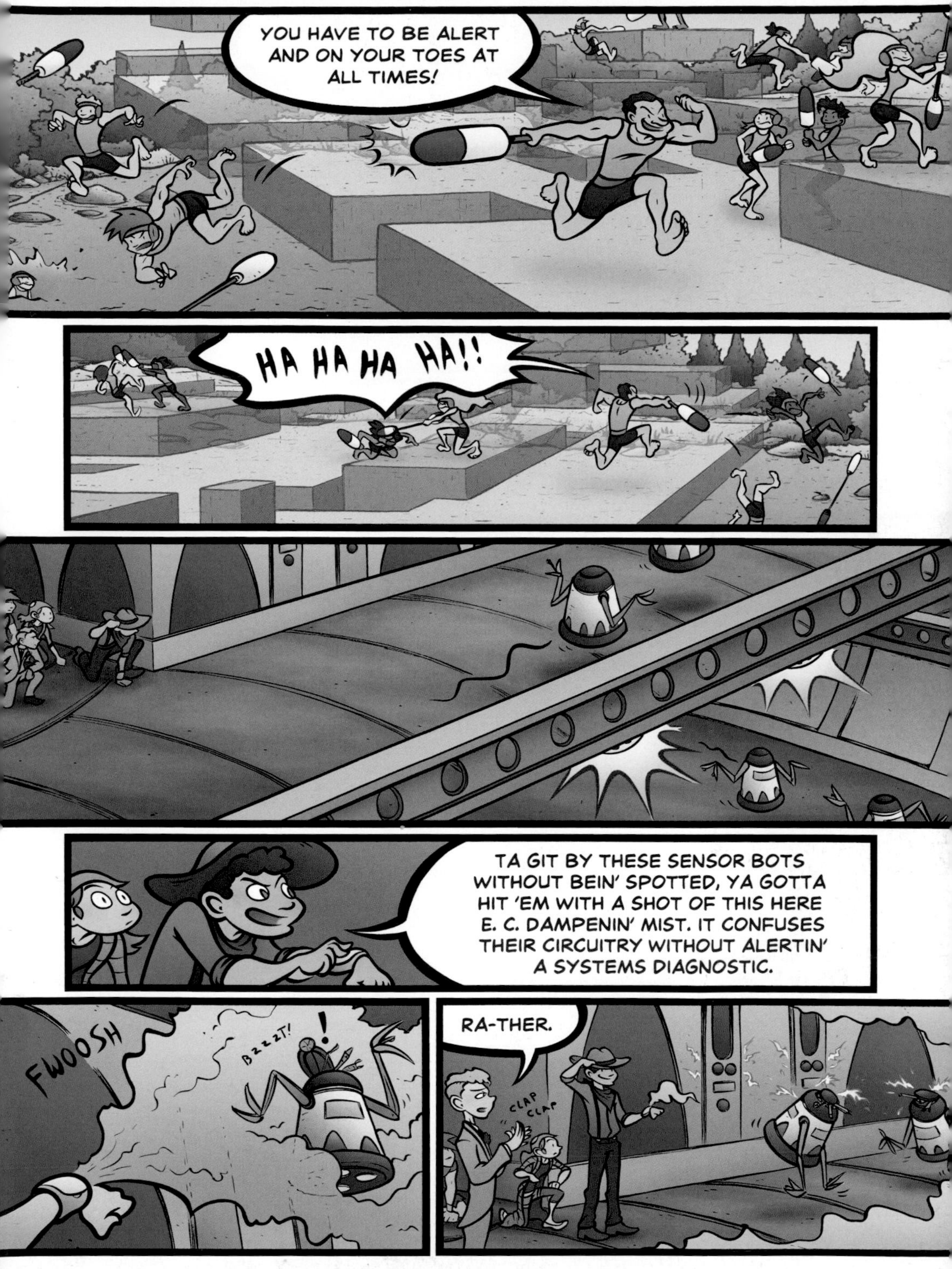
YOU HAVE TO BE ALERT AND ON YOUR TOES AT ALL TIMES!
HA HA HA HA!!
TA GIT BY THESE SENSOR BOTS WITHOUT BEIN' SPOTTED, YA GOTTA HIT 'EM WITH A SHOT OF THIS HERE E. C. DAMPENIN' MIST. IT CONFUSES THEIR CIRCUITRY WITHOUT ALERTIN' A SYSTEMS DIAGNOSTIC.
FWOOSH
BZZZT!
!
RA-THER.
CLAP CLAP

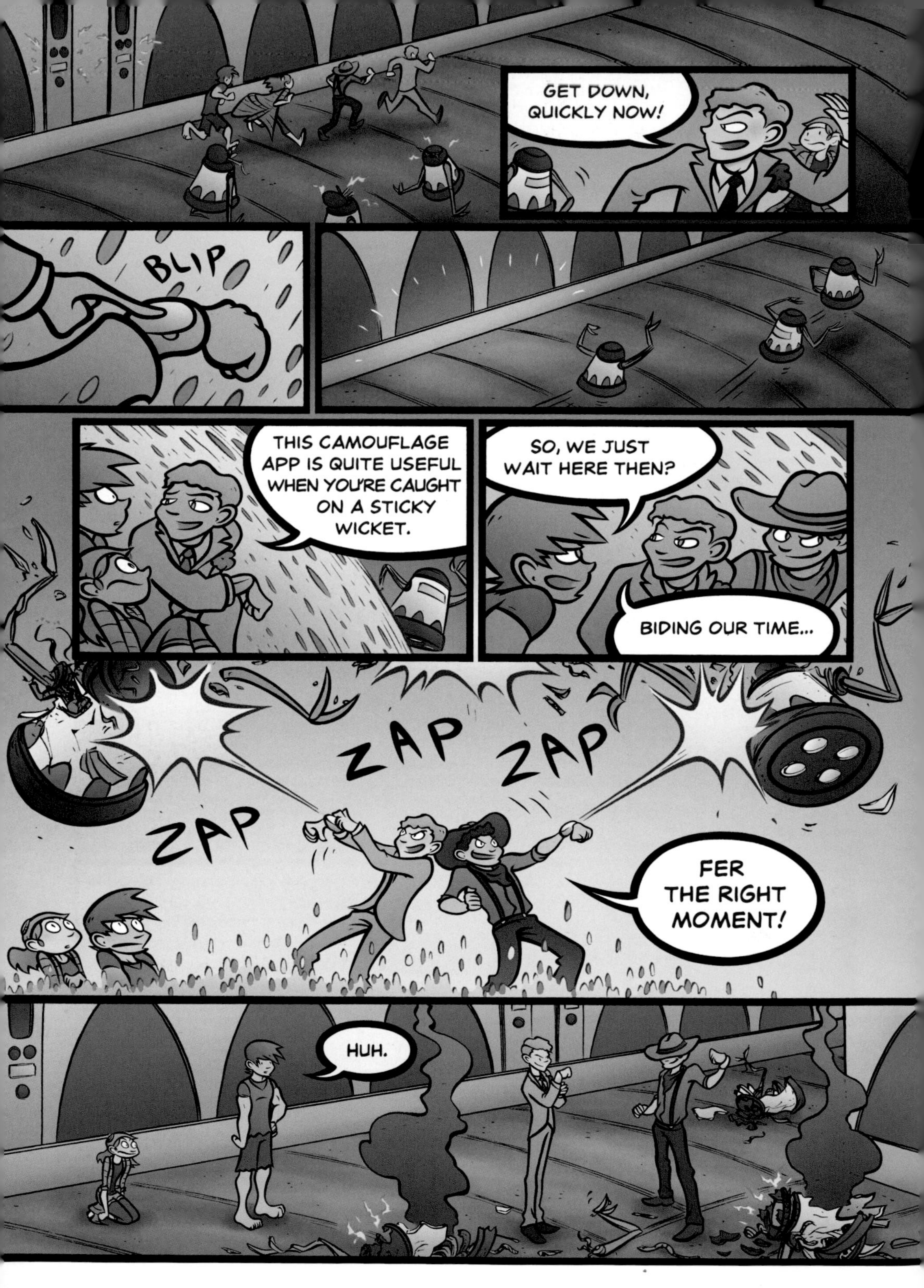
GET DOWN, QUICKLY NOW!
BLIP
THIS CAMOUFLAGE APP IS QUITE USEFUL WHEN YOU'RE CAUGHT ON A STICKY WICKET.
SO, WE JUST WAIT HERE THEN?
BIDING OUR TIME...
ZAP
ZAP
ZAP
FER THE RIGHT MOMENT!
HUH.

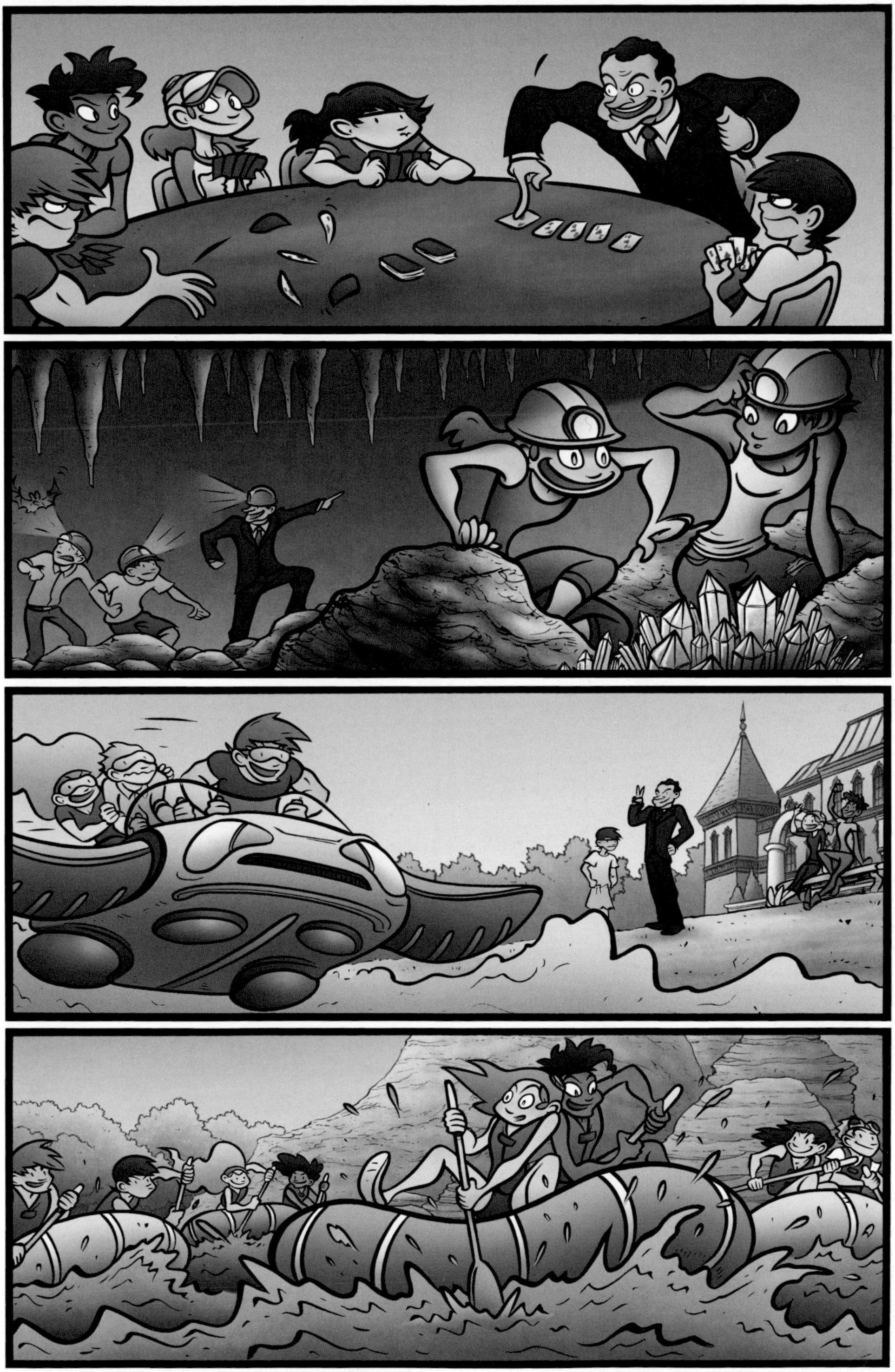

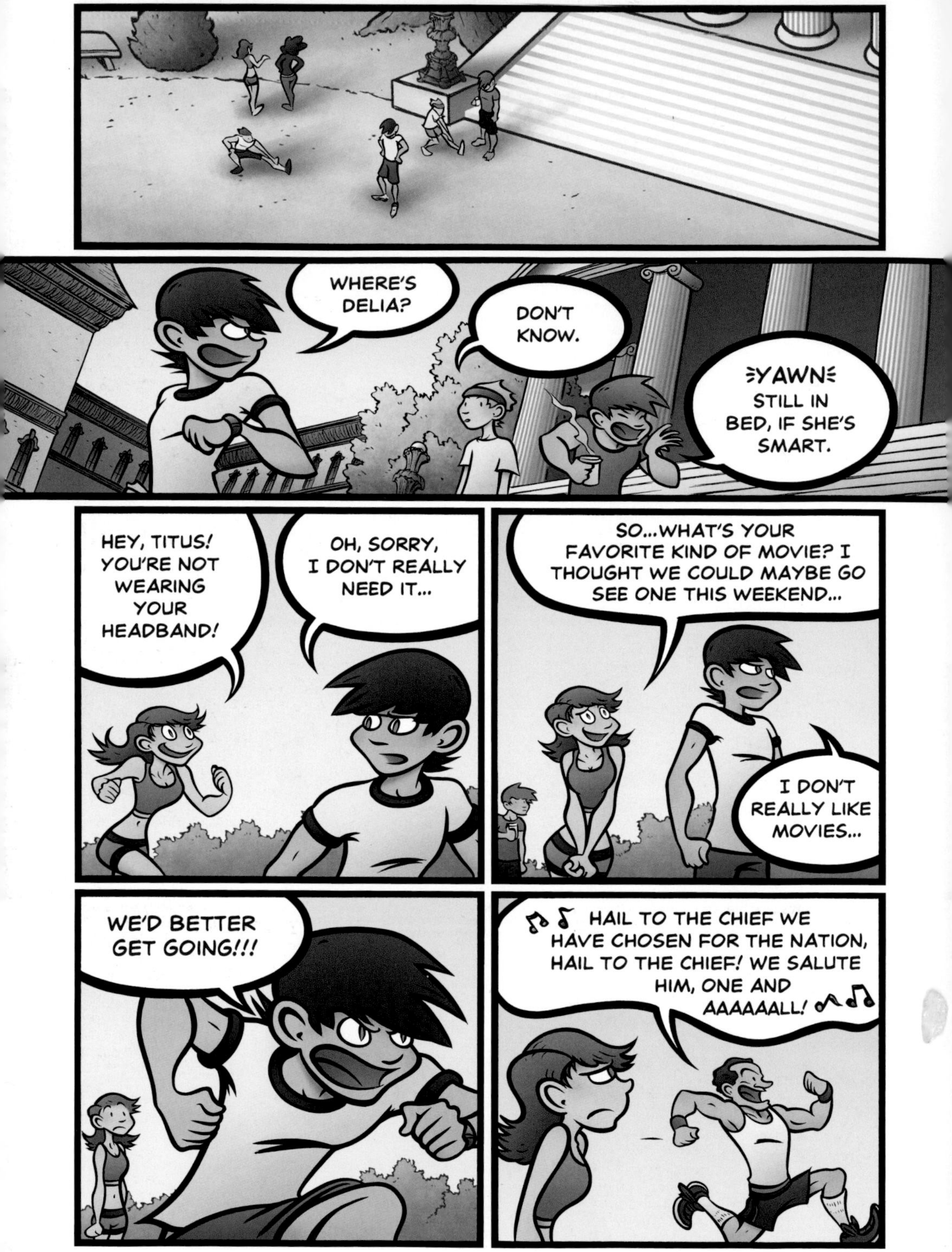
WHERE'S DELIA?
DON'T KNOW.
≡YAWN≡ STILL IN BED, IF SHE'S SMART.
HEY, TITUS! YOU'RE NOT WEARING YOUR HEADBAND!
OH, SORRY, I DON'T REALLY NEED IT...
SO...WHAT'S YOUR FAVORITE KIND OF MOVIE? I THOUGHT WE COULD MAYBE GO SEE ONE THIS WEEKEND...
I DON'T REALLY LIKE MOVIES...
WE'D BETTER GET GOING!!!
♫ HAIL TO THE CHIEF WE HAVE CHOSEN FOR THE NATION, HAIL TO THE CHIEF! WE SALUTE HIM, ONE AND AAAAAALL! ♫

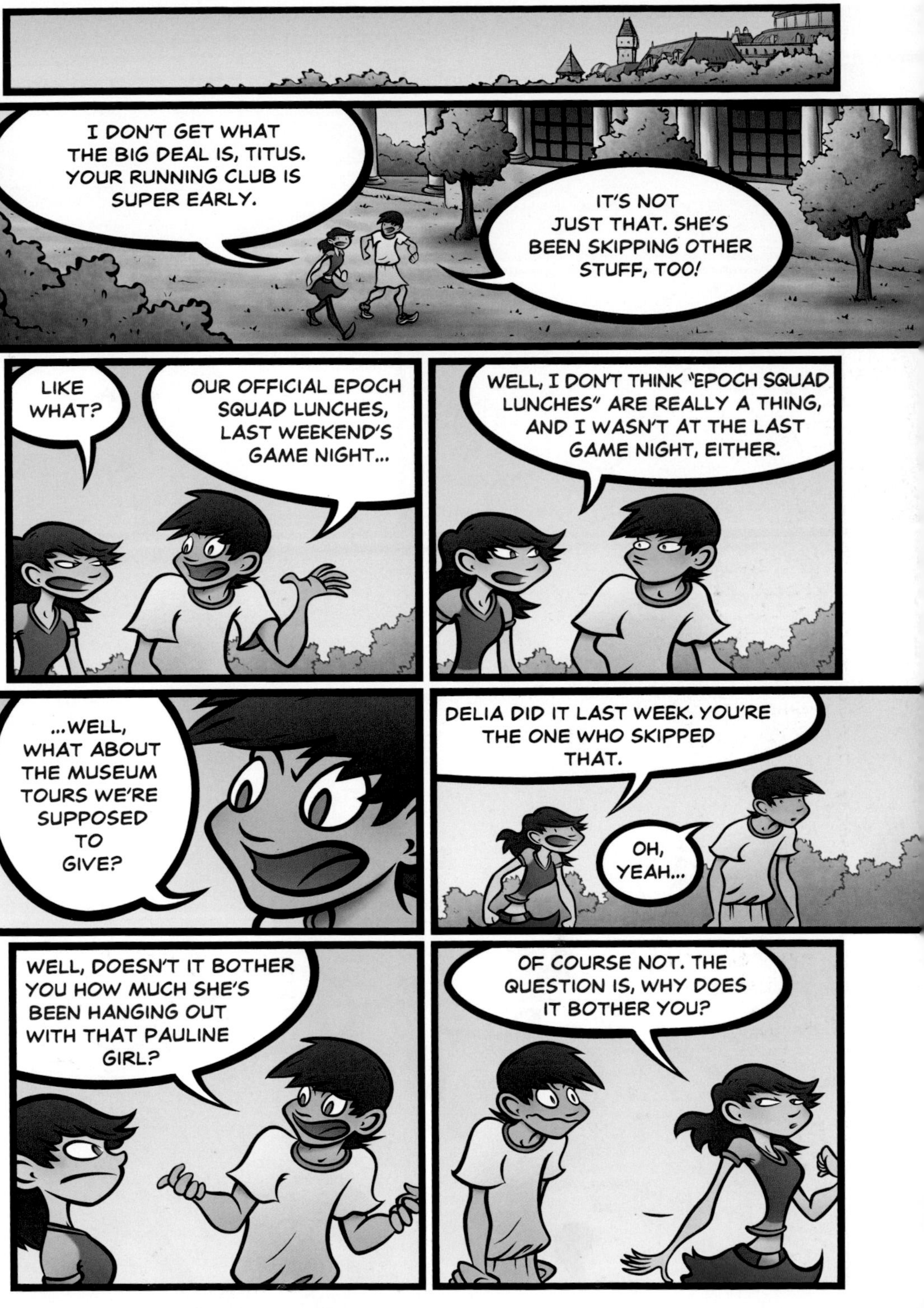
I DON'T GET WHAT THE BIG DEAL IS, TITUS. YOUR RUNNING CLUB IS SUPER EARLY.
IT'S NOT JUST THAT. SHE'S BEEN SKIPPING OTHER STUFF, TOO!
LIKE WHAT?
OUR OFFICIAL EPOCH SQUAD LUNCHES, LAST WEEKEND'S GAME NIGHT...
WELL, I DON'T THINK "EPOCH SQUAD LUNCHES" ARE REALLY A THING, AND I WASN'T AT THE LAST GAME NIGHT, EITHER.
...WELL, WHAT ABOUT THE MUSEUM TOURS WE'RE SUPPOSED TO GIVE?
DELIA DID IT LAST WEEK. YOU'RE THE ONE WHO SKIPPED THAT.
OH, YEAH...
WELL, DOESN'T IT BOTHER YOU HOW MUCH SHE'S BEEN HANGING OUT WITH THAT PAULINE GIRL?
OF COURSE NOT. THE QUESTION IS, WHY DOES IT BOTHER YOU?

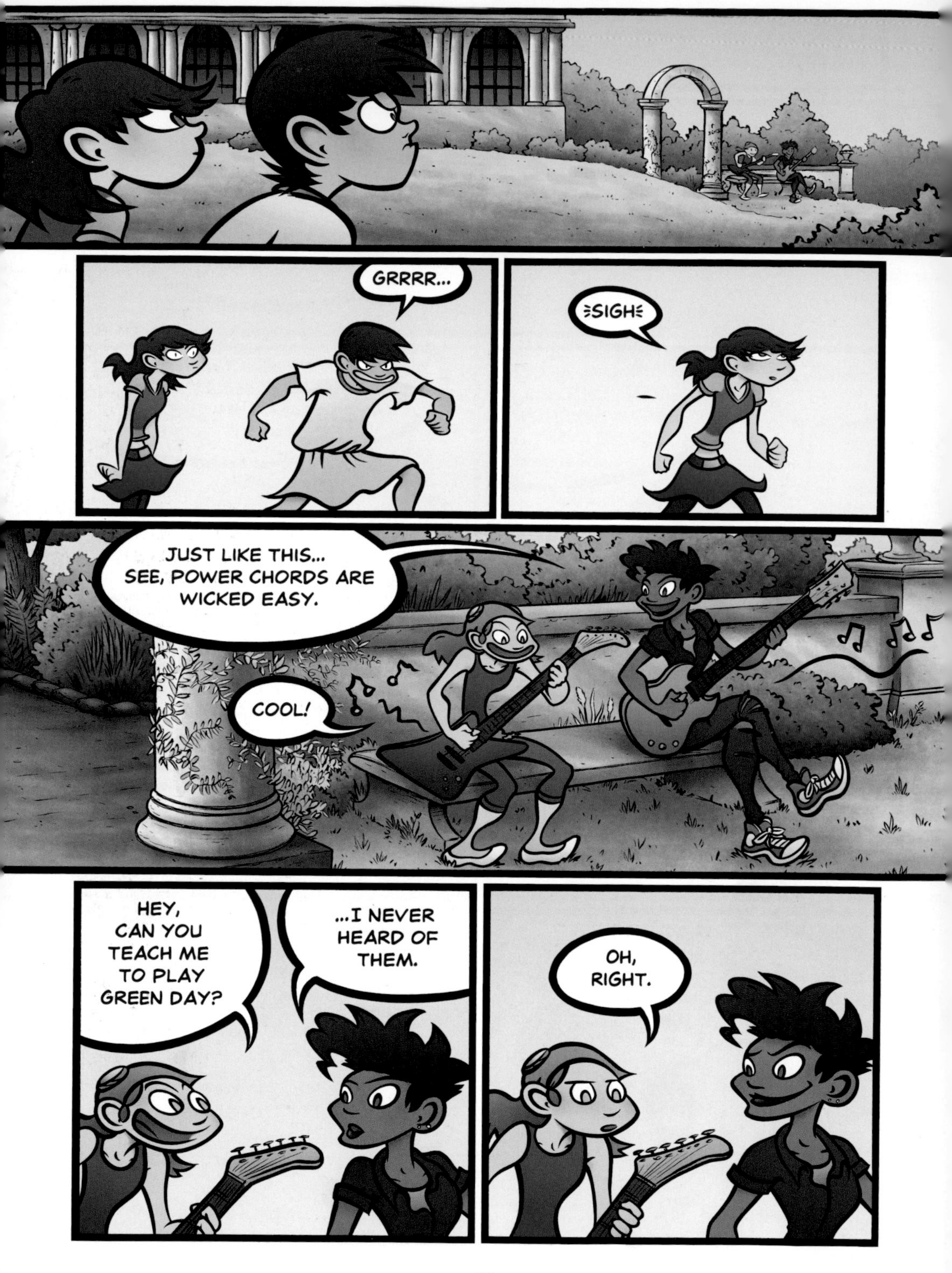
GRRRR...
SIGH
JUST LIKE THIS... SEE, POWER CHORDS ARE WICKED EASY.
COOL!
HEY, CAN YOU TEACH ME TO PLAY GREEN DAY?
...I NEVER HEARD OF THEM.
OH, RIGHT.

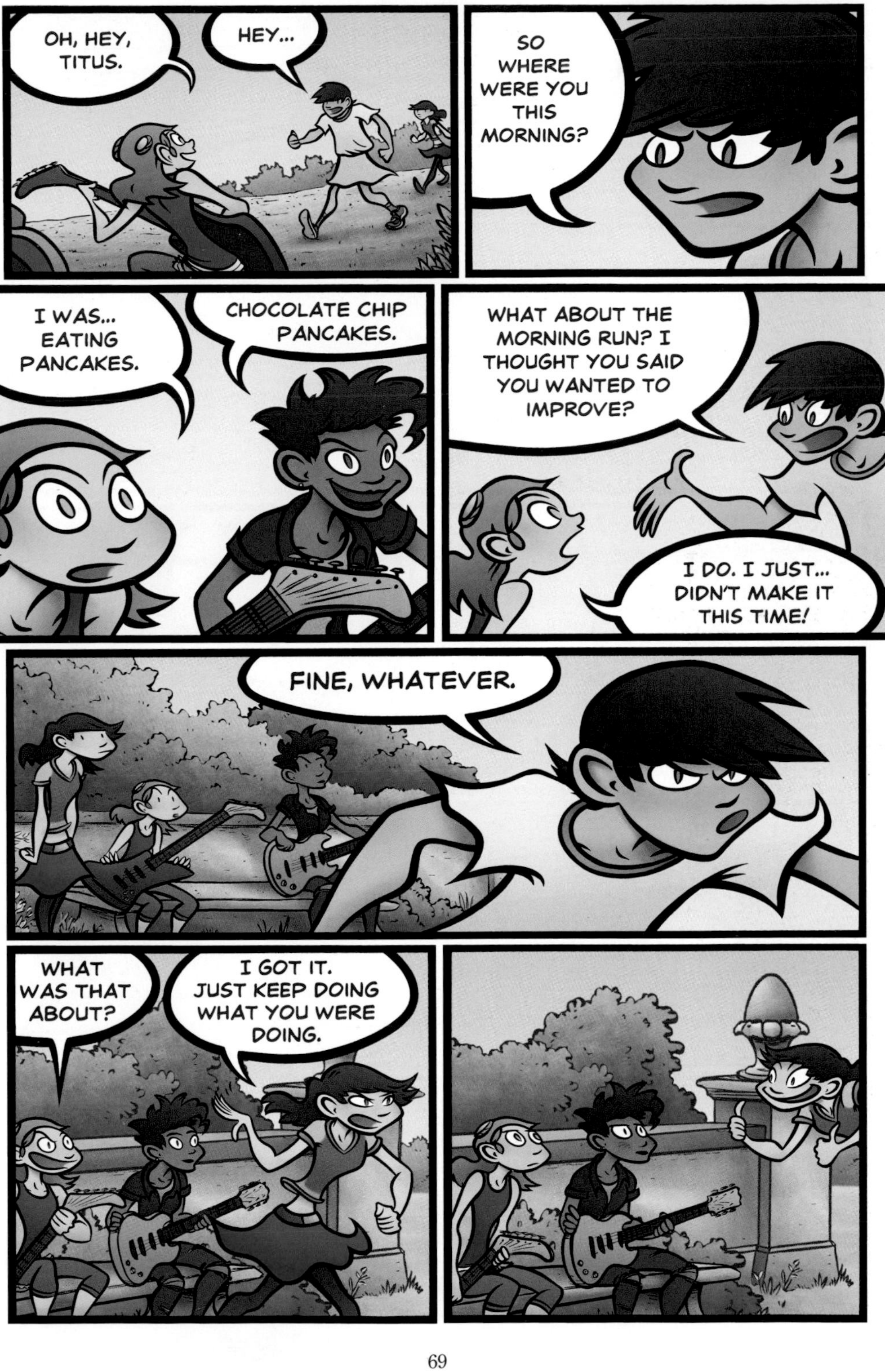
OH, HEY, TITUS.
HEY...
SO WHERE WERE YOU THIS MORNING?
I WAS... EATING PANCAKES.
CHOCOLATE CHIP PANCAKES.
WHAT ABOUT THE MORNING RUN? I THOUGHT YOU SAID YOU WANTED TO IMPROVE?
I DO. I JUST... DIDN'T MAKE IT THIS TIME!
FINE, WHATEVER.
WHAT WAS THAT ABOUT?
I GOT IT. JUST KEEP DOING WHAT YOU WERE DOING.

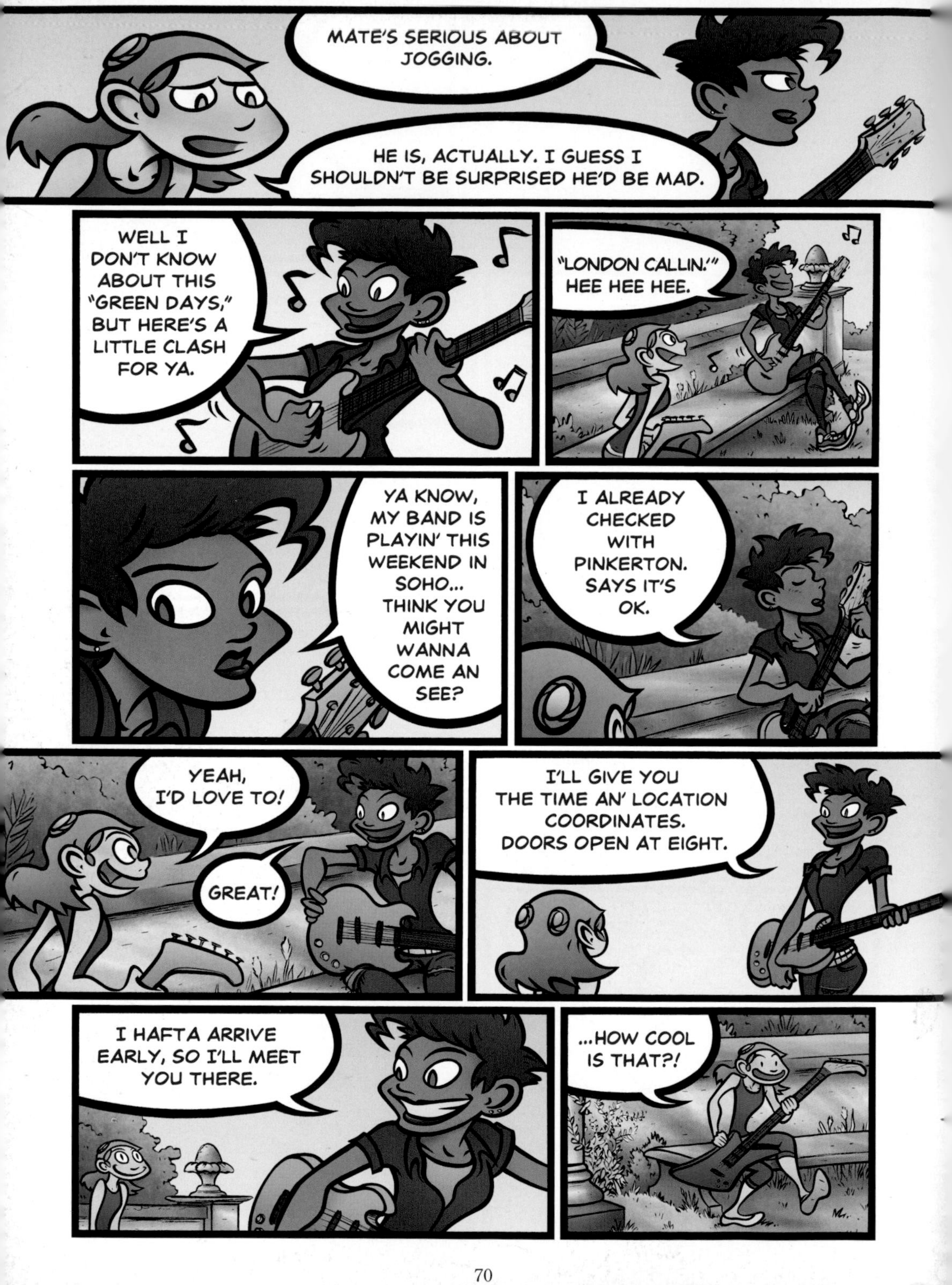
MATE'S SERIOUS ABOUT JOGGING.
HE IS, ACTUALLY. I GUESS I SHOULDN'T BE SURPRISED HE'D BE MAD.
WELL I DON'T KNOW ABOUT THIS "GREEN DAYS," BUT HERE'S A LITTLE CLASH FOR YA.
"LONDON CALLIN.'" HEE HEE HEE.
YA KNOW, MY BAND IS PLAYIN' THIS WEEKEND IN SOHO... THINK YOU MIGHT WANNA COME AN SEE?
I ALREADY CHECKED WITH PINKERTON. SAYS IT'S OK.
YEAH, I'D LOVE TO!
GREAT!
I'LL GIVE YOU THE TIME AN' LOCATION COORDINATES. DOORS OPEN AT EIGHT.
I HAFTA ARRIVE EARLY, SO I'LL MEET YOU THERE.
...HOW COOL IS THAT?!

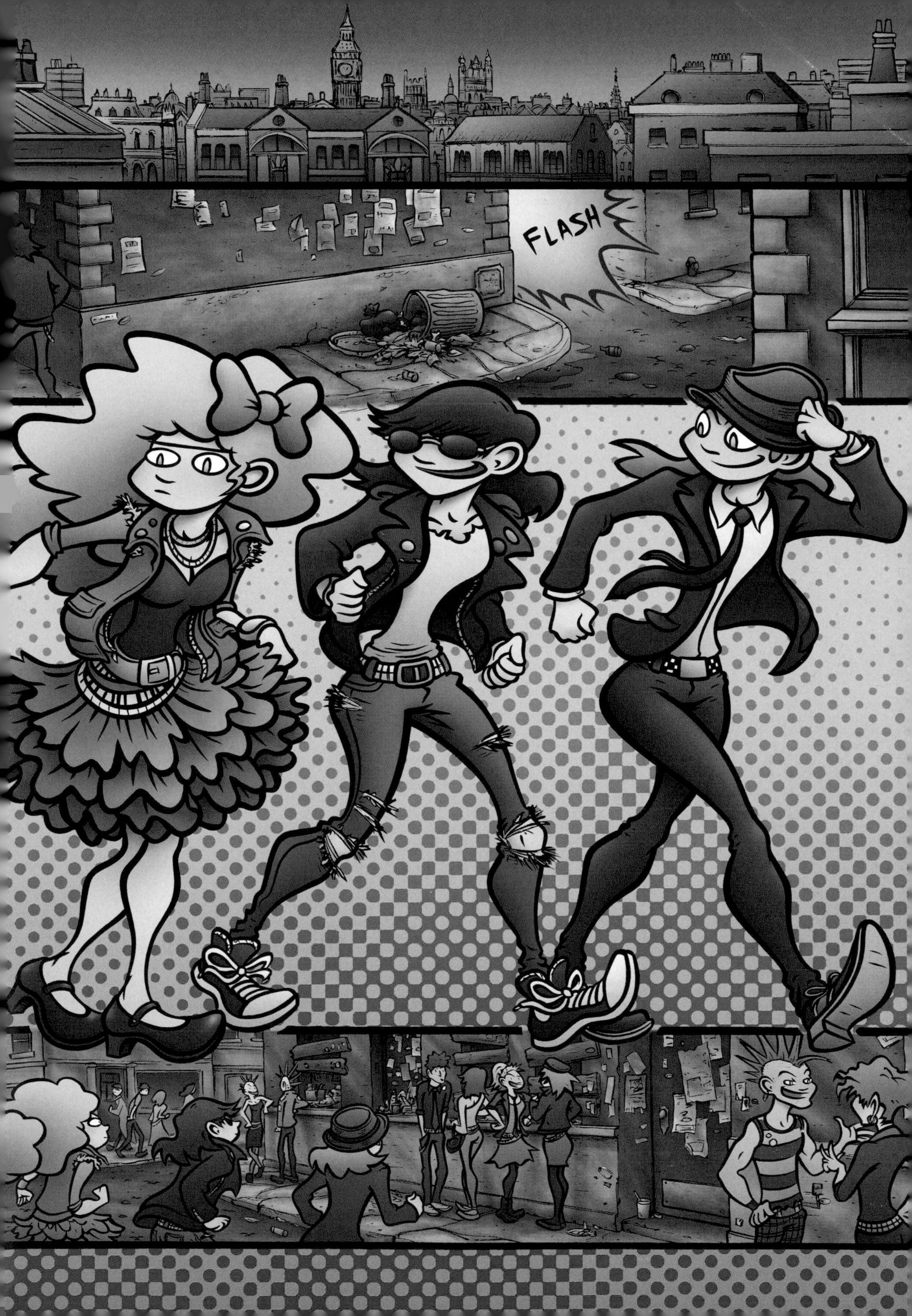
FLASH

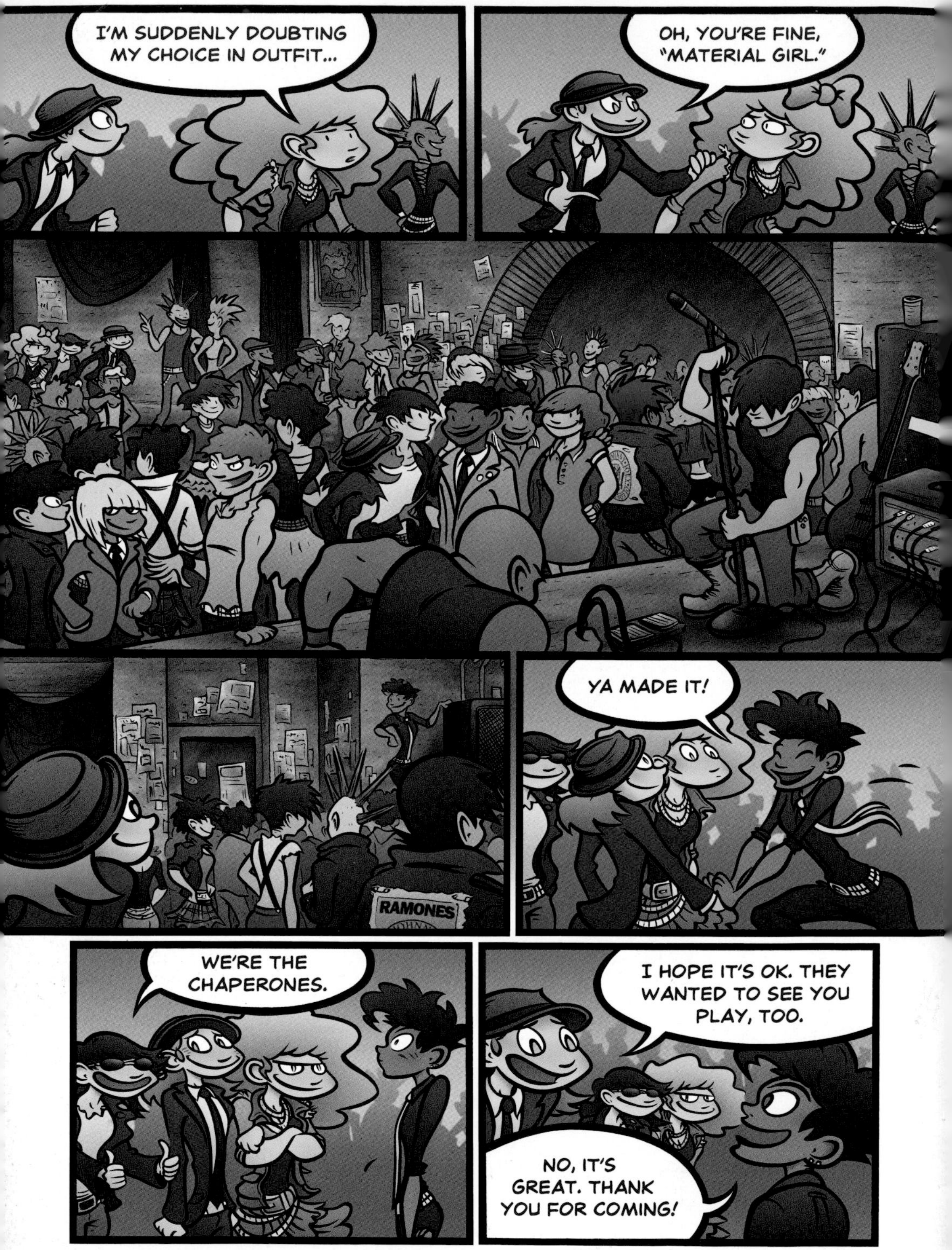
I'M SUDDENLY DOUBTING MY CHOICE IN OUTFIT...
OH, YOU'RE FINE, "MATERIAL GIRL."
RAMONES
YA MADE IT!
WE'RE THE CHAPERONES.
I HOPE IT'S OK. THEY WANTED TO SEE YOU PLAY, TOO.
NO, IT'S GREAT. THANK YOU FOR COMING!

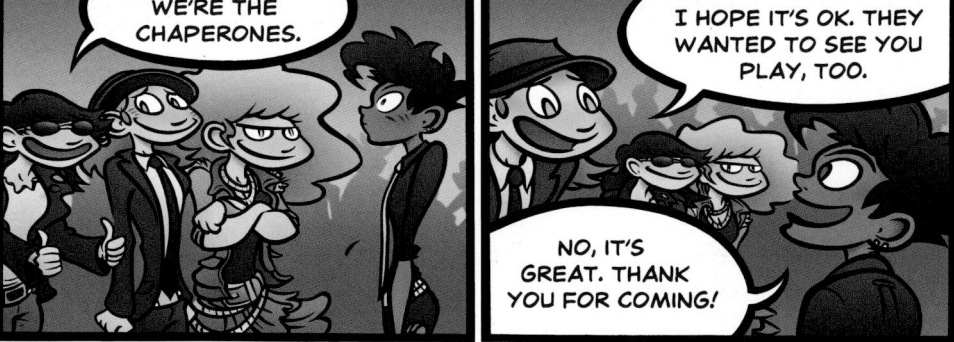

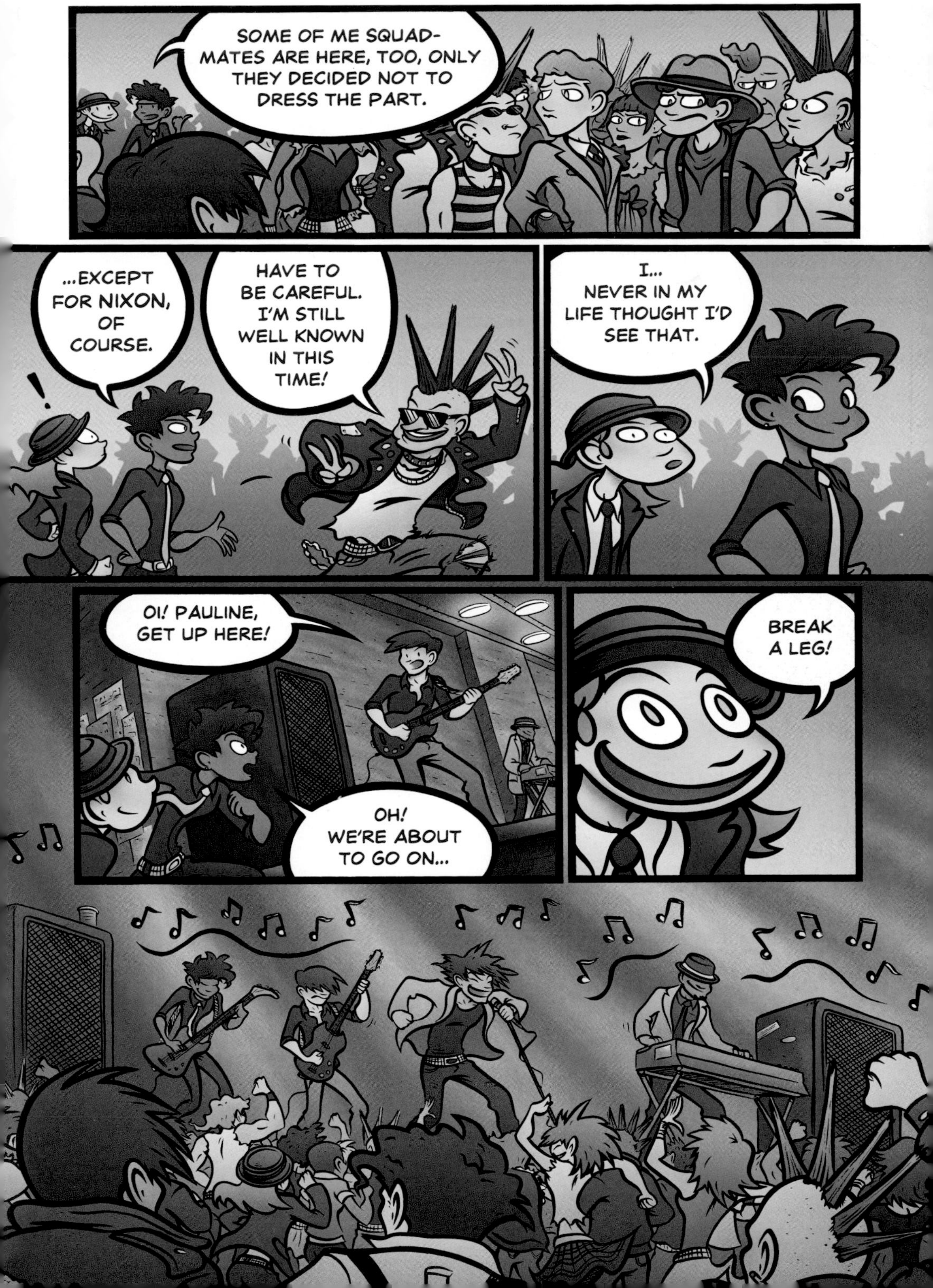
SOME OF ME SQUAD-MATES ARE HERE, TOO, ONLY THEY DECIDED NOT TO DRESS THE PART.
...EXCEPT FOR NIXON, OF COURSE.
HAVE TO BE CAREFUL. I'M STILL WELL KNOWN IN THIS TIME!
!
I... NEVER IN MY LIFE THOUGHT I'D SEE THAT.
OI! PAULINE, GET UP HERE!
OH! WE'RE ABOUT TO GO ON...
BREAK A LEG!

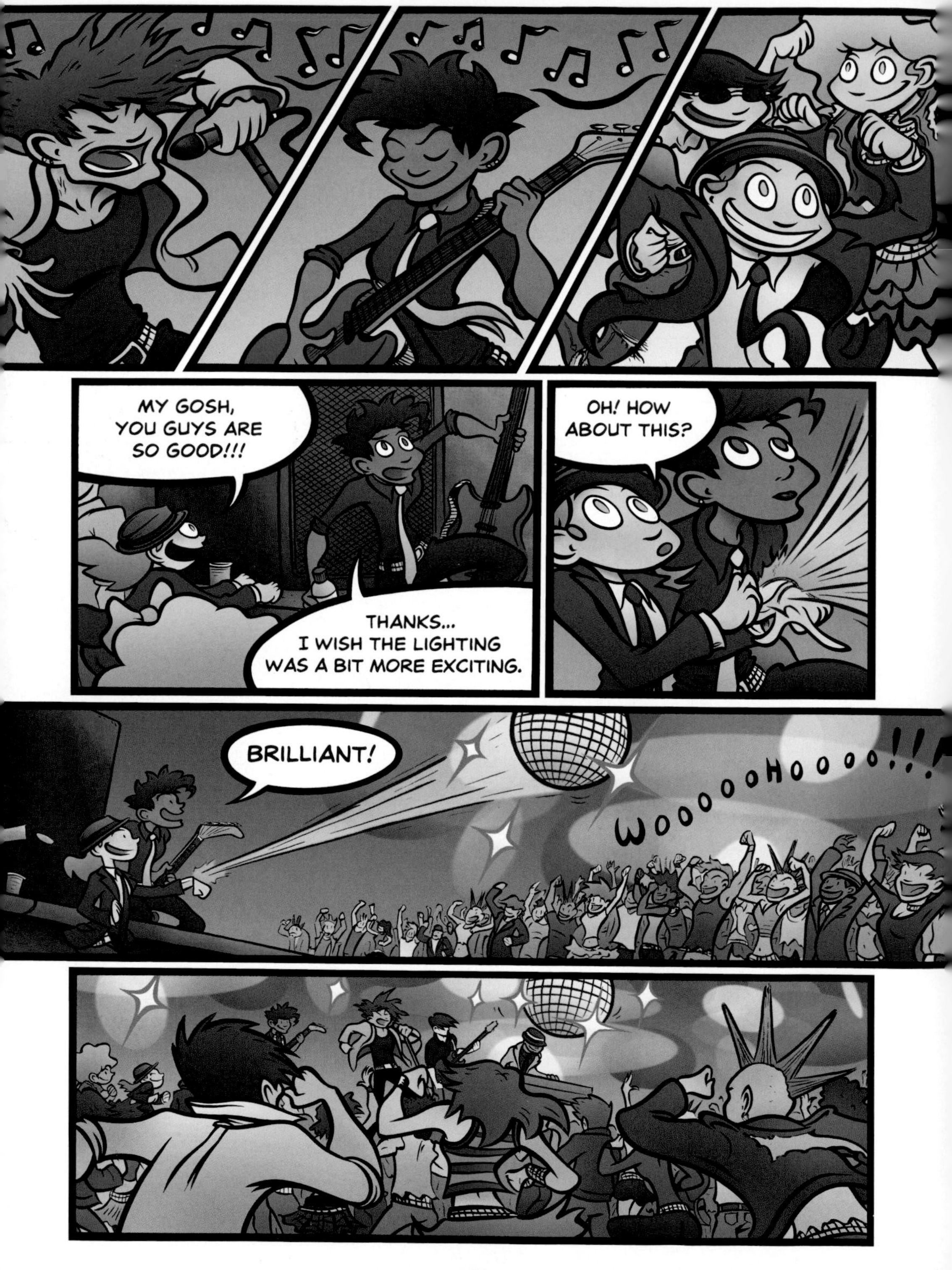

MY GOSH, YOU GUYS ARE SO GOOD!!!
THANKS... I WISH THE LIGHTING WAS A BIT MORE EXCITING.
OH! HOW ABOUT THIS?
BRILLIANT!
WOOOOOHOOOOO!!!

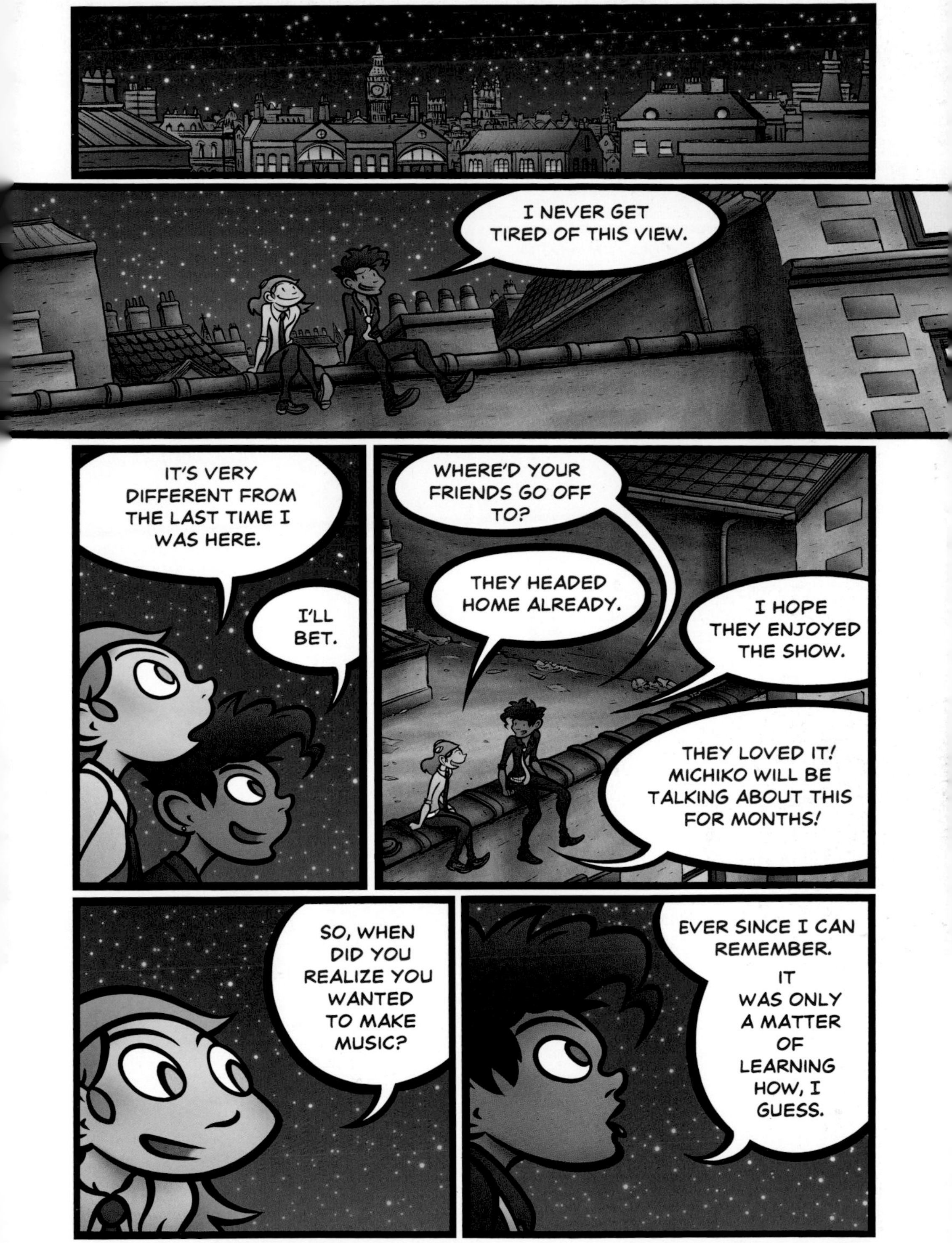
I NEVER GET TIRED OF THIS VIEW.
IT'S VERY DIFFERENT FROM THE LAST TIME I WAS HERE.
I'LL BET.
WHERE'D YOUR FRIENDS GO OFF TO?
THEY HEADED HOME ALREADY.
I HOPE THEY ENJOYED THE SHOW.
THEY LOVED IT! MICHIKO WILL BE TALKING ABOUT THIS FOR MONTHS!
SO, WHEN DID YOU REALIZE YOU WANTED TO MAKE MUSIC?
EVER SINCE I CAN REMEMBER.
IT WAS ONLY A MATTER OF LEARNING HOW, I GUESS.

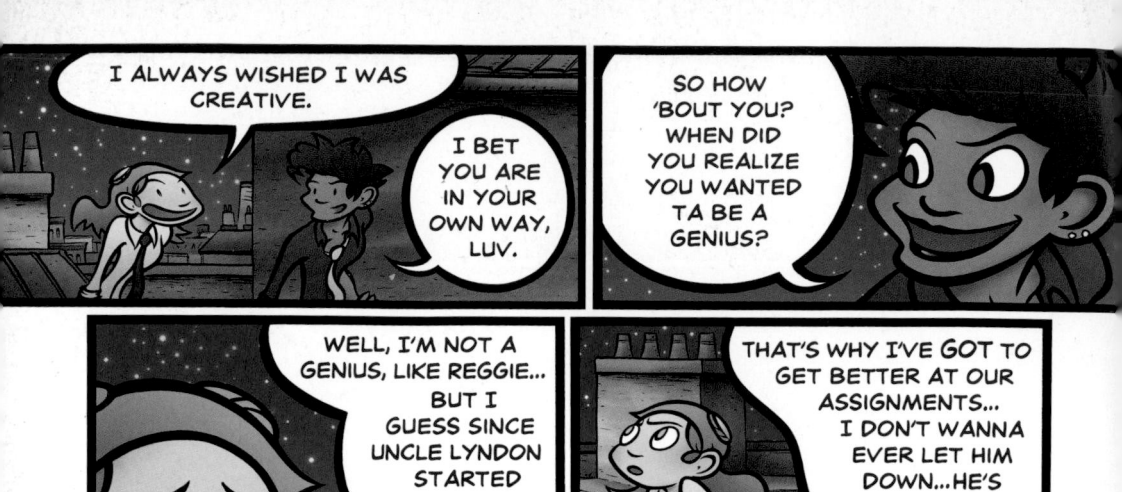

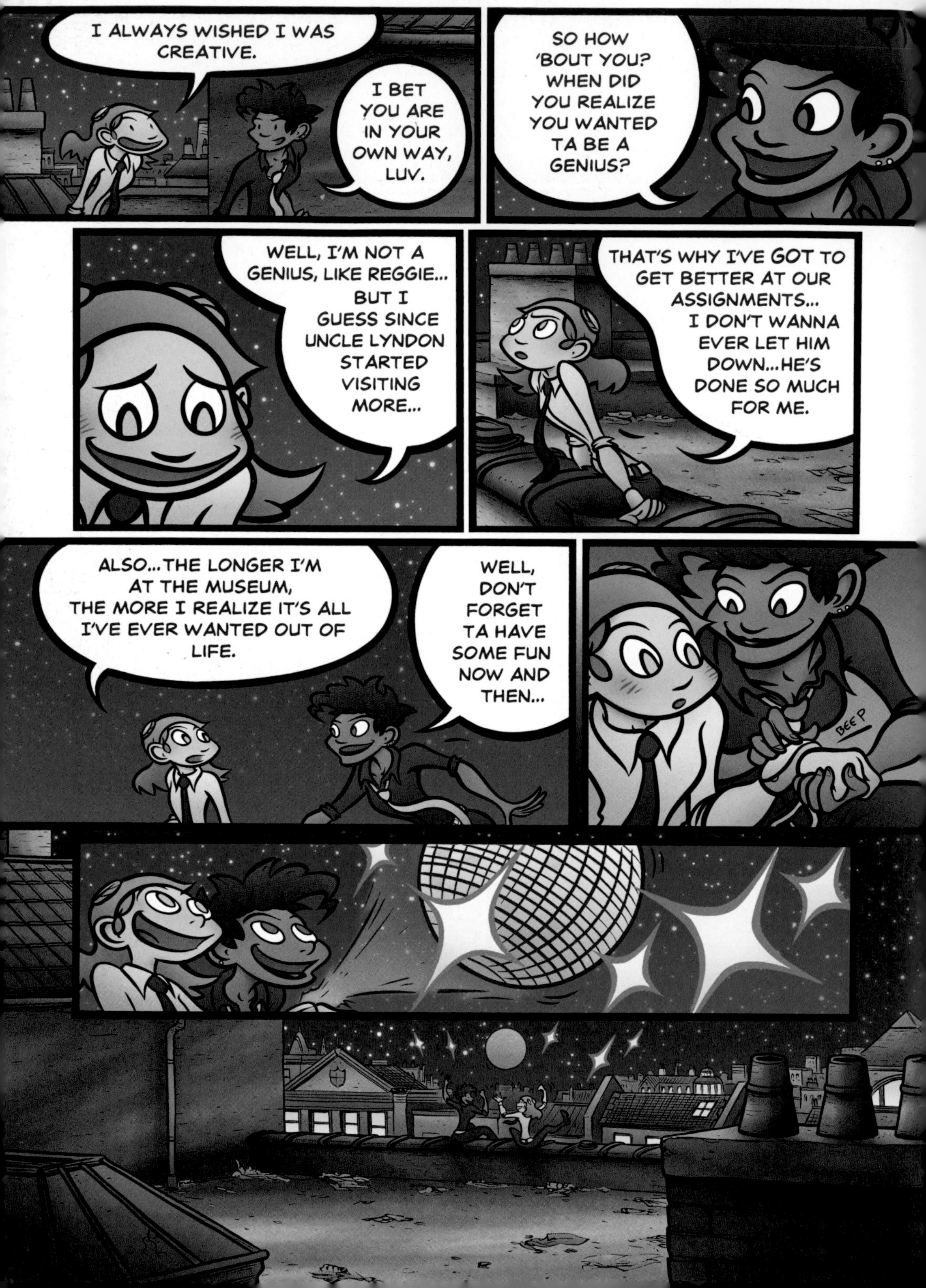
I ALWAYS WISHED I WAS CREATIVE.
I BET YOU ARE IN YOUR OWN WAY, LUV.
SO HOW 'BOUT YOU? WHEN DID YOU REALIZE YOU WANTED TA BE A GENIUS?
WELL, I'M NOT A GENIUS, LIKE REGGIE... BUT I GUESS SINCE UNCLE LYNDON STARTED VISITING MORE...
THAT'S WHY I'VE GOT TO GET BETTER AT OUR ASSIGNMENTS... I DON'T WANNA EVER LET HIM DOWN...HE'S DONE SO MUCH FOR ME.
ALSO...THE LONGER I'M AT THE MUSEUM, THE MORE I REALIZE IT'S ALL I'VE EVER WANTED OUT OF LIFE.
WELL, DON'T FORGET TA HAVE SOME FUN NOW AND THEN...
BEEP

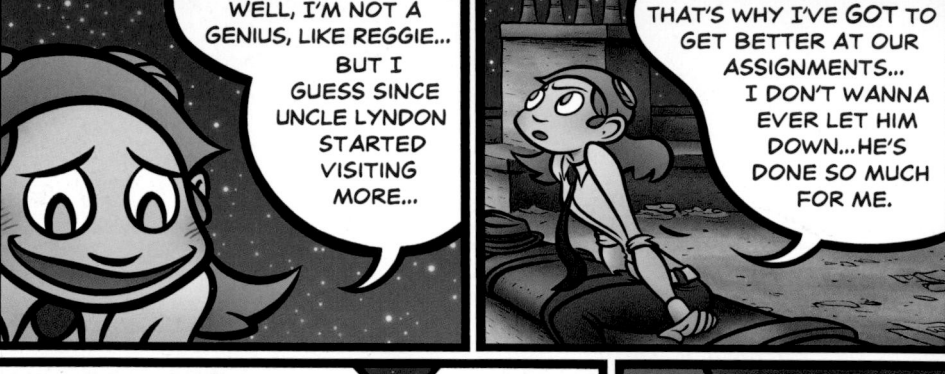

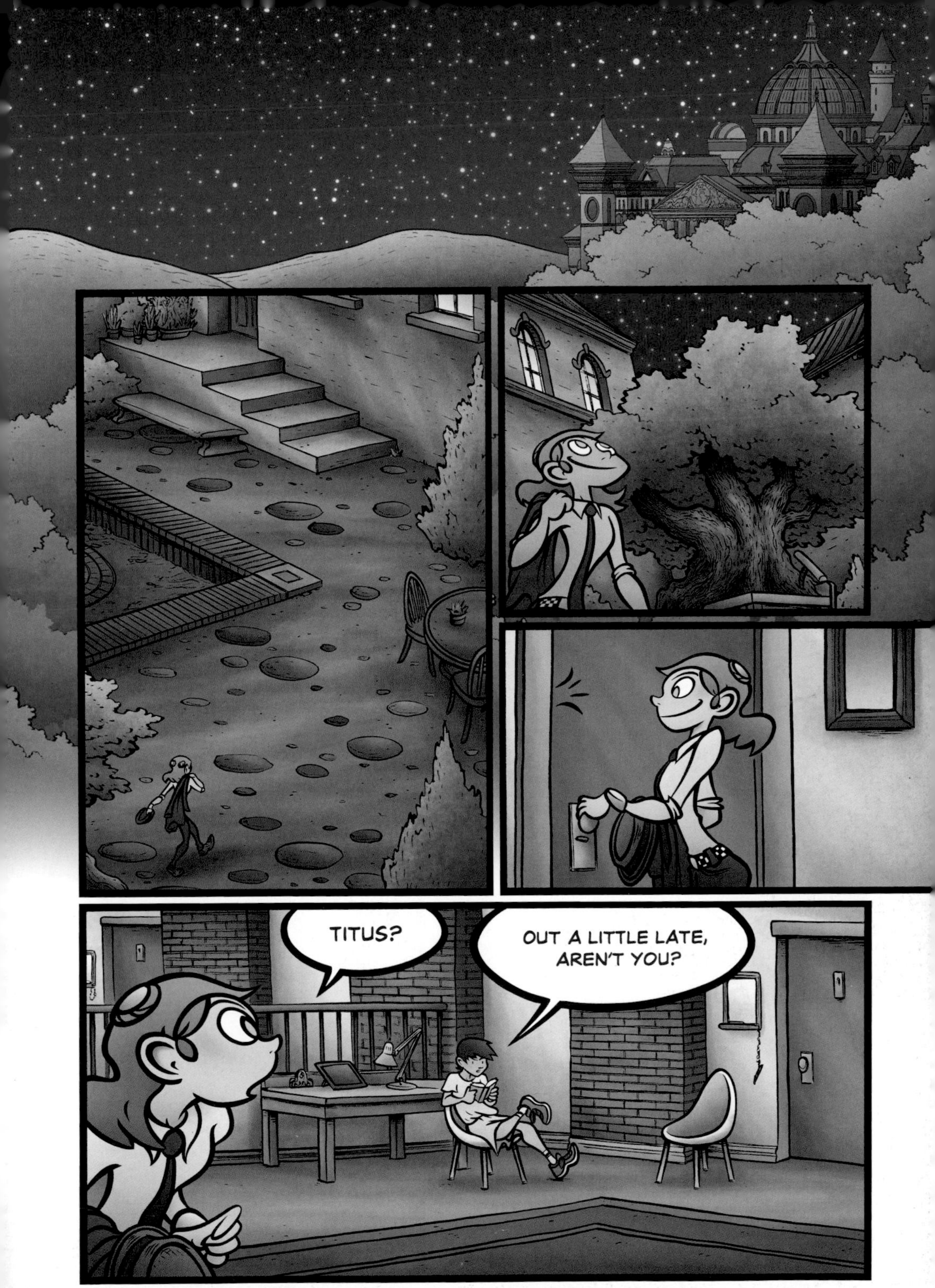
TITUS?
OUT A LITTLE LATE, AREN'T YOU?

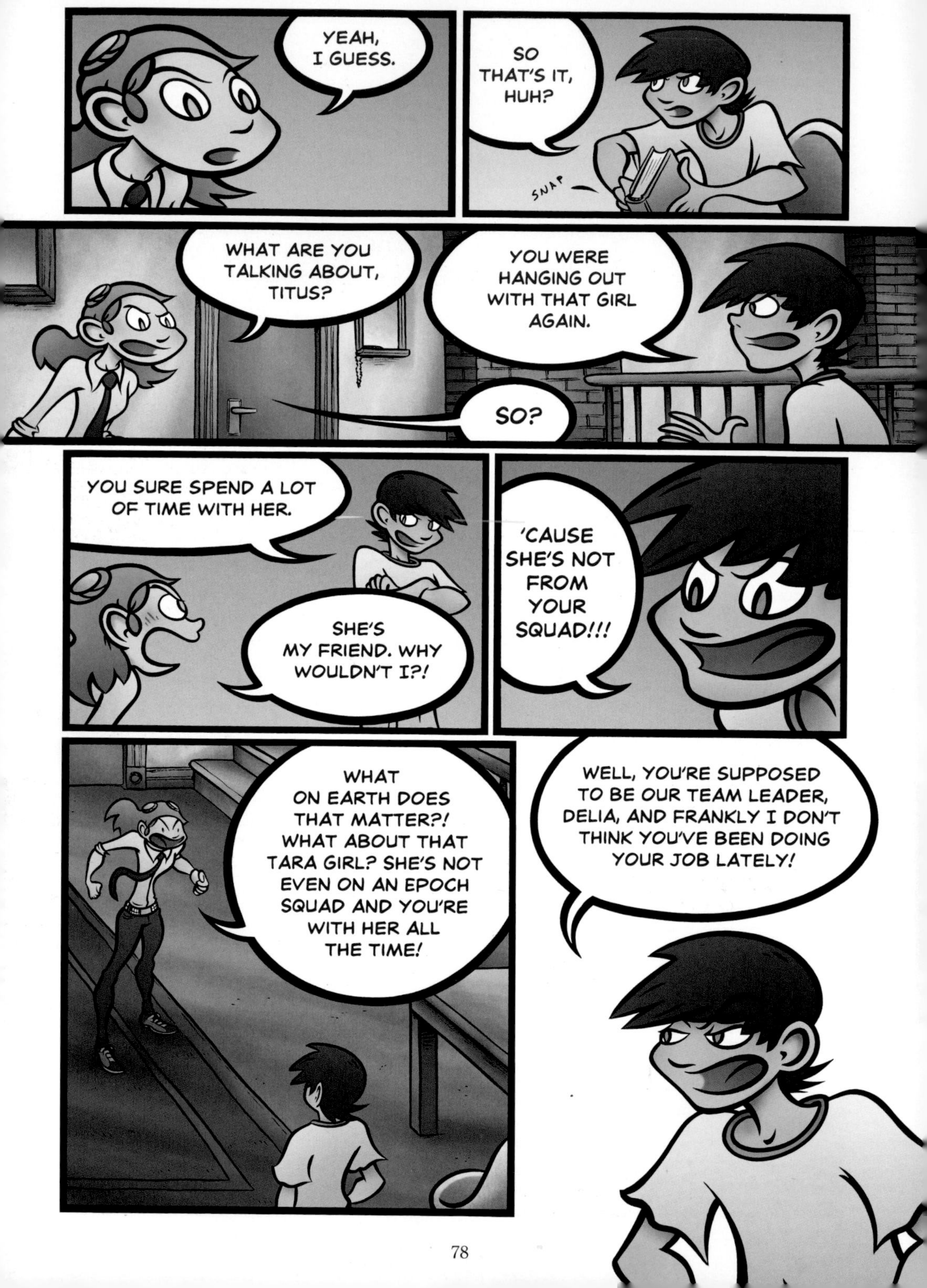
YEAH, I GUESS.
SO THAT'S IT, HUH?
SNAP
WHAT ARE YOU TALKING ABOUT, TITUS?
YOU WERE HANGING OUT WITH THAT GIRL AGAIN.
SO?
YOU SURE SPEND A LOT OF TIME WITH HER.
SHE'S MY FRIEND. WHY WOULDN'T I?!
'CAUSE SHE'S NOT FROM YOUR SQUAD!!!
WHAT ON EARTH DOES THAT MATTER?! WHAT ABOUT THAT TARA GIRL? SHE'S NOT EVEN ON AN EPOCH SQUAD AND YOU'RE WITH HER ALL THE TIME!
WELL, YOU'RE SUPPOSED TO BE OUR TEAM LEADER, DELIA, AND FRANKLY I DON'T THINK YOU'VE BEEN DOING YOUR JOB LATELY!

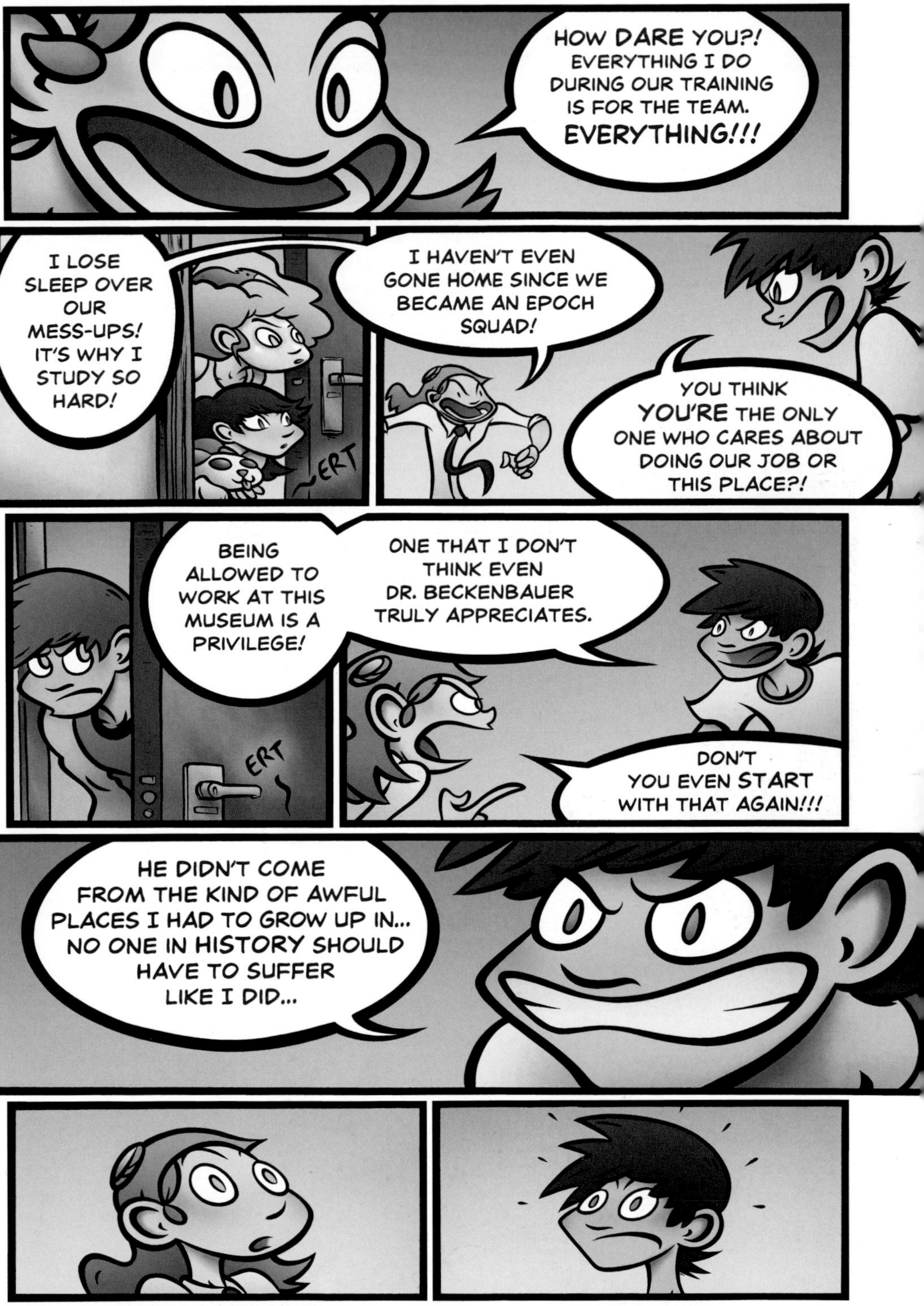
HOW DARE YOU?! EVERYTHING I DO DURING OUR TRAINING IS FOR THE TEAM. EVERYTHING!!!
I LOSE SLEEP OVER OUR MESS-UPS! IT'S WHY I STUDY SO HARD!
I HAVEN'T EVEN GONE HOME SINCE WE BECAME AN EPOCH SQUAD!
YOU THINK YOU'RE THE ONLY ONE WHO CARES ABOUT DOING OUR JOB OR THIS PLACE?!
ERT
BEING ALLOWED TO WORK AT THIS MUSEUM IS A PRIVILEGE!
ONE THAT I DON'T THINK EVEN DR. BECKENBAUER TRULY APPRECIATES.
ERT
DON'T YOU EVEN START WITH THAT AGAIN!!!
HE DIDN'T COME FROM THE KIND OF AWFUL PLACES I HAD TO GROW UP IN... NO ONE IN HISTORY SHOULD HAVE TO SUFFER LIKE I DID...

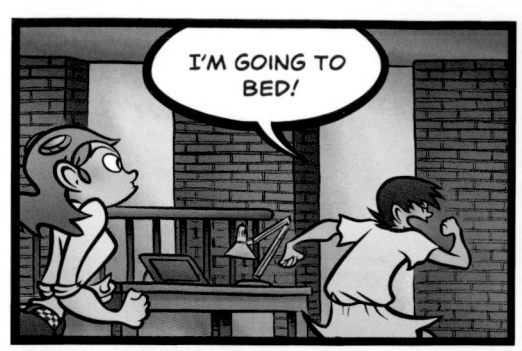

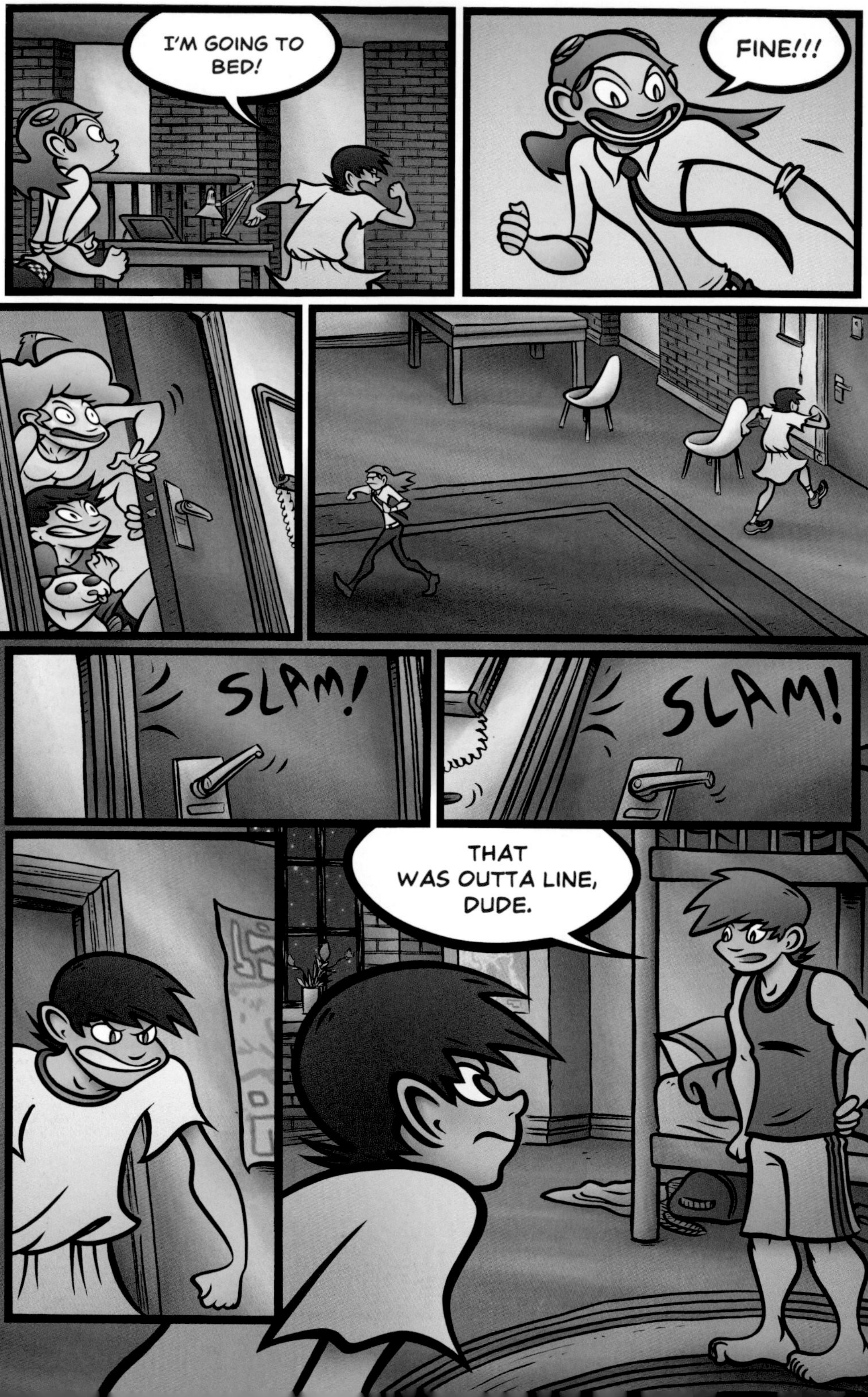
I'M GOING TO BED!
FINE!!!
SLAM!
SLAM!
THAT WAS OUTTA LINE, DUDE.

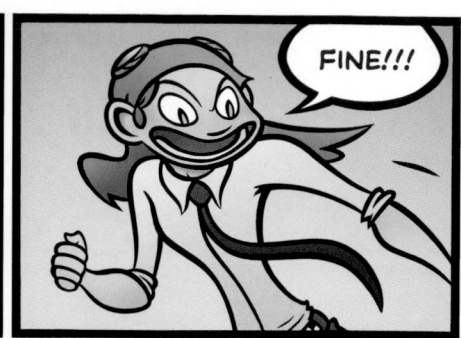

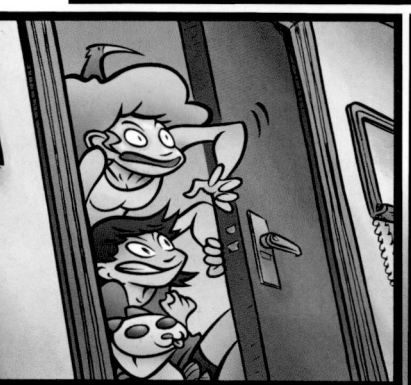

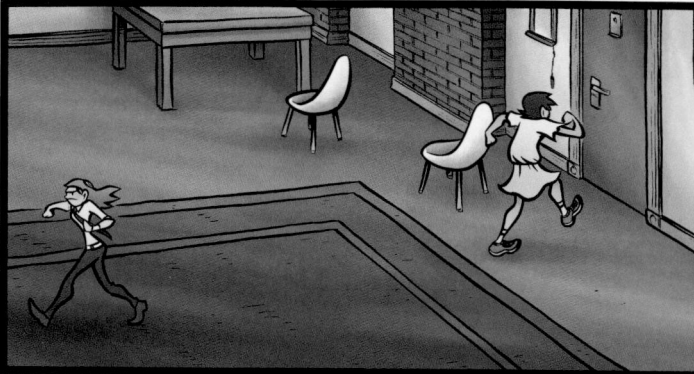

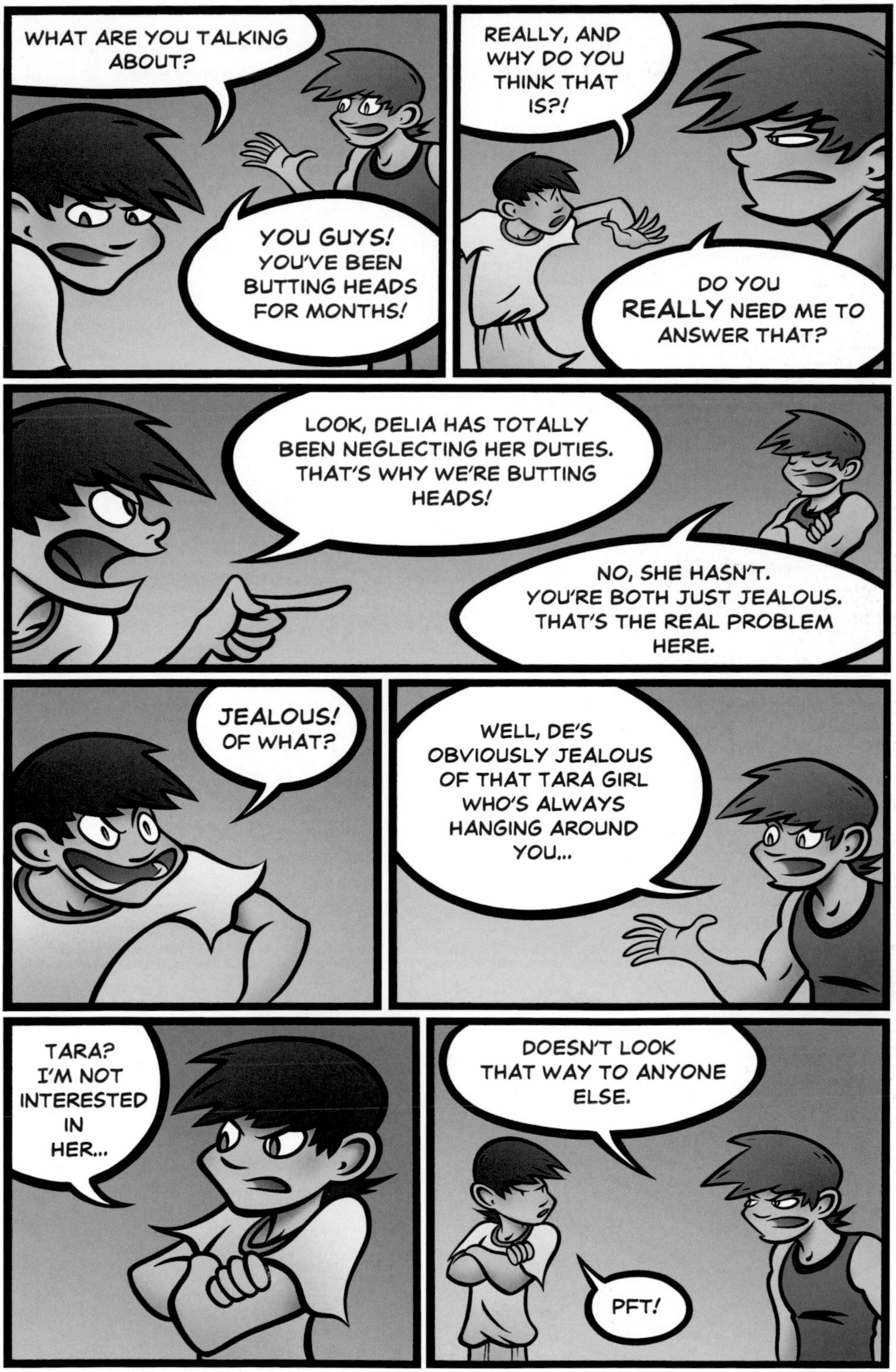
WHAT ARE YOU TALKING ABOUT?
YOU GUYS! YOU'VE BEEN BUTTING HEADS FOR MONTHS!
REALLY, AND WHY DO YOU THINK THAT IS?!
DO YOU REALLY NEED ME TO ANSWER THAT?
LOOK, DELIA HAS TOTALLY BEEN NEGLECTING HER DUTIES. THAT'S WHY WE'RE BUTTING HEADS!
NO, SHE HASN'T. YOU'RE BOTH JUST JEALOUS. THAT'S THE REAL PROBLEM HERE.
JEALOUS! OF WHAT?
WELL, DE'S OBVIOUSLY JEALOUS OF THAT TARA GIRL WHO'S ALWAYS HANGING AROUND YOU...
TARA? I'M NOT INTERESTED IN HER...
DOESN'T LOOK THAT WAY TO ANYONE ELSE.
PFT!

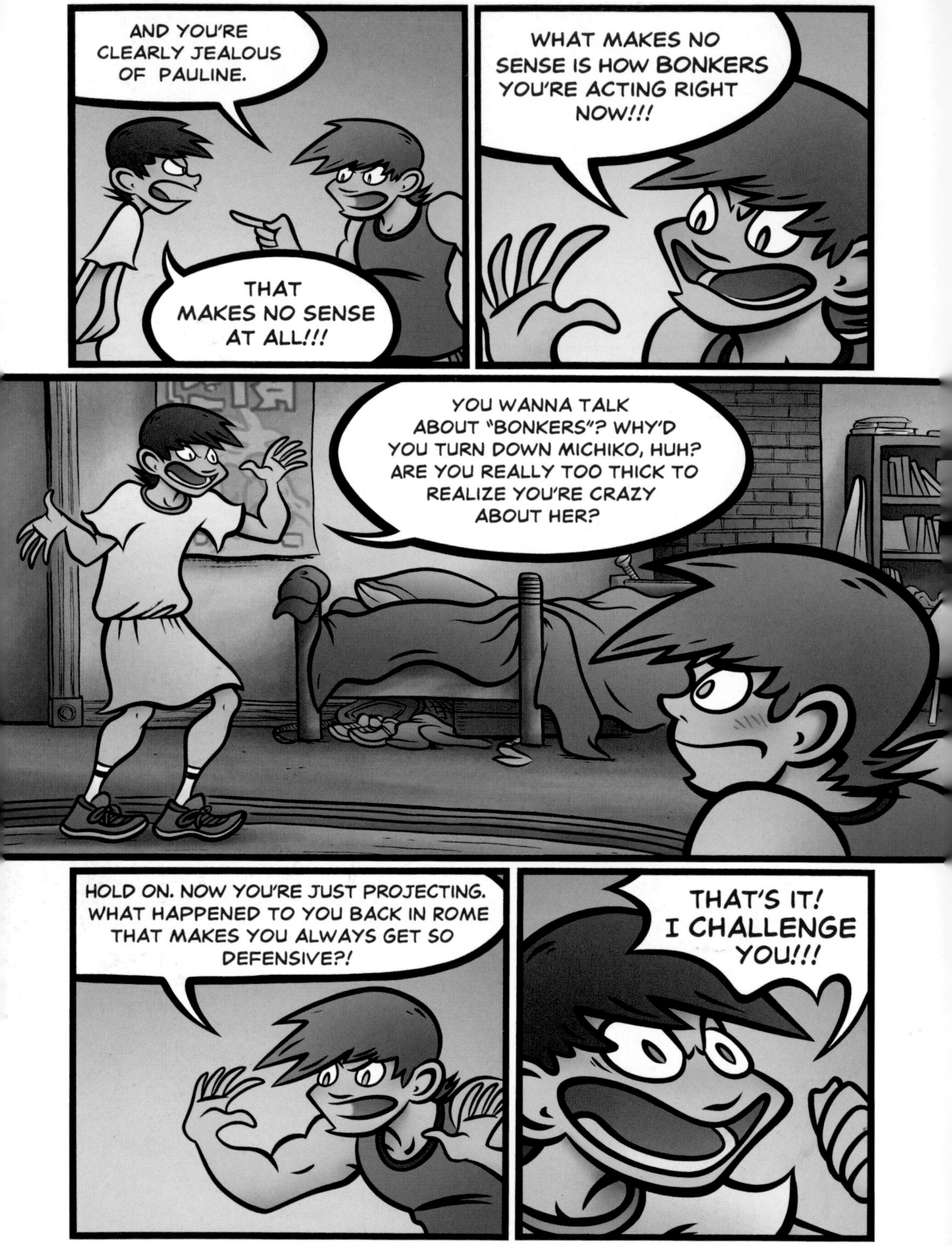
AND YOU'RE CLEARLY JEALOUS OF PAULINE.
THAT MAKES NO SENSE AT ALL!!!
WHAT MAKES NO SENSE IS HOW BONKERS YOU'RE ACTING RIGHT NOW!!!
YOU WANNA TALK ABOUT "BONKERS"? WHY'D YOU TURN DOWN MICHIKO, HUH? ARE YOU REALLY TOO THICK TO REALIZE YOU'RE CRAZY ABOUT HER?
HOLD ON. NOW YOU'RE JUST PROJECTING. WHAT HAPPENED TO YOU BACK IN ROME THAT MAKES YOU ALWAYS GET SO DEFENSIVE?!
THAT'S IT! I CHALLENGE YOU!!!

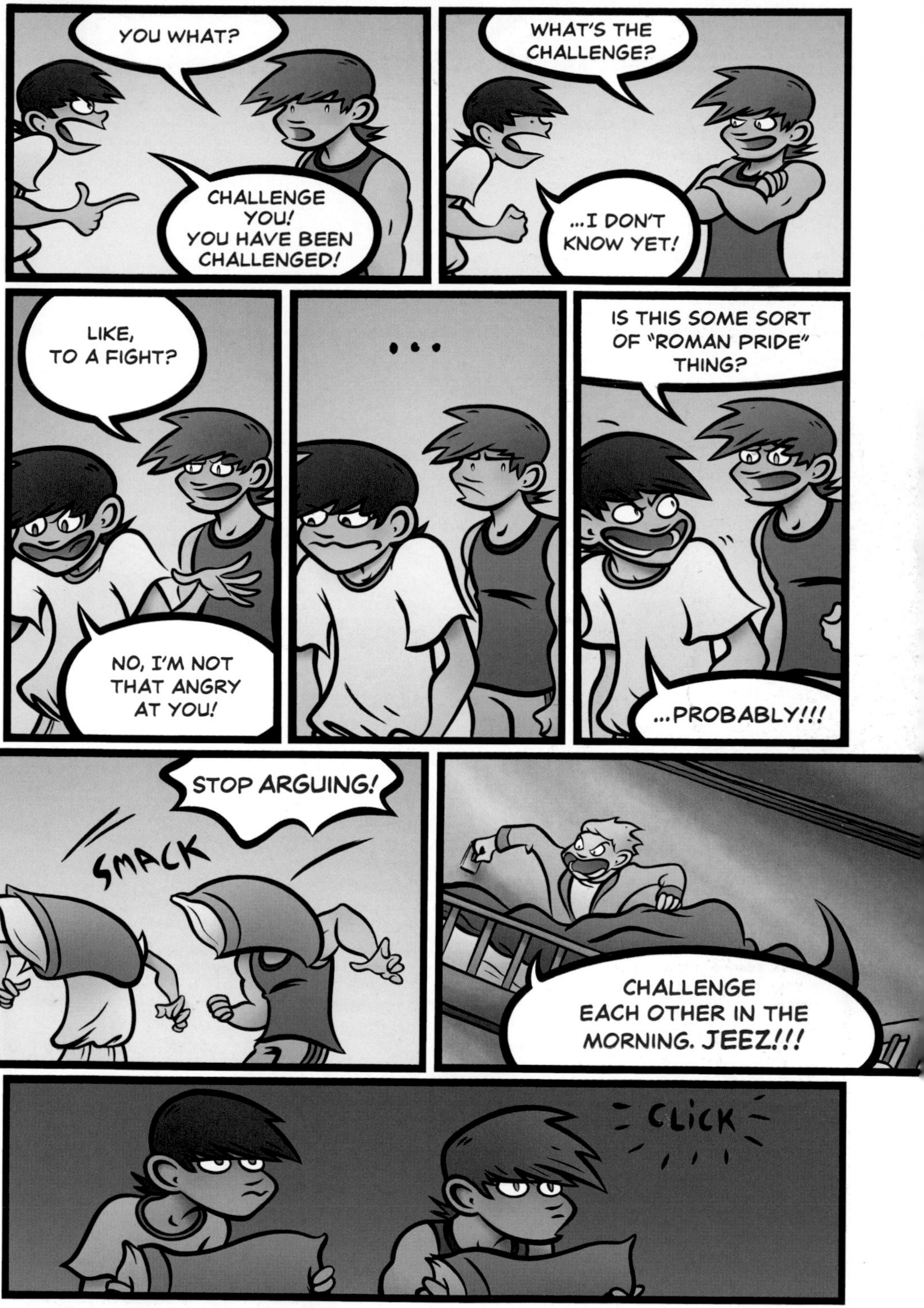
YOU WHAT?
CHALLENGE YOU! YOU HAVE BEEN CHALLENGED!
WHAT'S THE CHALLENGE?
...I DON'T KNOW YET!
LIKE, TO A FIGHT?
NO, I'M NOT THAT ANGRY AT YOU!
...
IS THIS SOME SORT OF "ROMAN PRIDE" THING?
...PROBABLY!!!
STOP ARGUING!
SMACK
CHALLENGE EACH OTHER IN THE MORNING. JEEZ!!!
CLICK

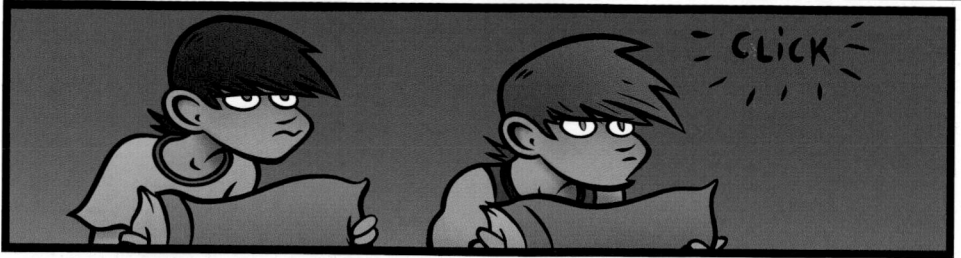

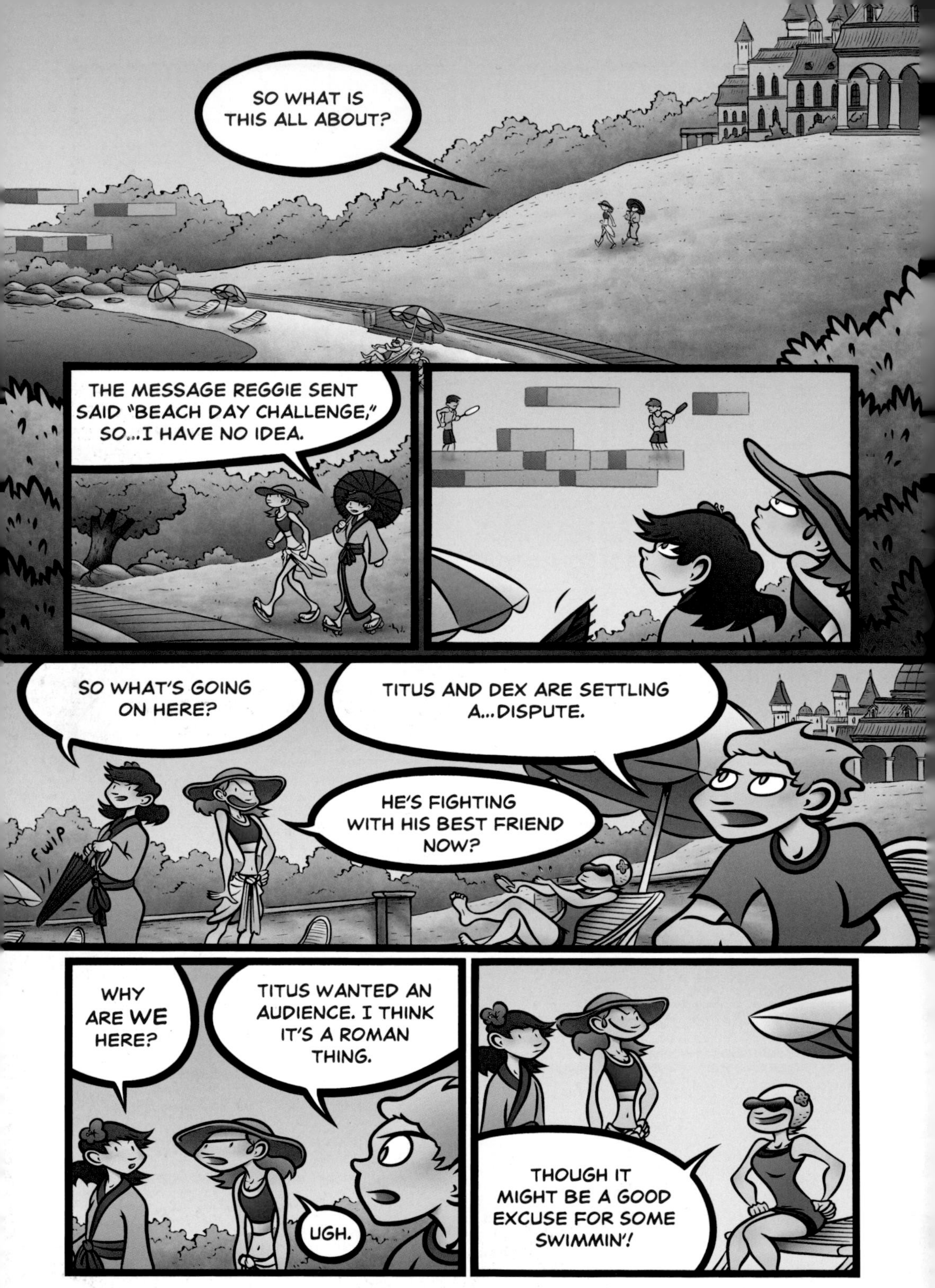

SO WHAT IS THIS ALL ABOUT?
THE MESSAGE REGGIE SENT SAID "BEACH DAY CHALLENGE," SO...I HAVE NO IDEA.
SO WHAT'S GOING ON HERE?
TITUS AND DEX ARE SETTLING A...DISPUTE.
FWIP
HE'S FIGHTING WITH HIS BEST FRIEND NOW?
WHY ARE WE HERE?
TITUS WANTED AN AUDIENCE. I THINK IT'S A ROMAN THING.
UGH.
THOUGH IT MIGHT BE A GOOD EXCUSE FOR SOME SWIMMIN'!

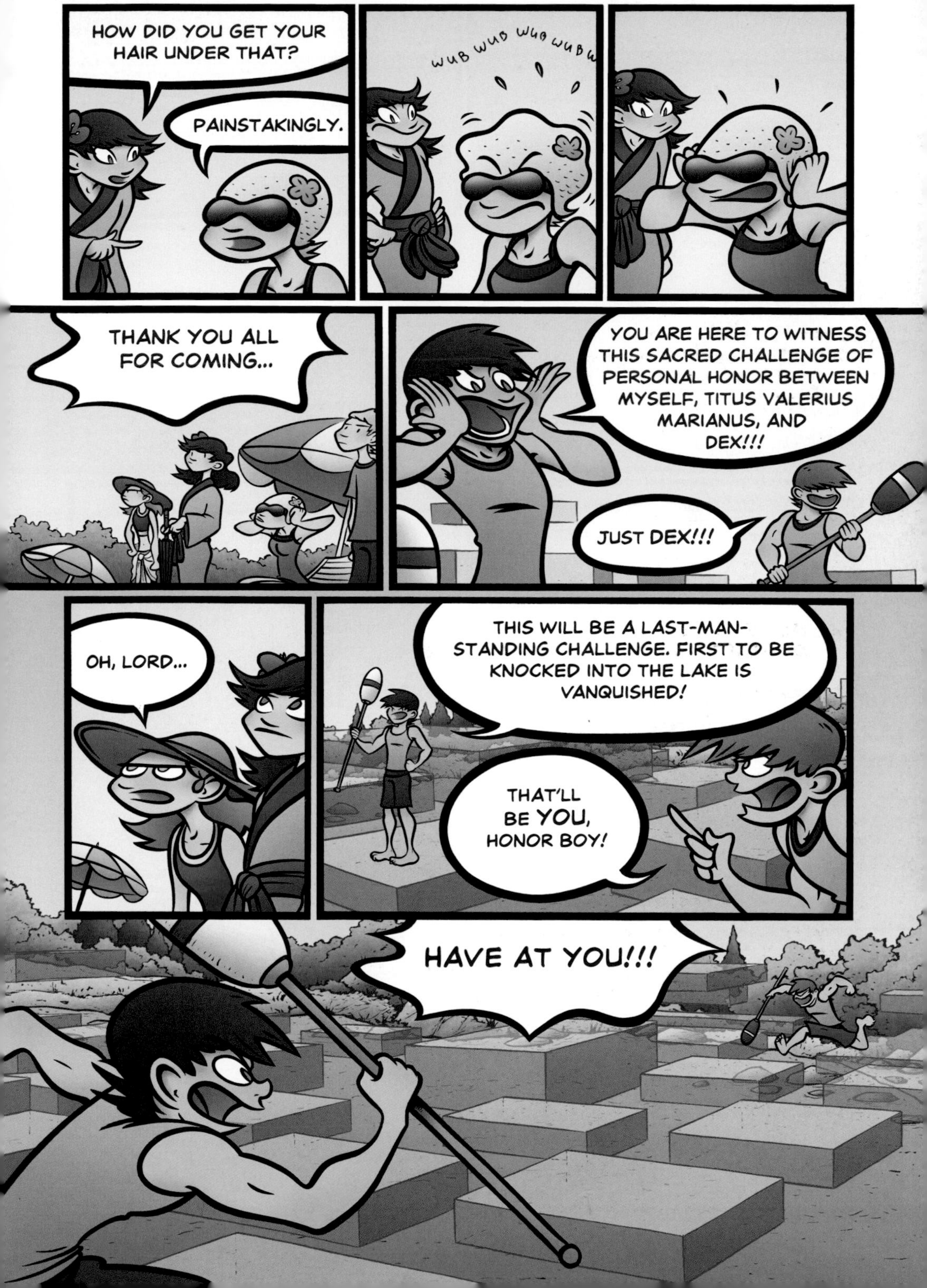
HOW DID YOU GET YOUR HAIR UNDER THAT?
PAINSTAKINGLY.
WUB WUB WUB WUB WUB W
THANK YOU ALL FOR COMING...
YOU ARE HERE TO WITNESS THIS SACRED CHALLENGE OF PERSONAL HONOR BETWEEN MYSELF, TITUS VALERIUS MARIANUS, AND DEX!!!
JUST DEX!!!
OH, LORD...
THIS WILL BE A LAST-MAN-STANDING CHALLENGE. FIRST TO BE KNOCKED INTO THE LAKE IS VANQUISHED!
THAT'LL BE YOU, HONOR BOY!
HAVE AT YOU!!!

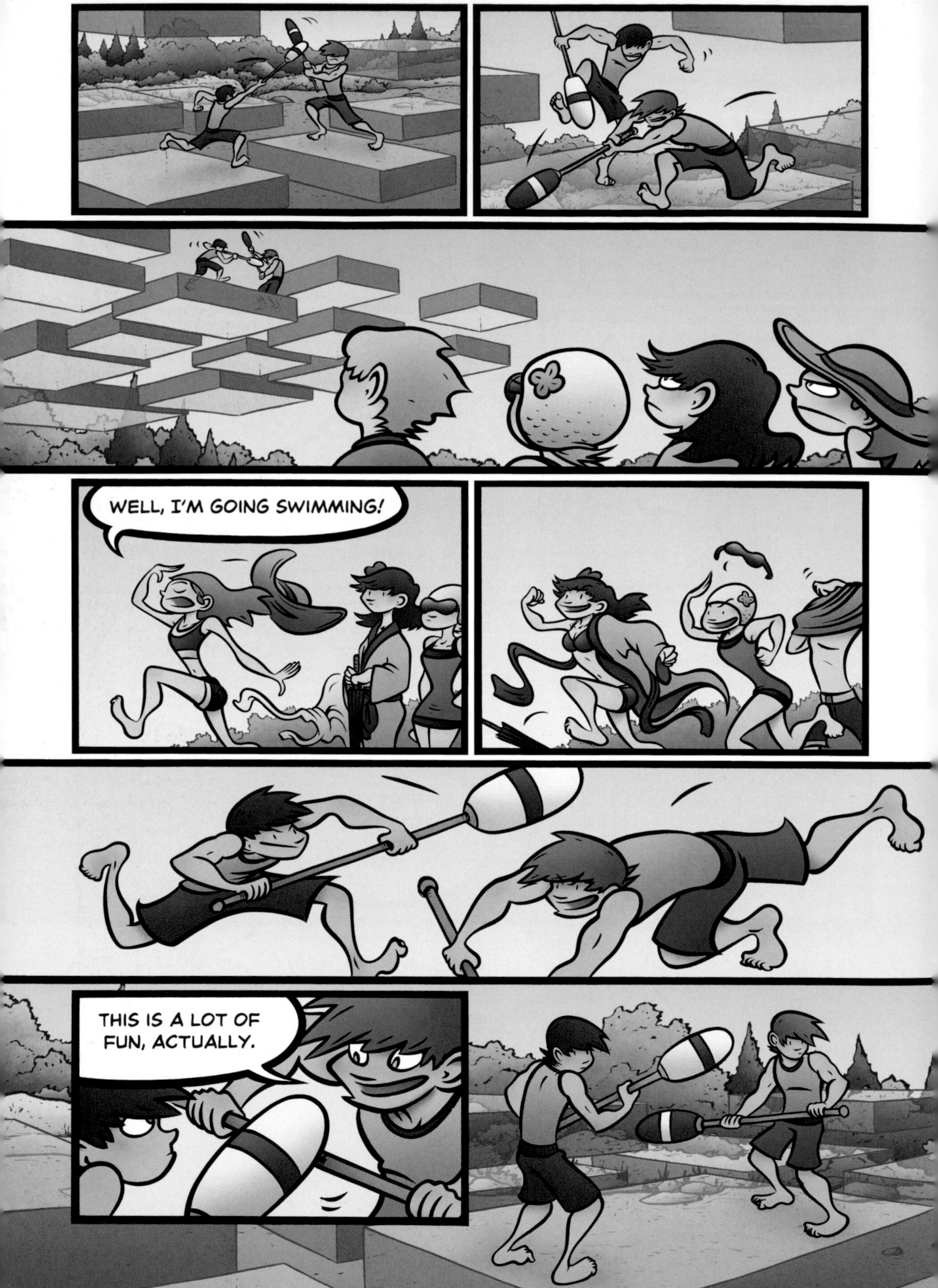
WELL, I'M GOING SWIMMING!
THIS IS A LOT OF FUN, ACTUALLY.

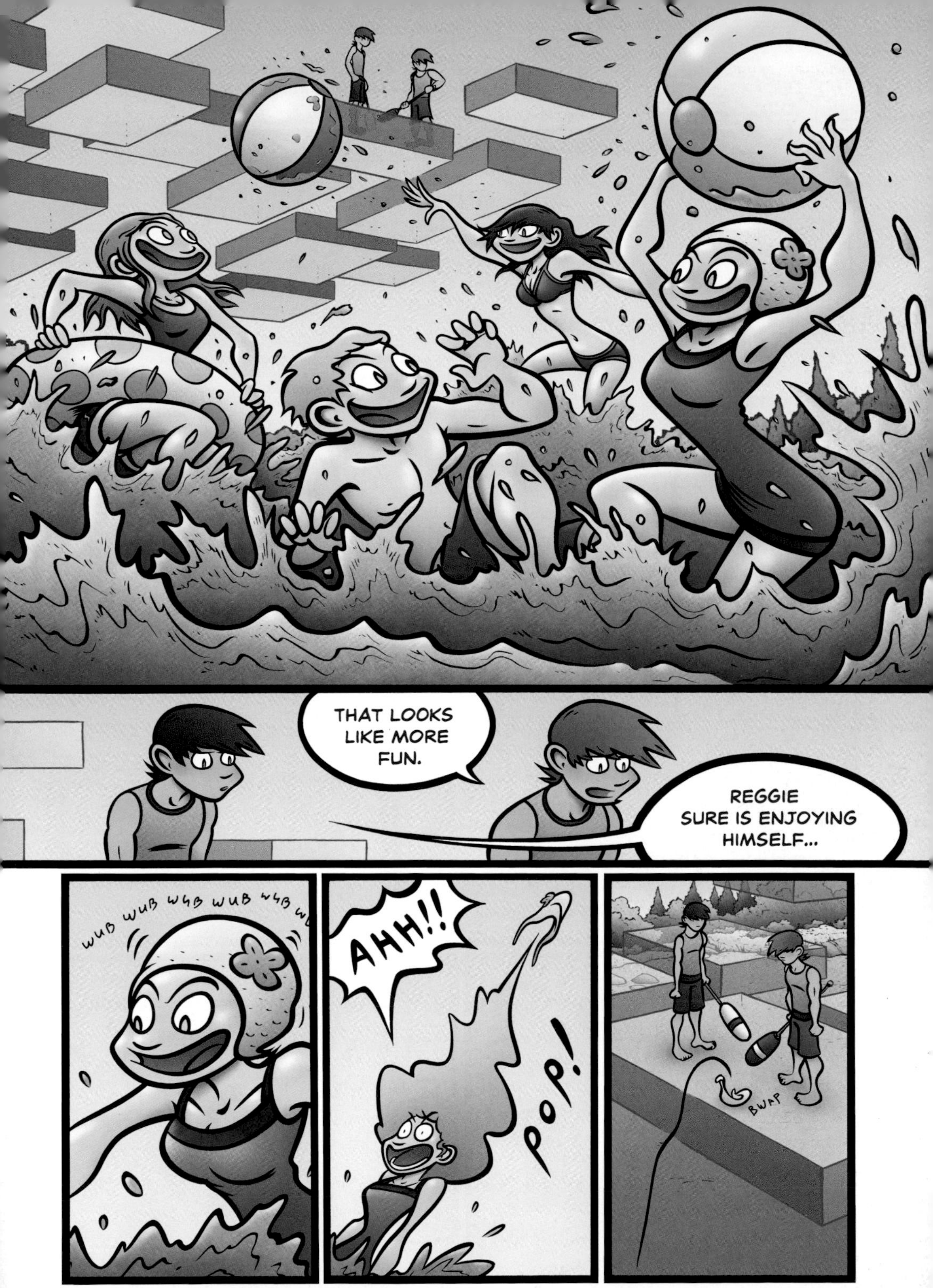
THAT LOOKS LIKE MORE FUN.
REGGIE SURE IS ENJOYING HIMSELF...
WUB WUB WUB WUB WUB
AHH!!
POP!
BWAP

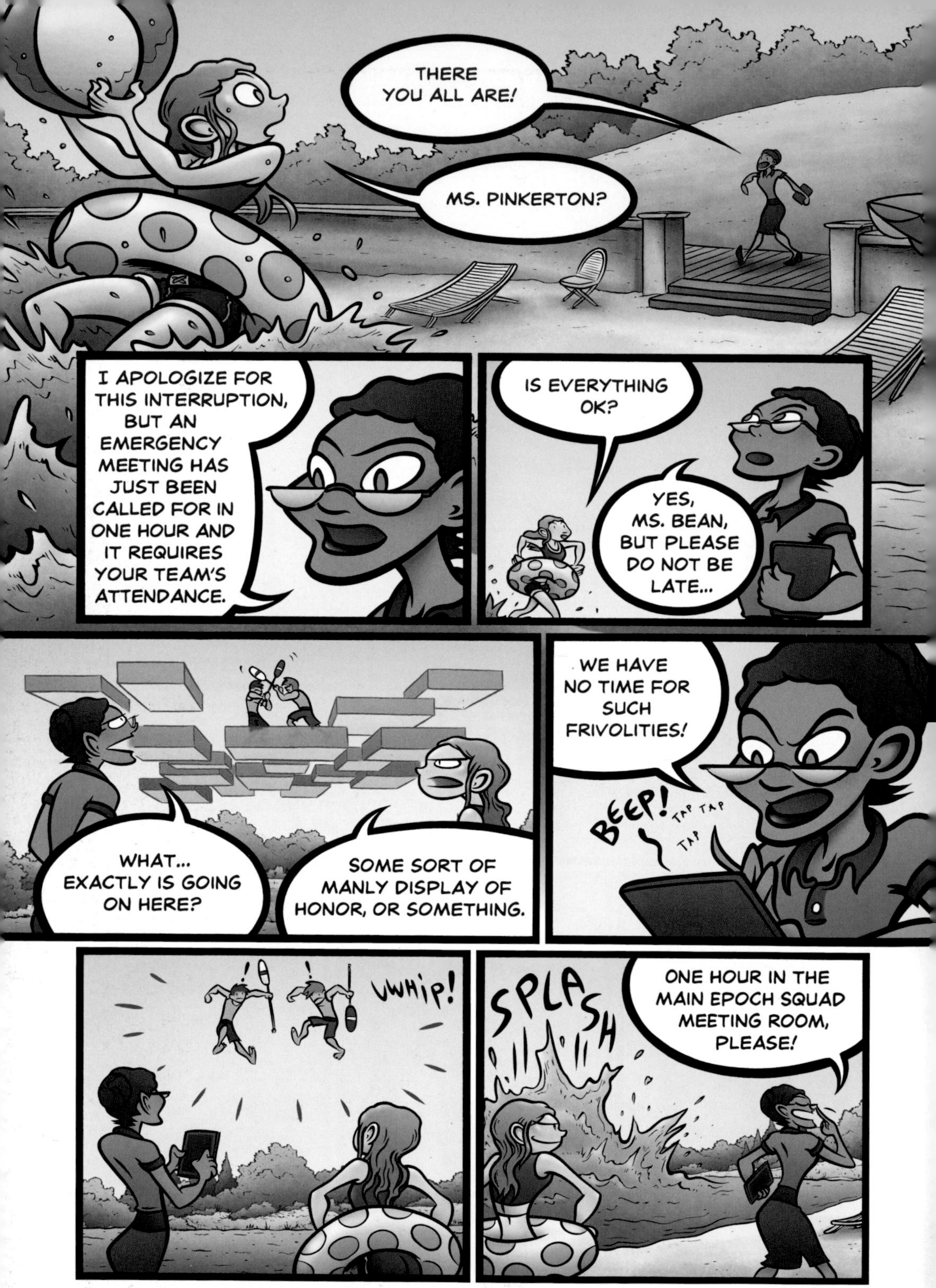
THERE YOU ALL ARE!
MS. PINKERTON?
I APOLOGIZE FOR THIS INTERRUPTION, BUT AN EMERGENCY MEETING HAS JUST BEEN CALLED FOR IN ONE HOUR AND IT REQUIRES YOUR TEAM'S ATTENDANCE.
IS EVERYTHING OK?
YES, MS. BEAN, BUT PLEASE DO NOT BE LATE...
WHAT... EXACTLY IS GOING ON HERE?
SOME SORT OF MANLY DISPLAY OF HONOR, OR SOMETHING.
WE HAVE NO TIME FOR SUCH FRIVOLITIES!
BEEP!
TAP TAP
TAP
VWHIP!
SPLASH
ONE HOUR IN THE MAIN EPOCH SQUAD MEETING ROOM, PLEASE!

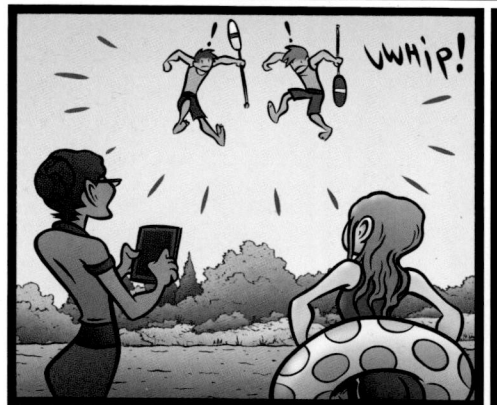

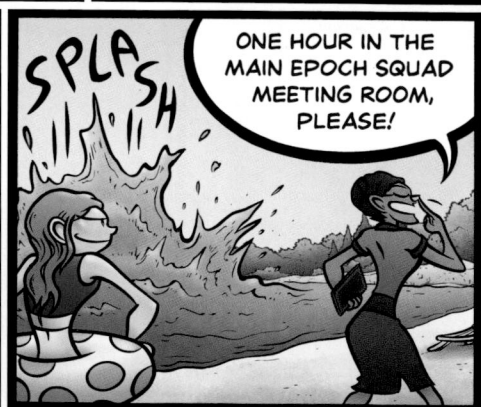

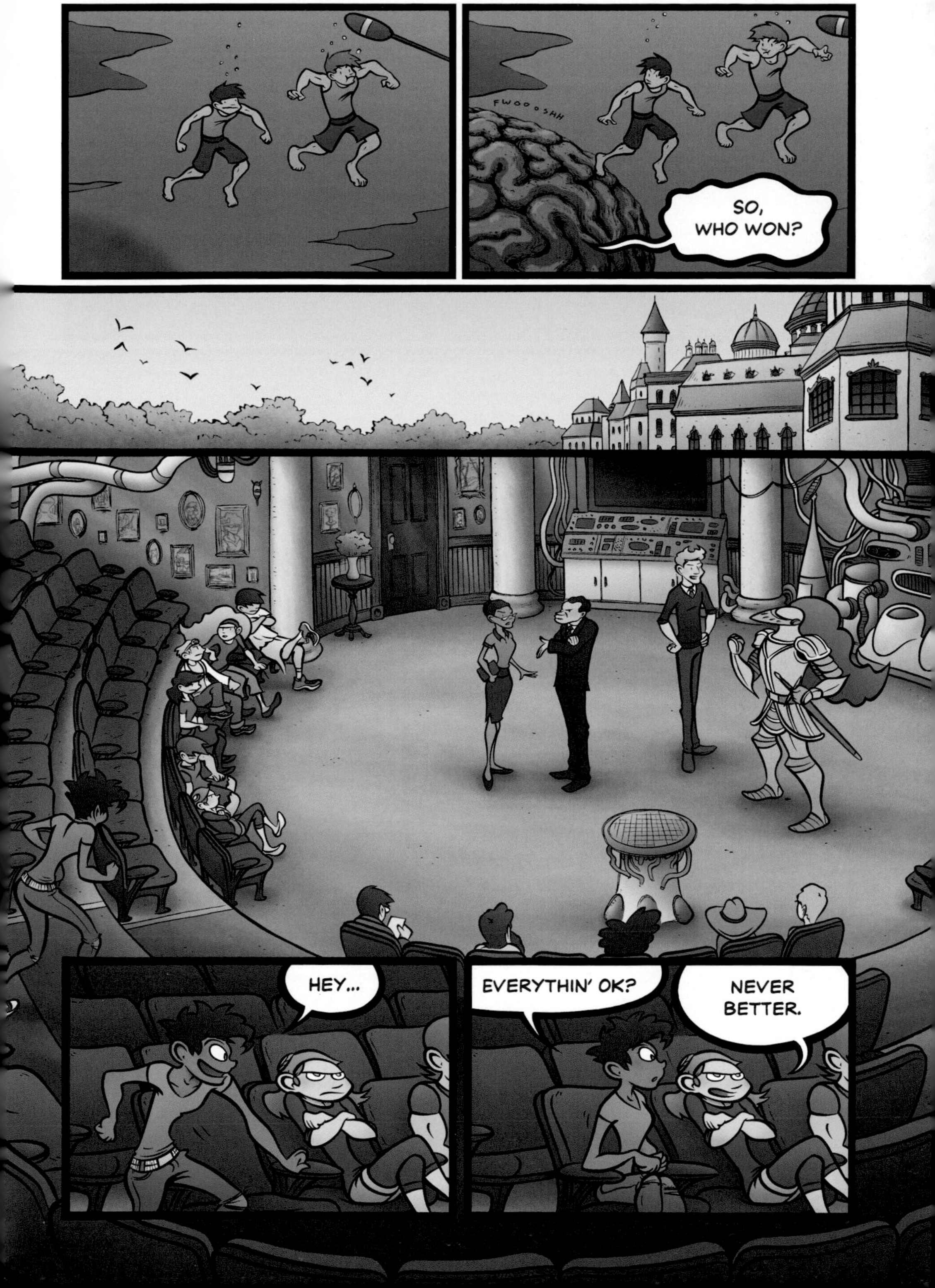
FWOOOSHH
SO, WHO WON?
HEY...
EVERYTHIN' OK?
NEVER BETTER.

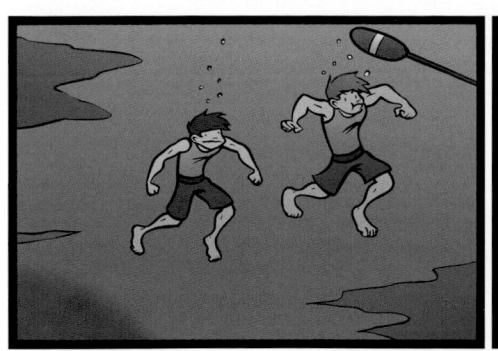

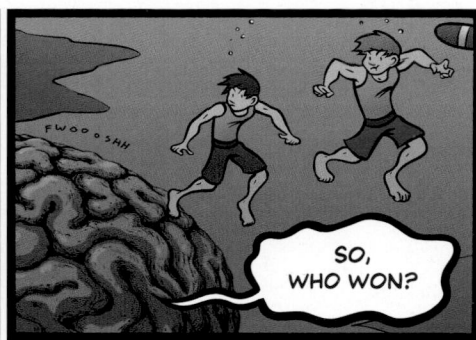

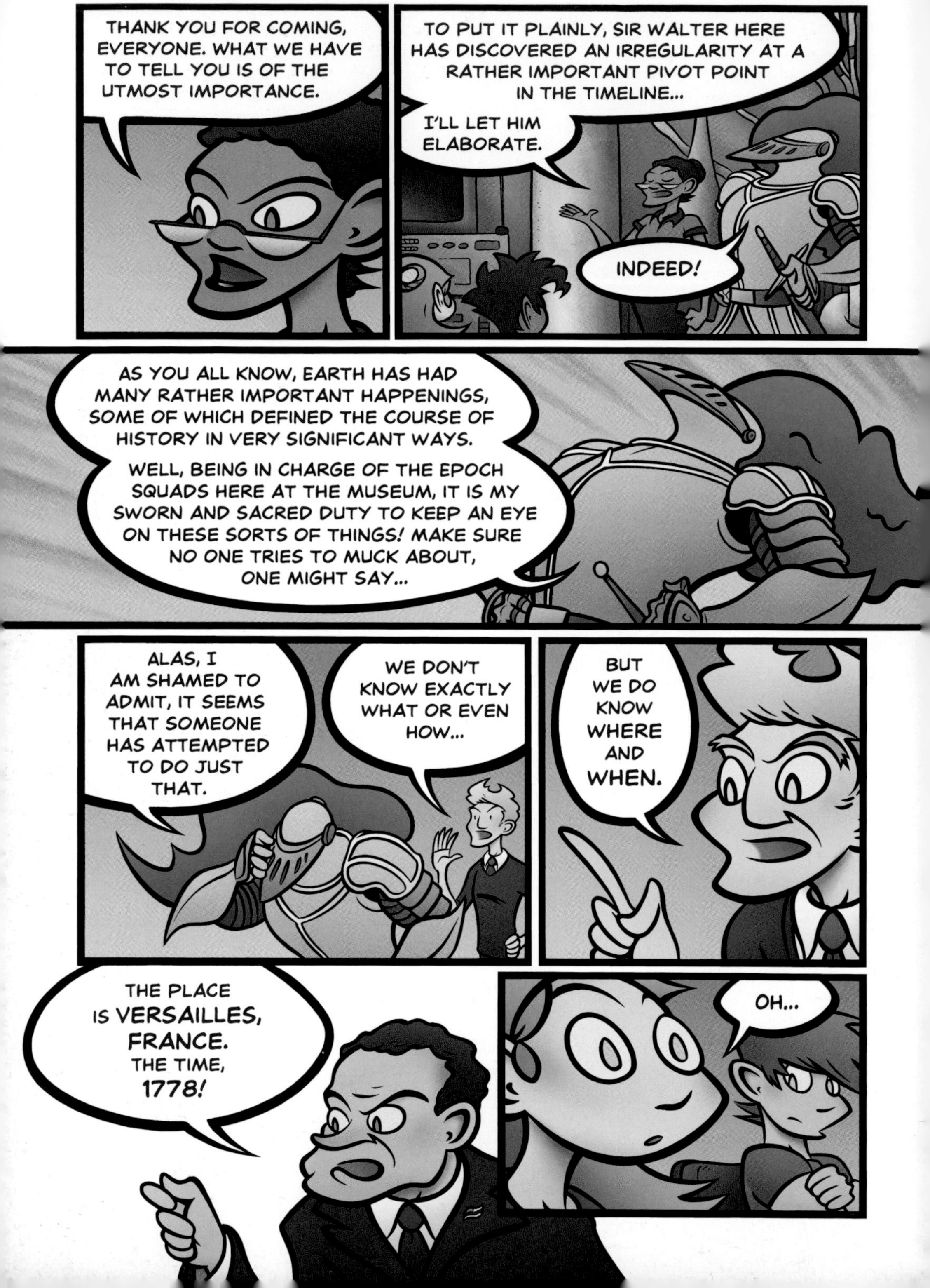
THANK YOU FOR COMING, EVERYONE. WHAT WE HAVE TO TELL YOU IS OF THE UTMOST IMPORTANCE.
TO PUT IT PLAINLY, SIR WALTER HERE HAS DISCOVERED AN IRREGULARITY AT A RATHER IMPORTANT PIVOT POINT IN THE TIMELINE...
I'LL LET HIM ELABORATE.
INDEED!
AS YOU ALL KNOW, EARTH HAS HAD MANY RATHER IMPORTANT HAPPENINGS, SOME OF WHICH DEFINED THE COURSE OF HISTORY IN VERY SIGNIFICANT WAYS.
WELL, BEING IN CHARGE OF THE EPOCH SQUADS HERE AT THE MUSEUM, IT IS MY SWORN AND SACRED DUTY TO KEEP AN EYE ON THESE SORTS OF THINGS! MAKE SURE NO ONE TRIES TO MUCK ABOUT, ONE MIGHT SAY...
ALAS, I AM SHAMED TO ADMIT, IT SEEMS THAT SOMEONE HAS ATTEMPTED TO DO JUST THAT.
WE DON'T KNOW EXACTLY WHAT OR EVEN HOW...
BUT WE DO KNOW WHERE AND WHEN.
THE PLACE IS VERSAILLES, FRANCE. THE TIME, 1778!
OH...

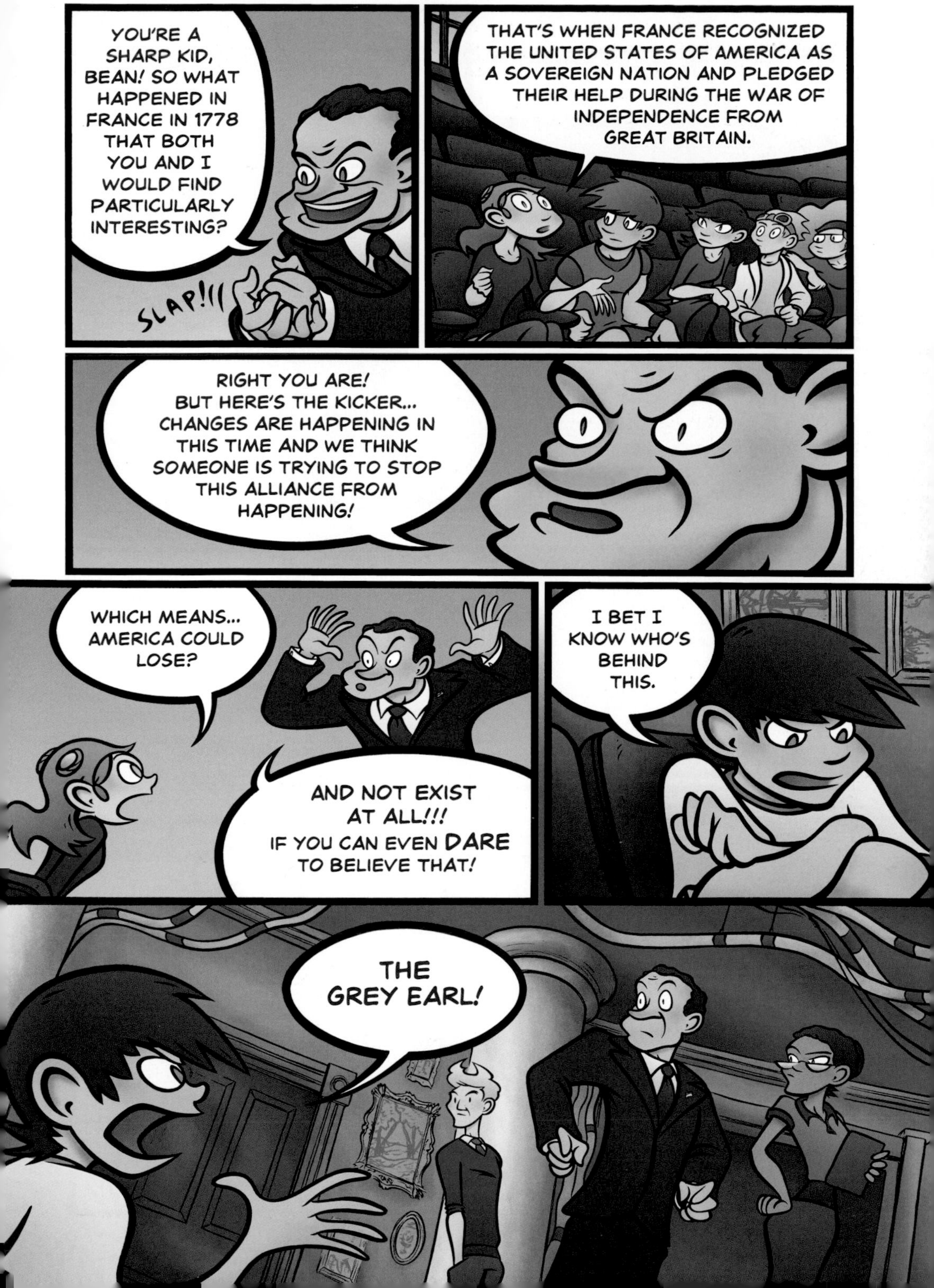
YOU'RE A SHARP KID, BEAN! SO WHAT HAPPENED IN FRANCE IN 1778 THAT BOTH YOU AND I WOULD FIND PARTICULARLY INTERESTING?
SLAP!!!
THAT'S WHEN FRANCE RECOGNIZED THE UNITED STATES OF AMERICA AS A SOVEREIGN NATION AND PLEDGED THEIR HELP DURING THE WAR OF INDEPENDENCE FROM GREAT BRITAIN.
RIGHT YOU ARE! BUT HERE'S THE KICKER... CHANGES ARE HAPPENING IN THIS TIME AND WE THINK SOMEONE IS TRYING TO STOP THIS ALLIANCE FROM HAPPENING!
WHICH MEANS... AMERICA COULD LOSE?
AND NOT EXIST AT ALL!!! IF YOU CAN EVEN DARE TO BELIEVE THAT!
I BET I KNOW WHO'S BEHIND THIS.
THE GREY EARL!

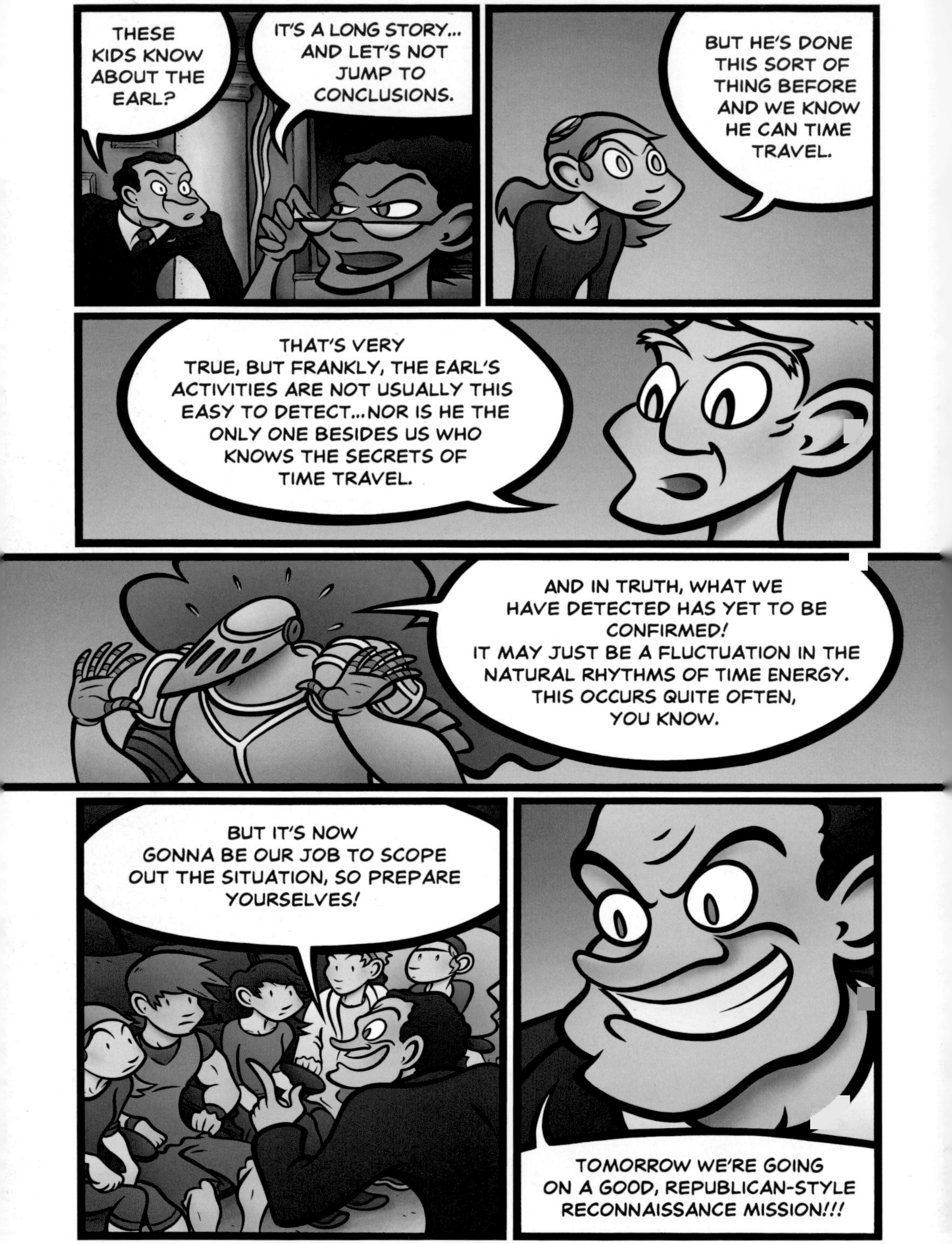
THESE KIDS KNOW ABOUT THE EARL?
IT'S A LONG STORY... AND LET'S NOT JUMP TO CONCLUSIONS.
BUT HE'S DONE THIS SORT OF THING BEFORE AND WE KNOW HE CAN TIME TRAVEL.
THAT'S VERY TRUE, BUT FRANKLY, THE EARL'S ACTIVITIES ARE NOT USUALLY THIS EASY TO DETECT...NOR IS HE THE ONLY ONE BESIDES US WHO KNOWS THE SECRETS OF TIME TRAVEL.
AND IN TRUTH, WHAT WE HAVE DETECTED HAS YET TO BE CONFIRMED! IT MAY JUST BE A FLUCTUATION IN THE NATURAL RHYTHMS OF TIME ENERGY. THIS OCCURS QUITE OFTEN, YOU KNOW.
BUT IT'S NOW GONNA BE OUR JOB TO SCOPE OUT THE SITUATION, SO PREPARE YOURSELVES!
TOMORROW WE'RE GOING ON A GOOD, REPUBLICAN-STYLE RECONNAISSANCE MISSION!!!

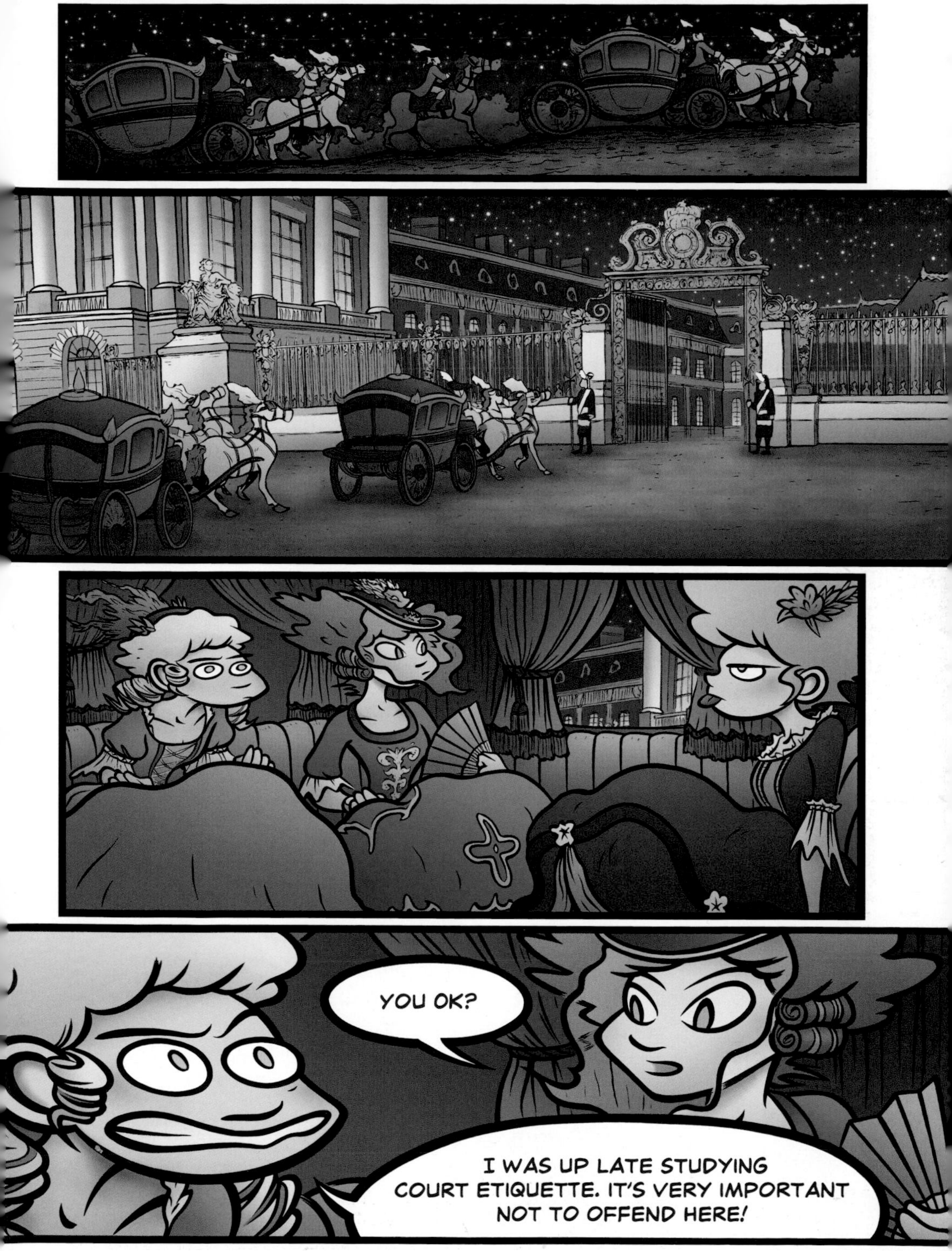
YOU OK?
I WAS UP LATE STUDYING COURT ETIQUETTE. IT'S VERY IMPORTANT NOT TO OFFEND HERE!

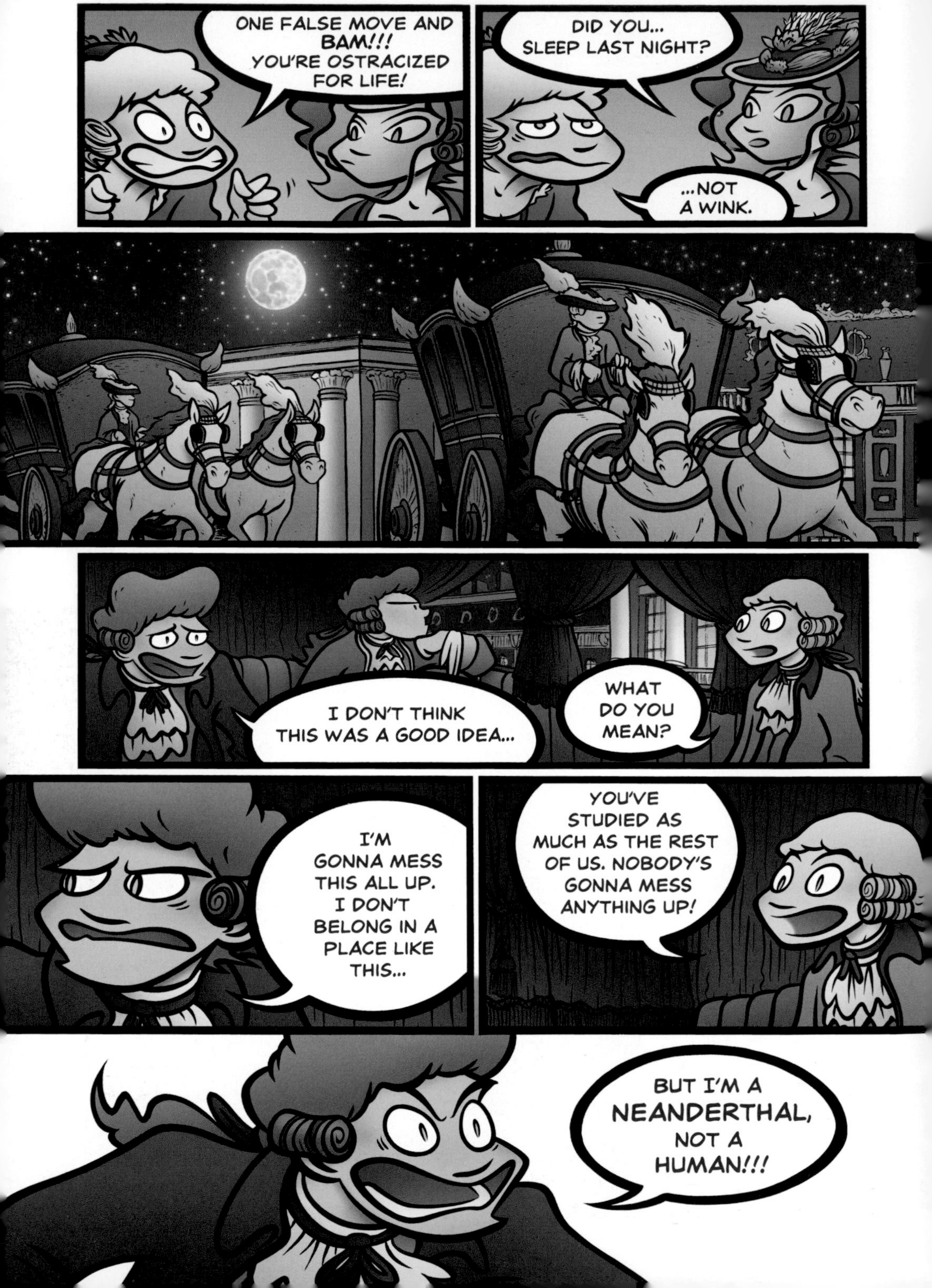

ONE FALSE MOVE AND BAM!!! YOU'RE OSTRACIZED FOR LIFE!
DID YOU... SLEEP LAST NIGHT?
...NOT A WINK.
I DON'T THINK THIS WAS A GOOD IDEA...
WHAT DO YOU MEAN?
I'M GONNA MESS THIS ALL UP. I DON'T BELONG IN A PLACE LIKE THIS...
YOU'VE STUDIED AS MUCH AS THE REST OF US. NOBODY'S GONNA MESS ANYTHING UP!
BUT I'M A NEANDERTHAL, NOT A HUMAN!!!

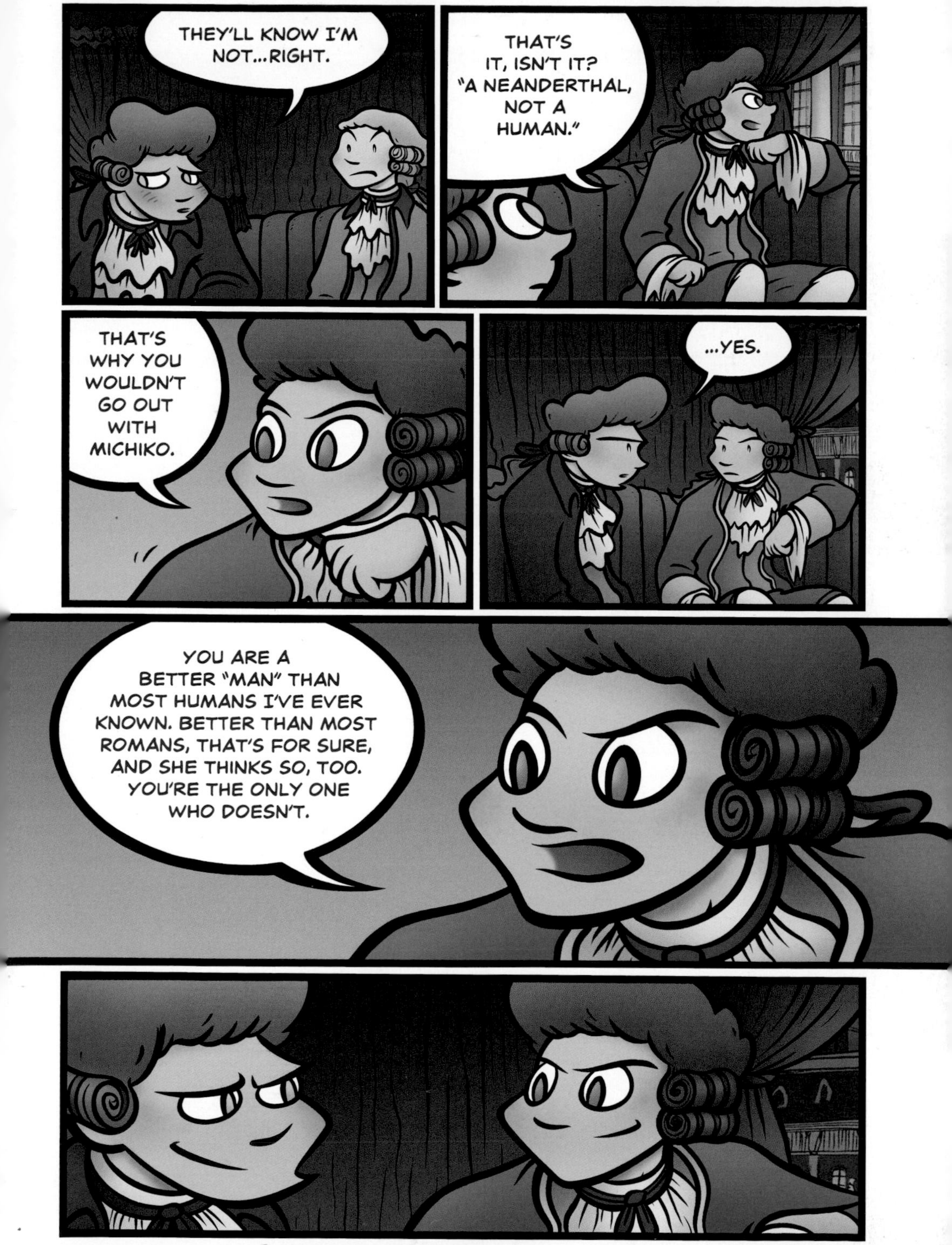
THEY'LL KNOW I'M NOT...RIGHT.
THAT'S IT, ISN'T IT? "A NEANDERTHAL, NOT A HUMAN."
THAT'S WHY YOU WOULDN'T GO OUT WITH MICHIKO.
...YES.
YOU ARE A BETTER "MAN" THAN MOST HUMANS I'VE EVER KNOWN. BETTER THAN MOST ROMANS, THAT'S FOR SURE, AND SHE THINKS SO, TOO. YOU'RE THE ONLY ONE WHO DOESN'T.

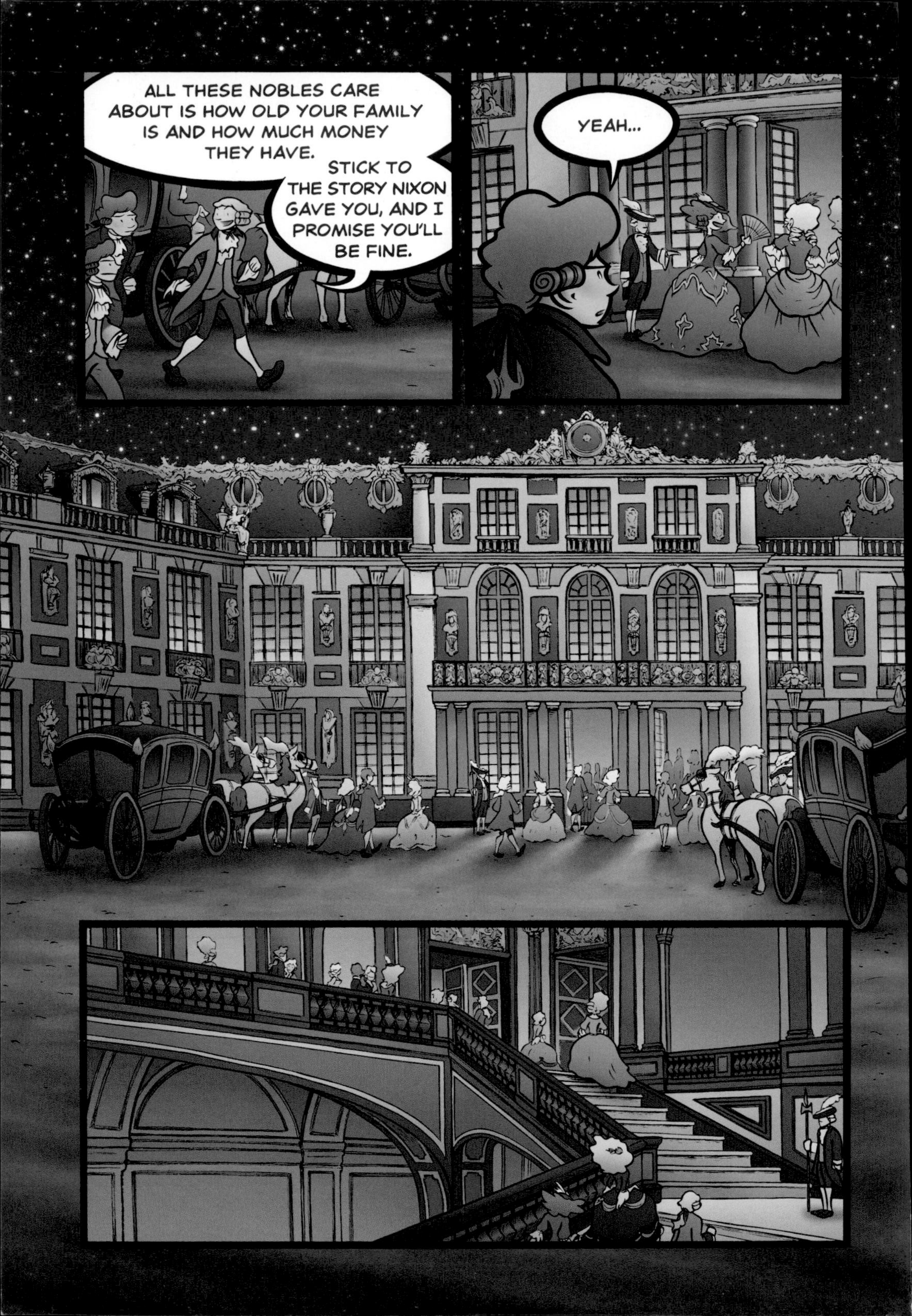
ALL THESE NOBLES CARE ABOUT IS HOW OLD YOUR FAMILY IS AND HOW MUCH MONEY THEY HAVE.
STICK TO THE STORY NIXON GAVE YOU, AND I PROMISE YOU'LL BE FINE.
YEAH...

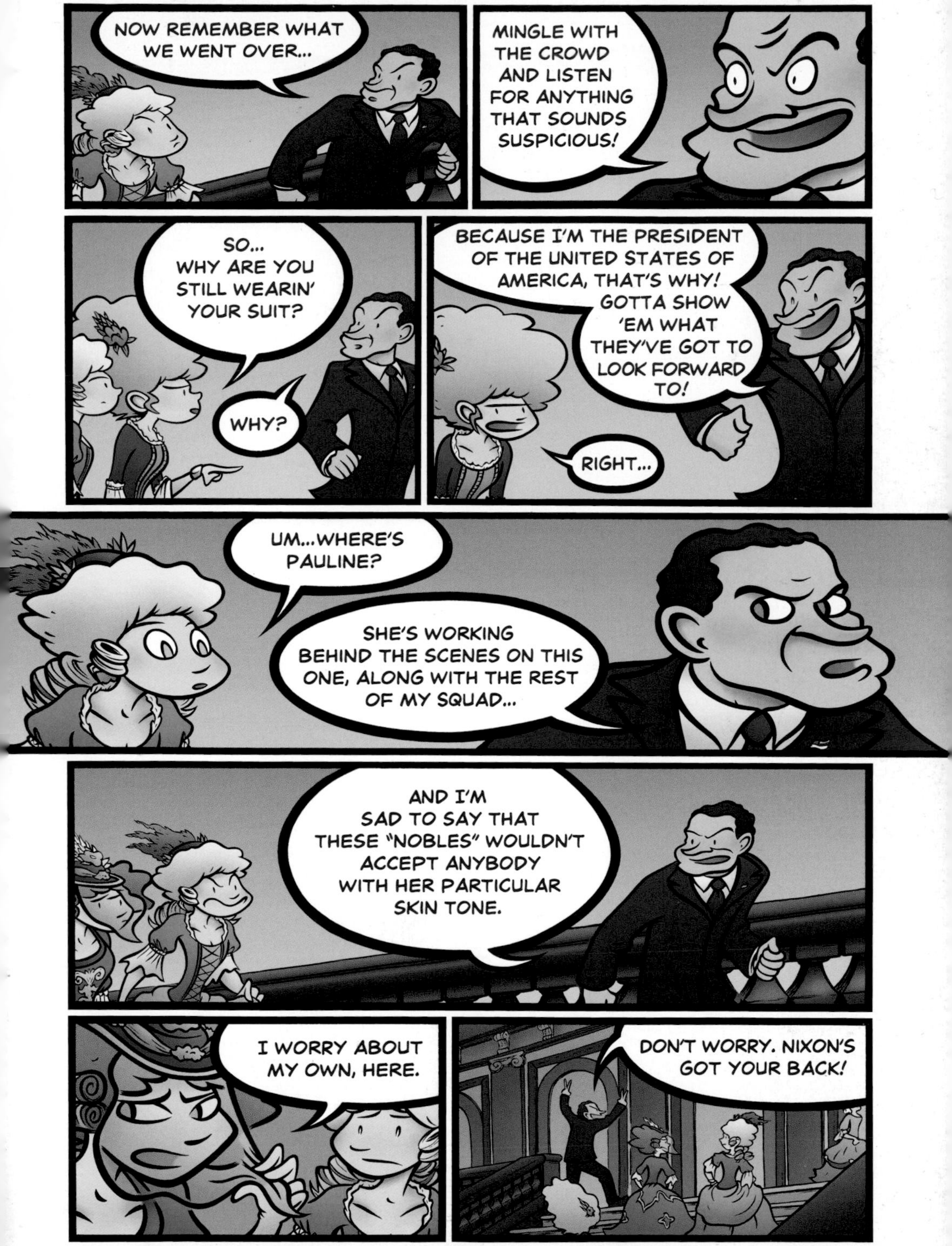
NOW REMEMBER WHAT WE WENT OVER...
MINGLE WITH THE CROWD AND LISTEN FOR ANYTHING THAT SOUNDS SUSPICIOUS!
SO... WHY ARE YOU STILL WEARIN' YOUR SUIT?
WHY?
BECAUSE I'M THE PRESIDENT OF THE UNITED STATES OF AMERICA, THAT'S WHY! GOTTA SHOW 'EM WHAT THEY'VE GOT TO LOOK FORWARD TO!
RIGHT...
UM...WHERE'S PAULINE?
SHE'S WORKING BEHIND THE SCENES ON THIS ONE, ALONG WITH THE REST OF MY SQUAD...
AND I'M SAD TO SAY THAT THESE "NOBLES" WOULDN'T ACCEPT ANYBODY WITH HER PARTICULAR SKIN TONE.
I WORRY ABOUT MY OWN, HERE.
DON'T WORRY. NIXON'S GOT YOUR BACK!

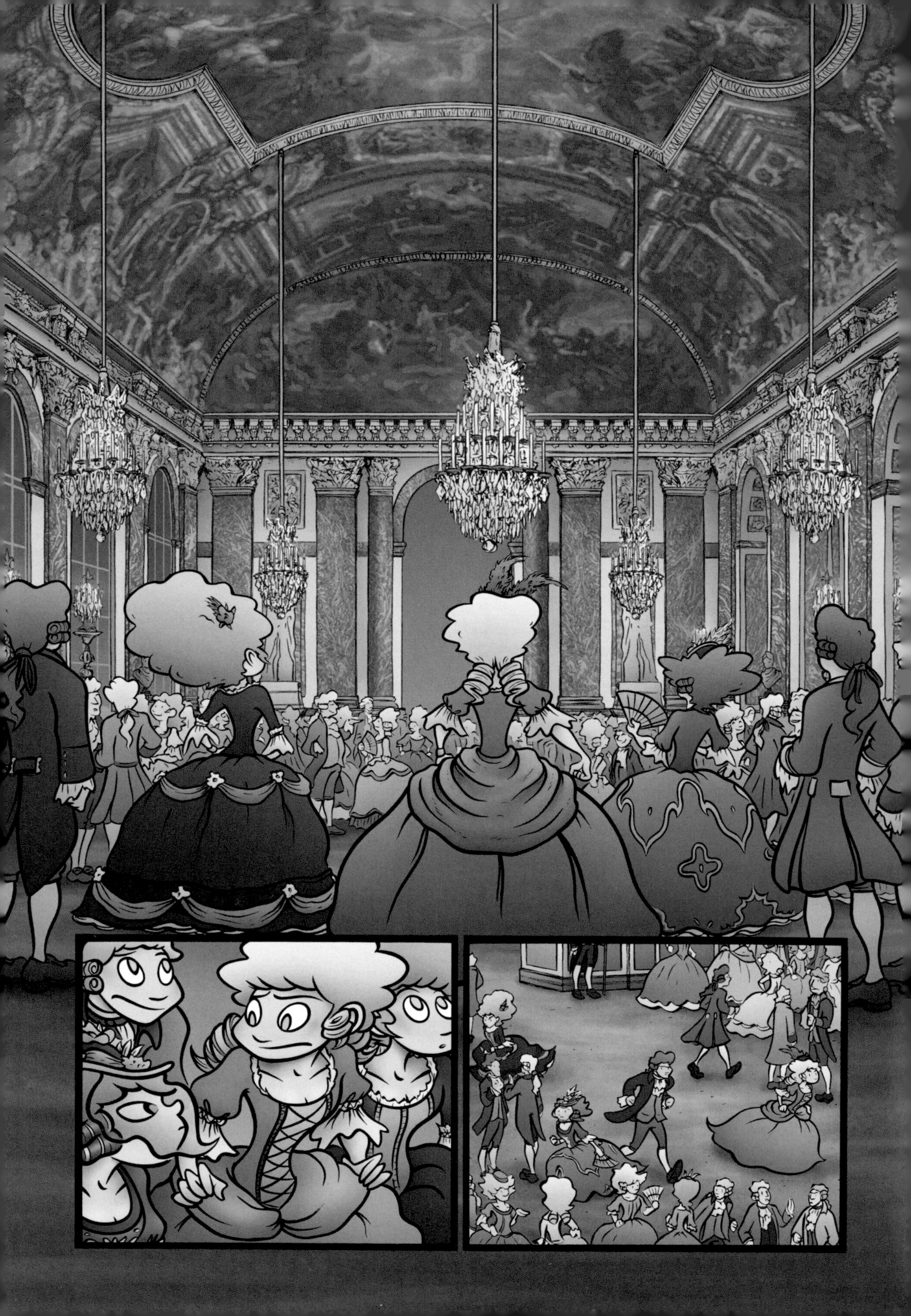

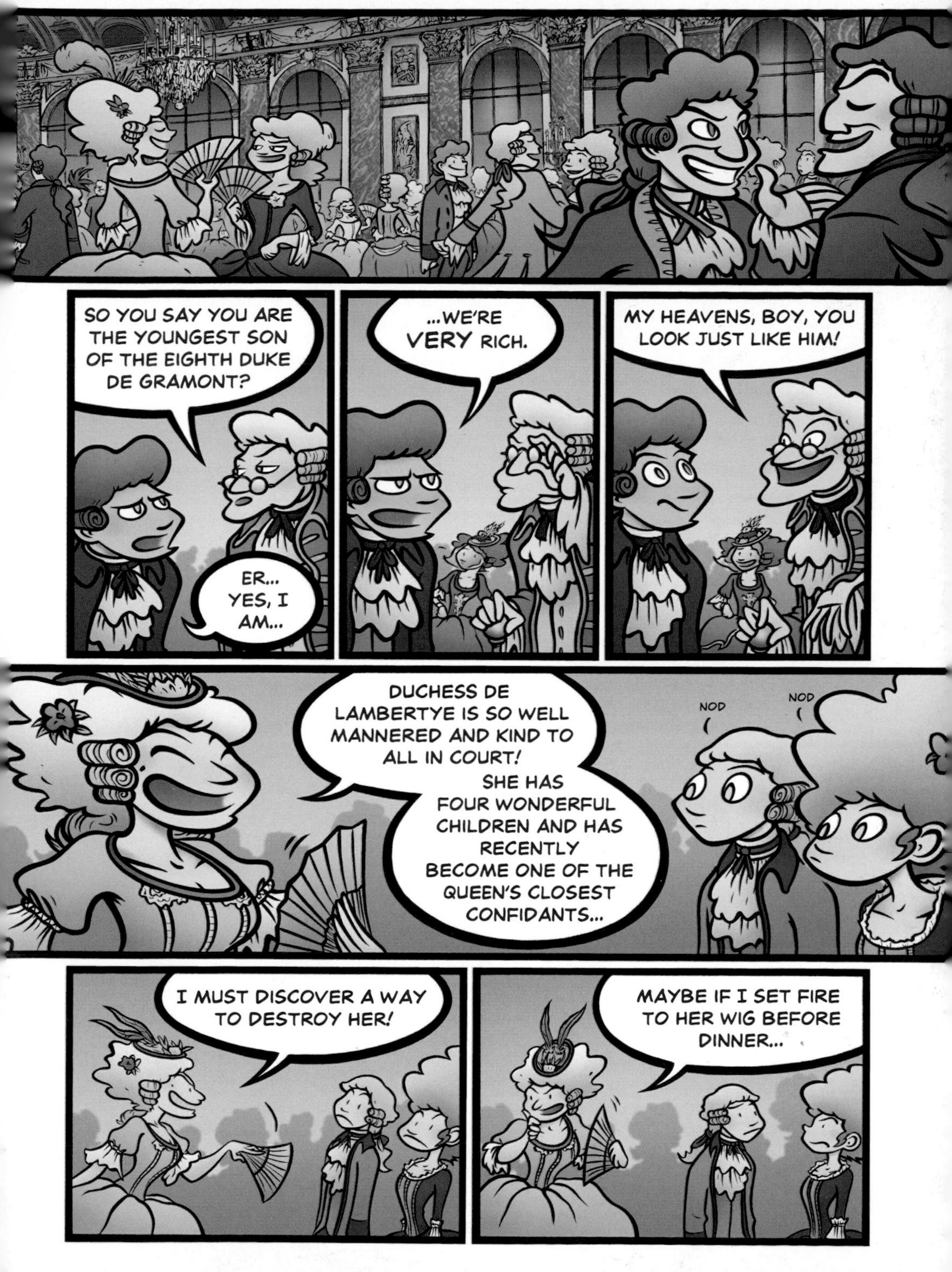
SO YOU SAY YOU ARE THE YOUNGEST SON OF THE EIGHTH DUKE DE GRAMONT?
ER... YES, I AM...
...WE'RE VERY RICH.
MY HEAVENS, BOY, YOU LOOK JUST LIKE HIM!
DUCHESS DE LAMBERTYE IS SO WELL MANNERED AND KIND TO ALL IN COURT!
SHE HAS FOUR WONDERFUL CHILDREN AND HAS RECENTLY BECOME ONE OF THE QUEEN'S CLOSEST CONFIDANTS...
NOD
NOD
I MUST DISCOVER A WAY TO DESTROY HER!
MAYBE IF I SET FIRE TO HER WIG BEFORE DINNER...

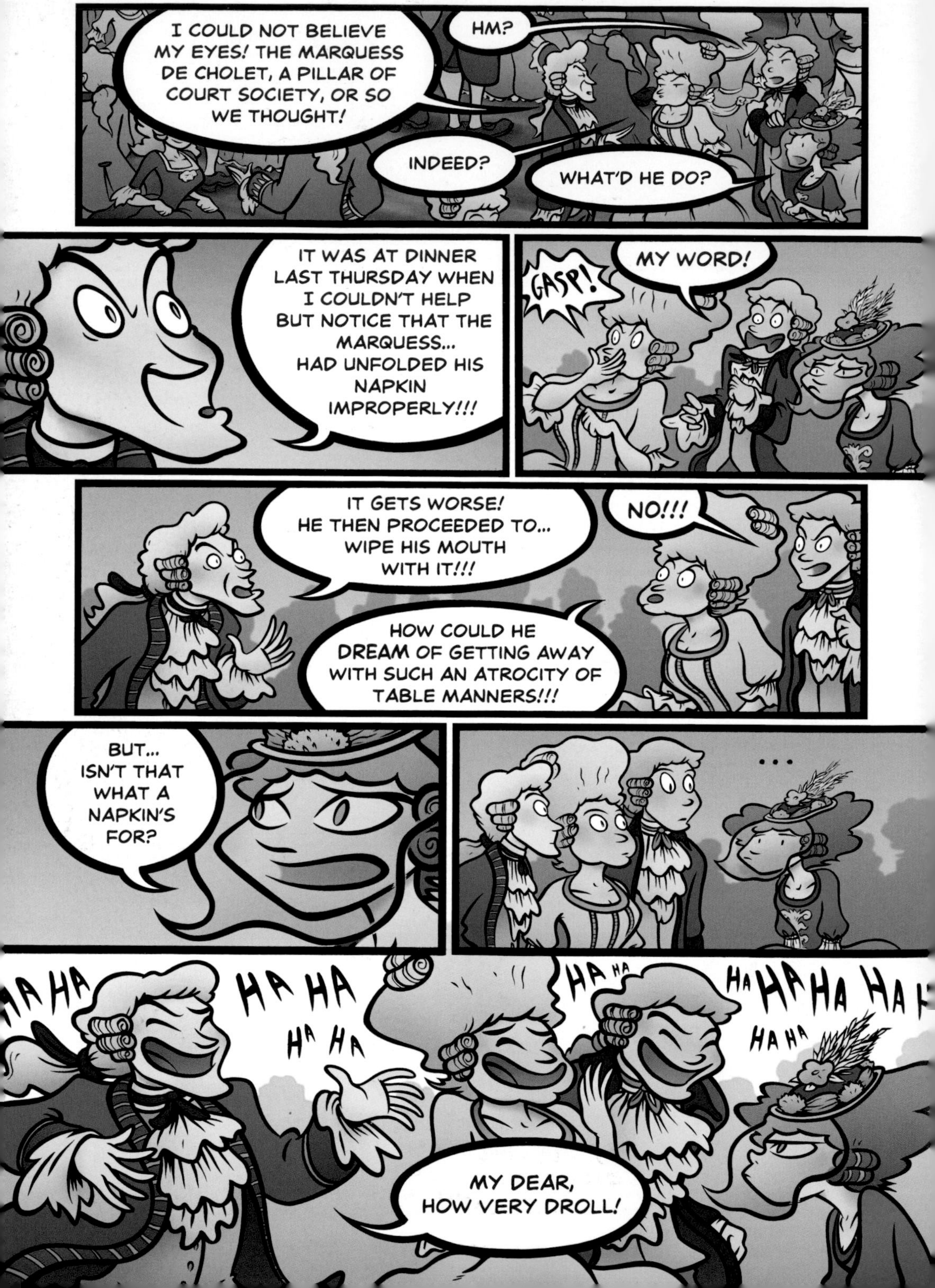
I COULD NOT BELIEVE MY EYES! THE MARQUESS DE CHOLET, A PILLAR OF COURT SOCIETY, OR SO WE THOUGHT!
HM?
INDEED?
WHAT'D HE DO?
IT WAS AT DINNER LAST THURSDAY WHEN I COULDN'T HELP BUT NOTICE THAT THE MARQUESS... HAD UNFOLDED HIS NAPKIN IMPROPERLY!!!
GASP!
MY WORD!
IT GETS WORSE! HE THEN PROCEEDED TO... WIPE HIS MOUTH WITH IT!!!
NO!!!
HOW COULD HE DREAM OF GETTING AWAY WITH SUCH AN ATROCITY OF TABLE MANNERS!!!
BUT... ISN'T THAT WHAT A NAPKIN'S FOR?
...
HA HA HA HA HA HA HA HA HA HA HA HA HA HA HA HA HA HA
MY DEAR, HOW VERY DROLL!

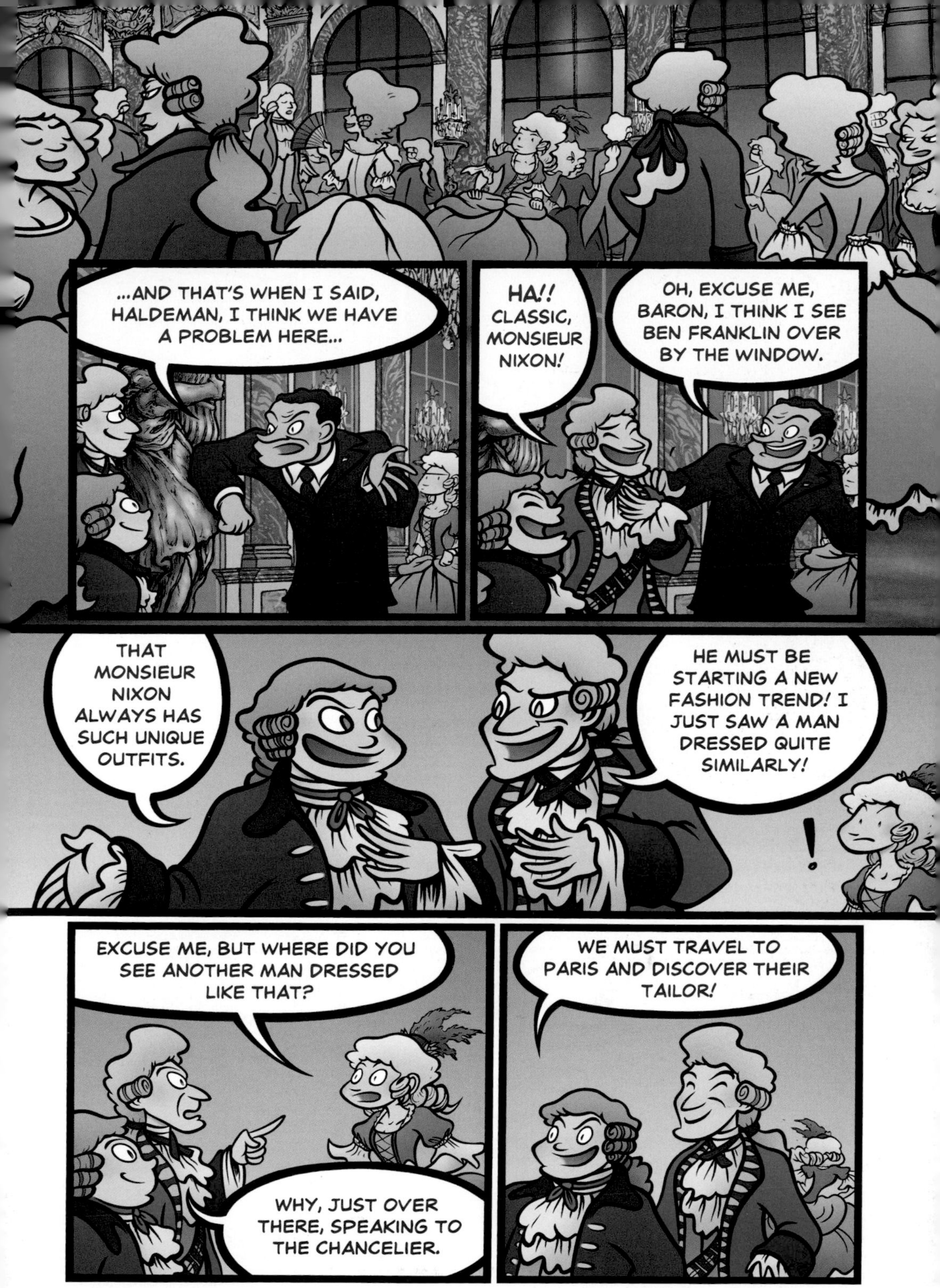

...AND THAT'S WHEN I SAID, HALDEMAN, I THINK WE HAVE A PROBLEM HERE...
HA!! CLASSIC, MONSIEUR NIXON!
OH, EXCUSE ME, BARON, I THINK I SEE BEN FRANKLIN OVER BY THE WINDOW.
THAT MONSIEUR NIXON ALWAYS HAS SUCH UNIQUE OUTFITS.
HE MUST BE STARTING A NEW FASHION TREND! I JUST SAW A MAN DRESSED QUITE SIMILARLY!
!
EXCUSE ME, BUT WHERE DID YOU SEE ANOTHER MAN DRESSED LIKE THAT?
WHY, JUST OVER THERE, SPEAKING TO THE CHANCELIER.
WE MUST TRAVEL TO PARIS AND DISCOVER THEIR TAILOR!

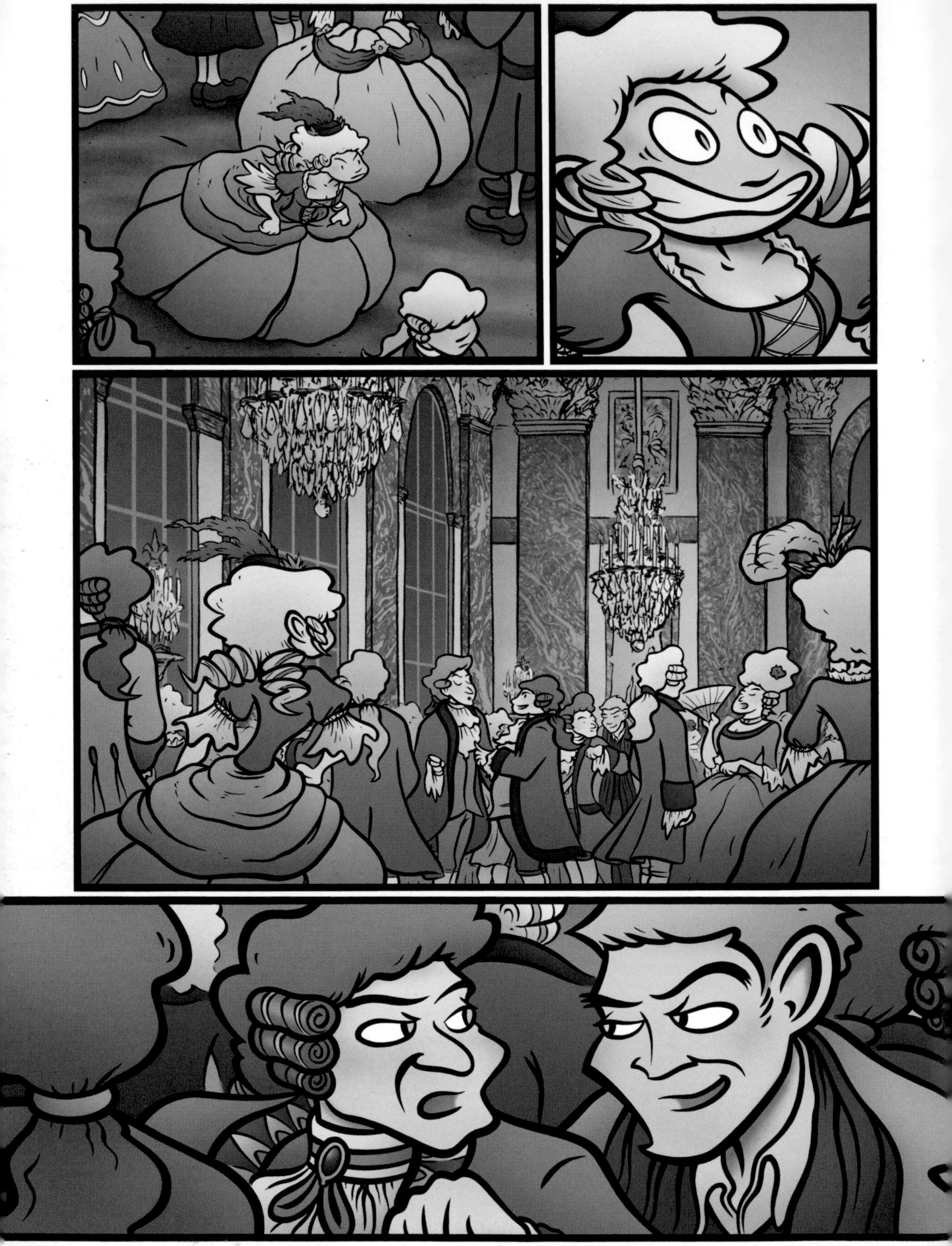

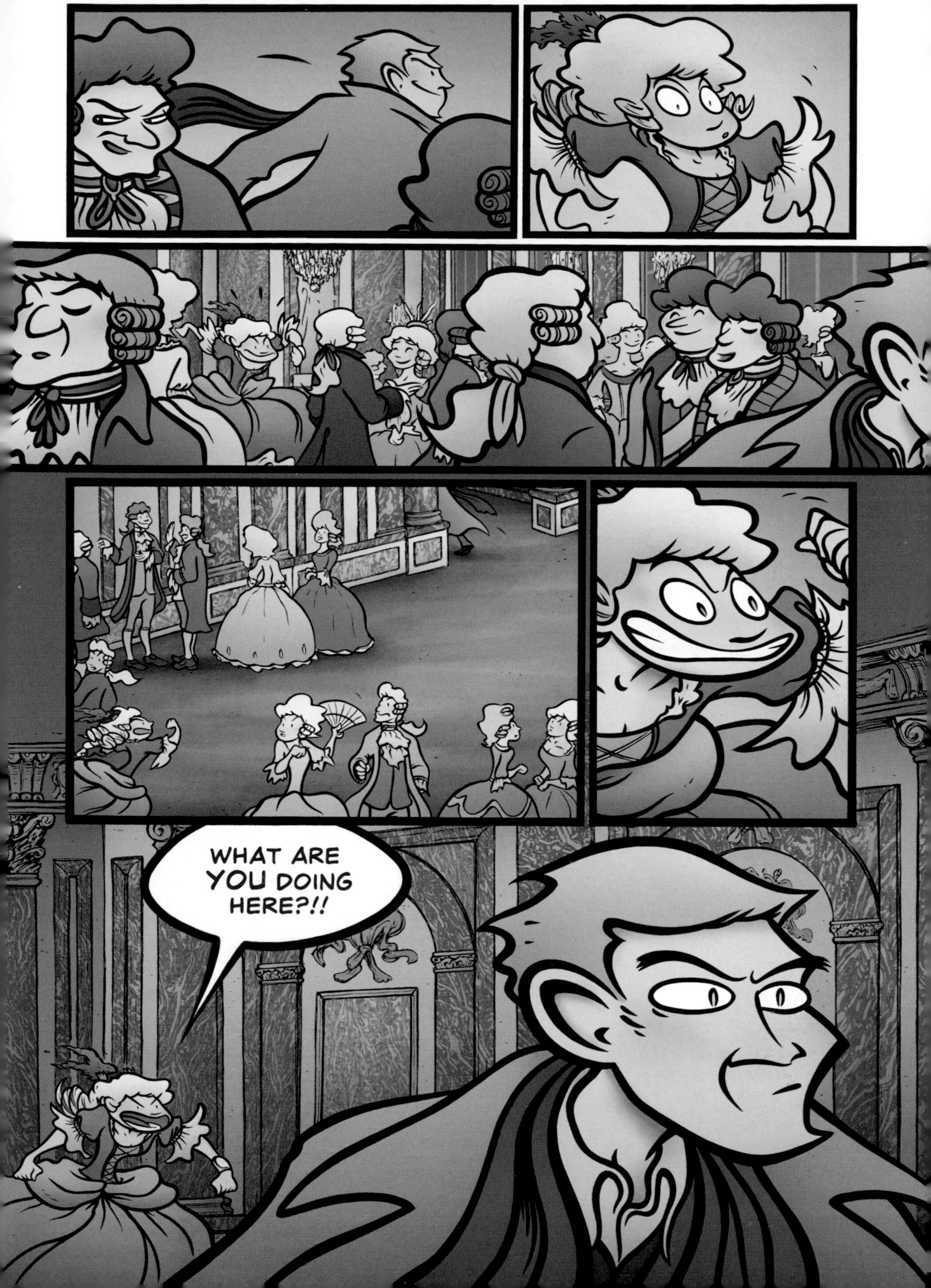
WHAT ARE YOU DOING HERE?!!

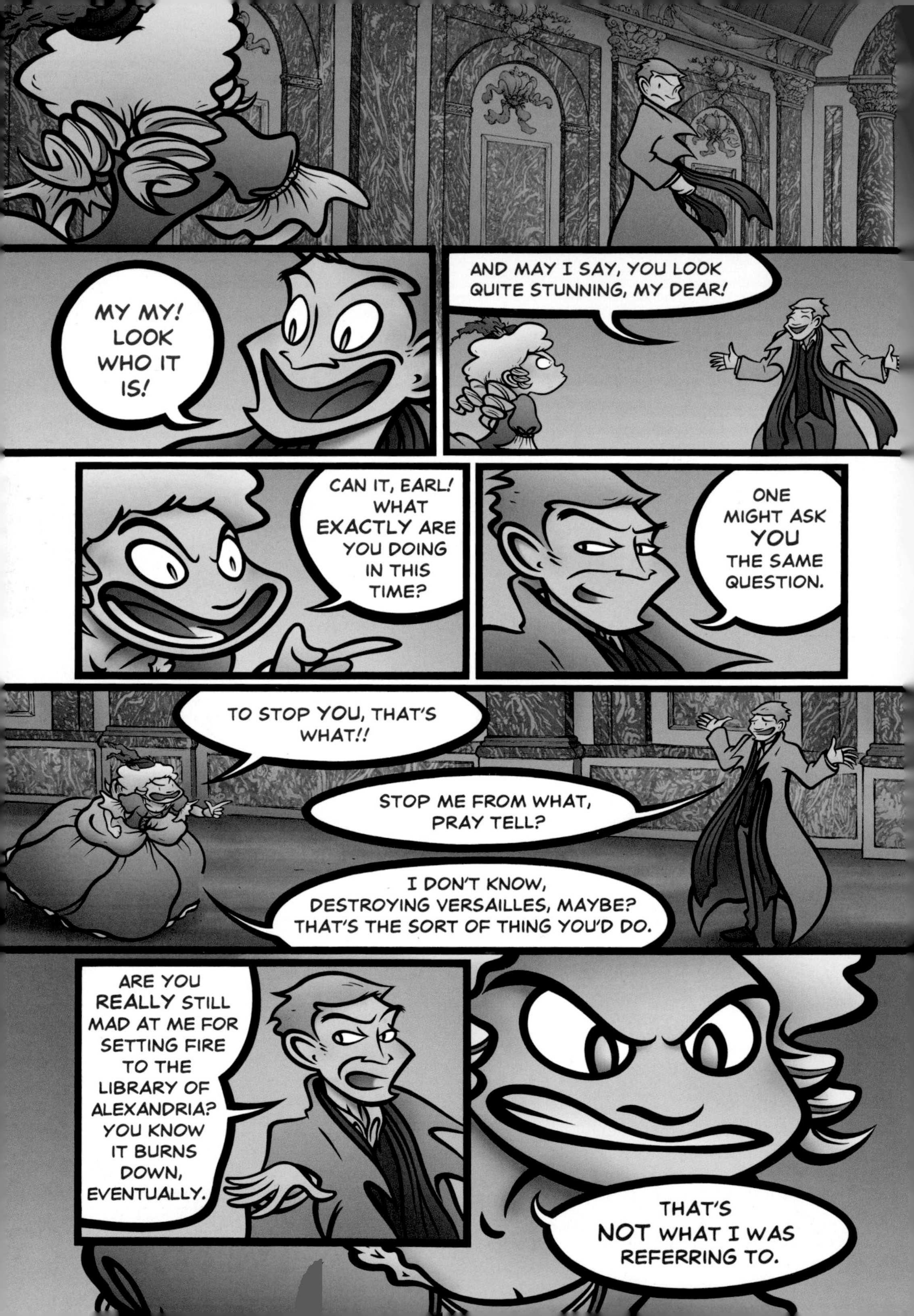
MY MY! LOOK WHO IT IS!
AND MAY I SAY, YOU LOOK QUITE STUNNING, MY DEAR!
CAN IT, EARL! WHAT EXACTLY ARE YOU DOING IN THIS TIME?
ONE MIGHT ASK YOU THE SAME QUESTION.
TO STOP YOU, THAT'S WHAT!!
STOP ME FROM WHAT, PRAY TELL?
I DON'T KNOW, DESTROYING VERSAILLES, MAYBE? THAT'S THE SORT OF THING YOU'D DO.
ARE YOU REALLY STILL MAD AT ME FOR SETTING FIRE TO THE LIBRARY OF ALEXANDRIA? YOU KNOW IT BURNS DOWN, EVENTUALLY.
THAT'S NOT WHAT I WAS REFERRING TO.

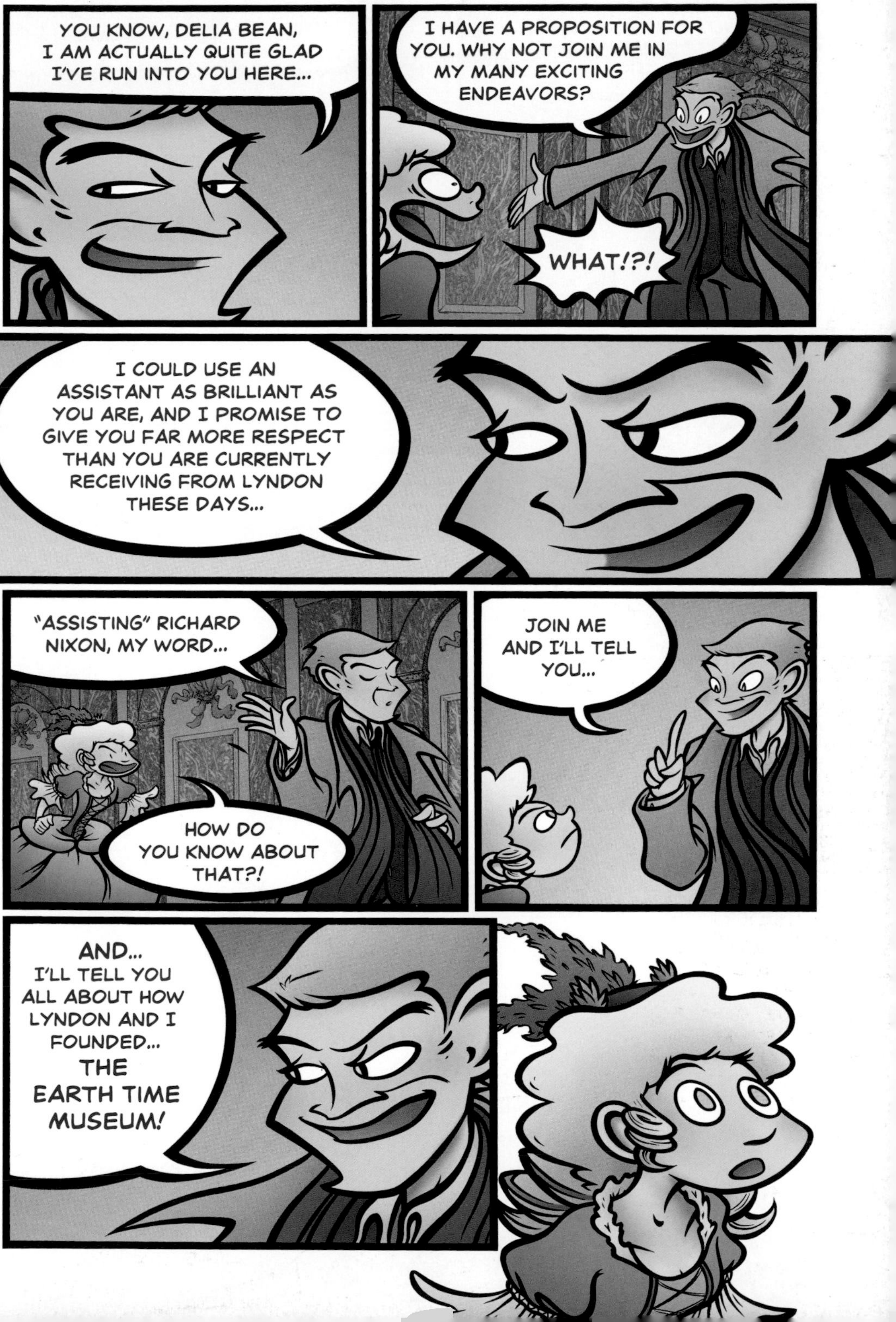

YOU KNOW, DELIA BEAN, I AM ACTUALLY QUITE GLAD I'VE RUN INTO YOU HERE...
I HAVE A PROPOSITION FOR YOU. WHY NOT JOIN ME IN MY MANY EXCITING ENDEAVORS?
WHAT!?!
I COULD USE AN ASSISTANT AS BRILLIANT AS YOU ARE, AND I PROMISE TO GIVE YOU FAR MORE RESPECT THAN YOU ARE CURRENTLY RECEIVING FROM LYNDON THESE DAYS...
"ASSISTING" RICHARD NIXON, MY WORD...
HOW DO YOU KNOW ABOUT THAT?!
JOIN ME AND I'LL TELL YOU...
AND... I'LL TELL YOU ALL ABOUT HOW LYNDON AND I FOUNDED... THE EARTH TIME MUSEUM!

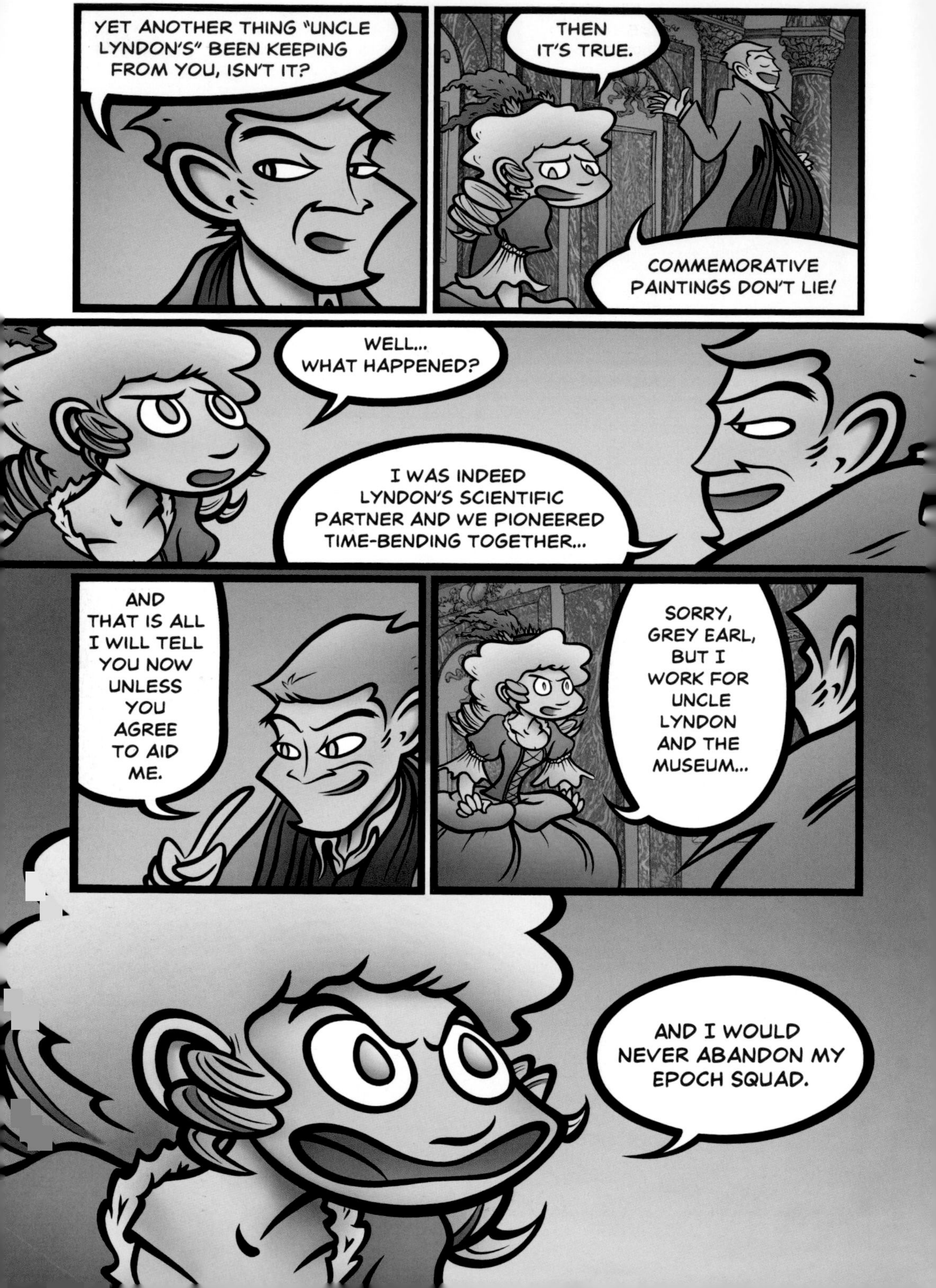
YET ANOTHER THING "UNCLE LYNDON'S" BEEN KEEPING FROM YOU, ISN'T IT?
THEN IT'S TRUE.
COMMEMORATIVE PAINTINGS DON'T LIE!
WELL... WHAT HAPPENED?
I WAS INDEED LYNDON'S SCIENTIFIC PARTNER AND WE PIONEERED TIME-BENDING TOGETHER...
AND THAT IS ALL I WILL TELL YOU NOW UNLESS YOU AGREE TO AID ME.
SORRY, GREY EARL, BUT I WORK FOR UNCLE LYNDON AND THE MUSEUM...
AND I WOULD NEVER ABANDON MY EPOCH SQUAD.

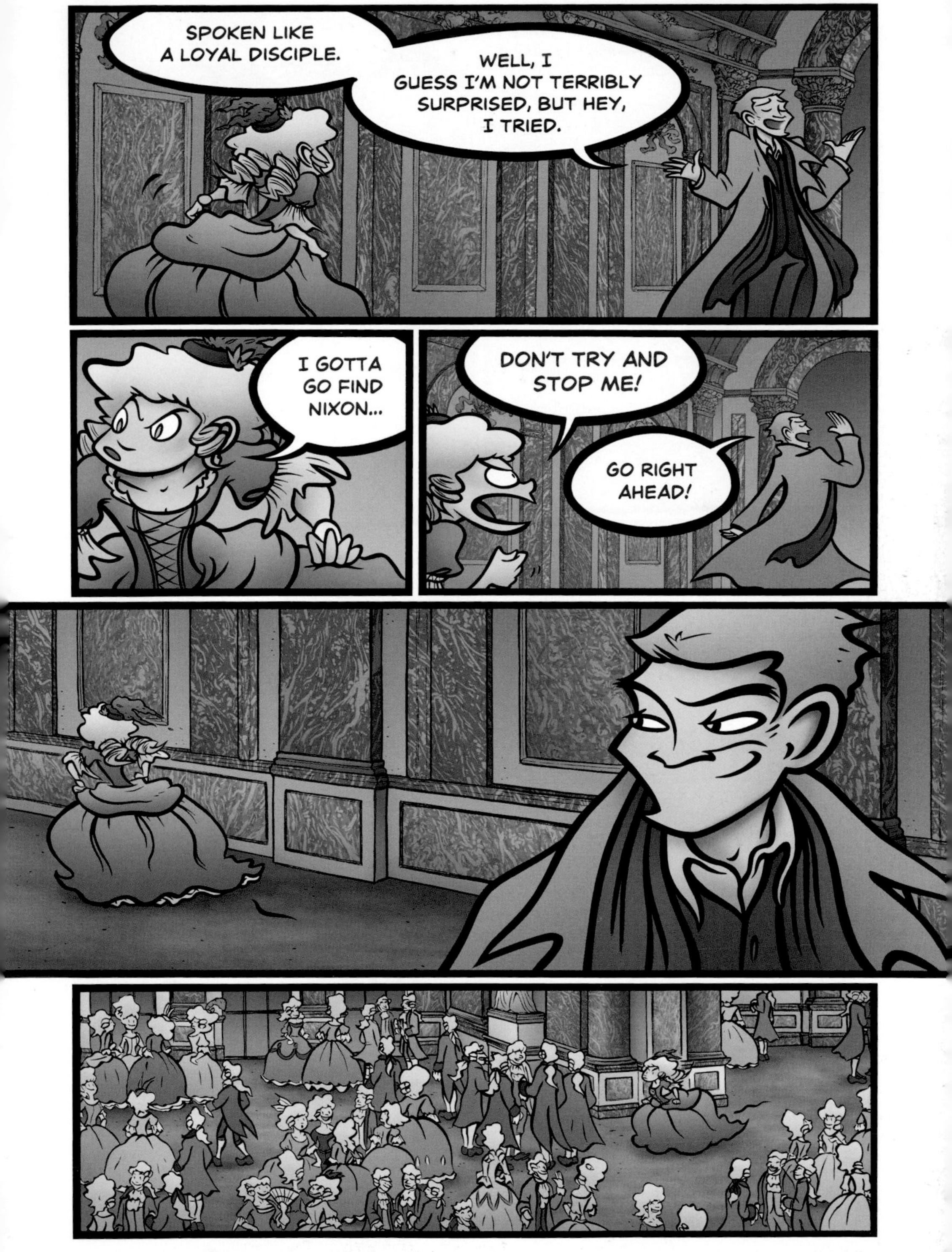
SPOKEN LIKE A LOYAL DISCIPLE.
WELL, I GUESS I'M NOT TERRIBLY SURPRISED, BUT HEY, I TRIED.
I GOTTA GO FIND NIXON...
DON'T TRY AND STOP ME!
GO RIGHT AHEAD!

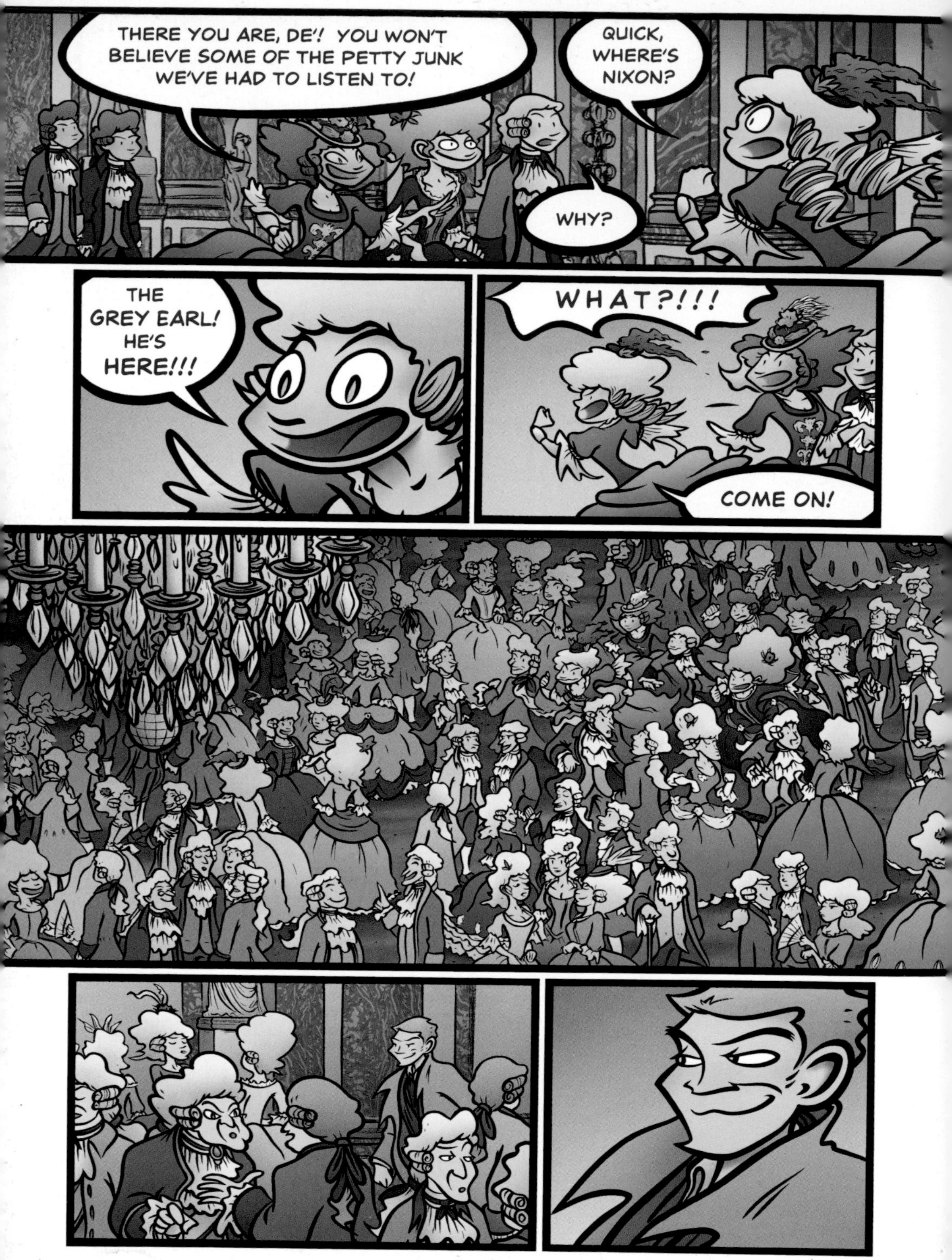
THERE YOU ARE, DE'! YOU WON'T BELIEVE SOME OF THE PETTY JUNK WE'VE HAD TO LISTEN TO!
QUICK, WHERE'S NIXON?
WHY?
THE GREY EARL! HE'S HERE!!!
WHAT?!!!
COME ON!

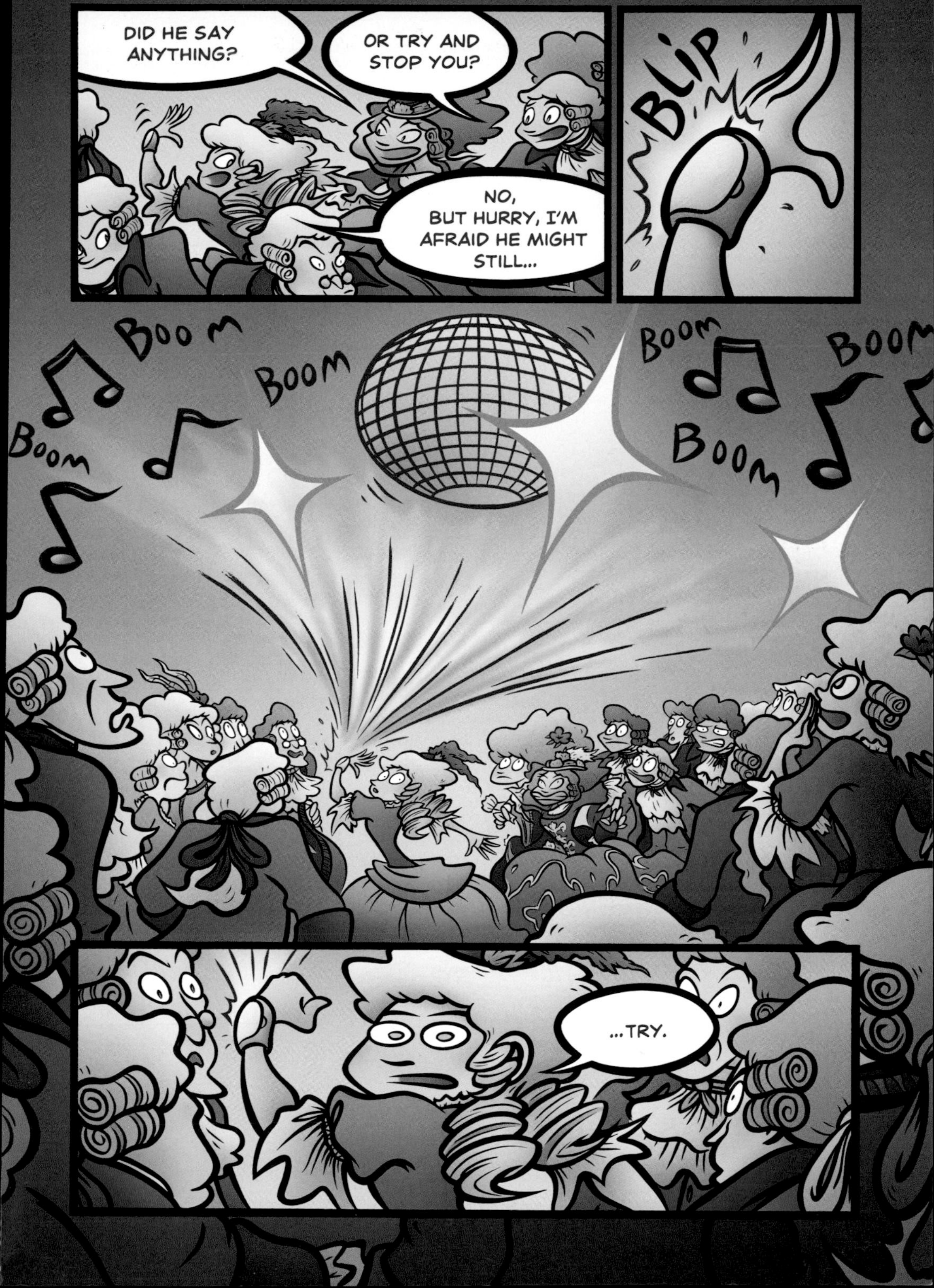
DID HE SAY ANYTHING?
OR TRY AND STOP YOU?
NO, BUT HURRY, I'M AFRAID HE MIGHT STILL...
BLIP
Boom
Boom
Boom
Boom
Boom
Boom
...TRY.

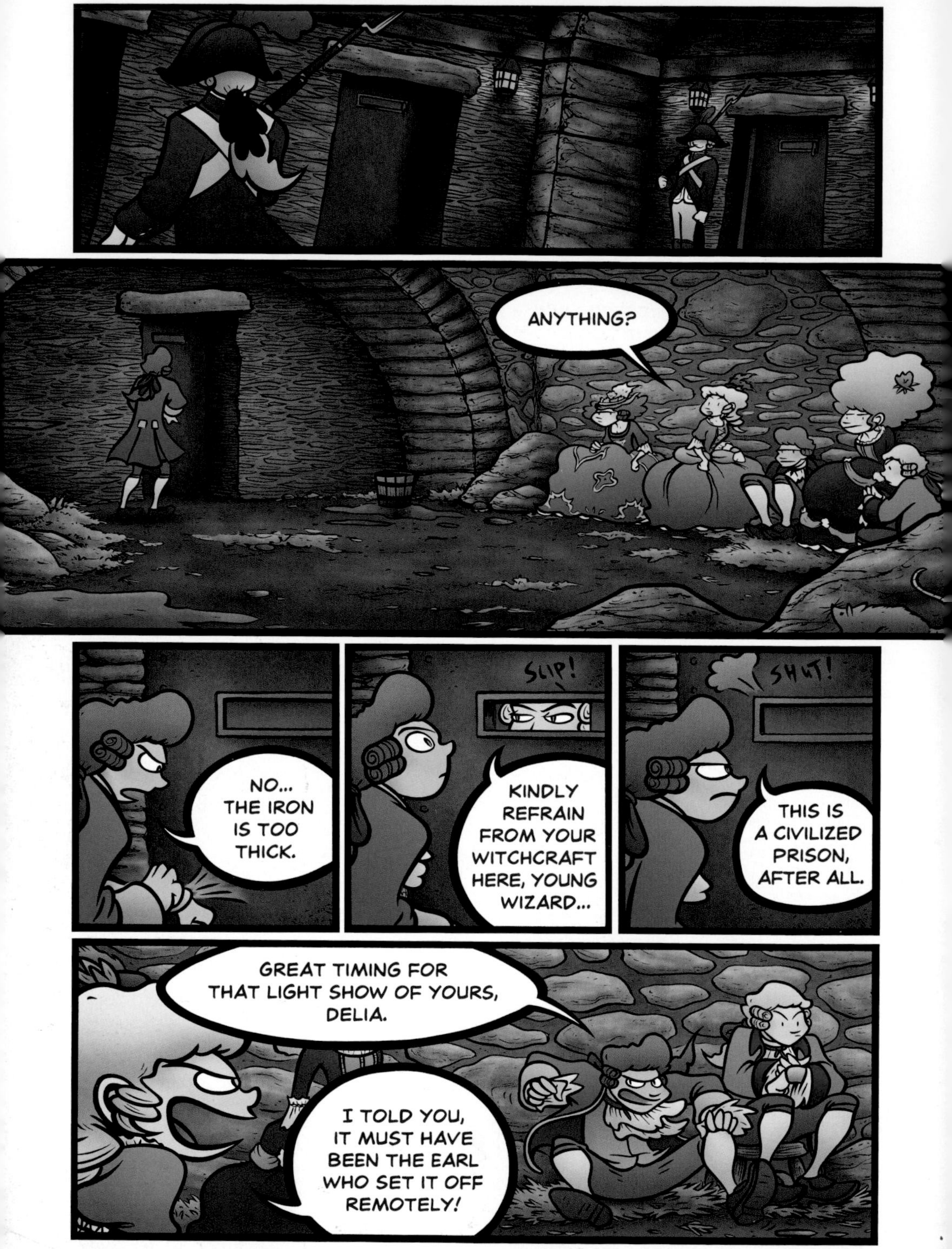
ANYTHING?
NO... THE IRON IS TOO THICK.
SLIP!
KINDLY REFRAIN FROM YOUR WITCHCRAFT HERE, YOUNG WIZARD...
SHUT!
THIS IS A CIVILIZED PRISON, AFTER ALL.
GREAT TIMING FOR THAT LIGHT SHOW OF YOURS, DELIA.
I TOLD YOU, IT MUST HAVE BEEN THE EARL WHO SET IT OFF REMOTELY!

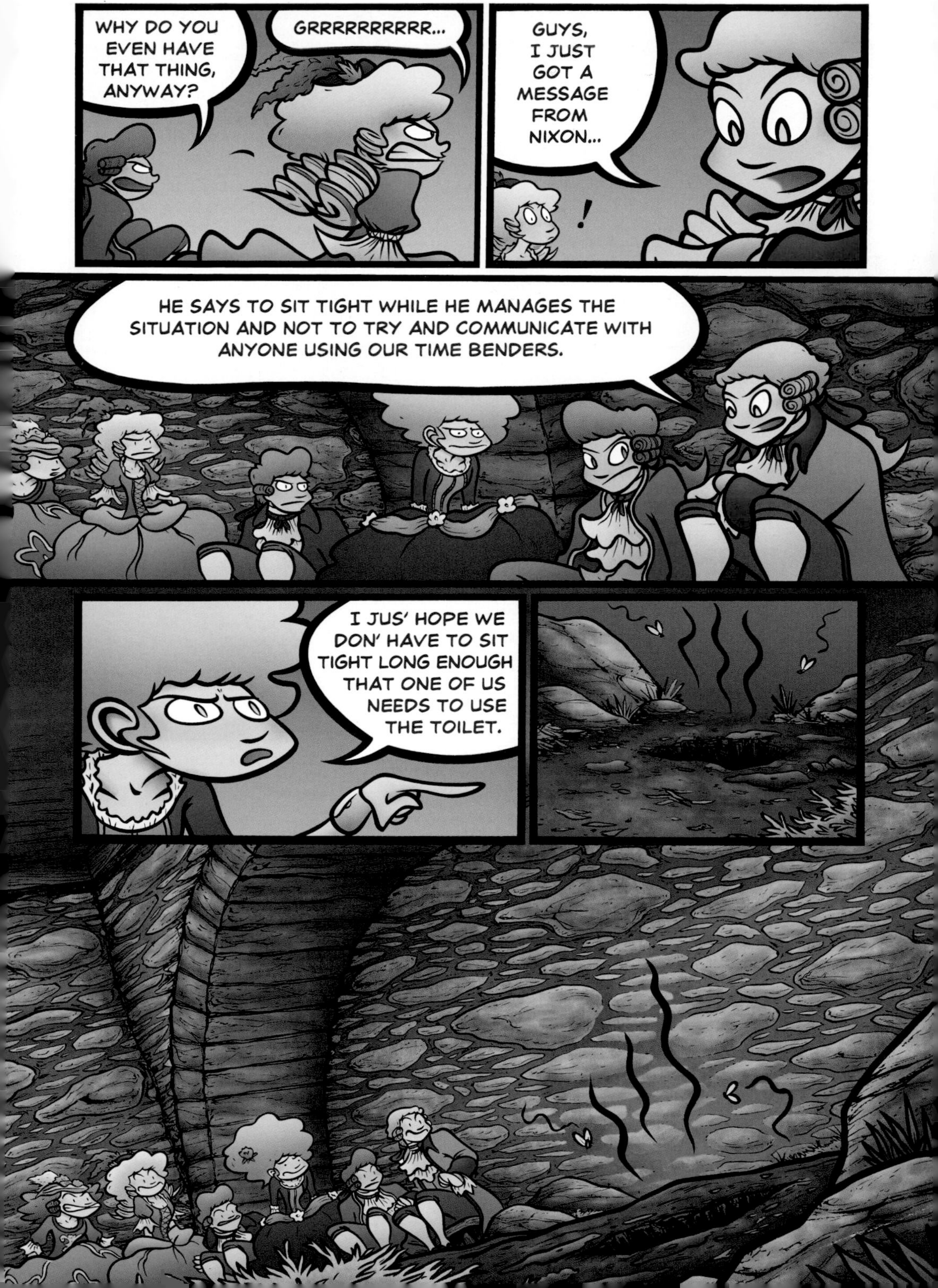

WHY DO YOU EVEN HAVE THAT THING, ANYWAY?
GRRRRRRRRR...
GUYS, I JUST GOT A MESSAGE FROM NIXON...
!
HE SAYS TO SIT TIGHT WHILE HE MANAGES THE SITUATION AND NOT TO TRY AND COMMUNICATE WITH ANYONE USING OUR TIME BENDERS.
I JUS' HOPE WE DON' HAVE TO SIT TIGHT LONG ENOUGH THAT ONE OF US NEEDS TO USE THE TOILET.

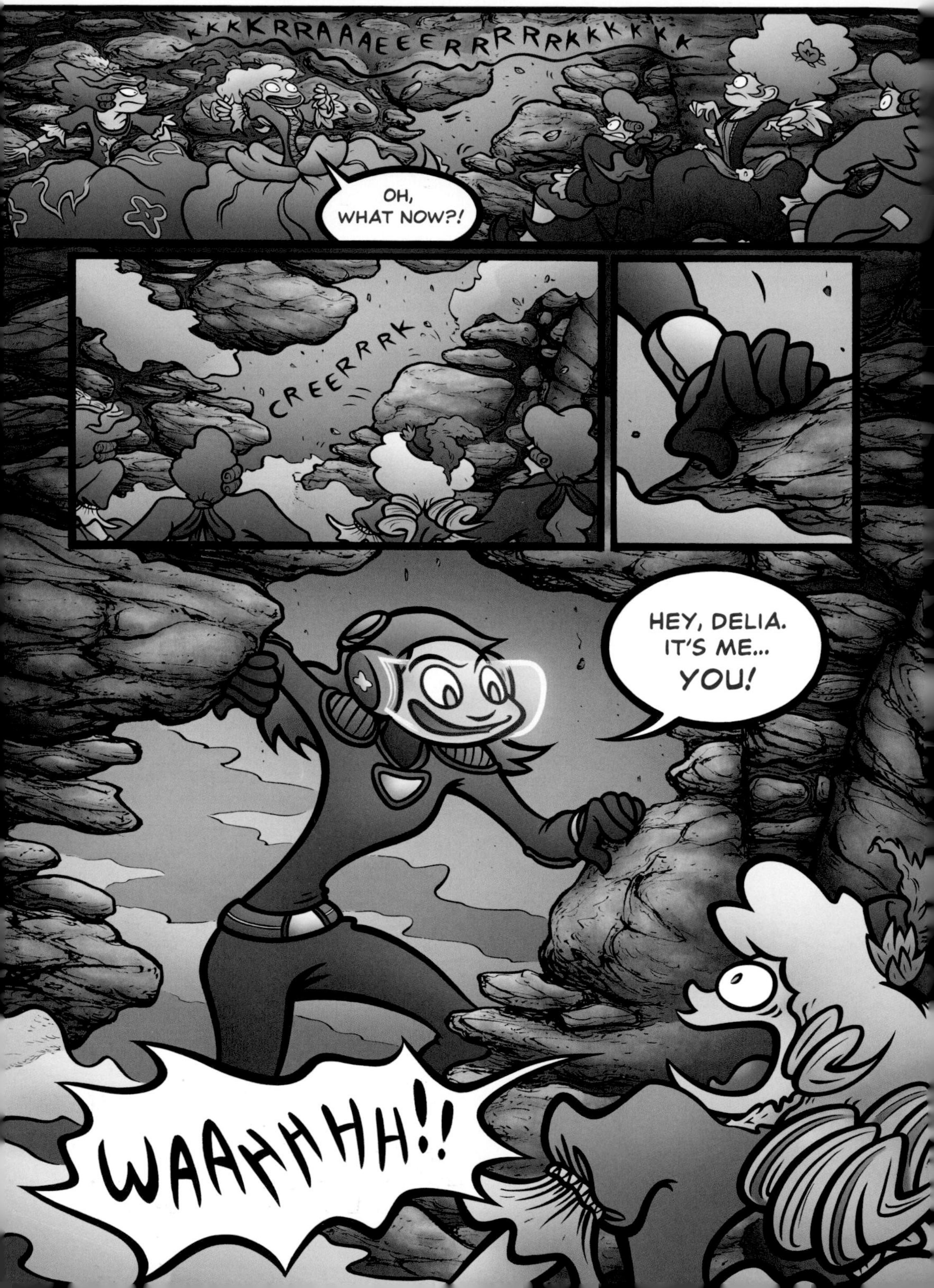
KKKKRRAAAAEEEERRRRRRKKKKKK
OH, WHAT NOW?!
CREERRRK
HEY, DELIA. IT'S ME... YOU!
WAAHHHH!!

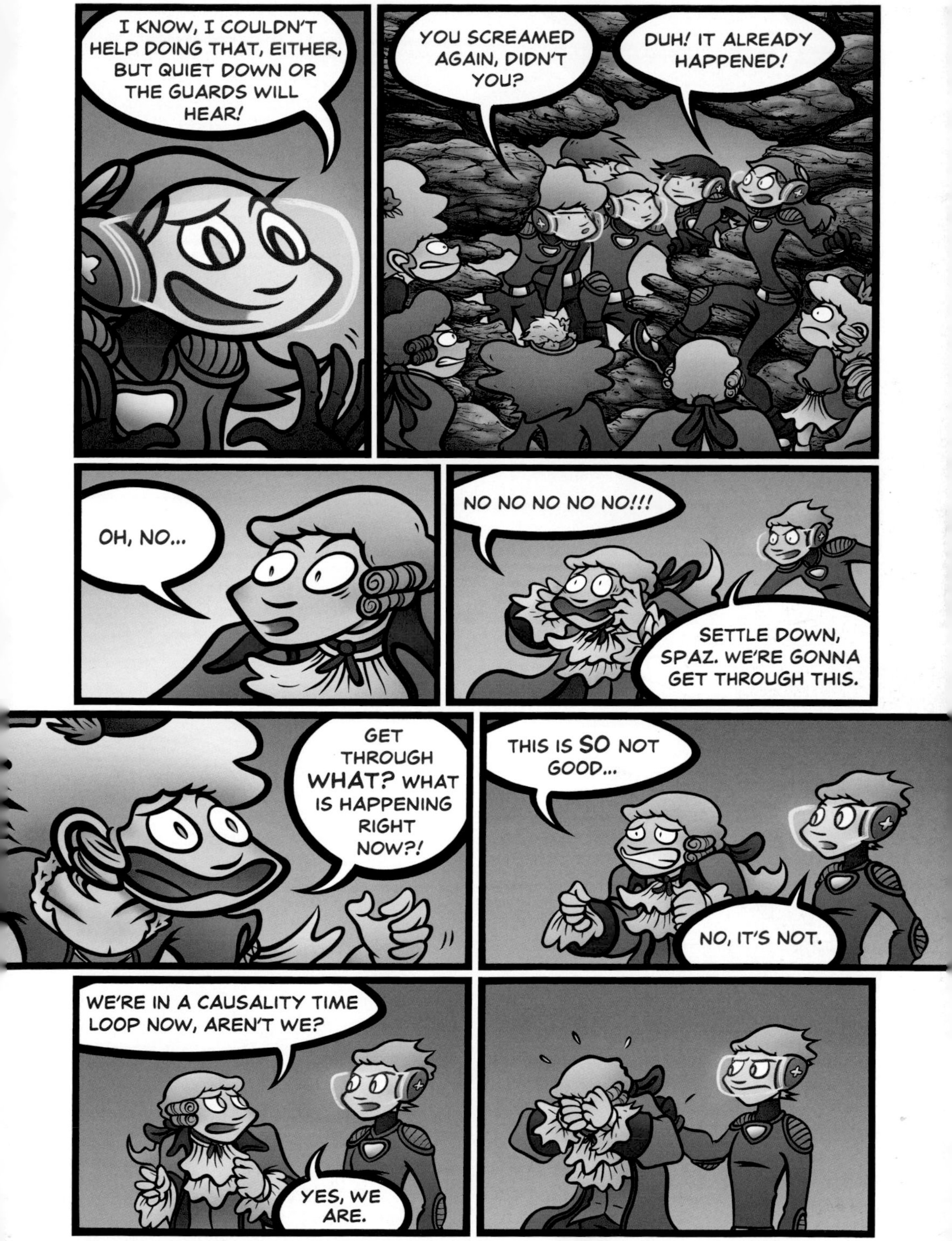
I KNOW, I COULDN'T HELP DOING THAT, EITHER, BUT QUIET DOWN OR THE GUARDS WILL HEAR!
YOU SCREAMED AGAIN, DIDN'T YOU?
DUH! IT ALREADY HAPPENED!
OH, NO...
NO NO NO NO NO!!!
SETTLE DOWN, SPAZ. WE'RE GONNA GET THROUGH THIS.
GET THROUGH WHAT? WHAT IS HAPPENING RIGHT NOW?!
THIS IS SO NOT GOOD...
NO, IT'S NOT.
WE'RE IN A CAUSALITY TIME LOOP NOW, AREN'T WE?
YES, WE ARE.

WHAT'S A CAUSALITY TIME LOOP?

THERE'S A LOT TO IT, BUT ESSENTIALLY IT'S A DESTABILIZATION OF THE TIMELINE OCCURRING WHEN A TIME TRAVELER BECOMES DIRECTLY INVOLVED IN THEIR OWN PAST EVENTS.

PARTICULARLY WHEN YOU END UP MEETING YOURSELF THERE.

RIGHT.

SO WHAT YOU'RE SAYING IS THAT YOU GUYS ARE US... FROM THE FUTURE?

YES, BUT ONLY ABOUT EIGHT HOURS.

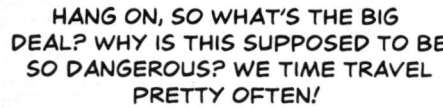

HANG ON, SO WHAT'S THE BIG DEAL? WHY IS THIS SUPPOSED TO BE SO DANGEROUS? WE TIME TRAVEL PRETTY OFTEN!

THIS IS DIFFERENT.
IF THE TIMELINE IS DESTABILIZED AND YOU ARE INTERACTING WITH YOUR PAST SELVES, THOSE SHARED EVENTS ARE NO LONGER GUARANTEED TO BE AS YOU REMEMBER THEM. IT THEN BECOMES SUPER EASY TO MESS IT ALL UP AND CAUSE A PARADOX!

SO?

OK, SAY I, FUTURE REGGIE, DECIDE TO KILL PAST REGGIE RIGHT NOW...

OW!

THUNK

I NOW WOULDN'T EXIST TO SHOW UP AND KILL PAST REGGIE HERE, AND THAT'S A PARADOX! IT'S SOMETHING THAT LITERALLY CAN'T HAPPEN!

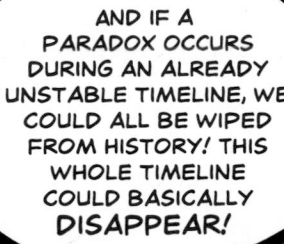

AND IF A PARADOX OCCURS DURING AN ALREADY UNSTABLE TIMELINE, WE COULD ALL BE WIPED FROM HISTORY! THIS WHOLE TIMELINE COULD BASICALLY **DISAPPEAR!**

AND THIS BEING A PIVOT POINT, THAT WOULD BE **EXTRA BAD!**

THOUGH THE MUSEUM HAS WAYS OF MINIMIZING SOME OF THE DAMAGES, BEING OUTSIDE THE TIMELINE AND ALL.

TRUE, BUT THERE'S NO GUARANTEE ANY OF US WOULD SURVIVE IT. IN FACT, I'M FAIRLY CERTAIN WE'D ALL TURN INTO SPACE DUST.

SO WE GOTTA GET THROUGH THIS "SHARED EVENT" WITHOUT **CHANGING ANYTHING!**

OK, JUST TELL US WHAT WE HAVE TA DO, THEN!

WE CANNAE TELL YOU TOO MUCH OR THAT ALSO MIGHT TRIGGER A PARADOX...

RIGHT?

YUP.

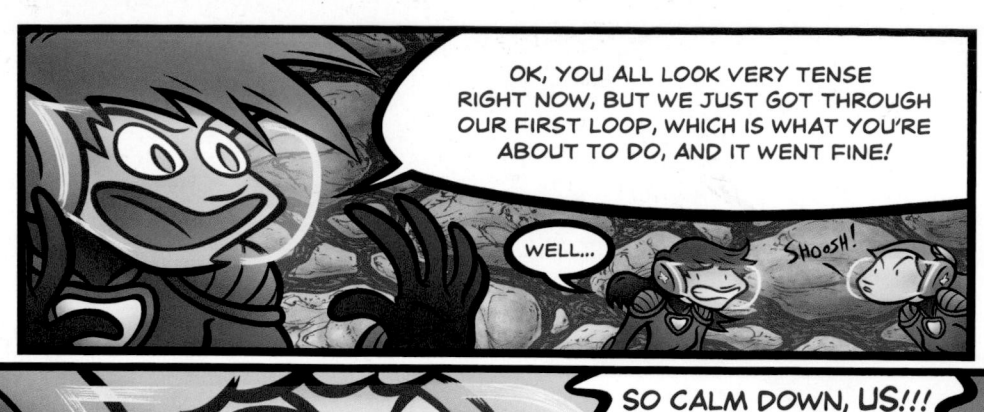

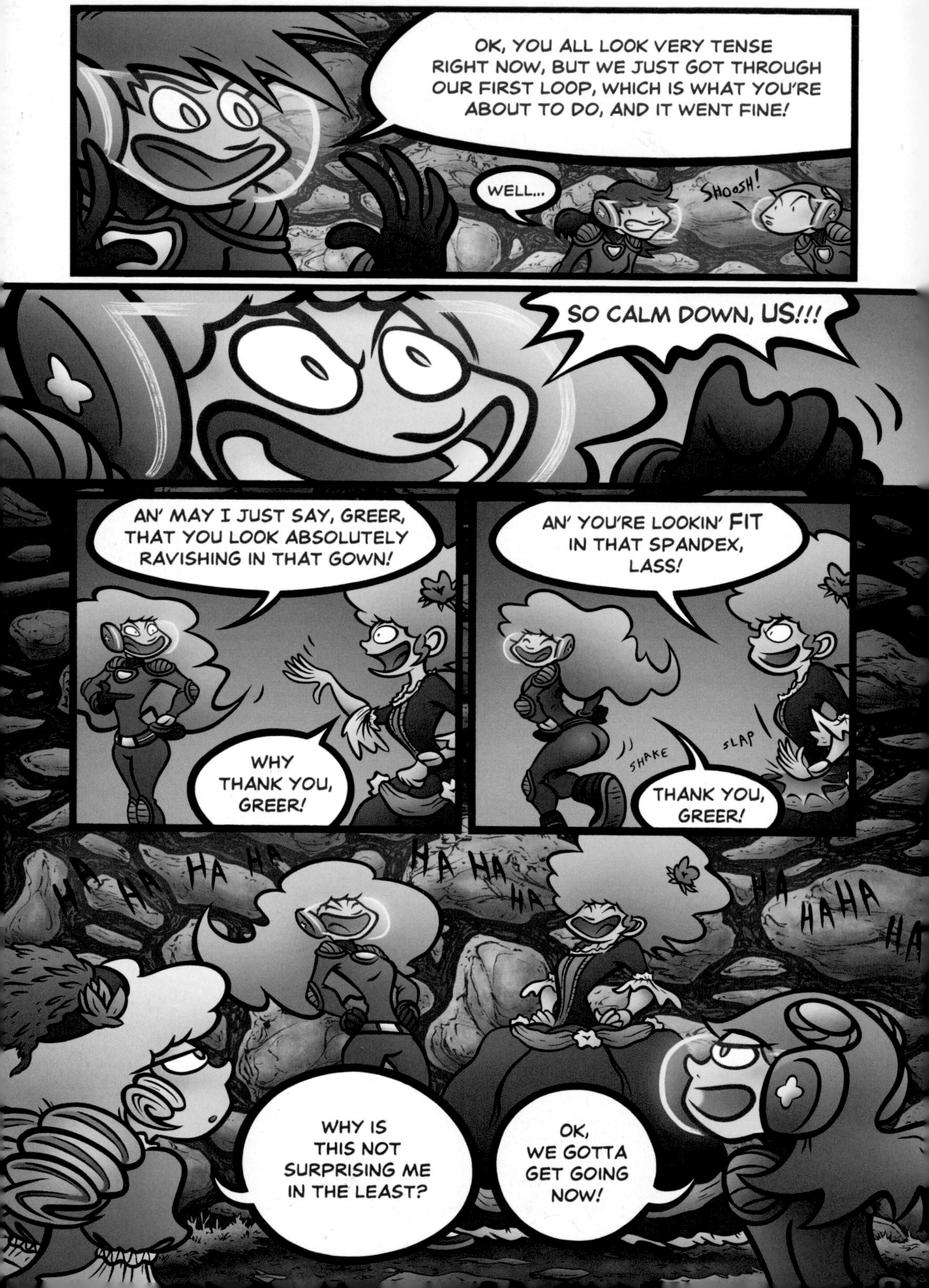
OK, YOU ALL LOOK VERY TENSE RIGHT NOW, BUT WE JUST GOT THROUGH OUR FIRST LOOP, WHICH IS WHAT YOU'RE ABOUT TO DO, AND IT WENT FINE!
WELL...
SHOOSH!
SO CALM DOWN, US!!!
AN' MAY I JUST SAY, GREER, THAT YOU LOOK ABSOLUTELY RAVISHING IN THAT GOWN!
WHY THANK YOU, GREER!
AN' YOU'RE LOOKIN' FIT IN THAT SPANDEX, LASS!
SHAKE
SLAP
THANK YOU, GREER!
HA HA HA HA HA HA HA HA HA HA HA HA HA HA
WHY IS THIS NOT SURPRISING ME IN THE LEAST?
OK, WE GOTTA GET GOING NOW!

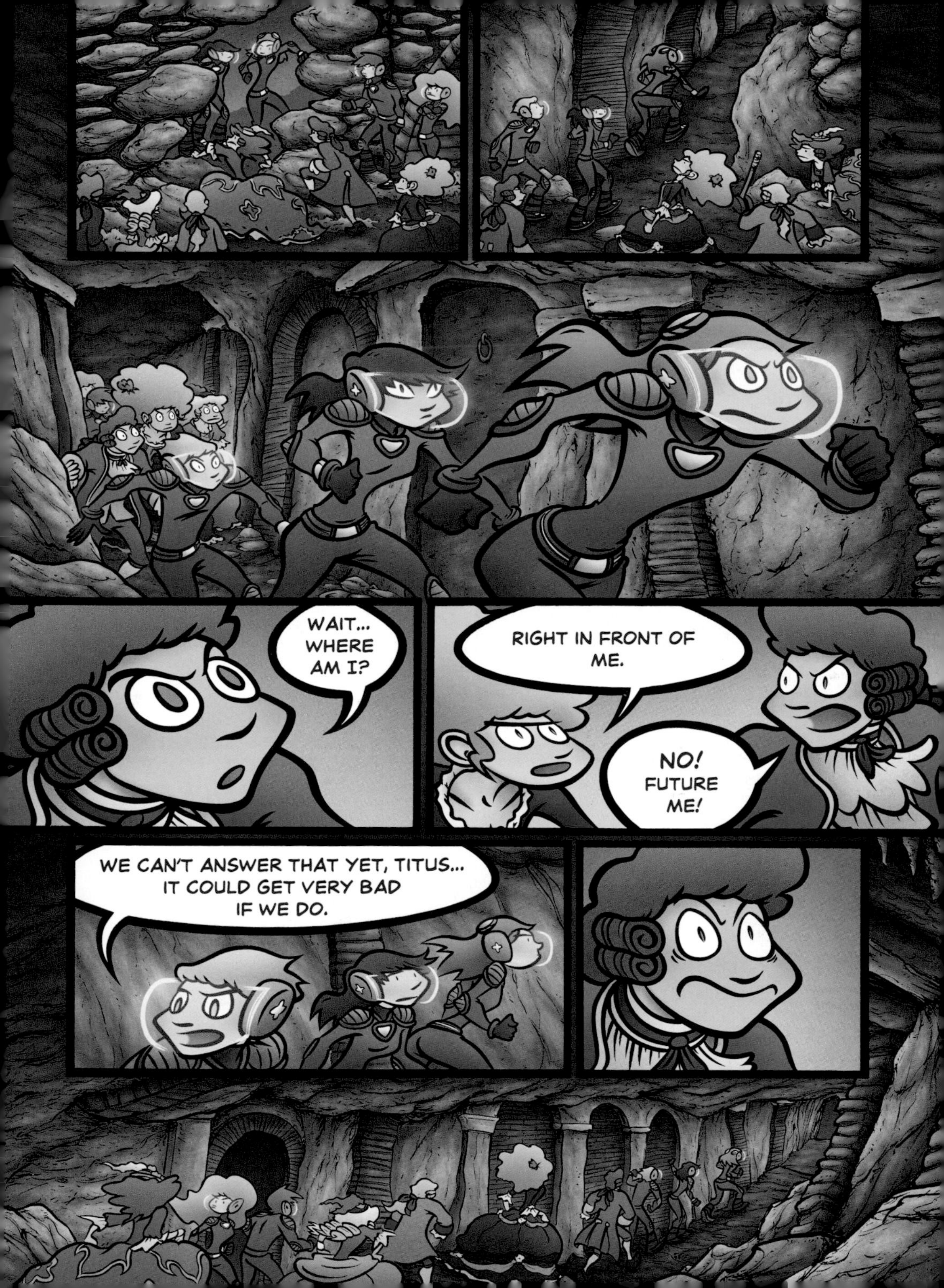
WAIT... WHERE AM I?
RIGHT IN FRONT OF ME.
NO! FUTURE ME!
WE CAN'T ANSWER THAT YET, TITUS... IT COULD GET VERY BAD IF WE DO.

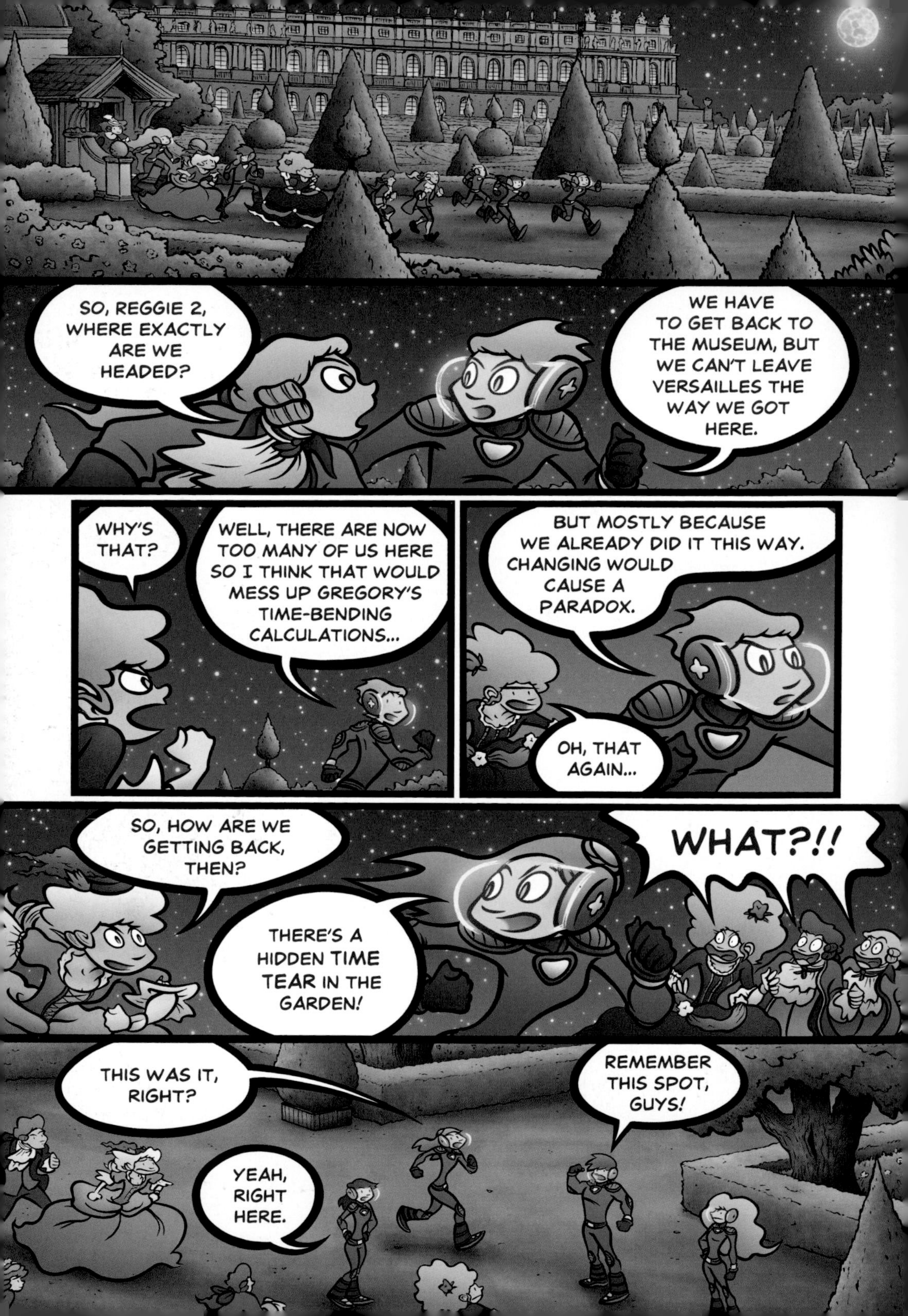
SO, REGGIE 2, WHERE EXACTLY ARE WE HEADED?
WE HAVE TO GET BACK TO THE MUSEUM, BUT WE CAN'T LEAVE VERSAILLES THE WAY WE GOT HERE.
WHY'S THAT?
WELL, THERE ARE NOW TOO MANY OF US HERE SO I THINK THAT WOULD MESS UP GREGORY'S TIME-BENDING CALCULATIONS...
BUT MOSTLY BECAUSE WE ALREADY DID IT THIS WAY. CHANGING WOULD CAUSE A PARADOX.
OH, THAT AGAIN...
SO, HOW ARE WE GETTING BACK, THEN?
THERE'S A HIDDEN TIME TEAR IN THE GARDEN!
WHAT?!!
THIS WAS IT, RIGHT?
REMEMBER THIS SPOT, GUYS!
YEAH, RIGHT HERE.

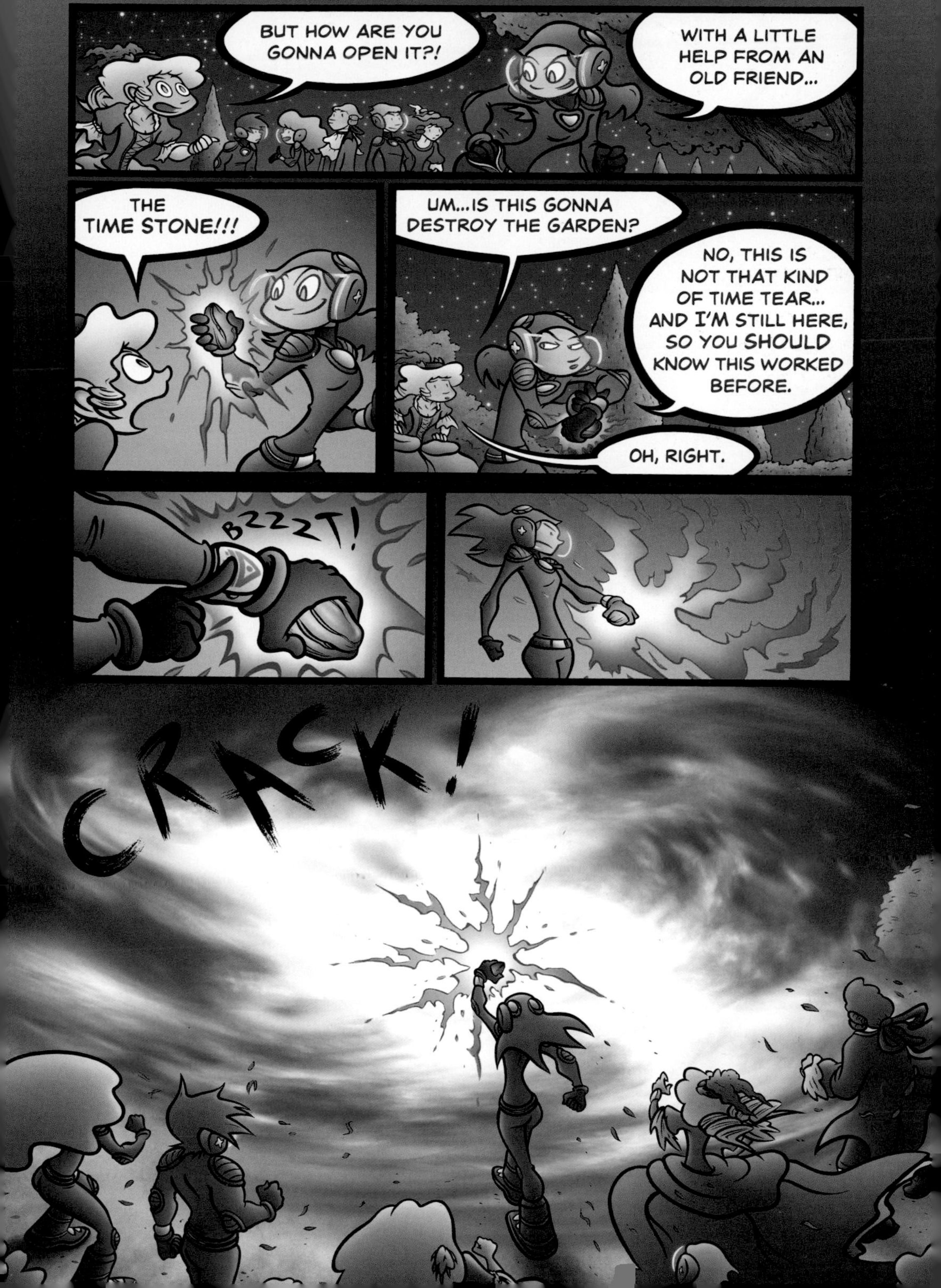
BUT HOW ARE YOU GONNA OPEN IT?!
WITH A LITTLE HELP FROM AN OLD FRIEND...
THE TIME STONE!!!
UM...IS THIS GONNA DESTROY THE GARDEN?
NO, THIS IS NOT THAT KIND OF TIME TEAR... AND I'M STILL HERE, SO YOU SHOULD KNOW THIS WORKED BEFORE.
OH, RIGHT.
BZZZT!
CRACK!

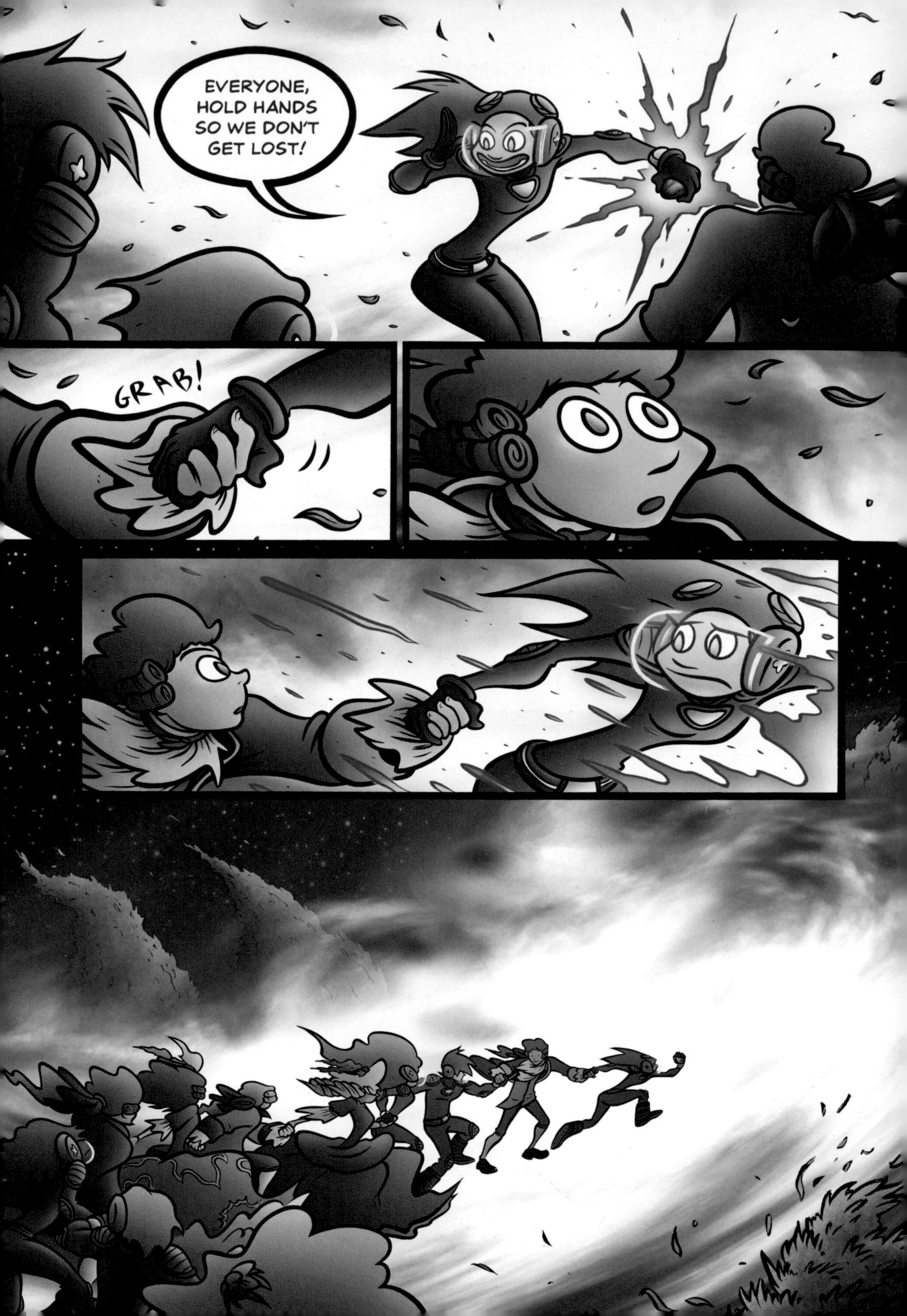
EVERYONE, HOLD HANDS SO WE DON'T GET LOST!
GRAB!

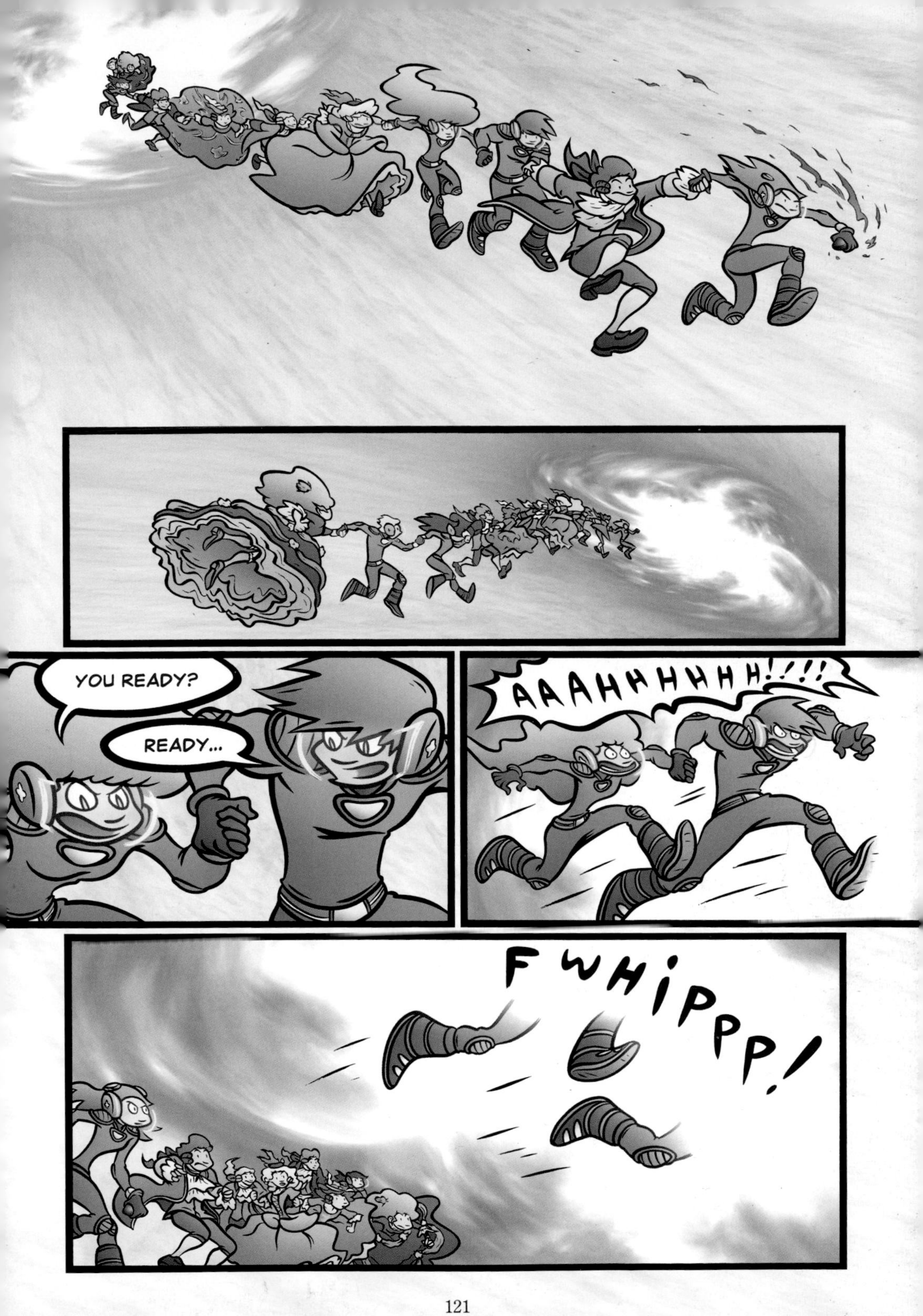

YOU READY?
READY...
AAAHHHHHH!!!!!
FWHIPPP!

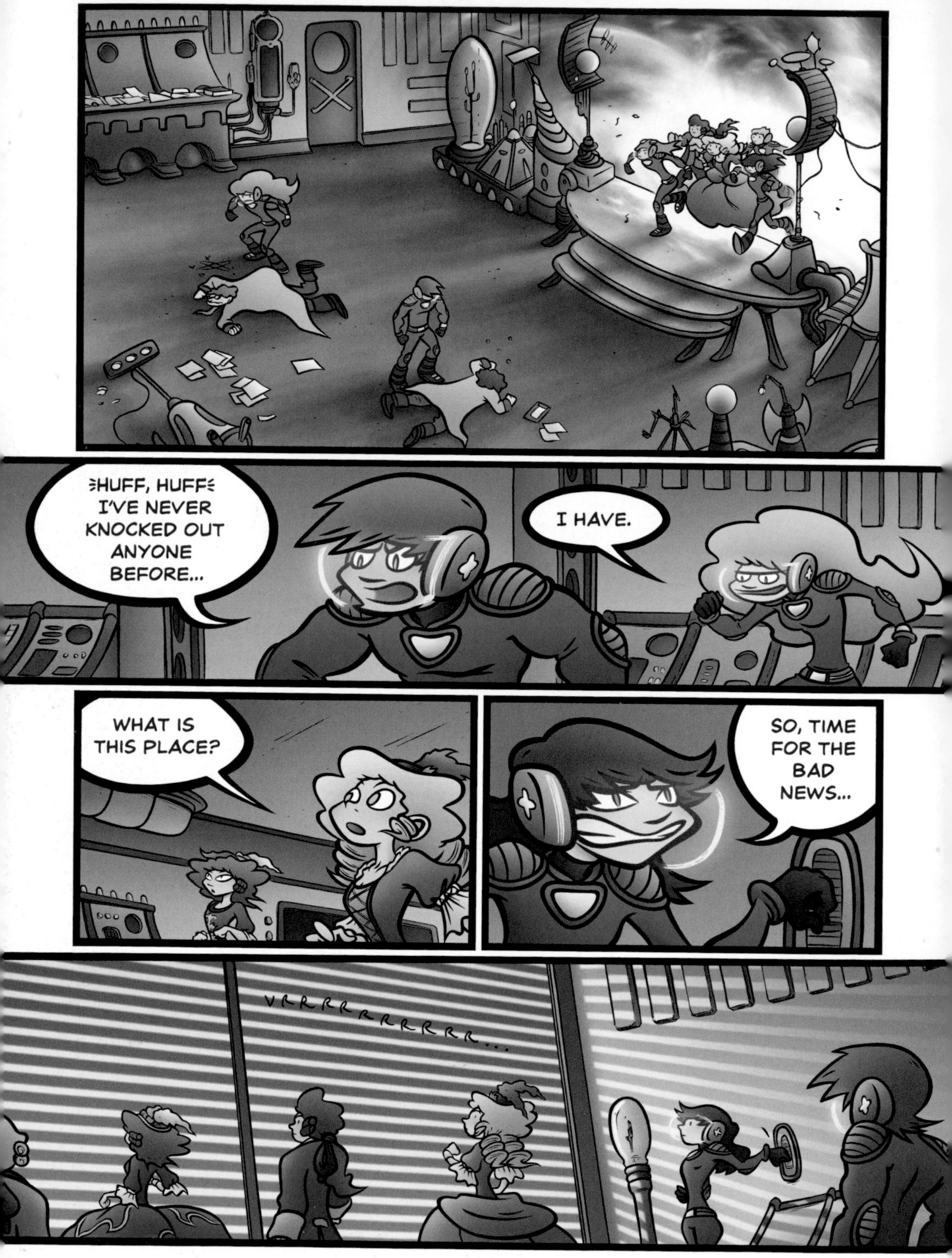

≡HUFF, HUFF≡ I'VE NEVER KNOCKED OUT ANYONE BEFORE...
I HAVE.
WHAT IS THIS PLACE?
SO, TIME FOR THE BAD NEWS...
VRRRRRRRRRRRRR...

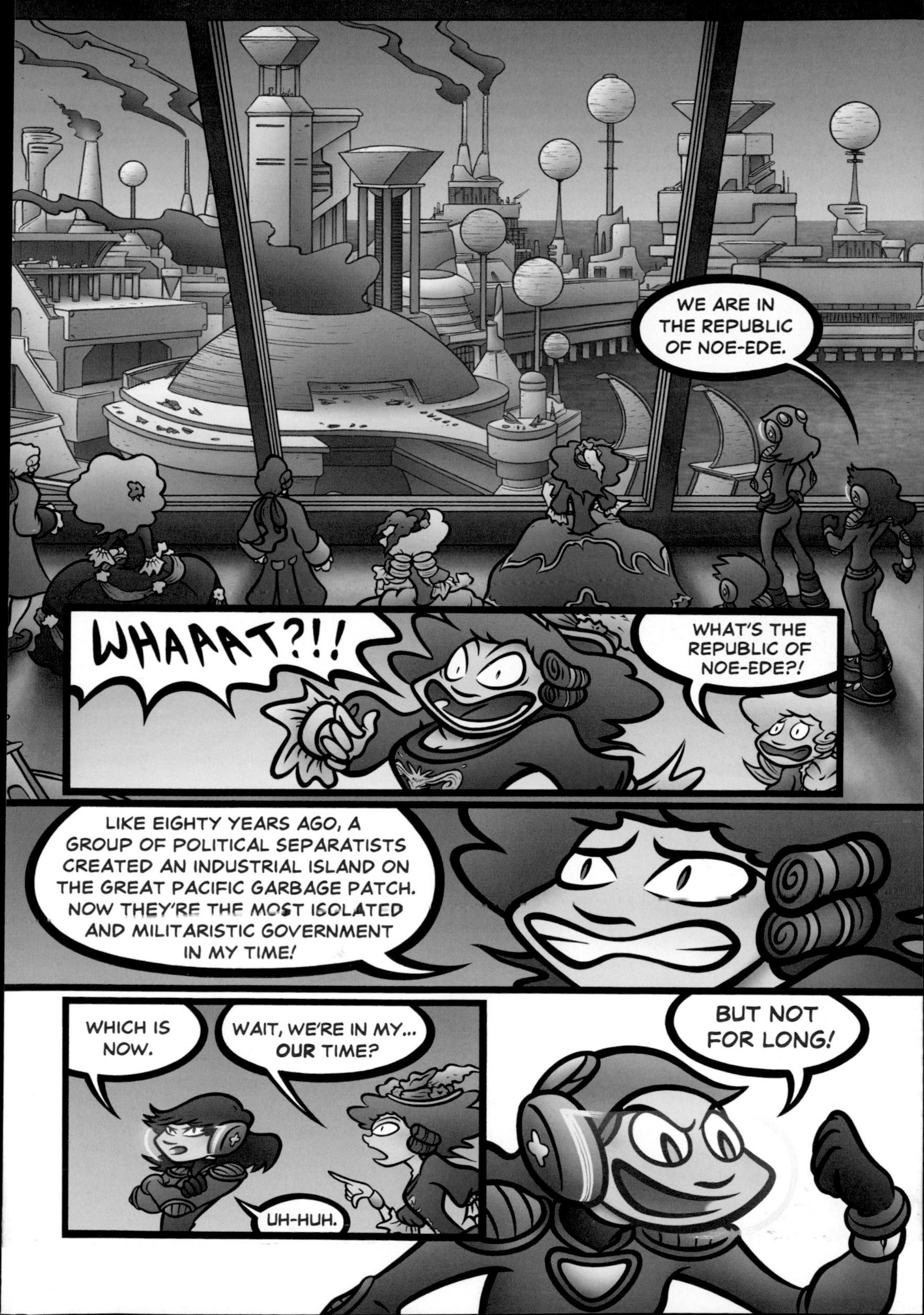
WE ARE IN THE REPUBLIC OF NOE-EDE.
WHAAAT?!!
WHAT'S THE REPUBLIC OF NOE-EDE?!
LIKE EIGHTY YEARS AGO, A GROUP OF POLITICAL SEPARATISTS CREATED AN INDUSTRIAL ISLAND ON THE GREAT PACIFIC GARBAGE PATCH. NOW THEY'RE THE MOST ISOLATED AND MILITARISTIC GOVERNMENT IN MY TIME!
WHICH IS NOW.
WAIT, WE'RE IN MY... OUR TIME?
UH-HUH.
BUT NOT FOR LONG!

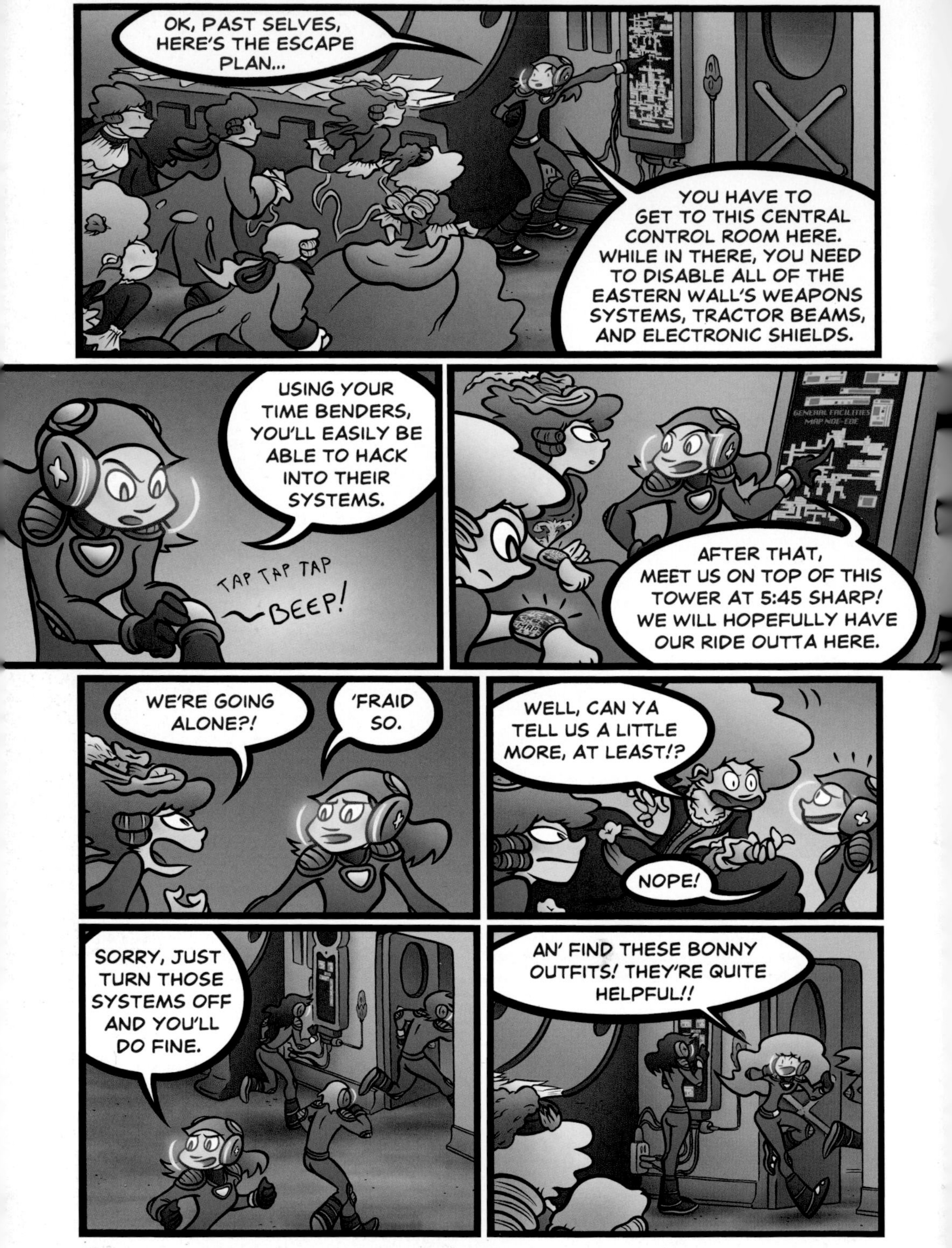
OK, PAST SELVES, HERE'S THE ESCAPE PLAN...
YOU HAVE TO GET TO THIS CENTRAL CONTROL ROOM HERE. WHILE IN THERE, YOU NEED TO DISABLE ALL OF THE EASTERN WALL'S WEAPONS SYSTEMS, TRACTOR BEAMS, AND ELECTRONIC SHIELDS.
USING YOUR TIME BENDERS, YOU'LL EASILY BE ABLE TO HACK INTO THEIR SYSTEMS.
TAP TAP TAP
BEEP!
AFTER THAT, MEET US ON TOP OF THIS TOWER AT 5:45 SHARP! WE WILL HOPEFULLY HAVE OUR RIDE OUTTA HERE.
WE'RE GOING ALONE?!
'FRAID SO.
WELL, CAN YA TELL US A LITTLE MORE, AT LEAST!?
NOPE!
SORRY, JUST TURN THOSE SYSTEMS OFF AND YOU'LL DO FINE.
AN' FIND THESE BONNY OUTFITS! THEY'RE QUITE HELPFUL!!

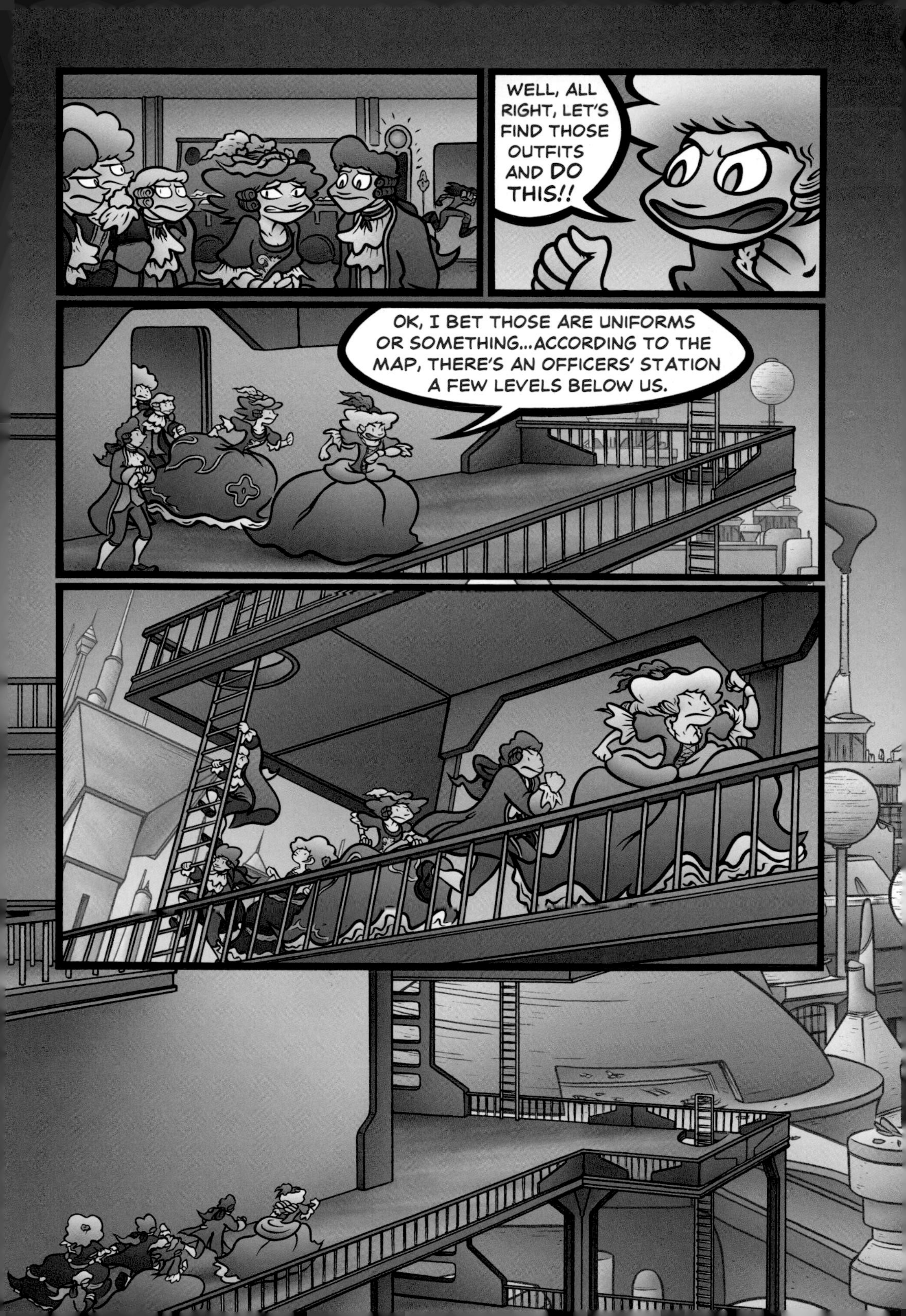
WELL, ALL RIGHT, LET'S FIND THOSE OUTFITS AND DO THIS!!
OK, I BET THOSE ARE UNIFORMS OR SOMETHING...ACCORDING TO THE MAP, THERE'S AN OFFICERS' STATION A FEW LEVELS BELOW US.

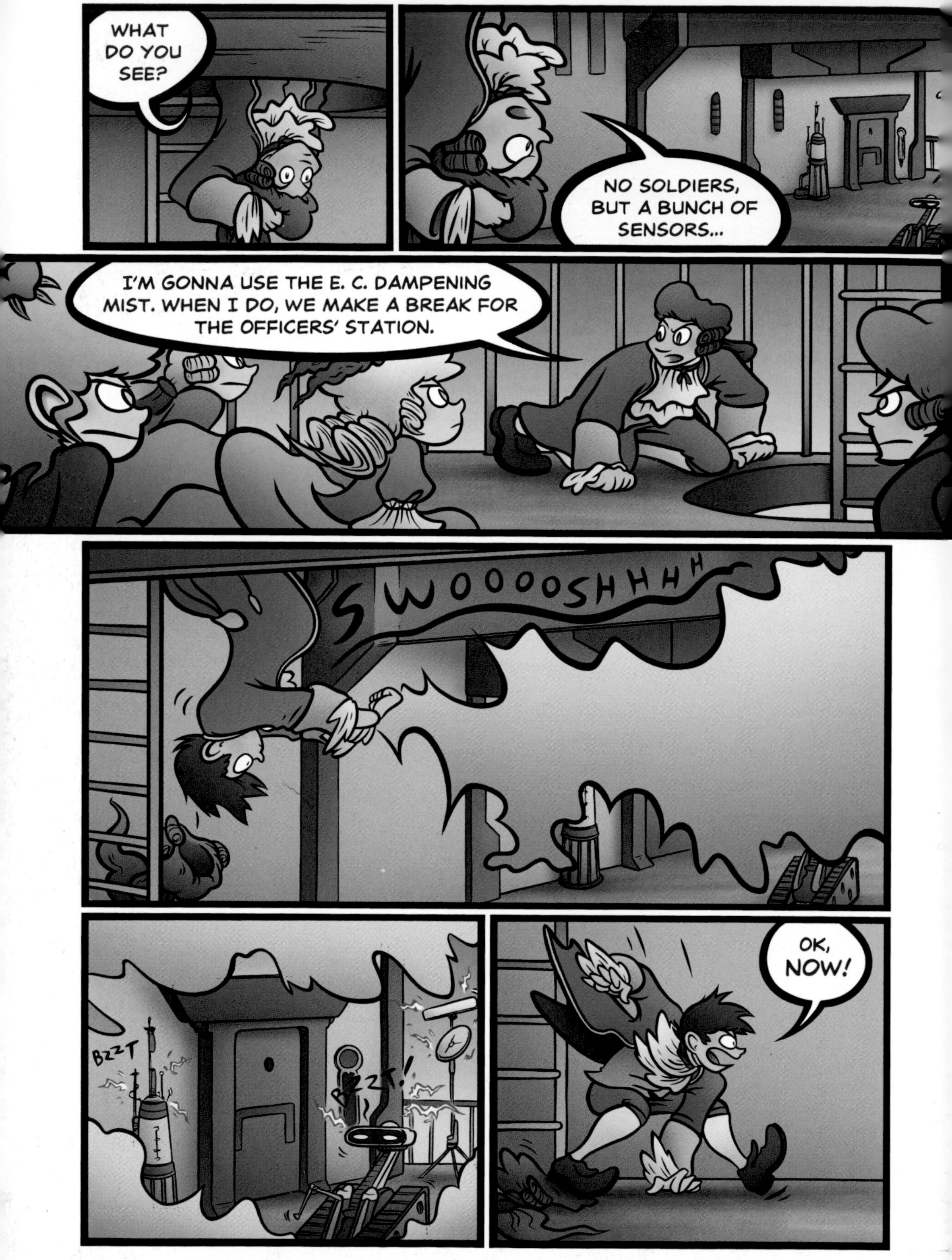
WHAT DO YOU SEE?
NO SOLDIERS, BUT A BUNCH OF SENSORS...
I'M GONNA USE THE E. C. DAMPENING MIST. WHEN I DO, WE MAKE A BREAK FOR THE OFFICERS' STATION.
SWOOOOSHHHH
BZZT
BZZT!
OK, NOW!

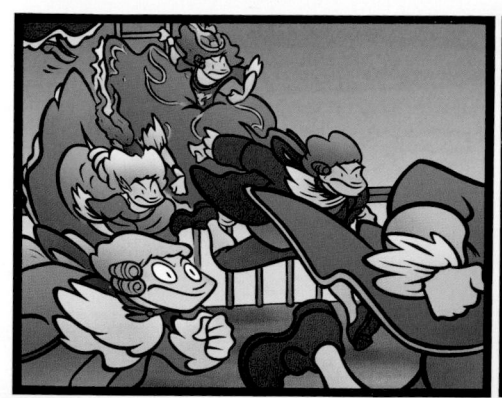

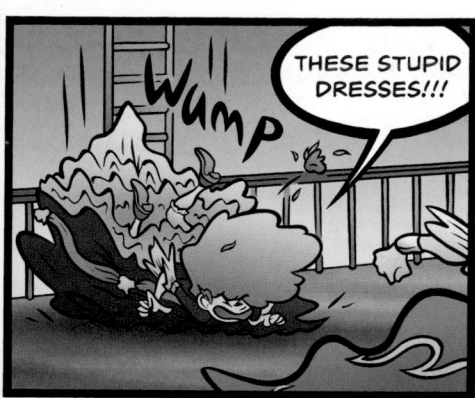

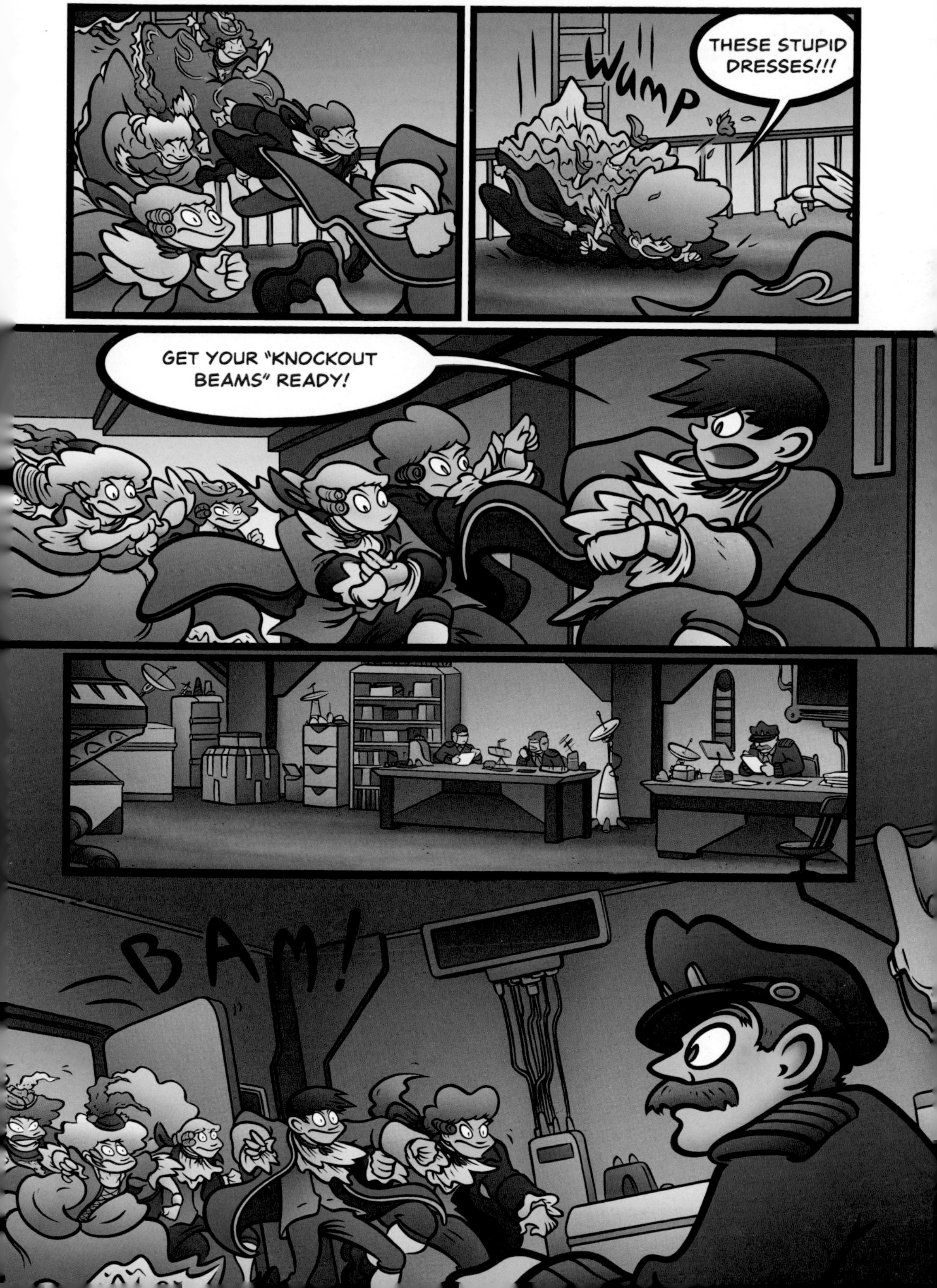
WUMP
THESE STUPID DRESSES!!!
GET YOUR "KNOCKOUT BEAMS" READY!
BAM!

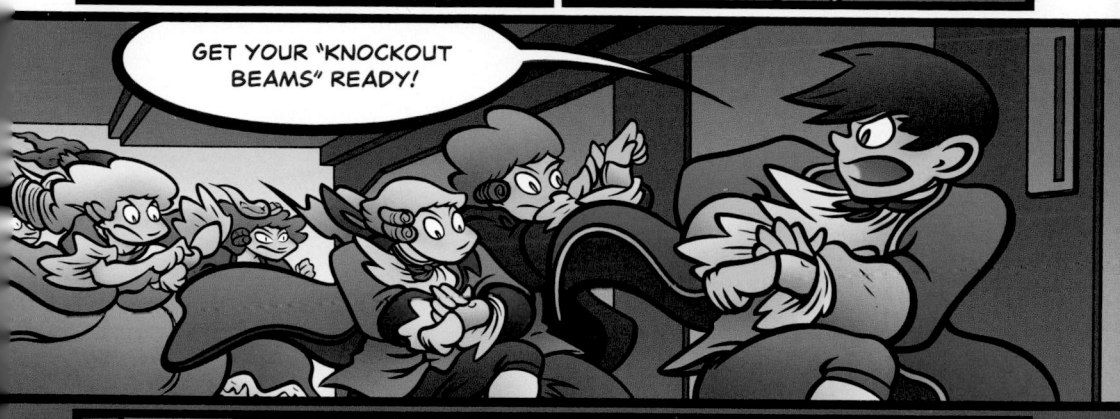

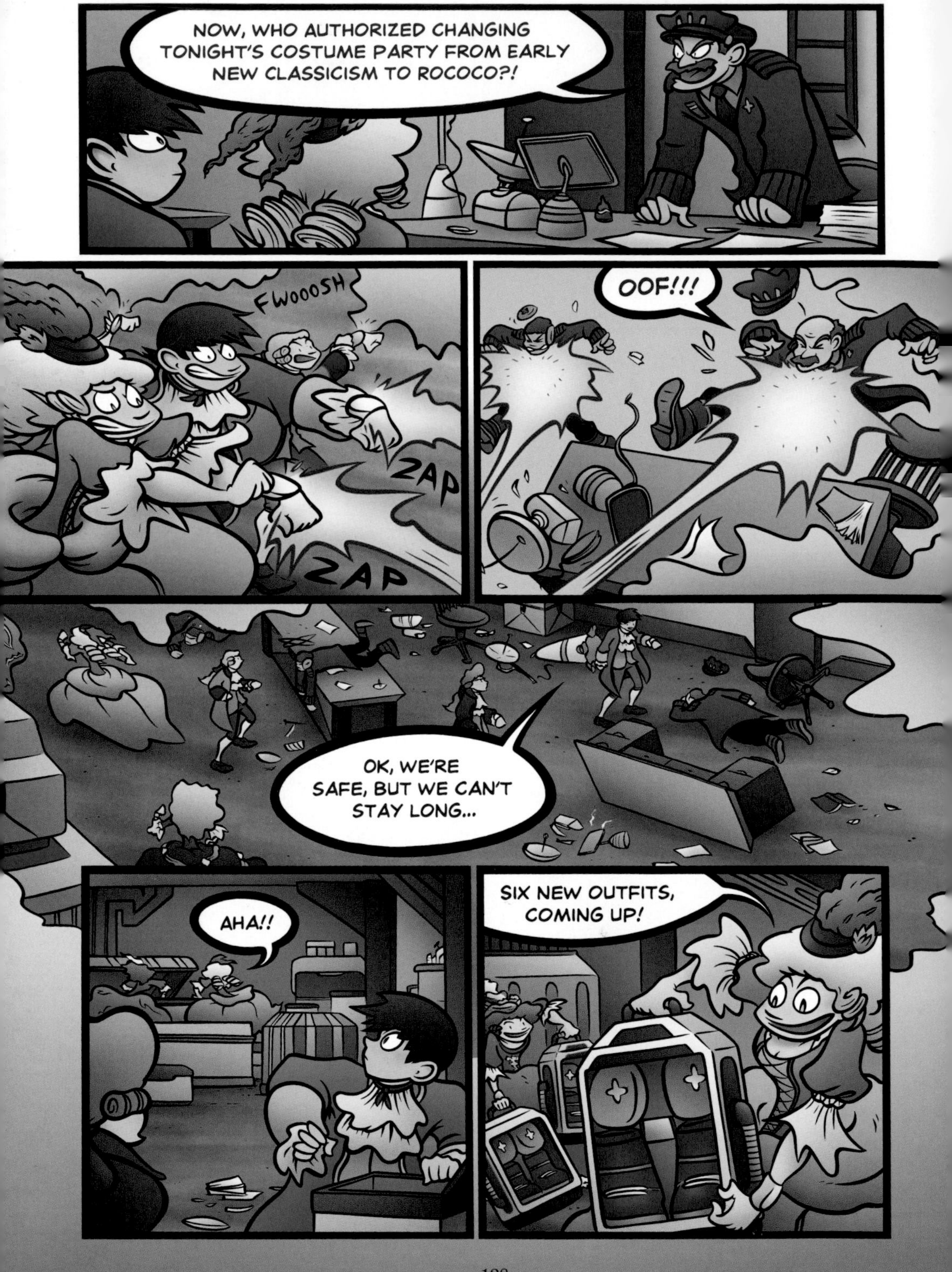
NOW, WHO AUTHORIZED CHANGING TONIGHT'S COSTUME PARTY FROM EARLY NEW CLASSICISM TO ROCOCO?!
FWOOOSH
ZAP
ZAP
OOF!!!
OK, WE'RE SAFE, BUT WE CAN'T STAY LONG...
AHA!!
SIX NEW OUTFITS, COMING UP!

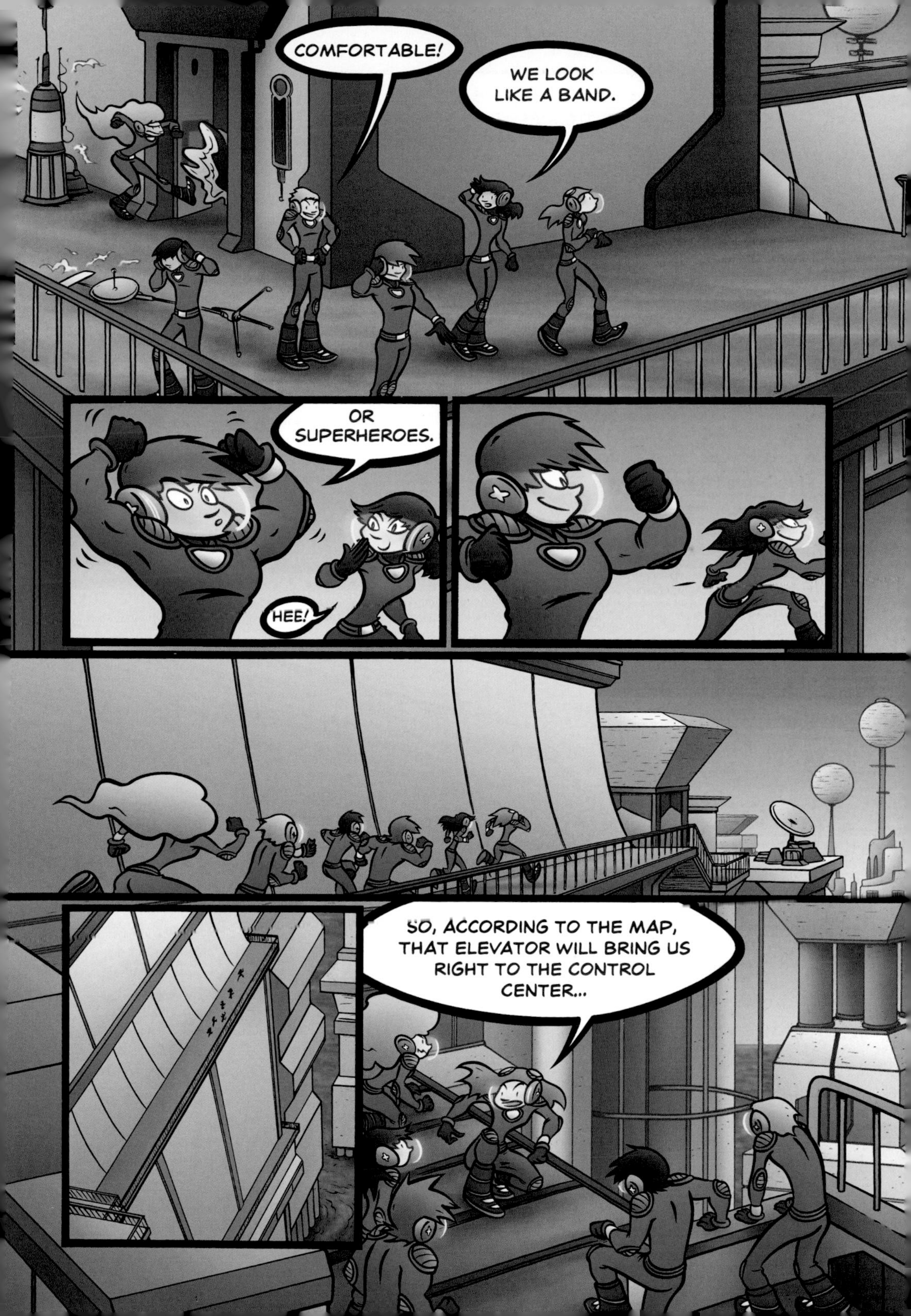
COMFORTABLE!
WE LOOK LIKE A BAND.
OR SUPERHEROES.
HEE!
SO, ACCORDING TO THE MAP, THAT ELEVATOR WILL BRING US RIGHT TO THE CONTROL CENTER...

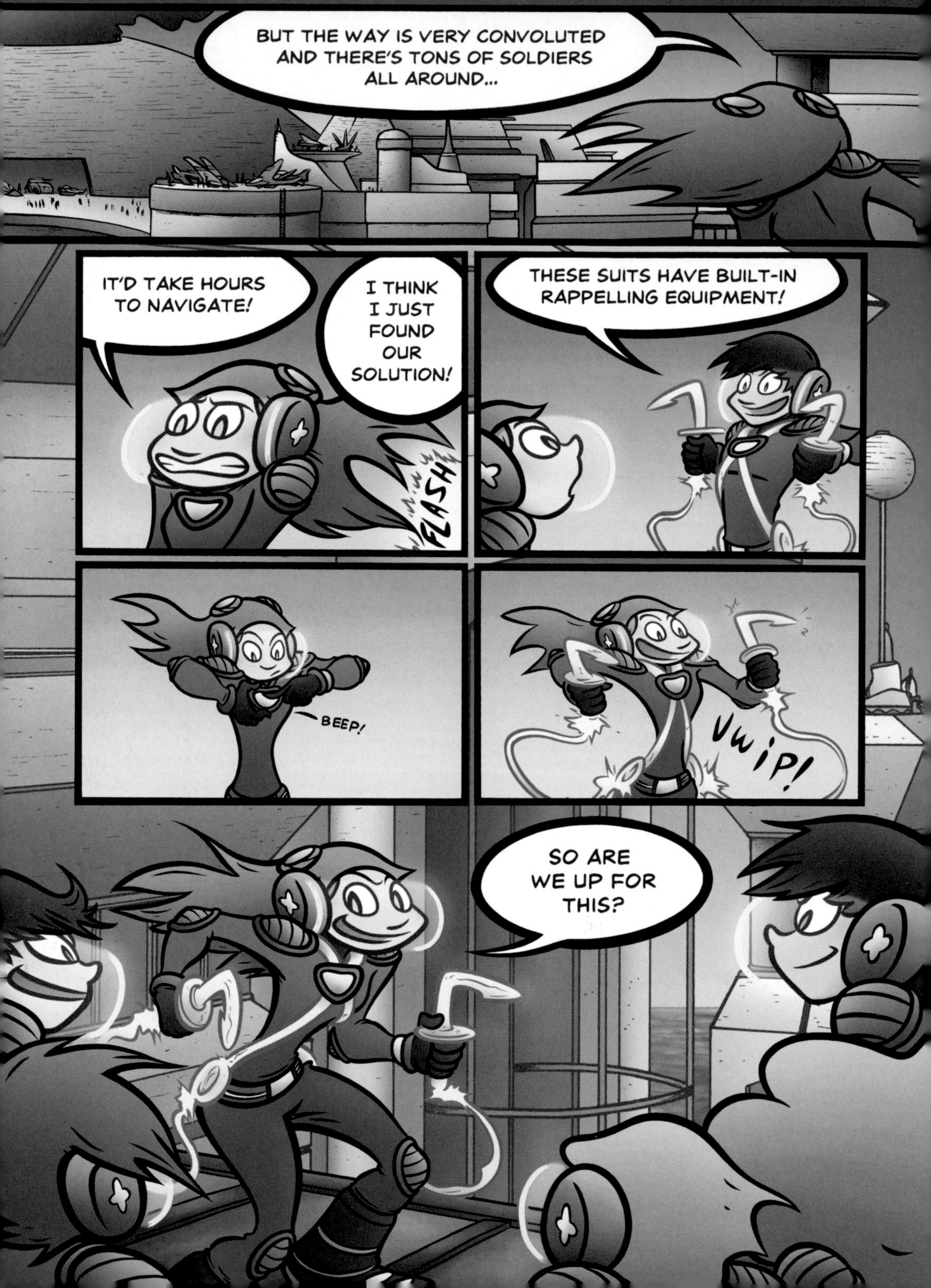

BUT THE WAY IS VERY CONVOLUTED AND THERE'S TONS OF SOLDIERS ALL AROUND...
IT'D TAKE HOURS TO NAVIGATE!
I THINK I JUST FOUND OUR SOLUTION!
FLASH
THESE SUITS HAVE BUILT-IN RAPPELLING EQUIPMENT!
BEEP!
VWIP!
SO ARE WE UP FOR THIS?

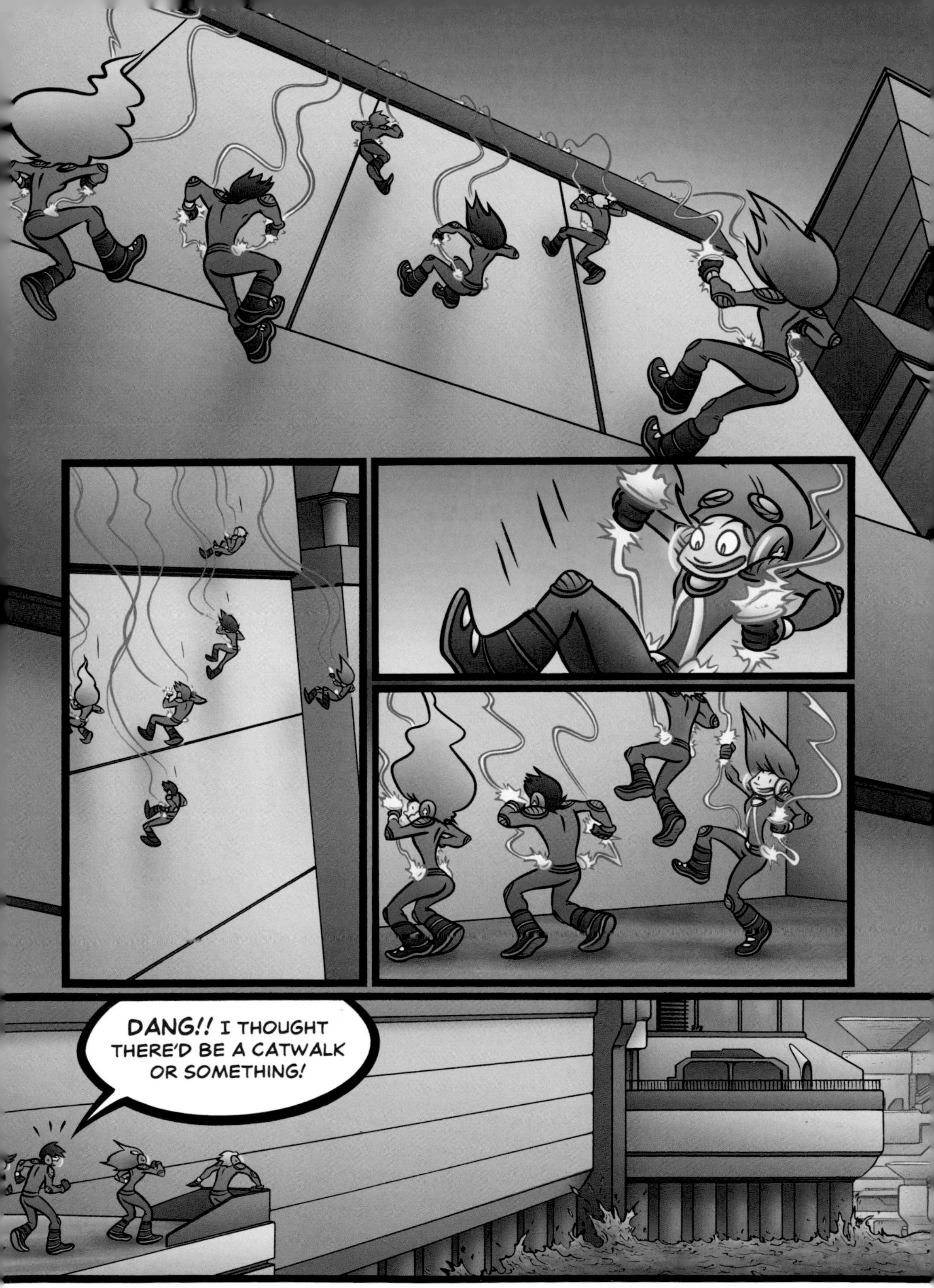
DANG!! I THOUGHT THERE'D BE A CATWALK OR SOMETHING!

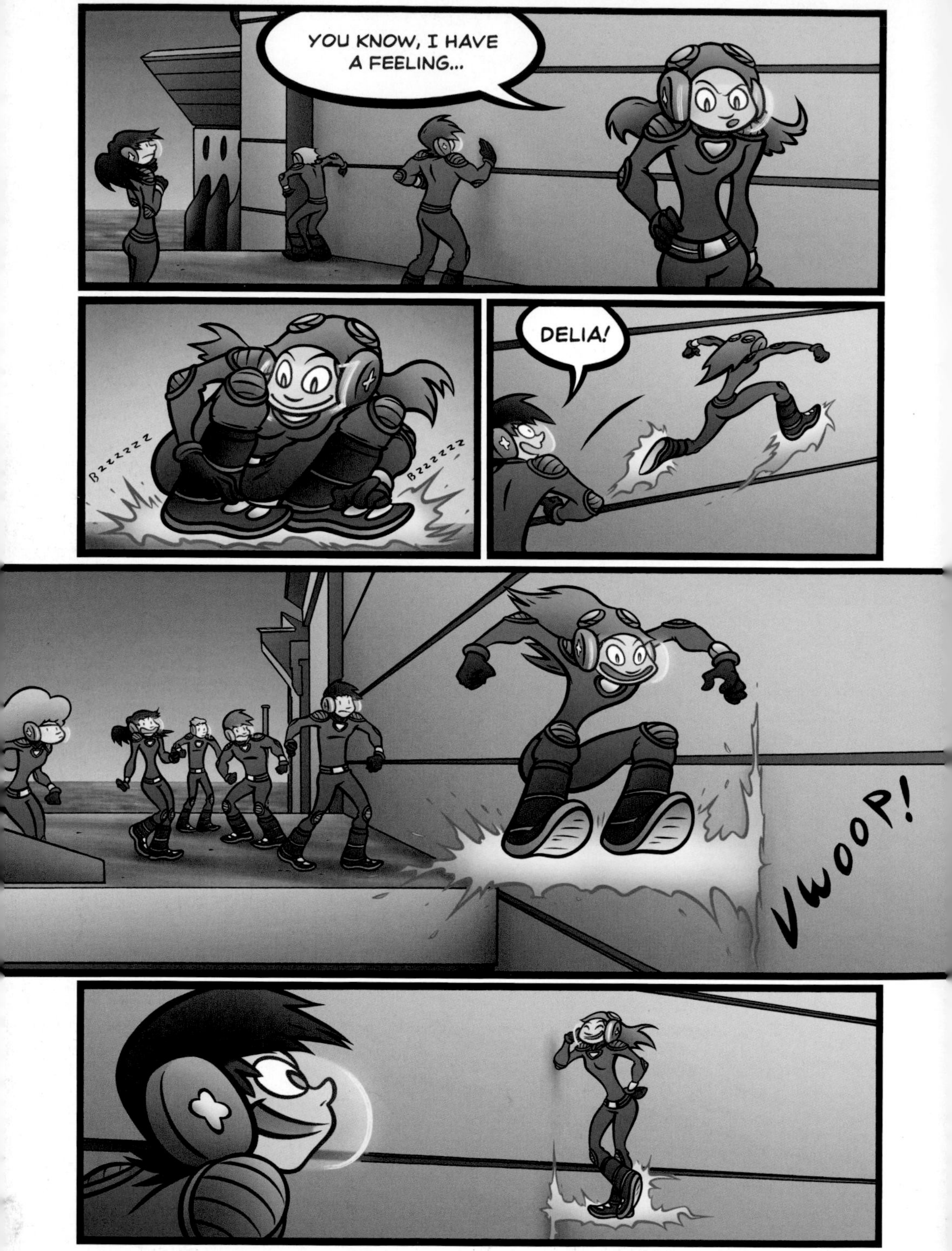
YOU KNOW, I HAVE A FEELING...
Bzzzzzz
Bzzzzzz
DELIA!
VWOOP!

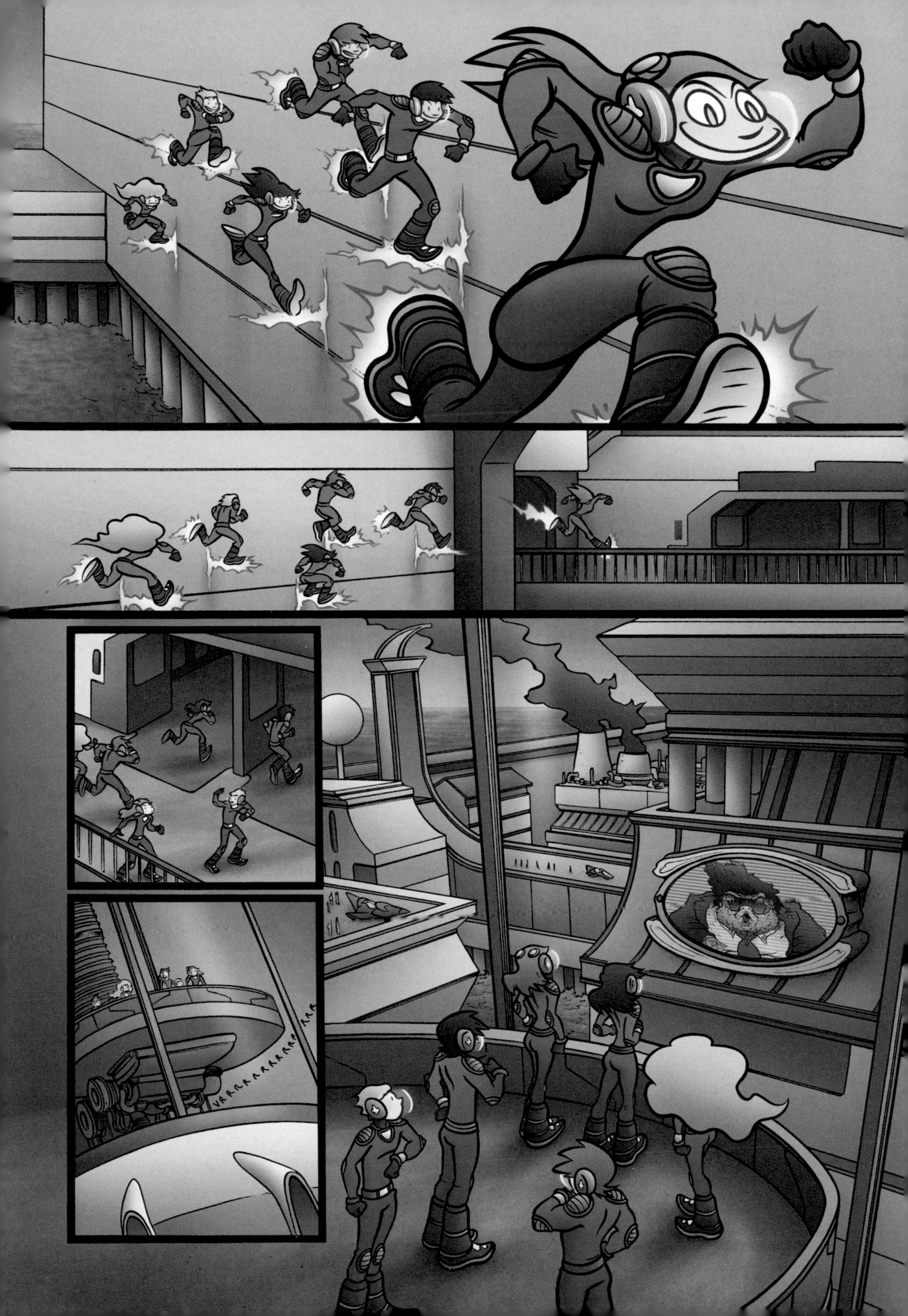
VRRRRRRRRRRRRRR

WHO'S THE BAWFACED OLD COOT?

THAT'S NOE-EDE'S PREEMINENT AND BENEVOLENT LEADER.

I HONESTLY DON'T EVEN KNOW HIS REAL NAME. THEY ONLY EVER REFER TO HIM AS THAT.

HE'S BEEN IN THE NEWS IN MY TIME A LOT LATELY 'CAUSE THIS PLACE WAS MOVING DANGEROUSLY CLOSE TO MY OWN ISLAND OF HONSHU, JAPAN. WHICH IS WHERE WE ARE NOW, I GUESS...

HM...

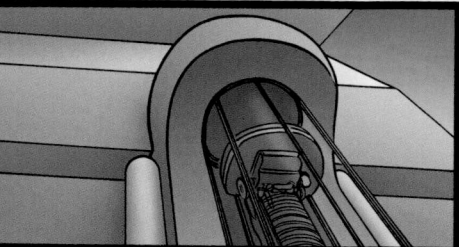

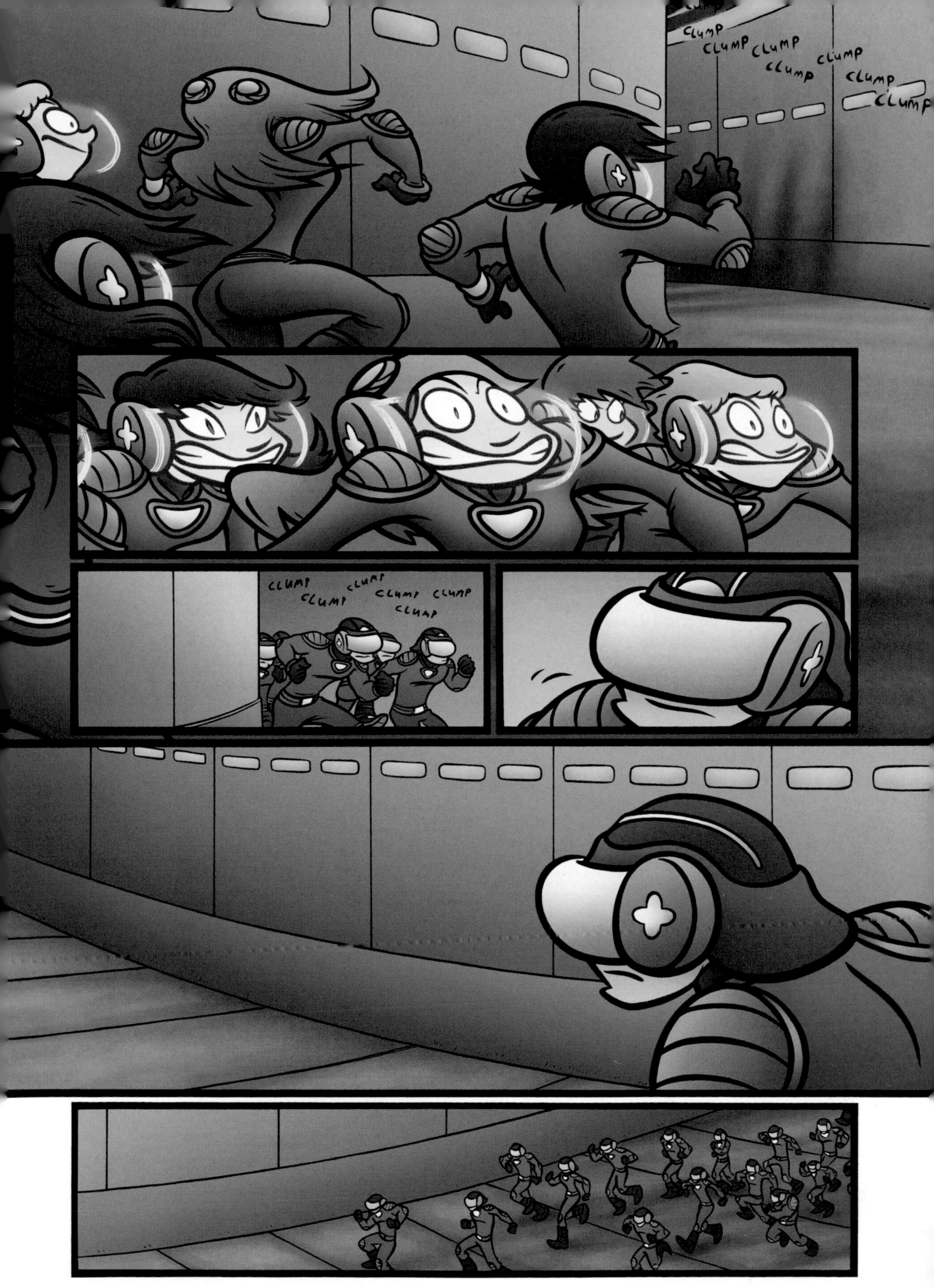
CLUMP
CLUMP CLUMP
CLUMP CLUMP
CLUMP
CLUMP
CLUMP
CLUMP CLUMP
CLUMP CLUMP CLUMP
CLUMP

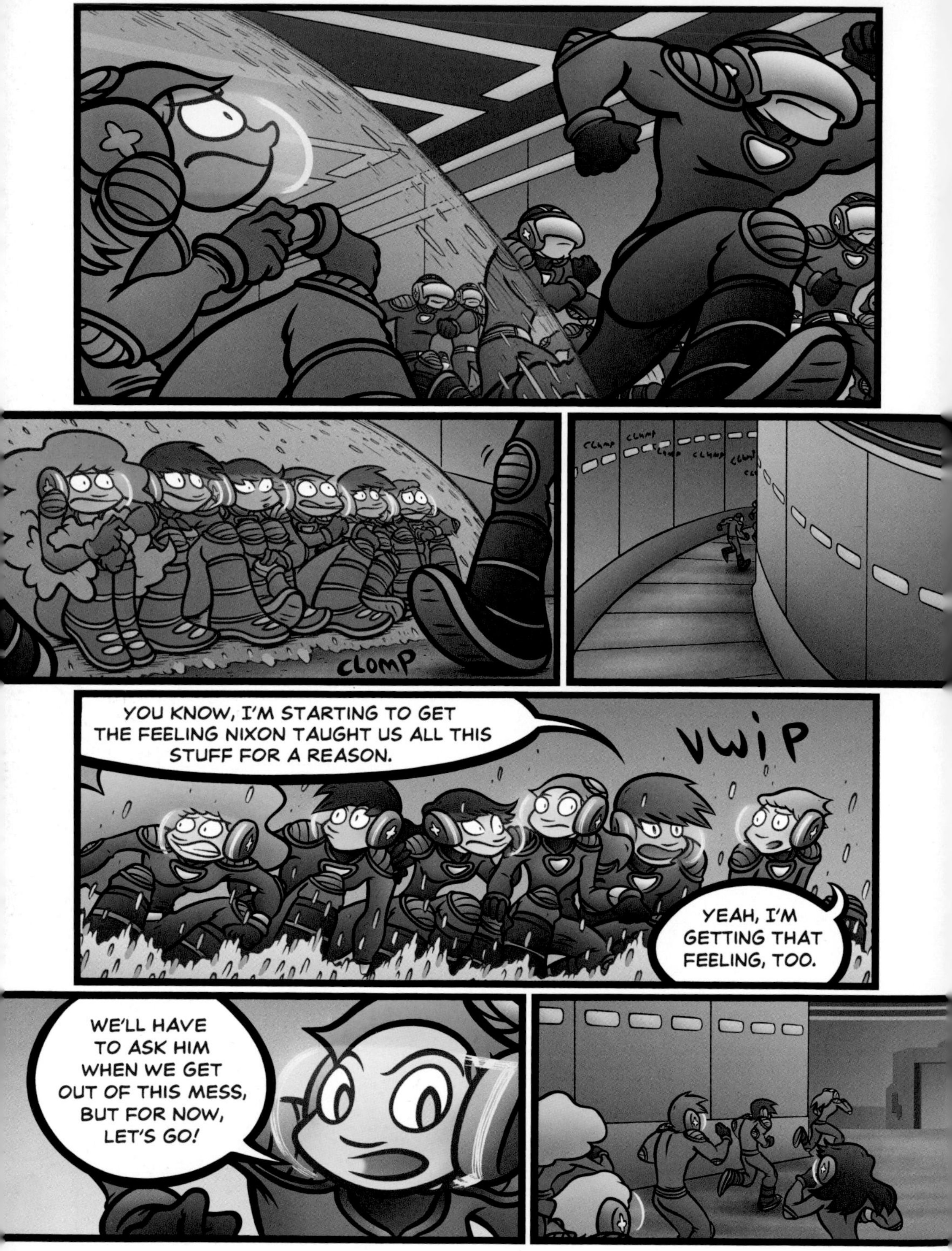
CLOMP
CLUMP CLUMP CLUMP CLUMP CLUMP
YOU KNOW, I'M STARTING TO GET THE FEELING NIXON TAUGHT US ALL THIS STUFF FOR A REASON.
VWIP
YEAH, I'M GETTING THAT FEELING, TOO.
WE'LL HAVE TO ASK HIM WHEN WE GET OUT OF THIS MESS, BUT FOR NOW, LET'S GO!

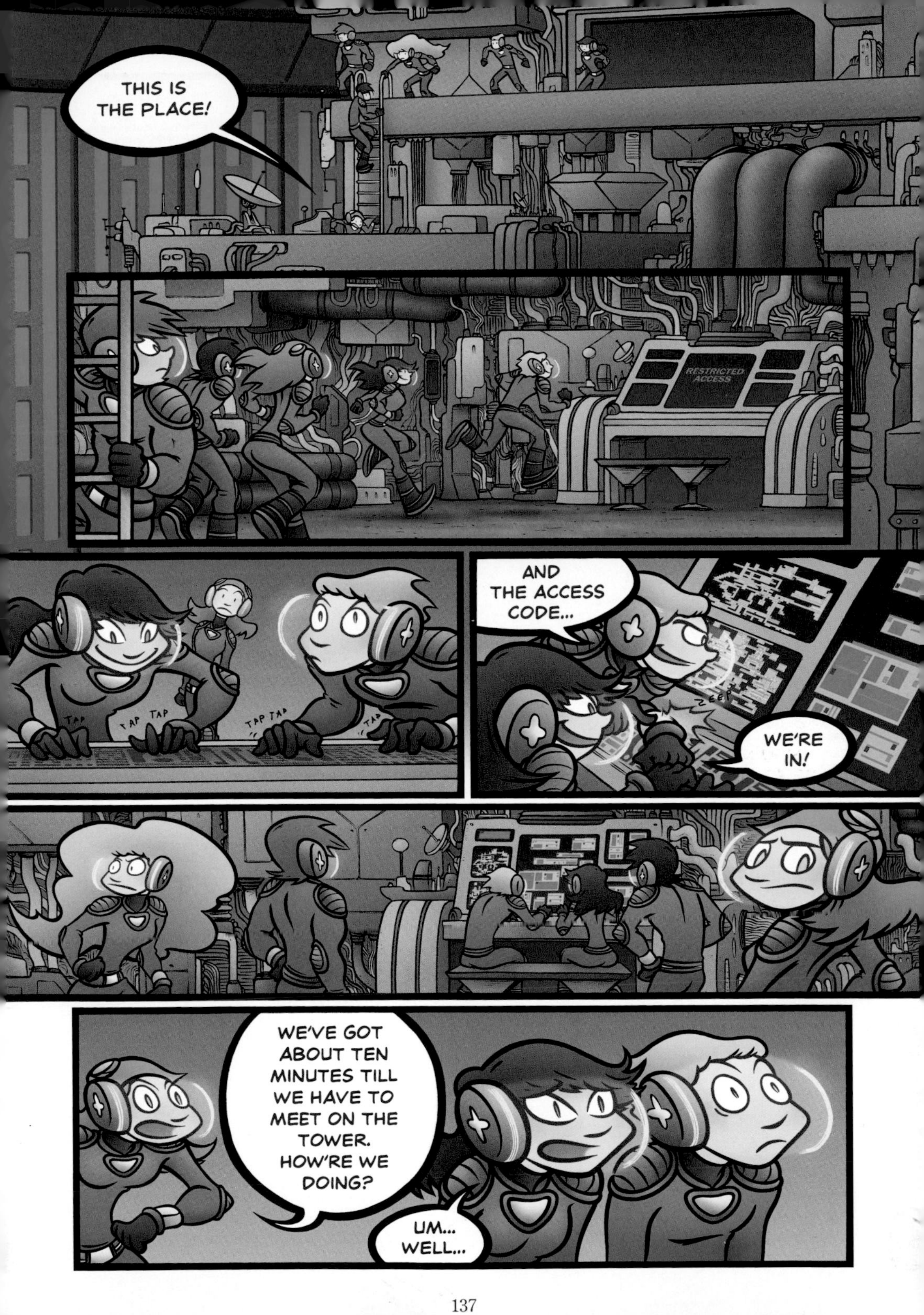
THIS IS THE PLACE!
RESTRICTED ACCESS
TAP TAP TAP
TAP TAP TAP
AND THE ACCESS CODE...
WE'RE IN!
WE'VE GOT ABOUT TEN MINUTES TILL WE HAVE TO MEET ON THE TOWER. HOW'RE WE DOING?
UM... WELL...

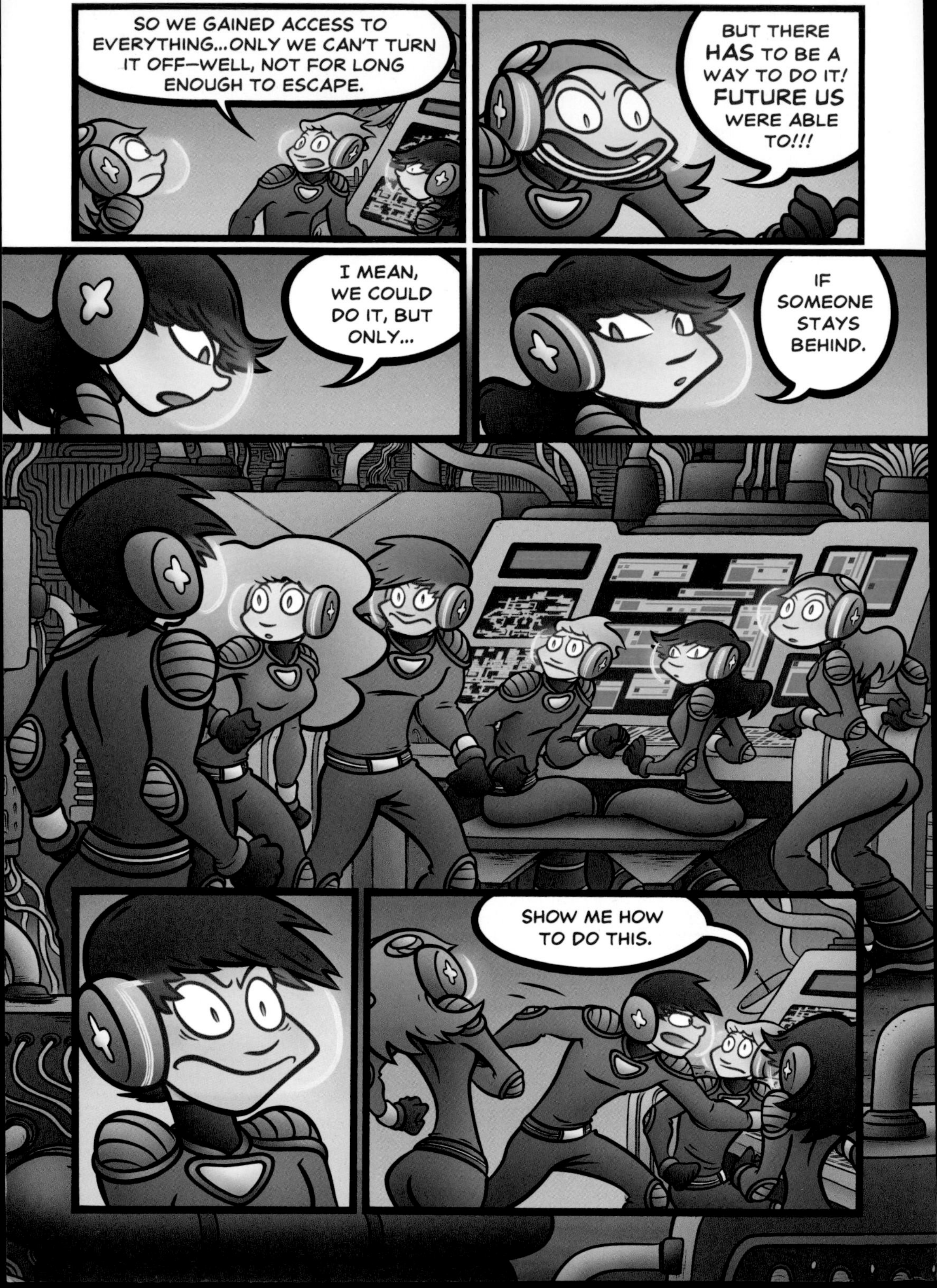
SO WE GAINED ACCESS TO EVERYTHING...ONLY WE CAN'T TURN IT OFF—WELL, NOT FOR LONG ENOUGH TO ESCAPE.
BUT THERE **HAS** TO BE A WAY TO DO IT! **FUTURE US** WERE ABLE TO!!!
I MEAN, WE COULD DO IT, BUT ONLY...
IF SOMEONE STAYS BEHIND.
SHOW ME HOW TO DO THIS.

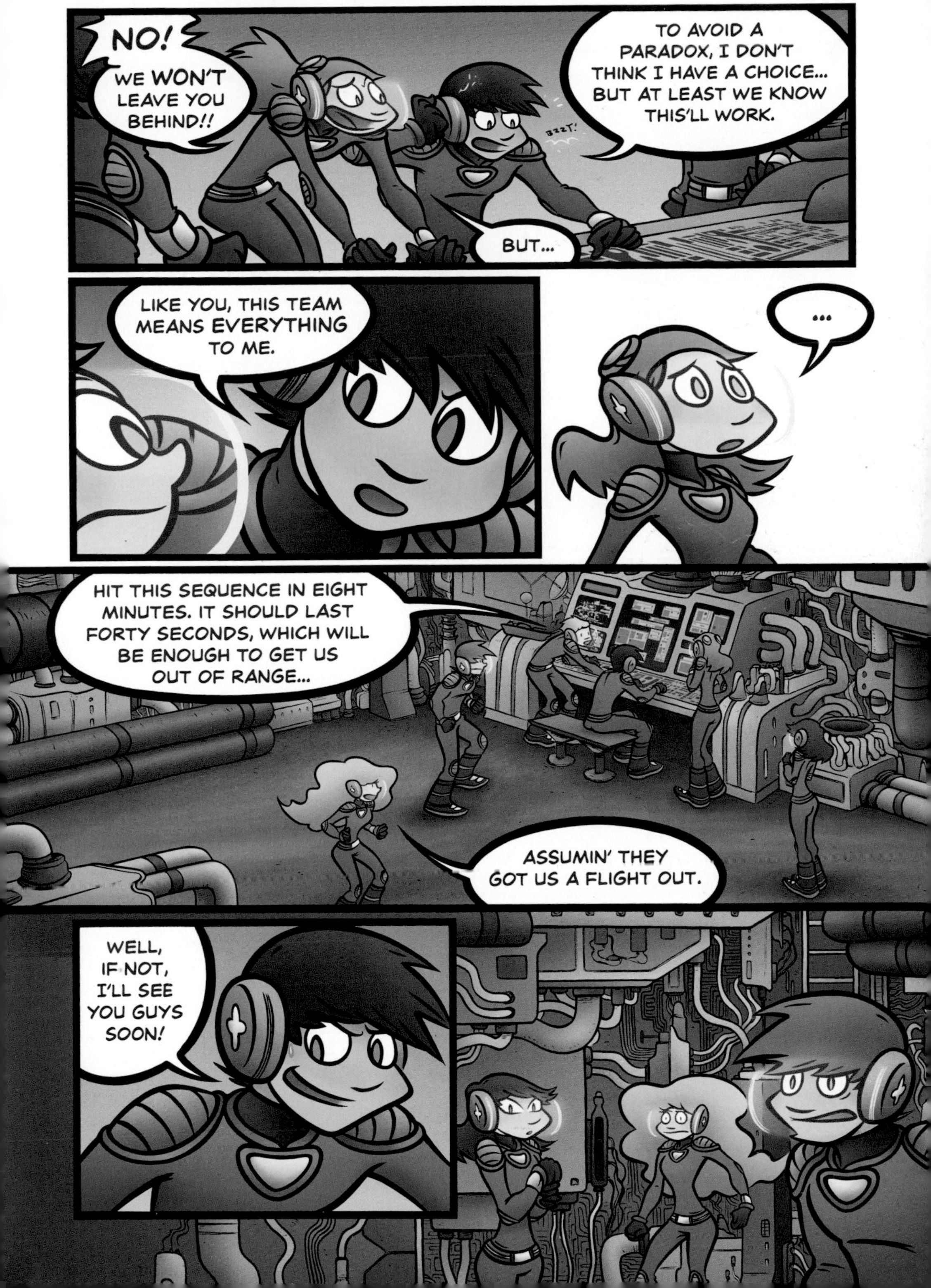
NO!
WE WON'T LEAVE YOU BEHIND!!
TO AVOID A PARADOX, I DON'T THINK I HAVE A CHOICE... BUT AT LEAST WE KNOW THIS'LL WORK.
BZZT!
BUT...
LIKE YOU, THIS TEAM MEANS EVERYTHING TO ME.
...
HIT THIS SEQUENCE IN EIGHT MINUTES. IT SHOULD LAST FORTY SECONDS, WHICH WILL BE ENOUGH TO GET US OUT OF RANGE...
ASSUMIN' THEY GOT US A FLIGHT OUT.
WELL, IF NOT, I'LL SEE YOU GUYS SOON!

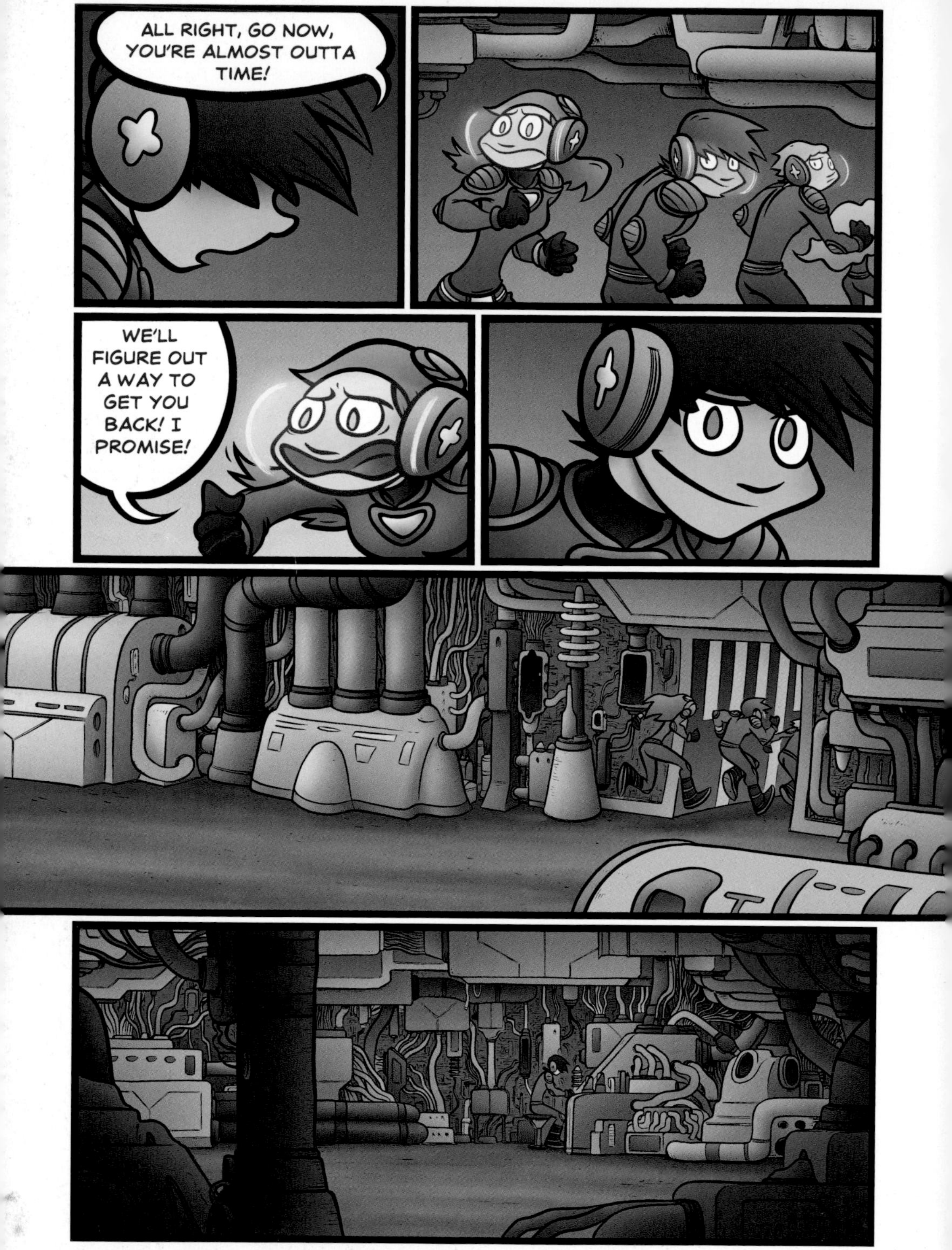

ALL RIGHT, GO NOW, YOU'RE ALMOST OUTTA TIME!
WE'LL FIGURE OUT A WAY TO GET YOU BACK! I PROMISE!

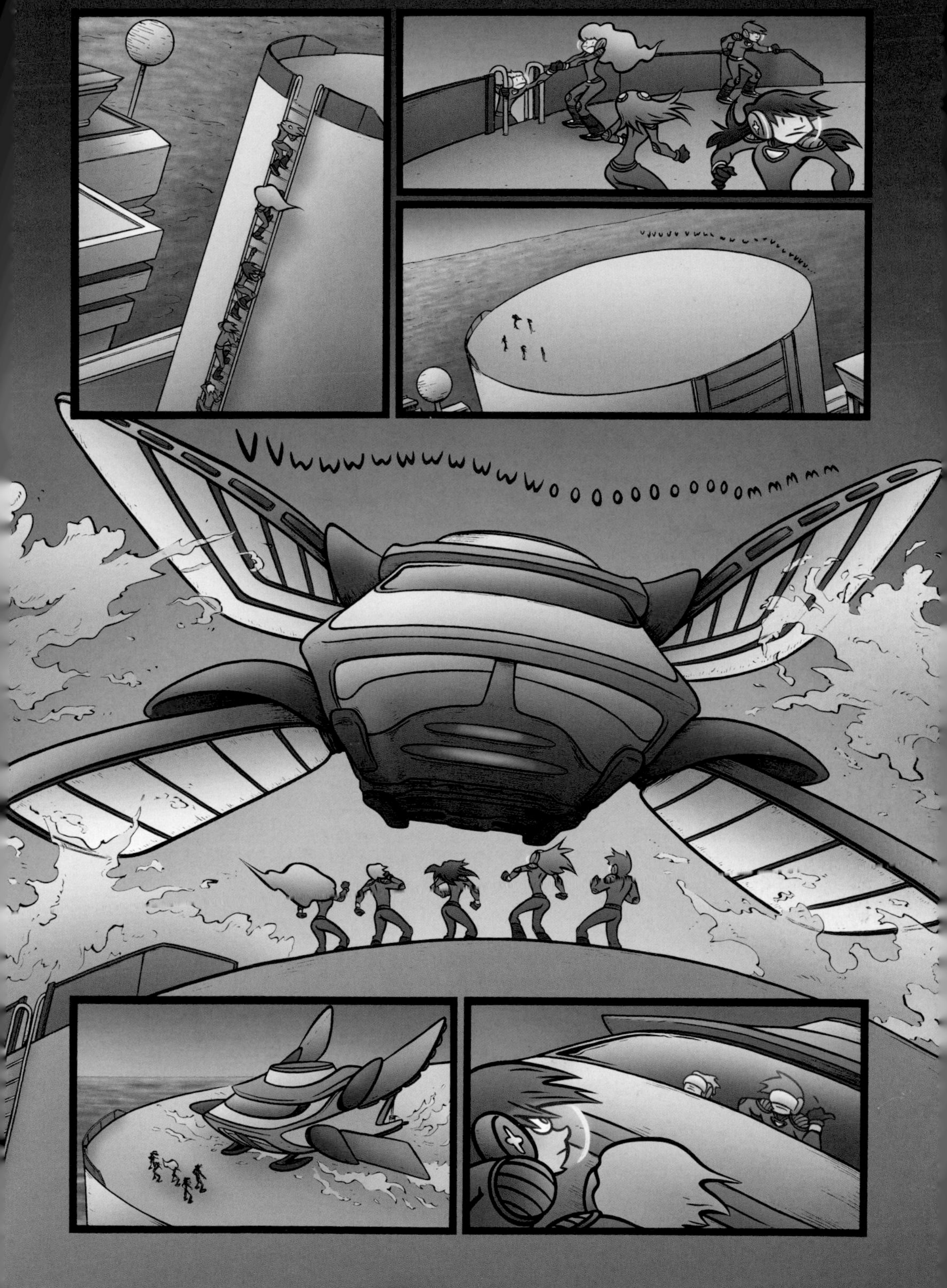
VVwwwwwwwwwwwWooooooooooooommmmm

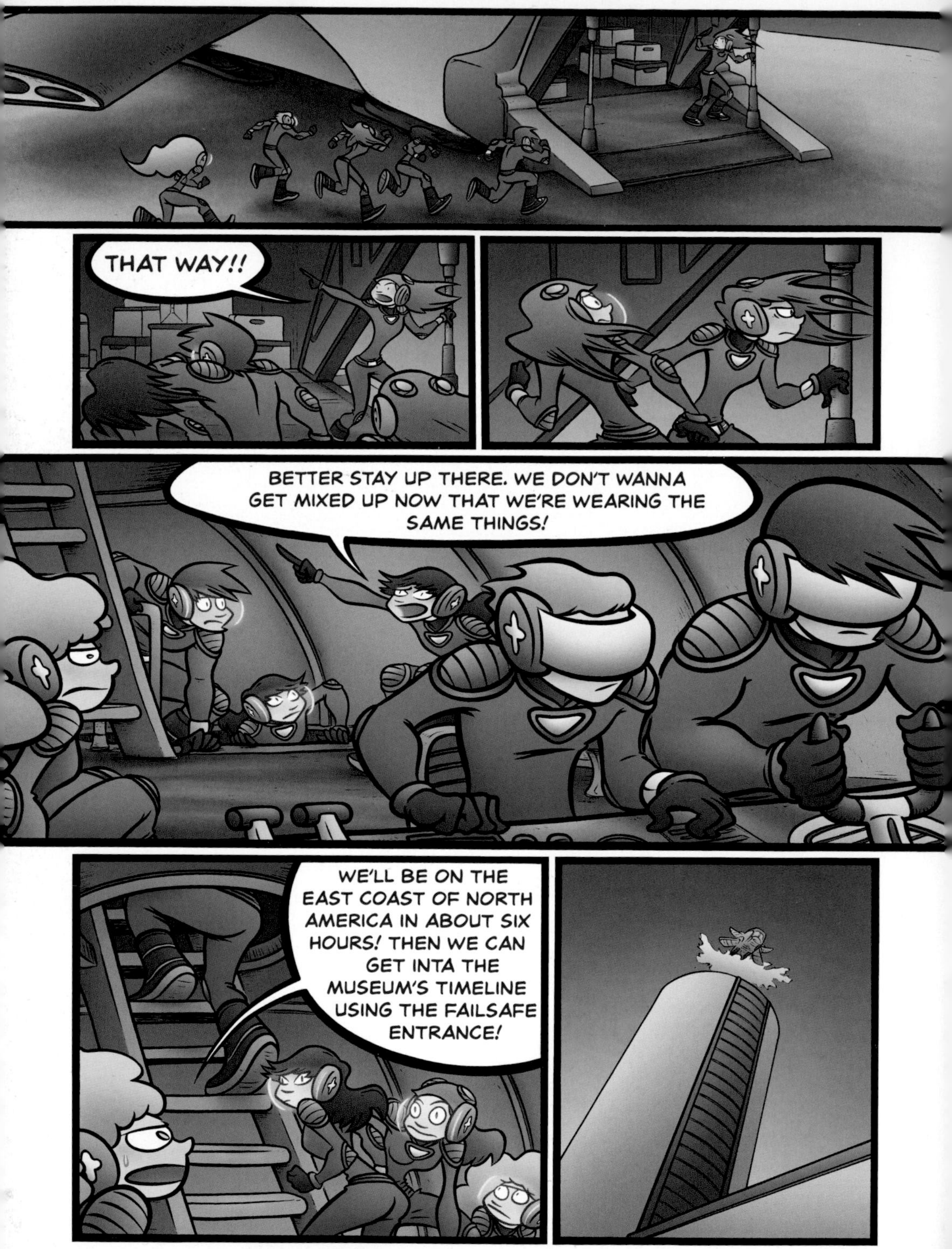
THAT WAY!!
BETTER STAY UP THERE. WE DON'T WANNA GET MIXED UP NOW THAT WE'RE WEARING THE SAME THINGS!
WE'LL BE ON THE EAST COAST OF NORTH AMERICA IN ABOUT SIX HOURS! THEN WE CAN GET INTA THE MUSEUM'S TIMELINE USING THE FAILSAFE ENTRANCE!

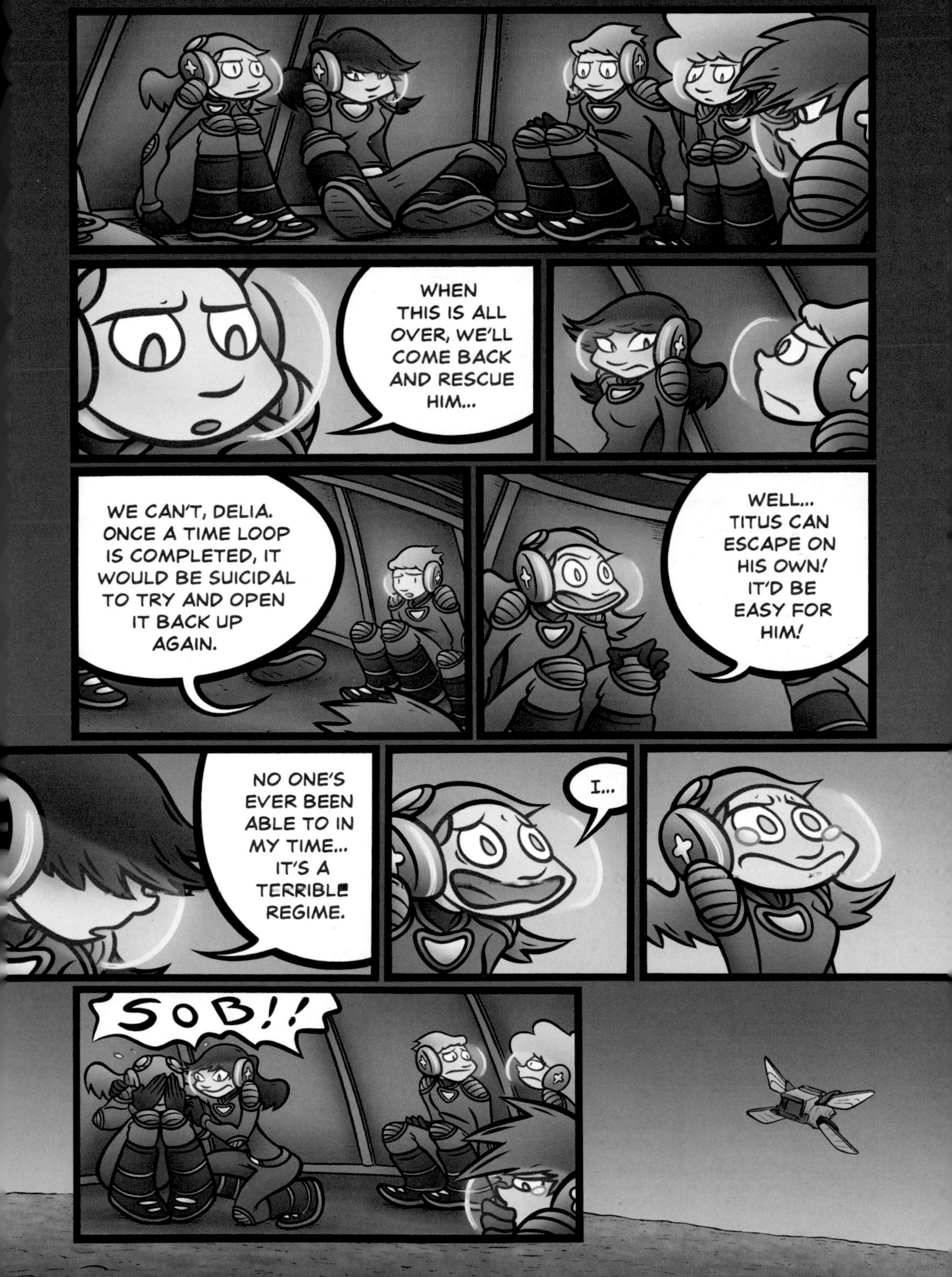
WHEN THIS IS ALL OVER, WE'LL COME BACK AND RESCUE HIM...
WE CAN'T, DELIA. ONCE A TIME LOOP IS COMPLETED, IT WOULD BE SUICIDAL TO TRY AND OPEN IT BACK UP AGAIN.
WELL... TITUS CAN ESCAPE ON HIS OWN! IT'D BE EASY FOR HIM!
NO ONE'S EVER BEEN ABLE TO IN MY TIME... IT'S A TERRIBLE REGIME.
I...
SOB!!

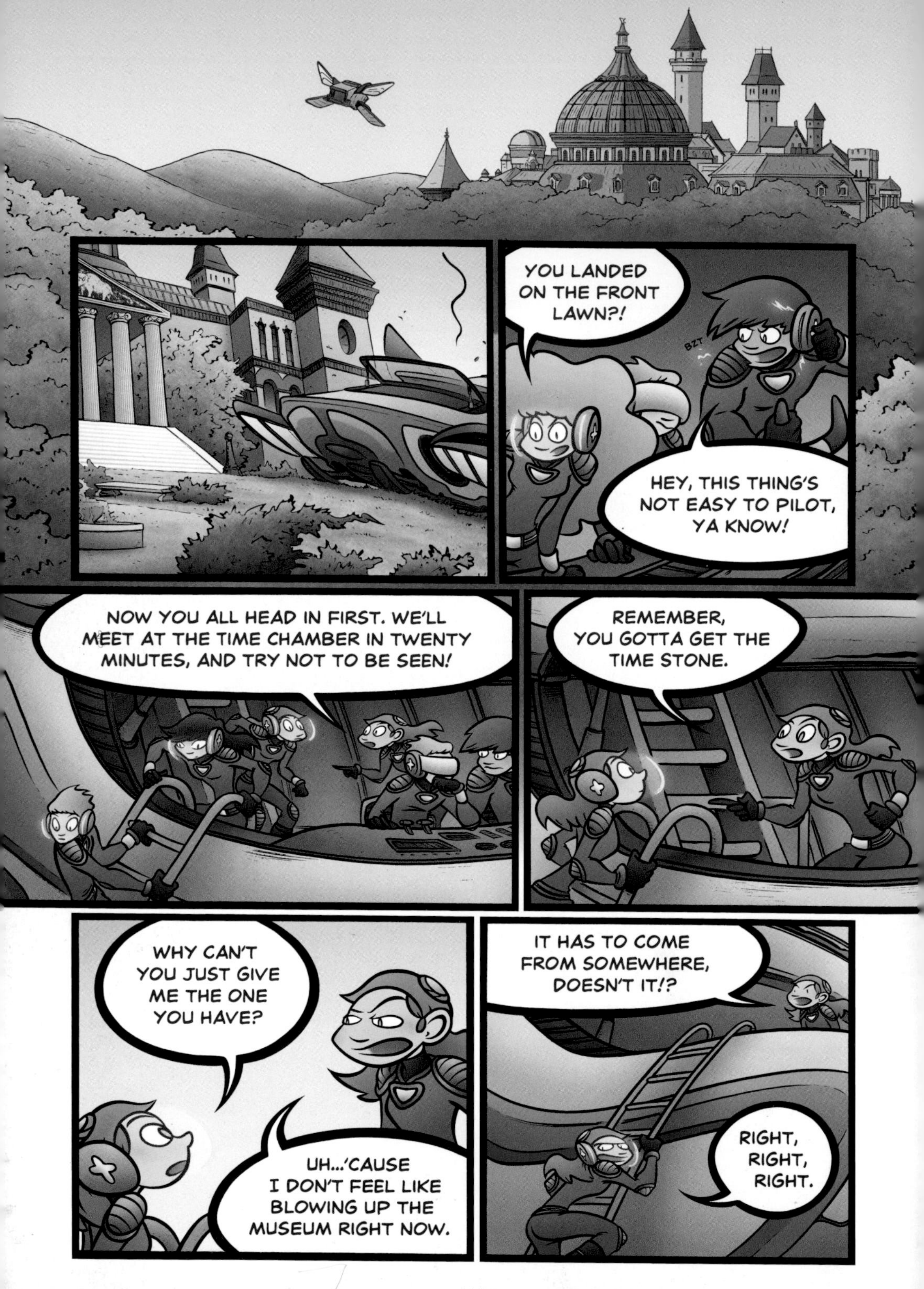
YOU LANDED ON THE FRONT LAWN?!
BZT
HEY, THIS THING'S NOT EASY TO PILOT, YA KNOW!
NOW YOU ALL HEAD IN FIRST. WE'LL MEET AT THE TIME CHAMBER IN TWENTY MINUTES, AND TRY NOT TO BE SEEN!
REMEMBER, YOU GOTTA GET THE TIME STONE.
WHY CAN'T YOU JUST GIVE ME THE ONE YOU HAVE?
UH...'CAUSE I DON'T FEEL LIKE BLOWING UP THE MUSEUM RIGHT NOW.
IT HAS TO COME FROM SOMEWHERE, DOESN'T IT!?
RIGHT, RIGHT, RIGHT.

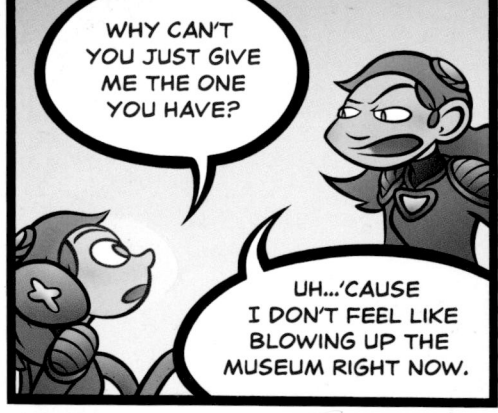

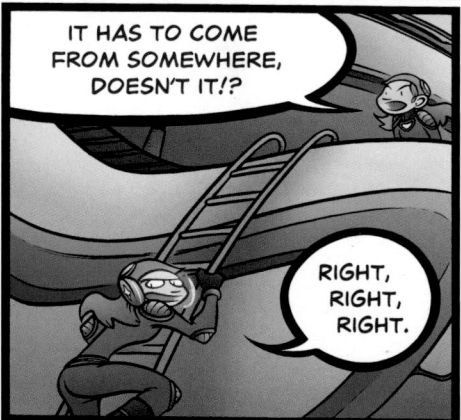

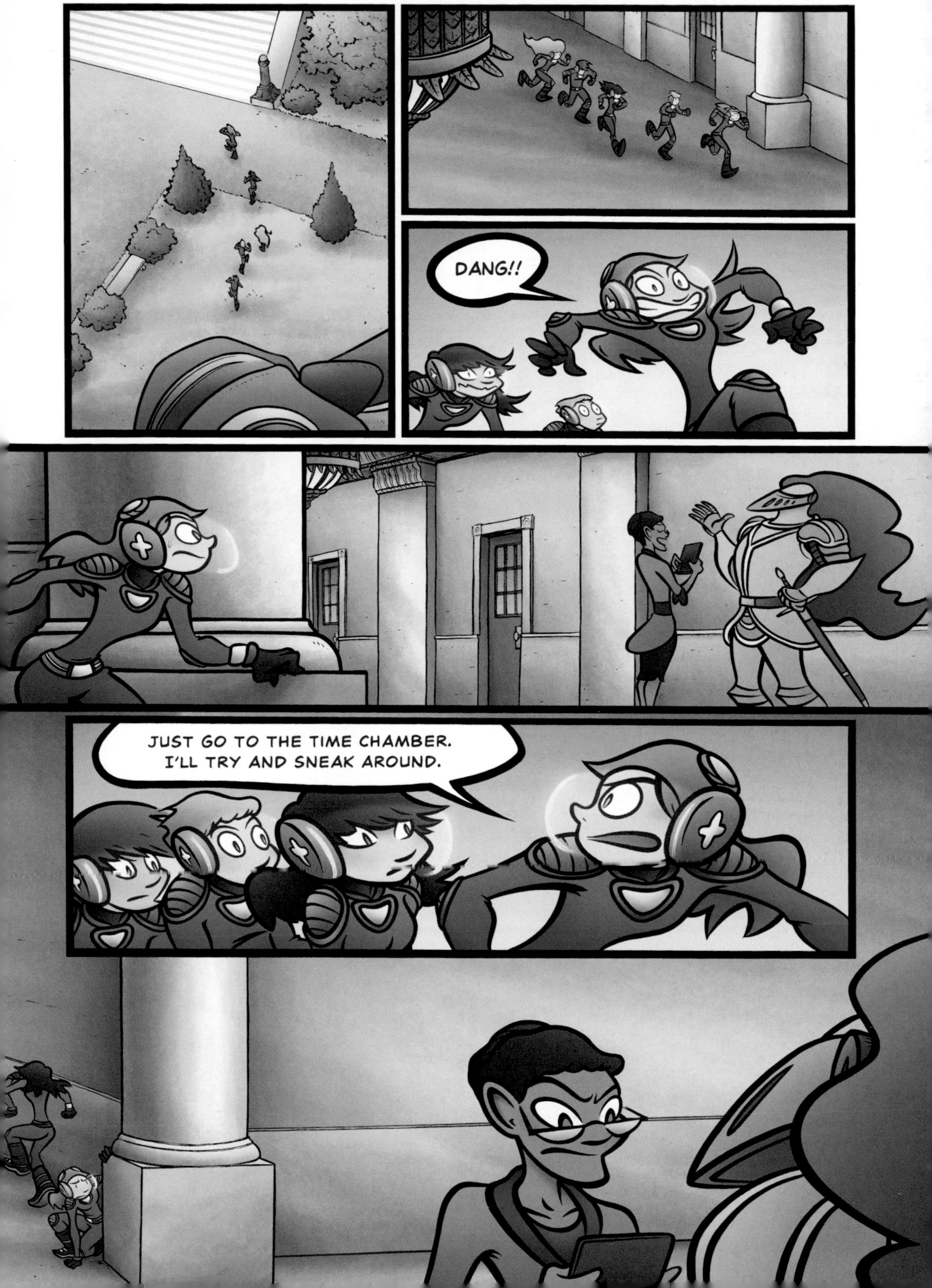
DANG!!
JUST GO TO THE TIME CHAMBER. I'LL TRY AND SNEAK AROUND.

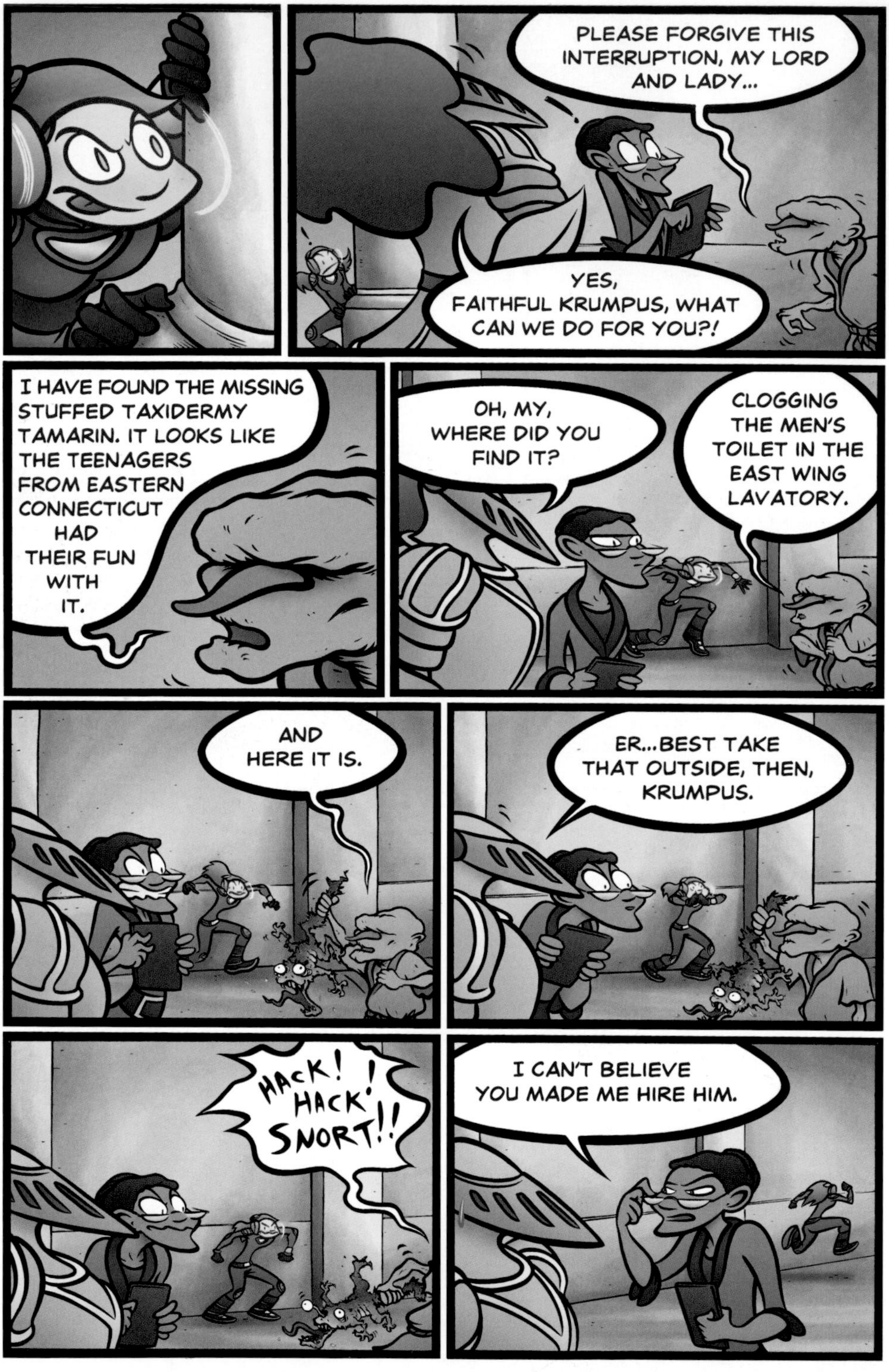

PLEASE FORGIVE THIS INTERRUPTION, MY LORD AND LADY...
YES, FAITHFUL KRUMPUS, WHAT CAN WE DO FOR YOU?!
I HAVE FOUND THE MISSING STUFFED TAXIDERMY TAMARIN. IT LOOKS LIKE THE TEENAGERS FROM EASTERN CONNECTICUT HAD THEIR FUN WITH IT.
OH, MY, WHERE DID YOU FIND IT?
CLOGGING THE MEN'S TOILET IN THE EAST WING LAVATORY.
AND HERE IT IS.
ER...BEST TAKE THAT OUTSIDE, THEN, KRUMPUS.
HACK! HACK! SNORT!!!
I CAN'T BELIEVE YOU MADE ME HIRE HIM.

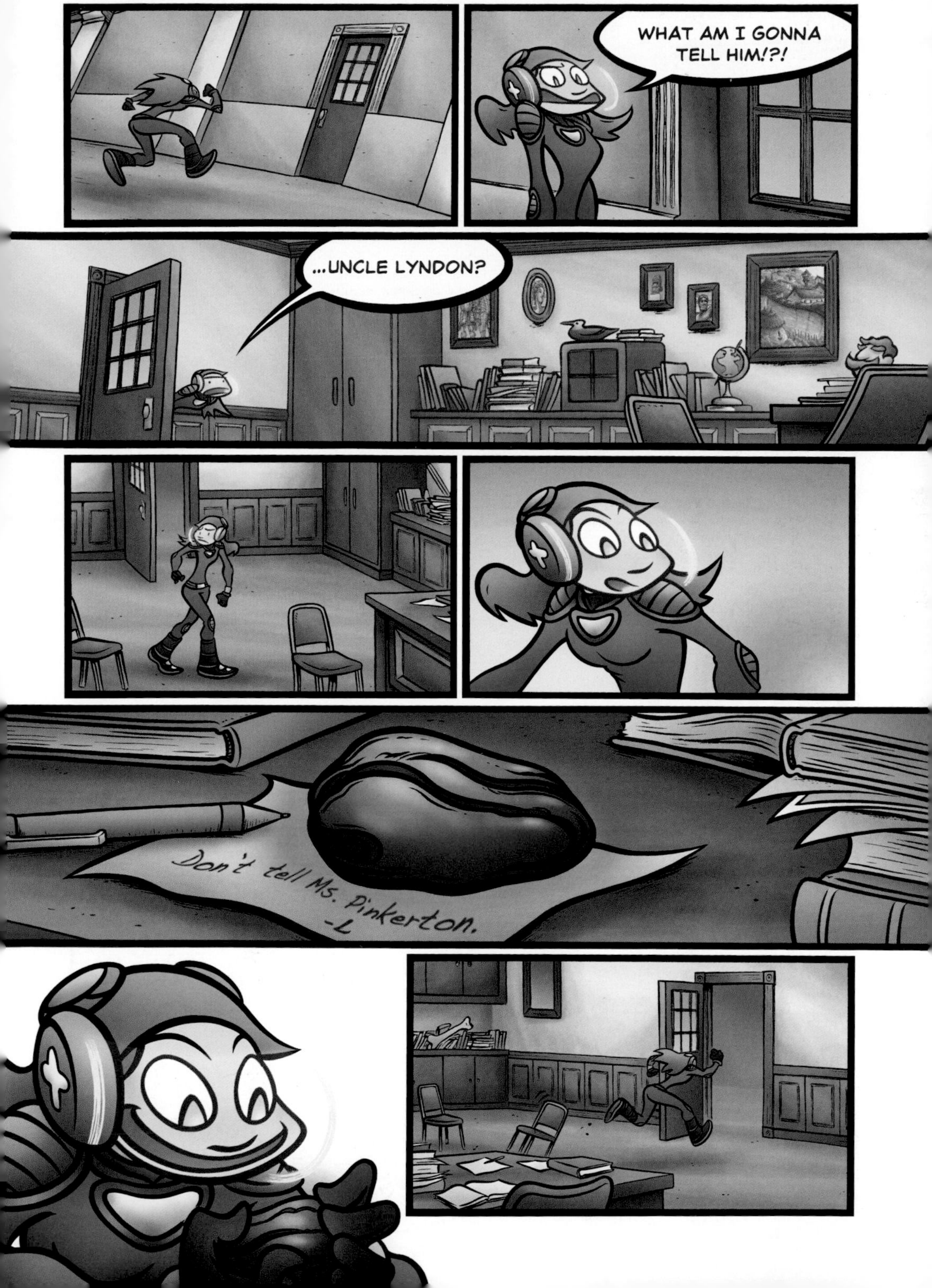
WHAT AM I GONNA TELL HIM!?!
...UNCLE LYNDON?
Don't tell Ms. Pinkerton.
-L

Panel:

OK, LET'S ALL HEAD DOWN TOGETHER NOW.

Panel:

GREGORY WILL TRY AND ASK QUESTIONS, SO I'LL DO THE TALKING.

WAIT, WHERE'S THE OTHER ME?

Panel:

YOU HAD TO TAKE CARE OF SOMETHING. DON'T WORRY ABOUT IT.

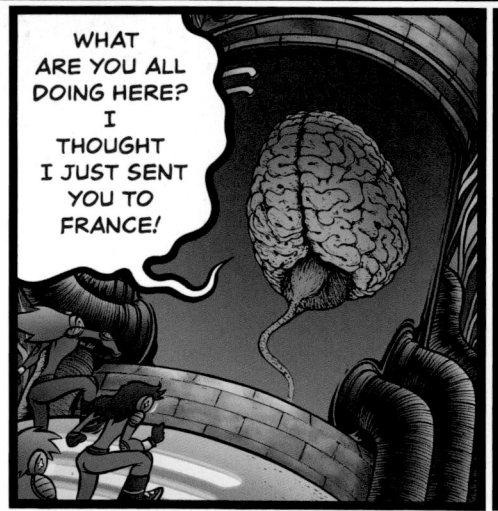

WHAT ARE YOU ALL DOING HERE? I THOUGHT I JUST SENT YOU TO FRANCE!

DOUBLES?! HANG ON, NOW, YOU GUYS ARE ENTERING SOME DANGEROUS TERRITORY HERE!

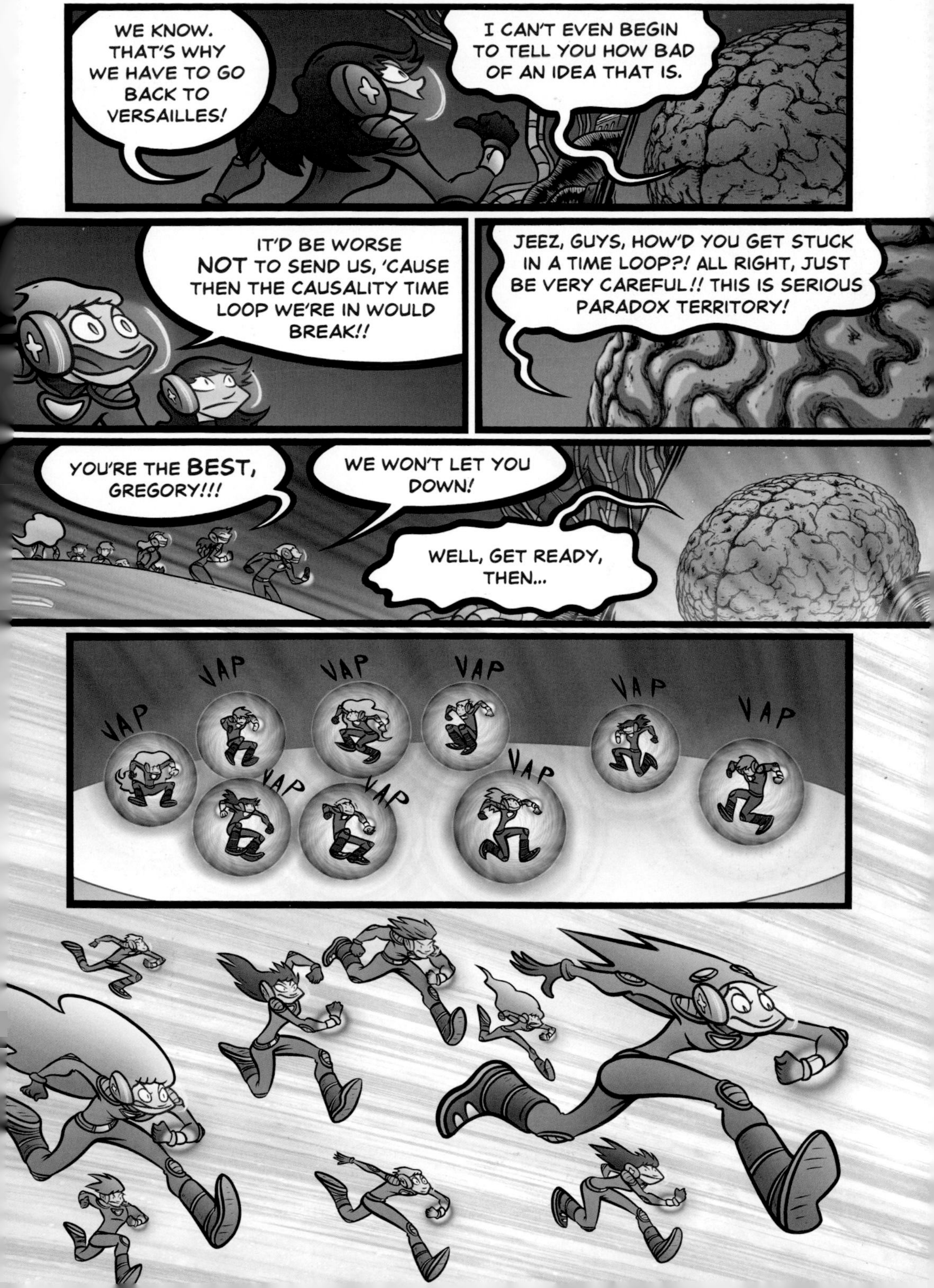
WE KNOW. THAT'S WHY WE HAVE TO GO BACK TO VERSAILLES!
I CAN'T EVEN BEGIN TO TELL YOU HOW BAD OF AN IDEA THAT IS.
IT'D BE WORSE NOT TO SEND US, 'CAUSE THEN THE CAUSALITY TIME LOOP WE'RE IN WOULD BREAK!!
JEEZ, GUYS, HOW'D YOU GET STUCK IN A TIME LOOP?! ALL RIGHT, JUST BE VERY CAREFUL!! THIS IS SERIOUS PARADOX TERRITORY!
YOU'RE THE BEST, GREGORY!!!
WE WON'T LET YOU DOWN!
WELL, GET READY, THEN...
VAP
VAP
VAP
VAP
VAP
VAP
VAP
VAP
VAP
VAP

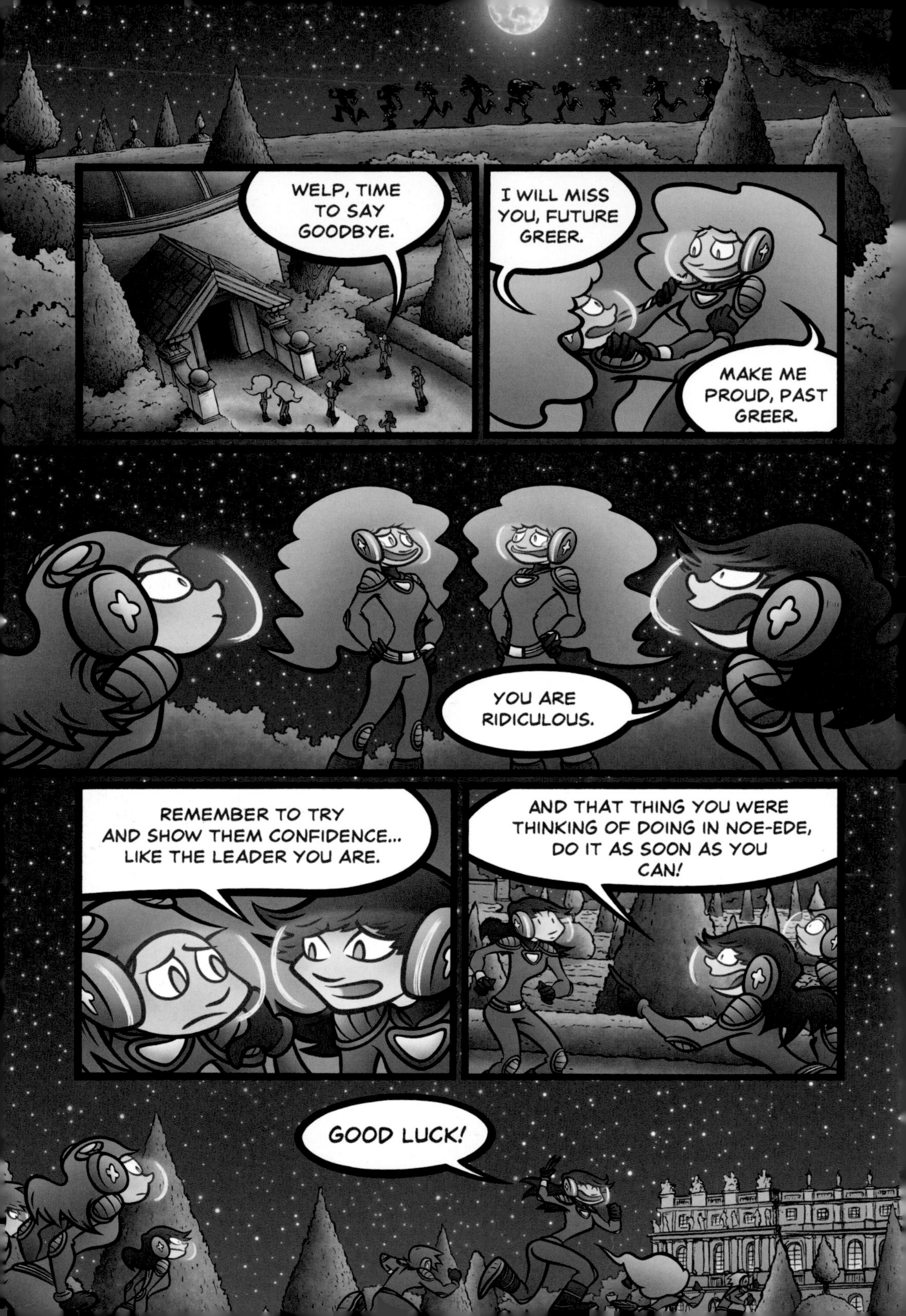
WELP, TIME TO SAY GOODBYE.
I WILL MISS YOU, FUTURE GREER.
MAKE ME PROUD, PAST GREER.
YOU ARE RIDICULOUS.
REMEMBER TO TRY AND SHOW THEM CONFIDENCE... LIKE THE LEADER YOU ARE.
AND THAT THING YOU WERE THINKING OF DOING IN NOE-EDE, DO IT AS SOON AS YOU CAN!
GOOD LUCK!

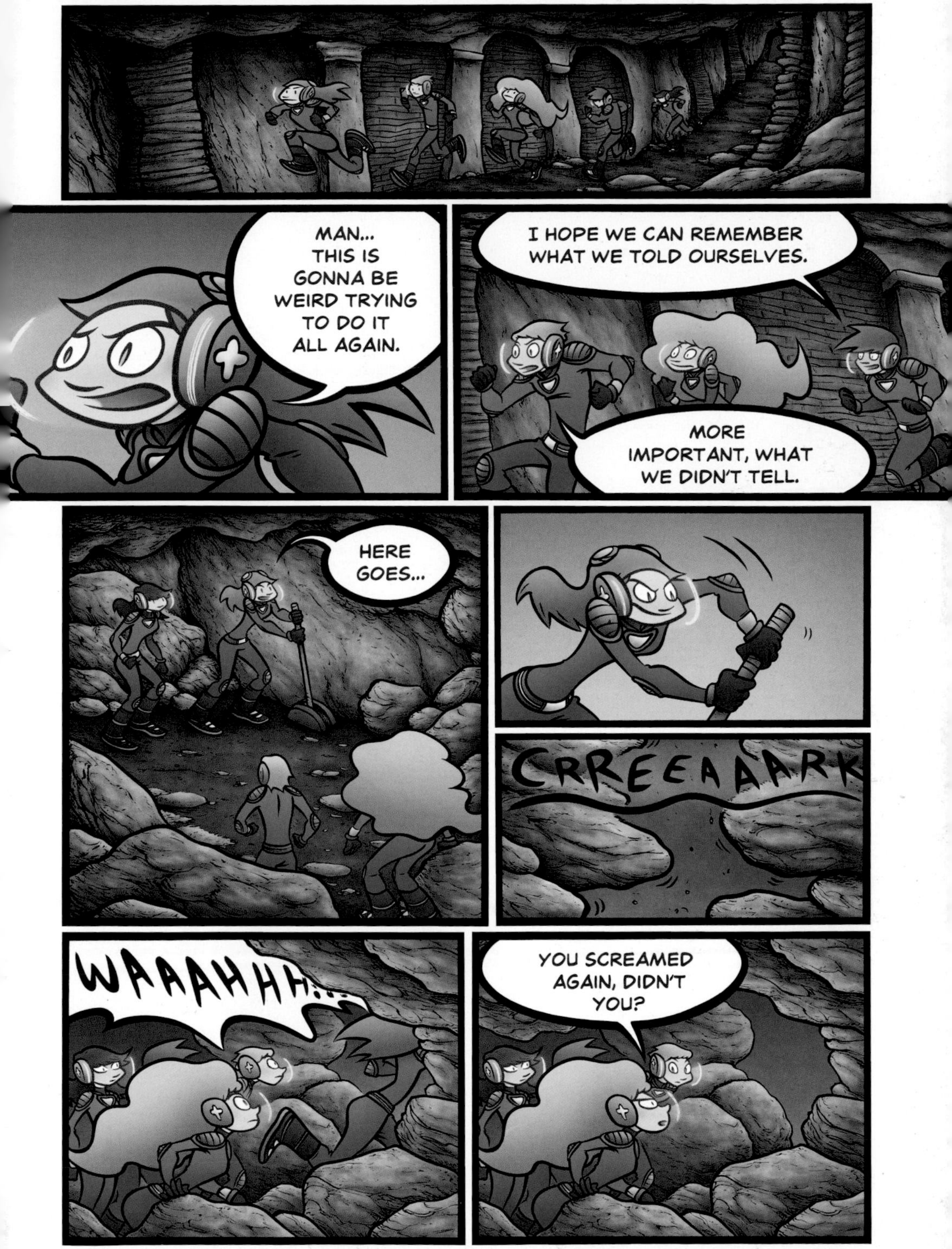
MAN... THIS IS GONNA BE WEIRD TRYING TO DO IT ALL AGAIN.
I HOPE WE CAN REMEMBER WHAT WE TOLD OURSELVES.
MORE IMPORTANT, WHAT WE DIDN'T TELL.
HERE GOES...
CRREEAAARK
WAAAHHH!...
YOU SCREAMED AGAIN, DIDN'T YOU?

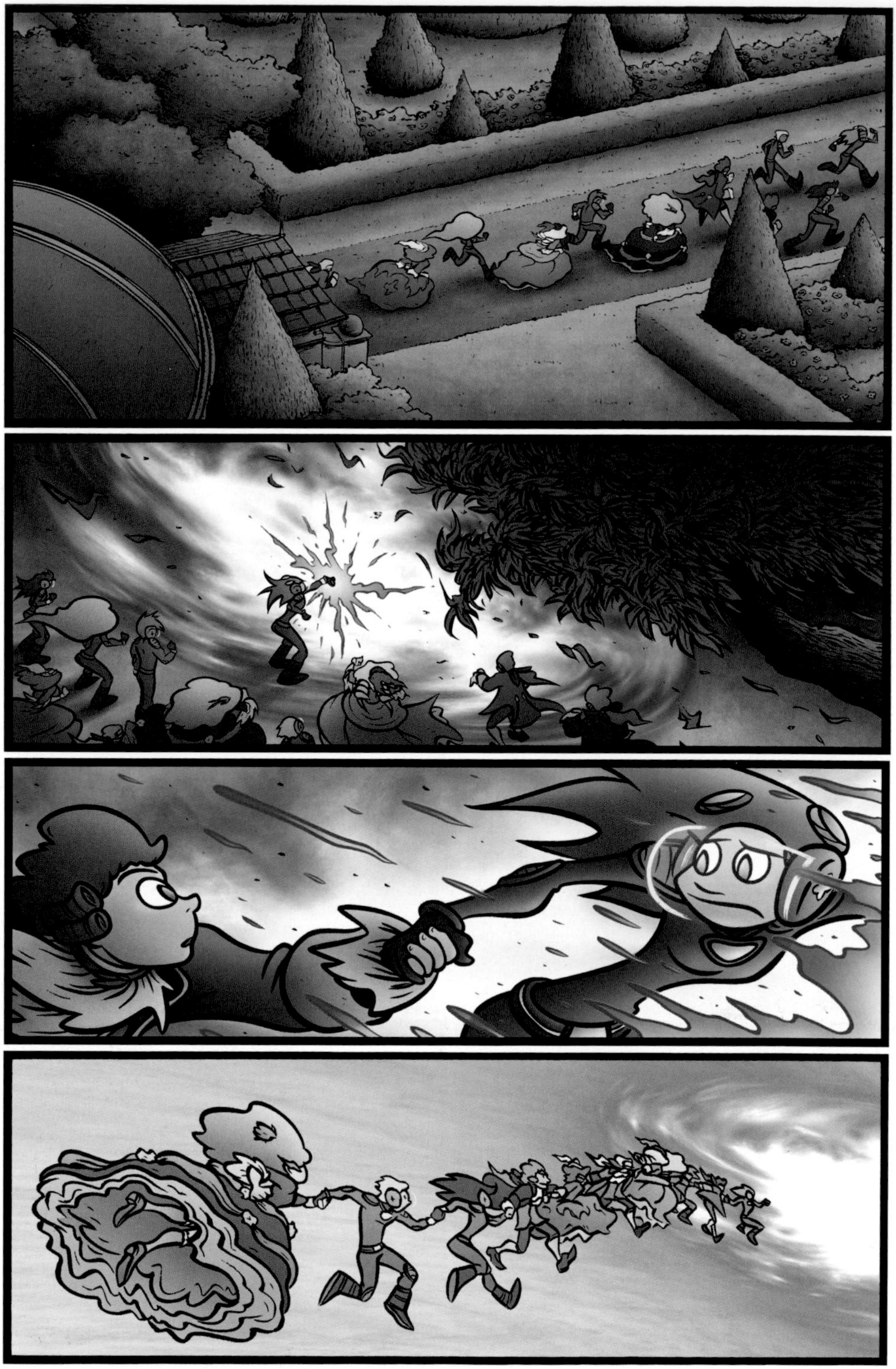

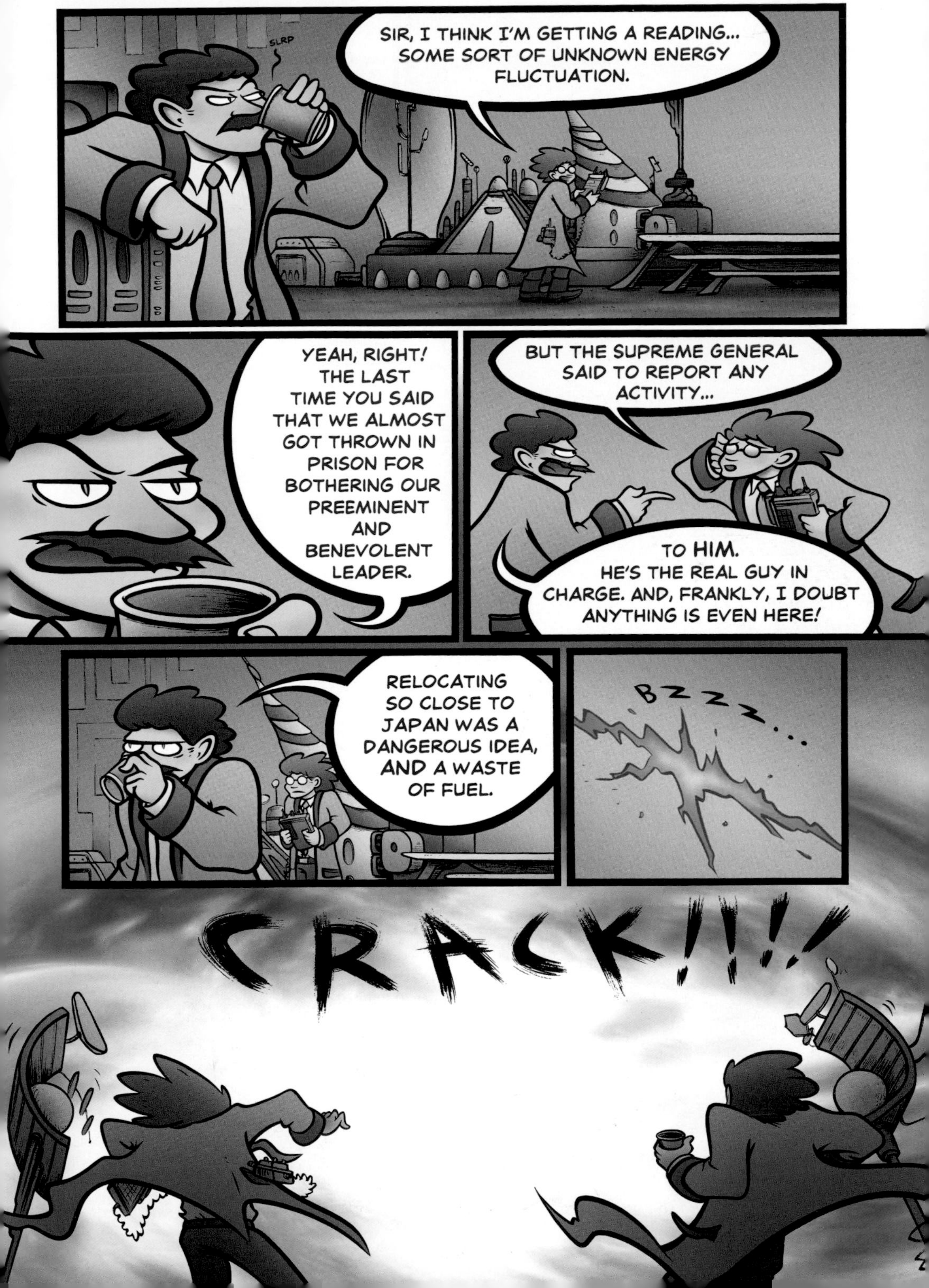
SLRP
SIR, I THINK I'M GETTING A READING... SOME SORT OF UNKNOWN ENERGY FLUCTUATION.
YEAH, RIGHT! THE LAST TIME YOU SAID THAT WE ALMOST GOT THROWN IN PRISON FOR BOTHERING OUR PREEMINENT AND BENEVOLENT LEADER.
BUT THE SUPREME GENERAL SAID TO REPORT ANY ACTIVITY...
TO HIM. HE'S THE REAL GUY IN CHARGE. AND, FRANKLY, I DOUBT ANYTHING IS EVEN HERE!
RELOCATING SO CLOSE TO JAPAN WAS A DANGEROUS IDEA, AND A WASTE OF FUEL.
BZZZ...
CRACK!!!!

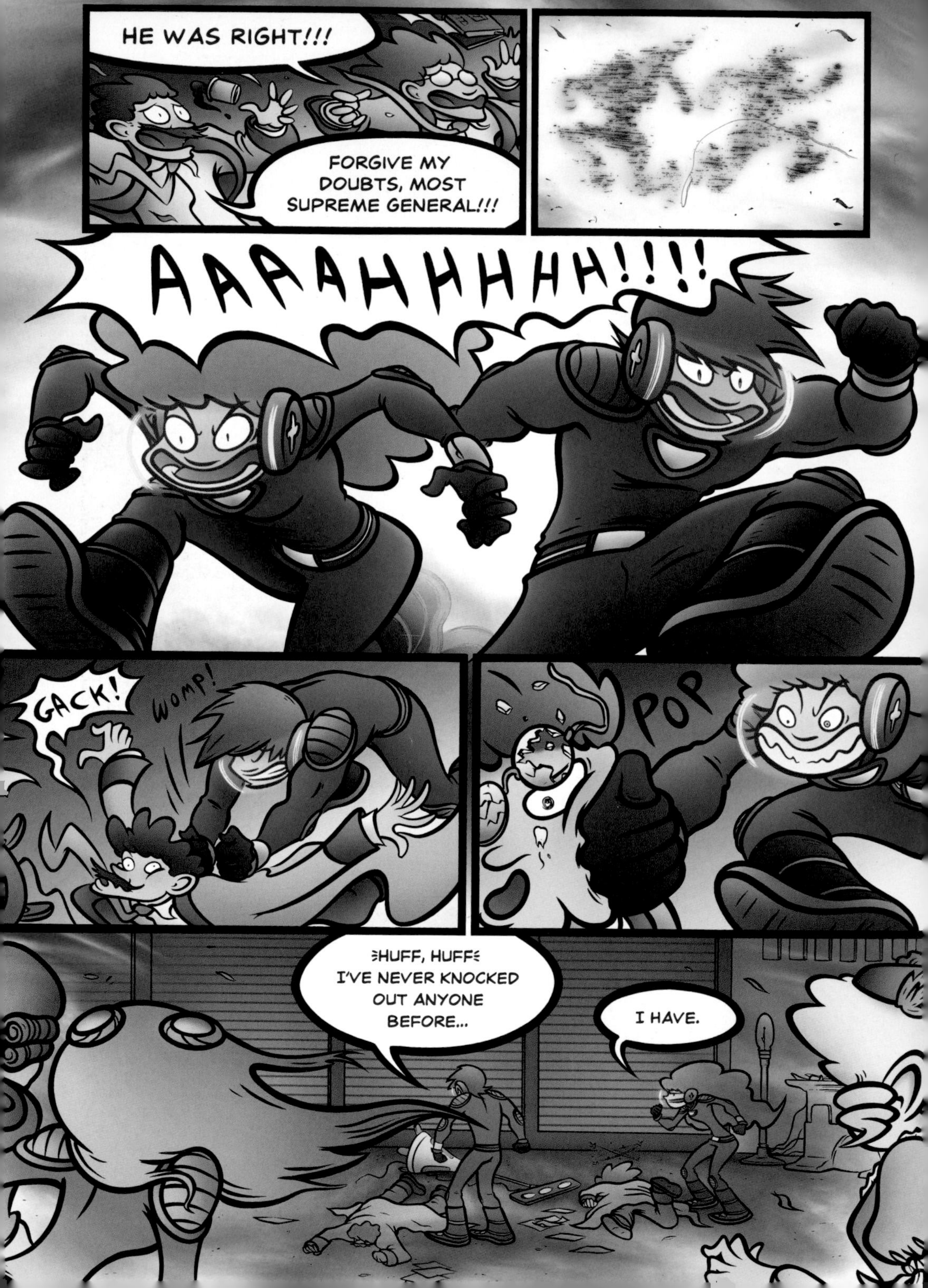

HE WAS RIGHT!!!
FORGIVE MY DOUBTS, MOST SUPREME GENERAL!!!
AAAAHHHHH!!!!
GACK!
WOMP!
POP
HUFF, HUFF
I'VE NEVER KNOCKED OUT ANYONE BEFORE...
I HAVE.

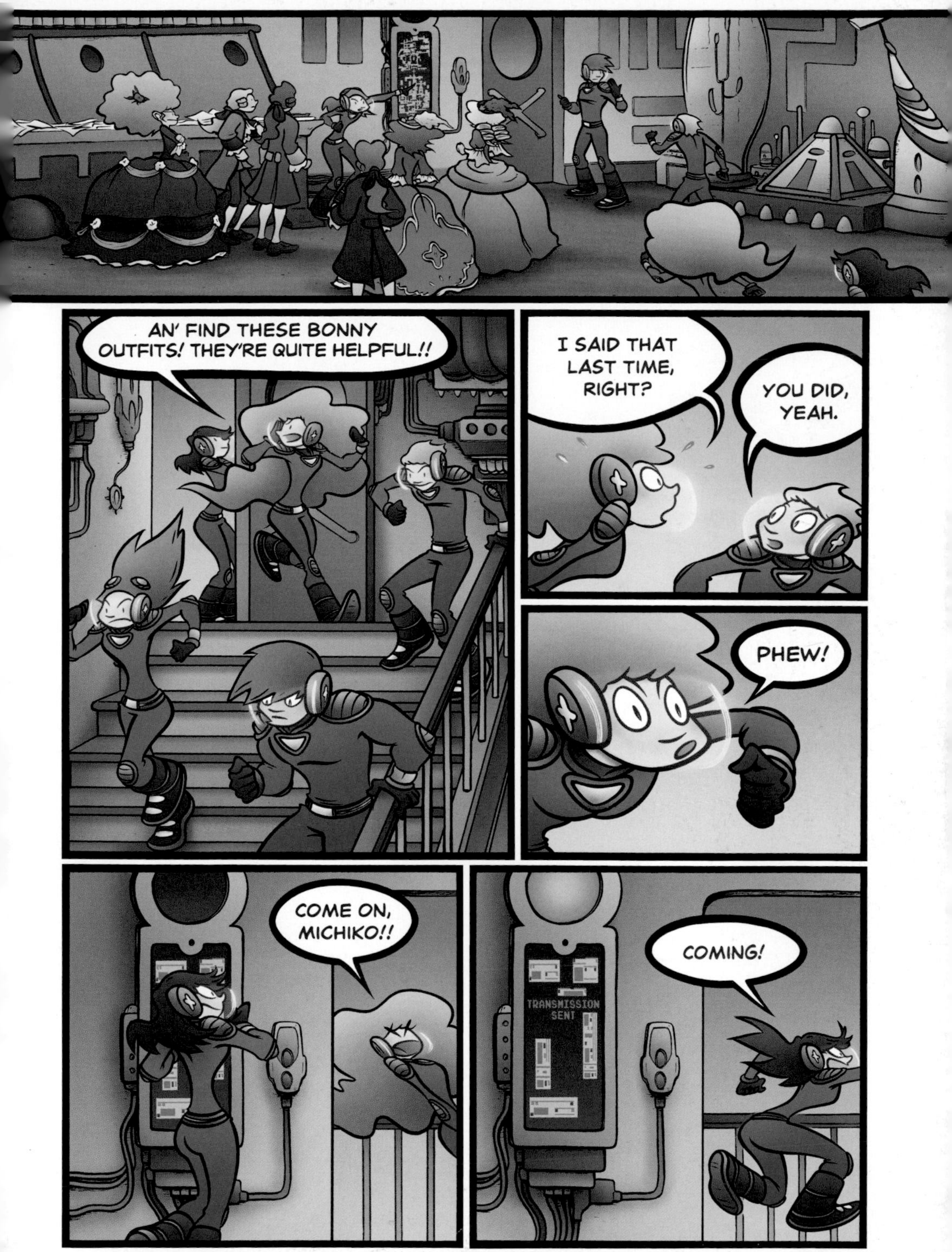
AN' FIND THESE BONNY OUTFITS! THEY'RE QUITE HELPFUL!!
I SAID THAT LAST TIME, RIGHT?
YOU DID, YEAH.
PHEW!
COME ON, MICHIKO!!
TRANSMISSION SENT
COMING!

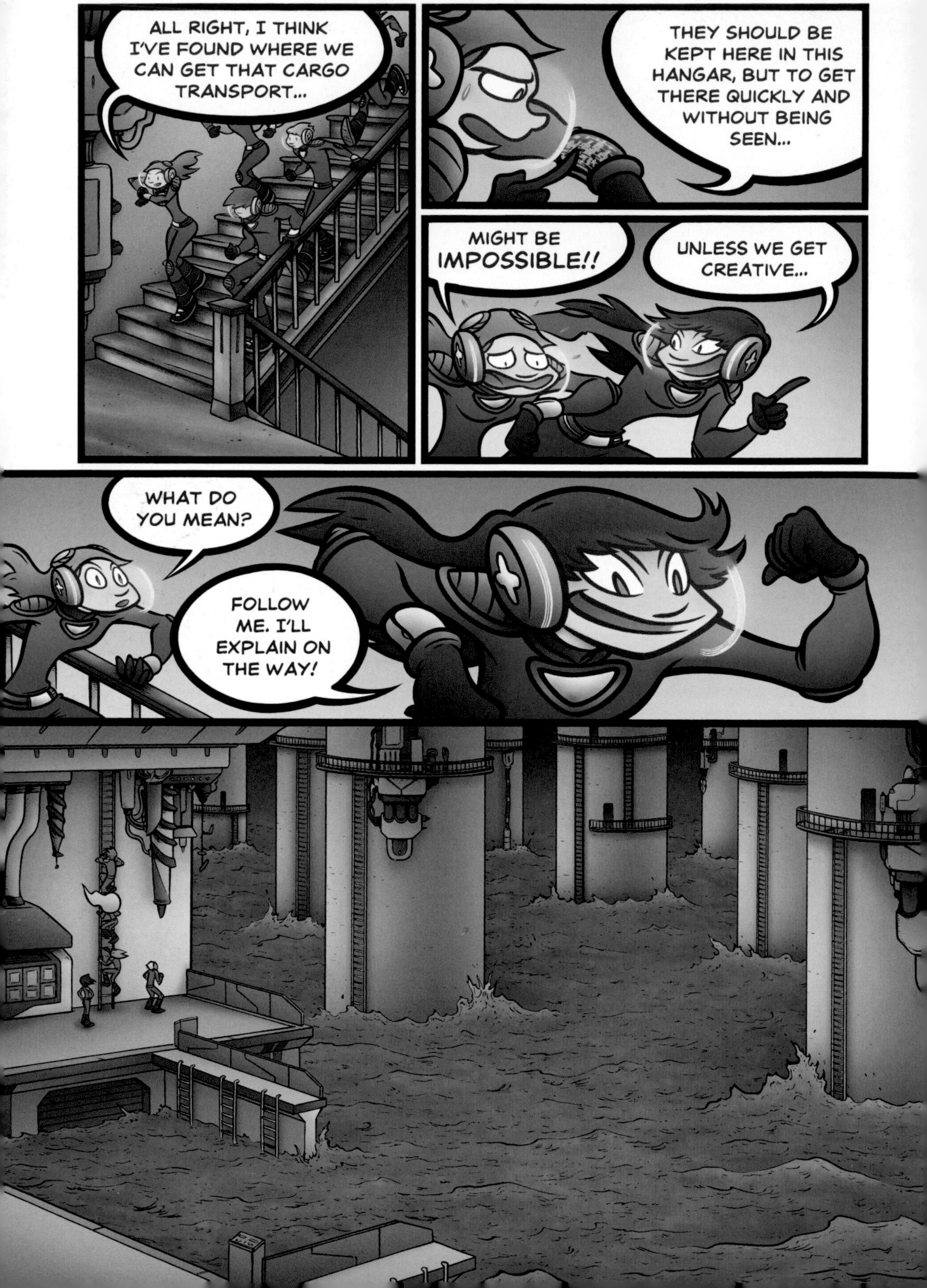
ALL RIGHT, I THINK I'VE FOUND WHERE WE CAN GET THAT CARGO TRANSPORT...
THEY SHOULD BE KEPT HERE IN THIS HANGAR, BUT TO GET THERE QUICKLY AND WITHOUT BEING SEEN...
MIGHT BE IMPOSSIBLE!!
UNLESS WE GET CREATIVE...
WHAT DO YOU MEAN?
FOLLOW ME. I'LL EXPLAIN ON THE WAY!

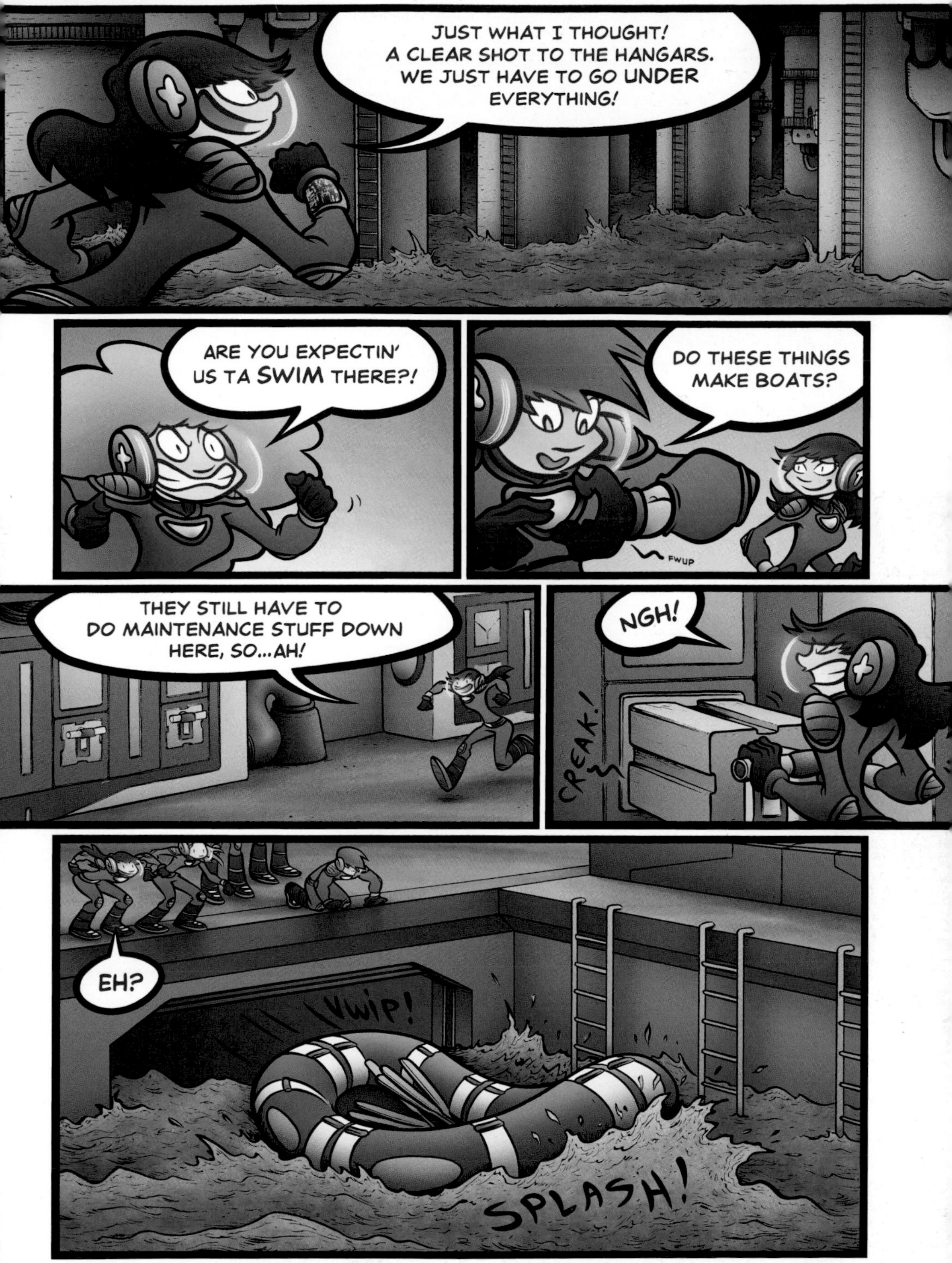

JUST WHAT I THOUGHT! A CLEAR SHOT TO THE HANGARS. WE JUST HAVE TO GO UNDER EVERYTHING!
ARE YOU EXPECTIN' US TA SWIM THERE?!
DO THESE THINGS MAKE BOATS?
FWUP
THEY STILL HAVE TO DO MAINTENANCE STUFF DOWN HERE, SO...AH!
NGH!
CREAK!
EH?
VWIP!
SPLASH!

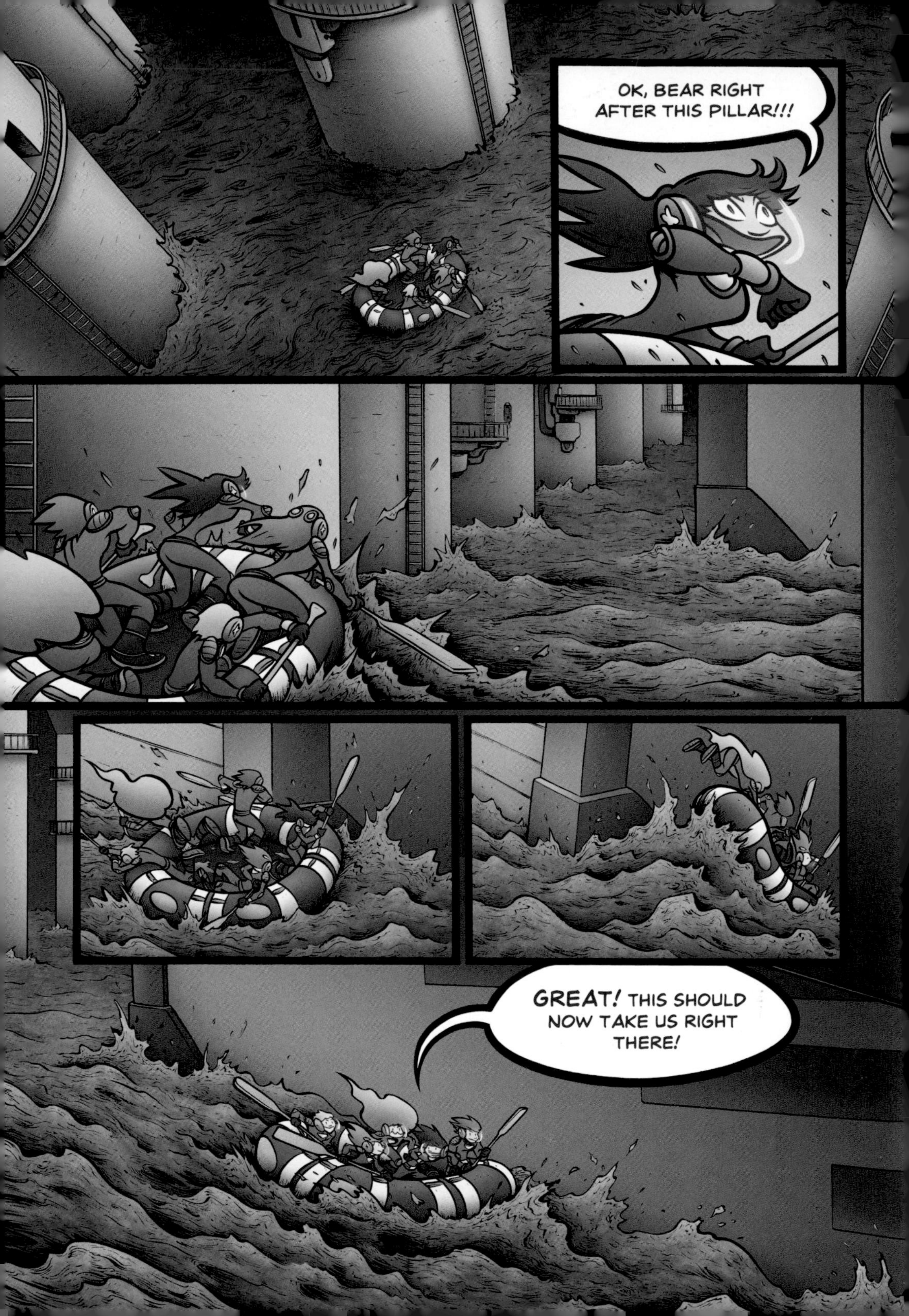
OK, BEAR RIGHT AFTER THIS PILLAR!!!
GREAT! THIS SHOULD NOW TAKE US RIGHT THERE!

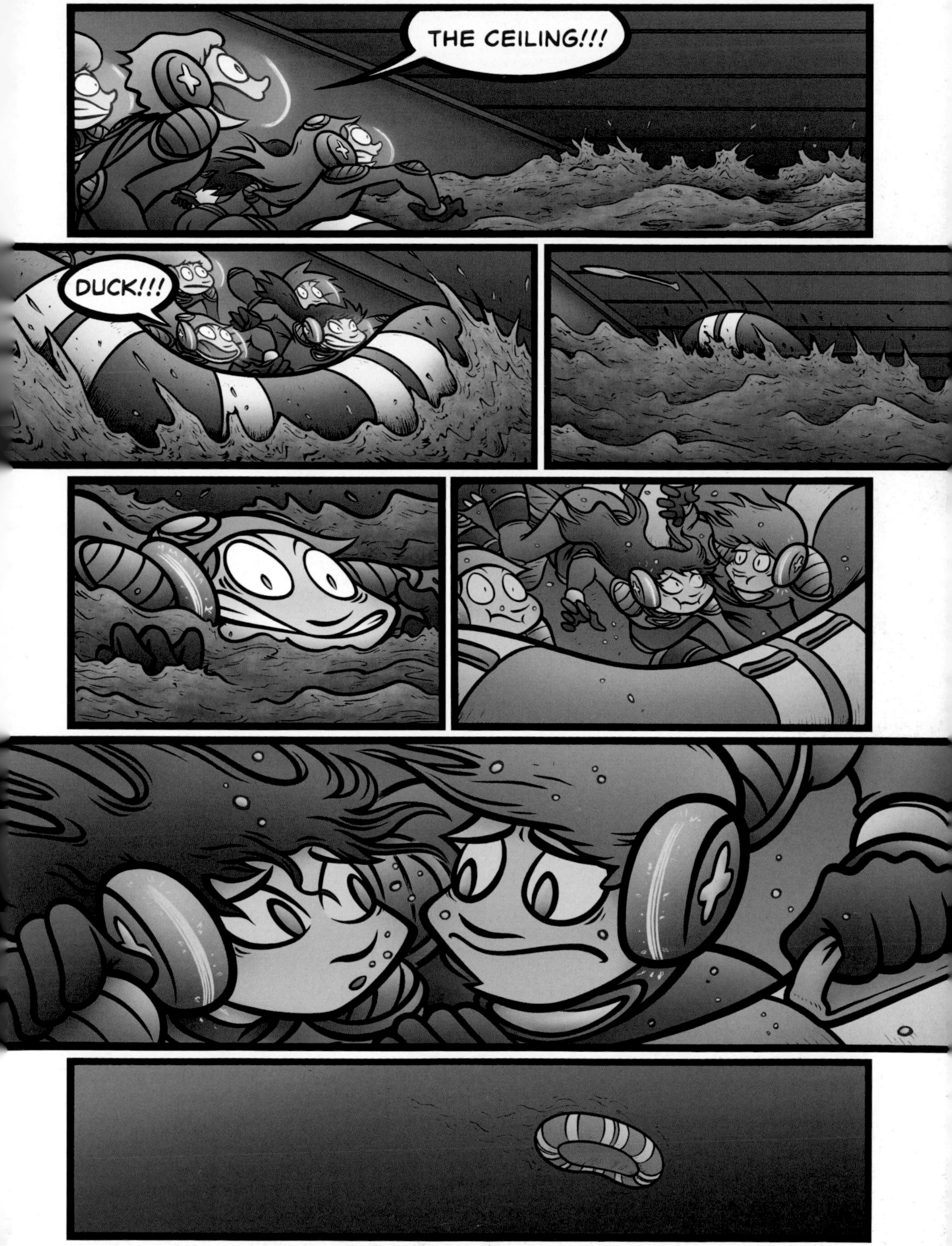
THE CEILING!!!
DUCK!!!

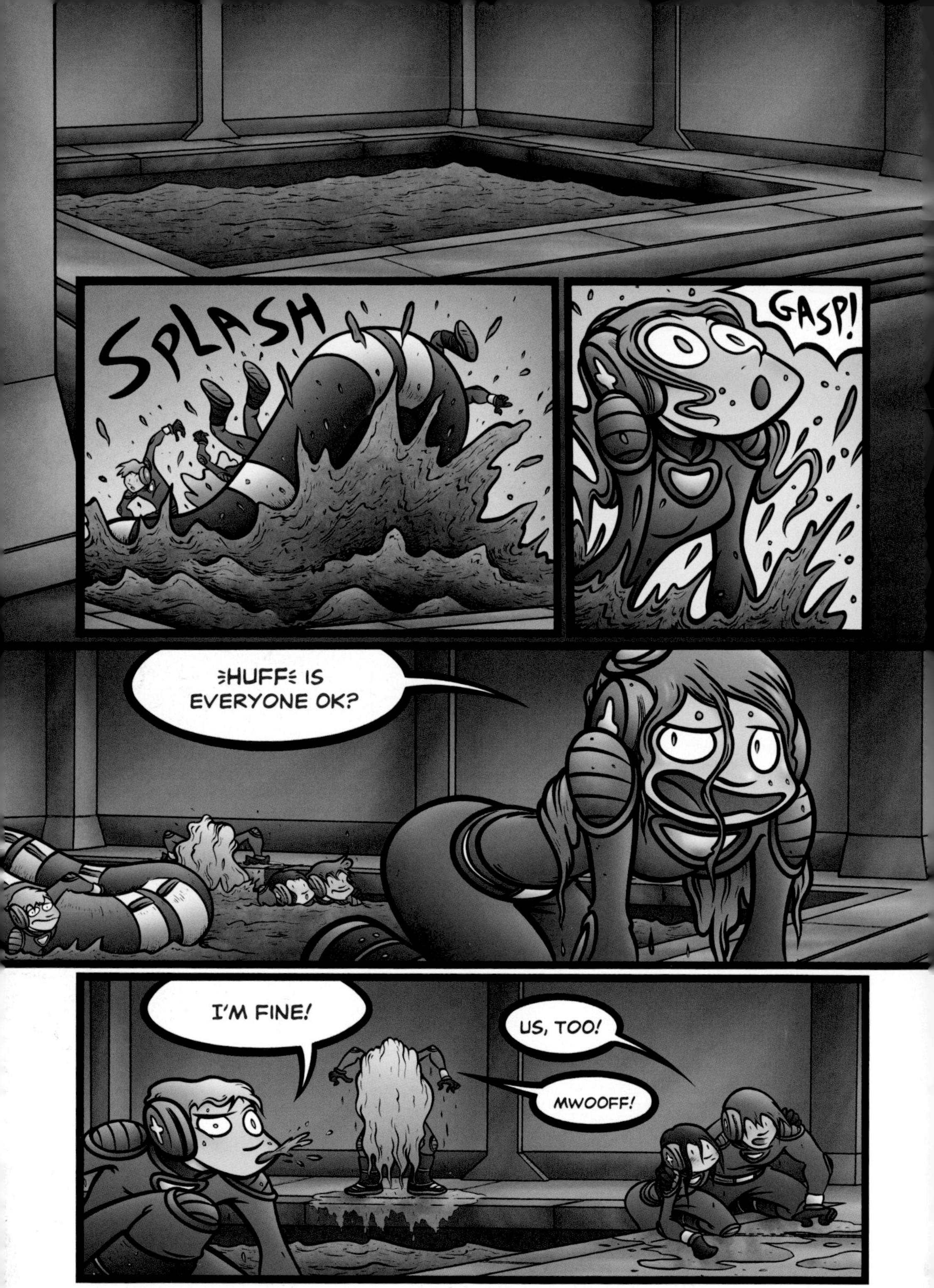
SPLASH
GASP!
HUFF IS EVERYONE OK?
I'M FINE!
US, TOO!
MWOOFF!

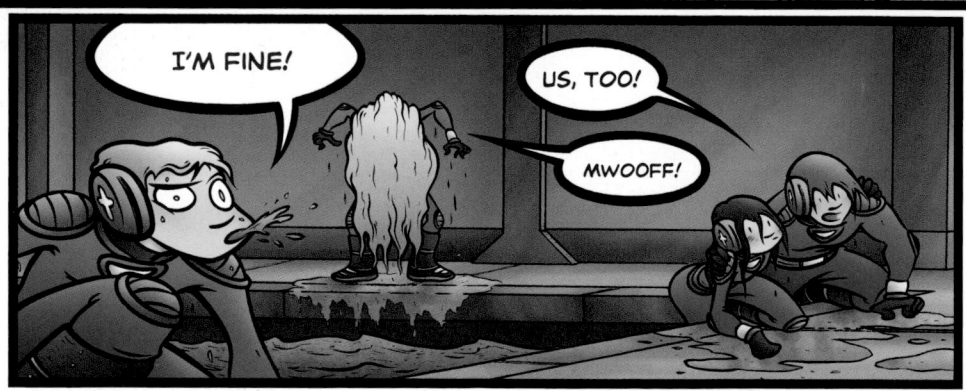

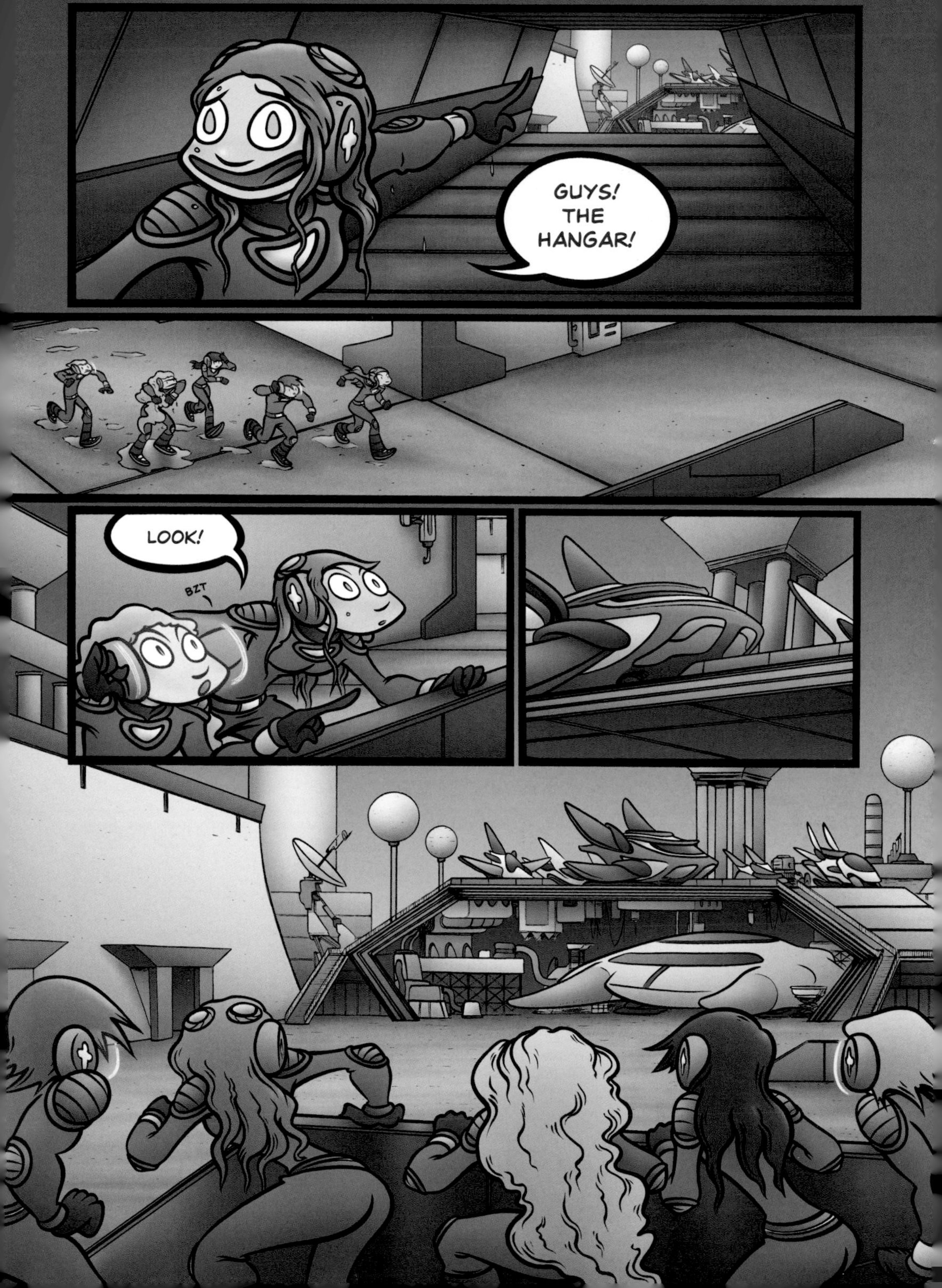
GUYS! THE HANGAR!
LOOK!
BZT

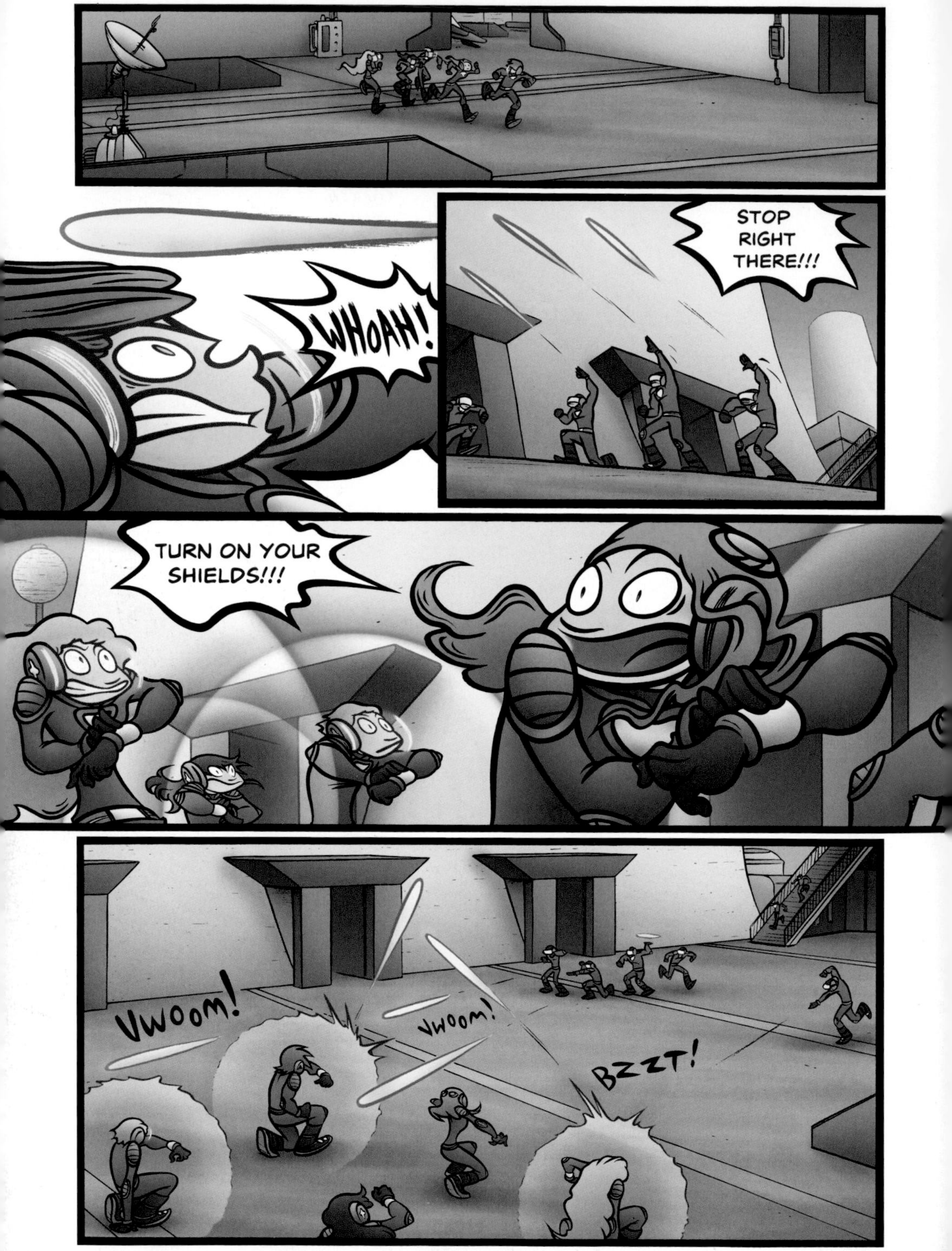

WHOAH!
STOP RIGHT THERE!!!
TURN ON YOUR SHIELDS!!!
VWOOM!
VWOOM!
BZZT!

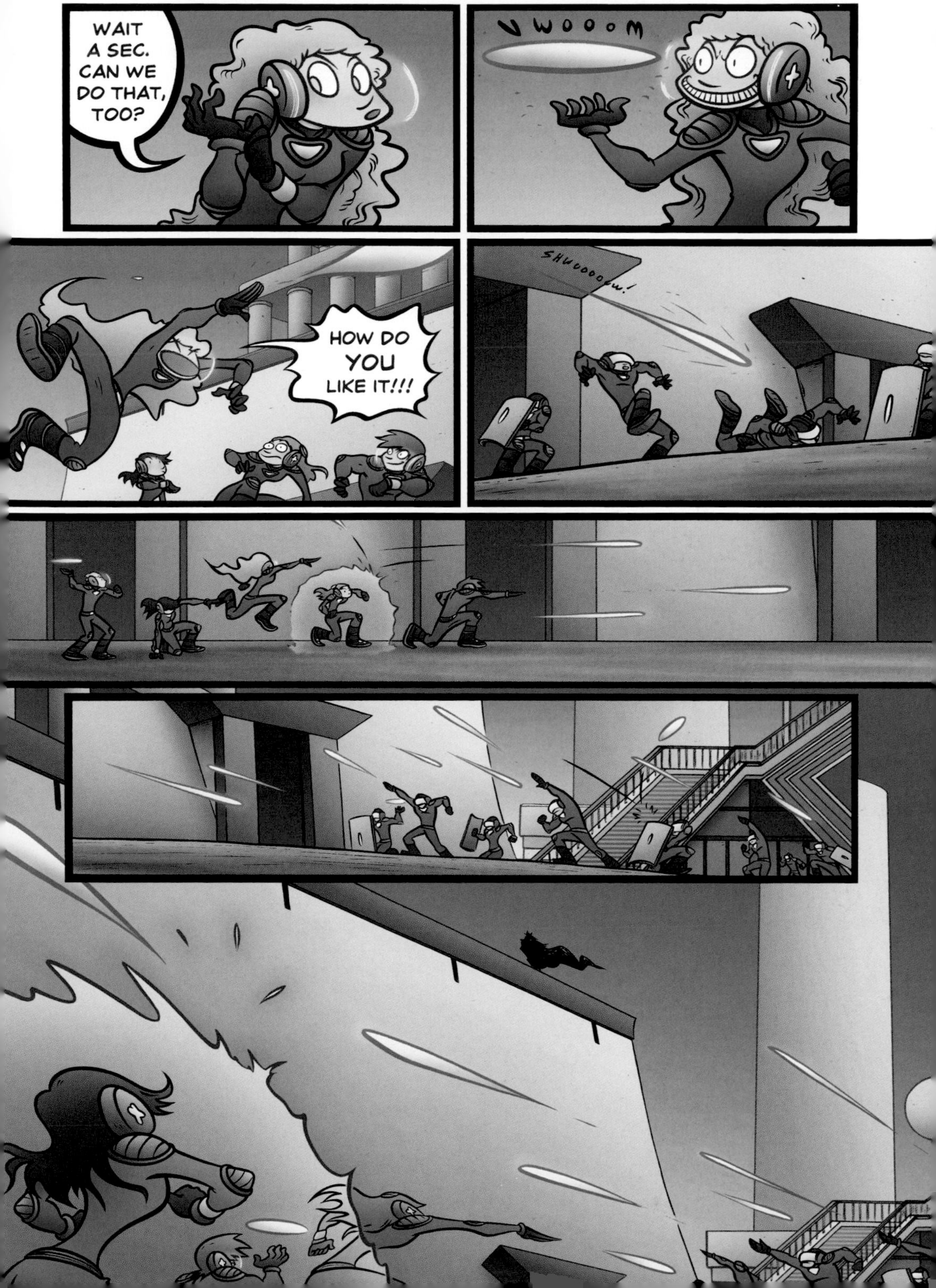
WAIT A SEC. CAN WE DO THAT, TOO?
VWOOOM
HOW DO YOU LIKE IT!!!
SHWOOOOOW!

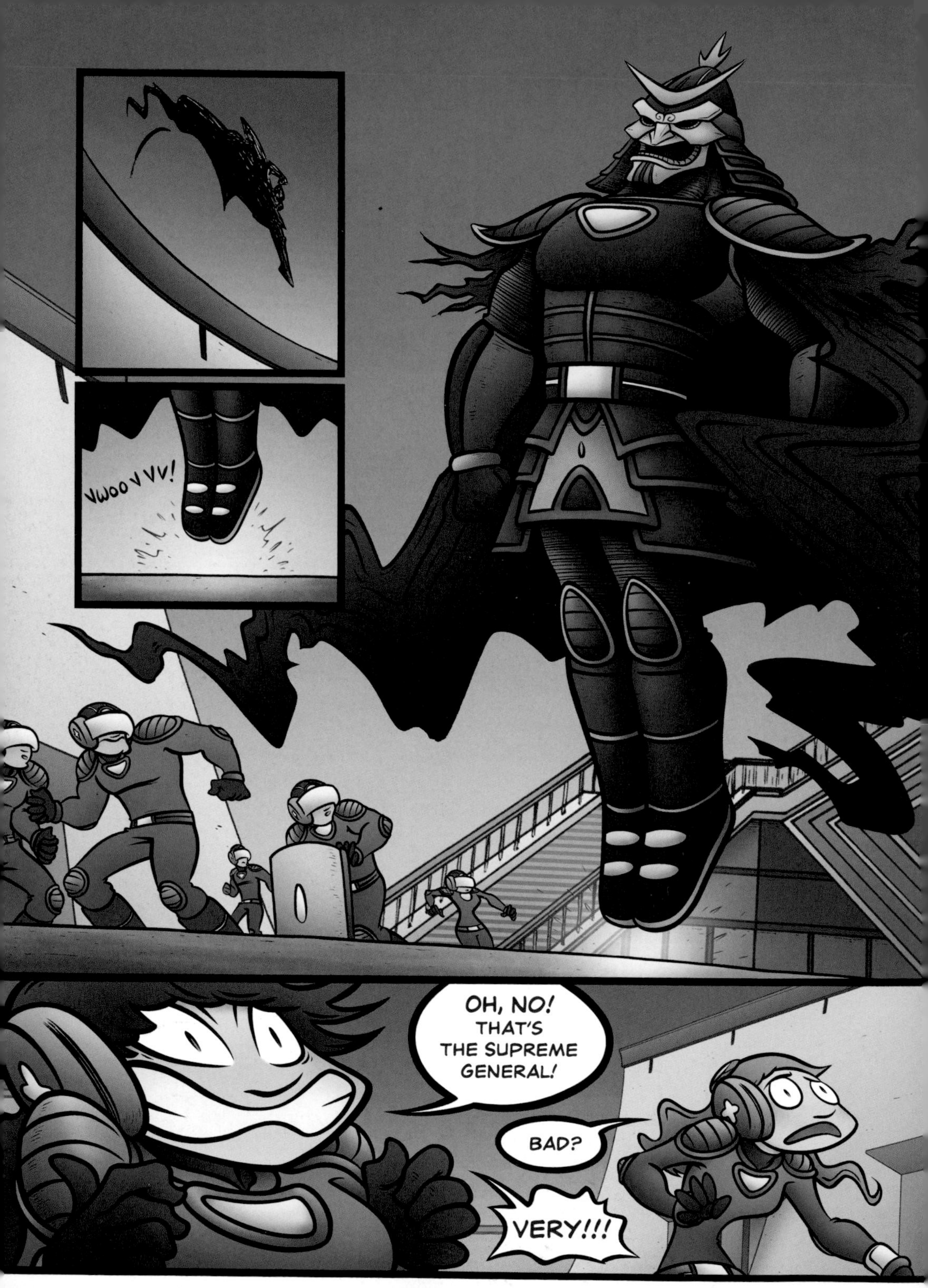
VWOOVVV!
OH, NO! THAT'S THE SUPREME GENERAL!
BAD?
VERY!!!

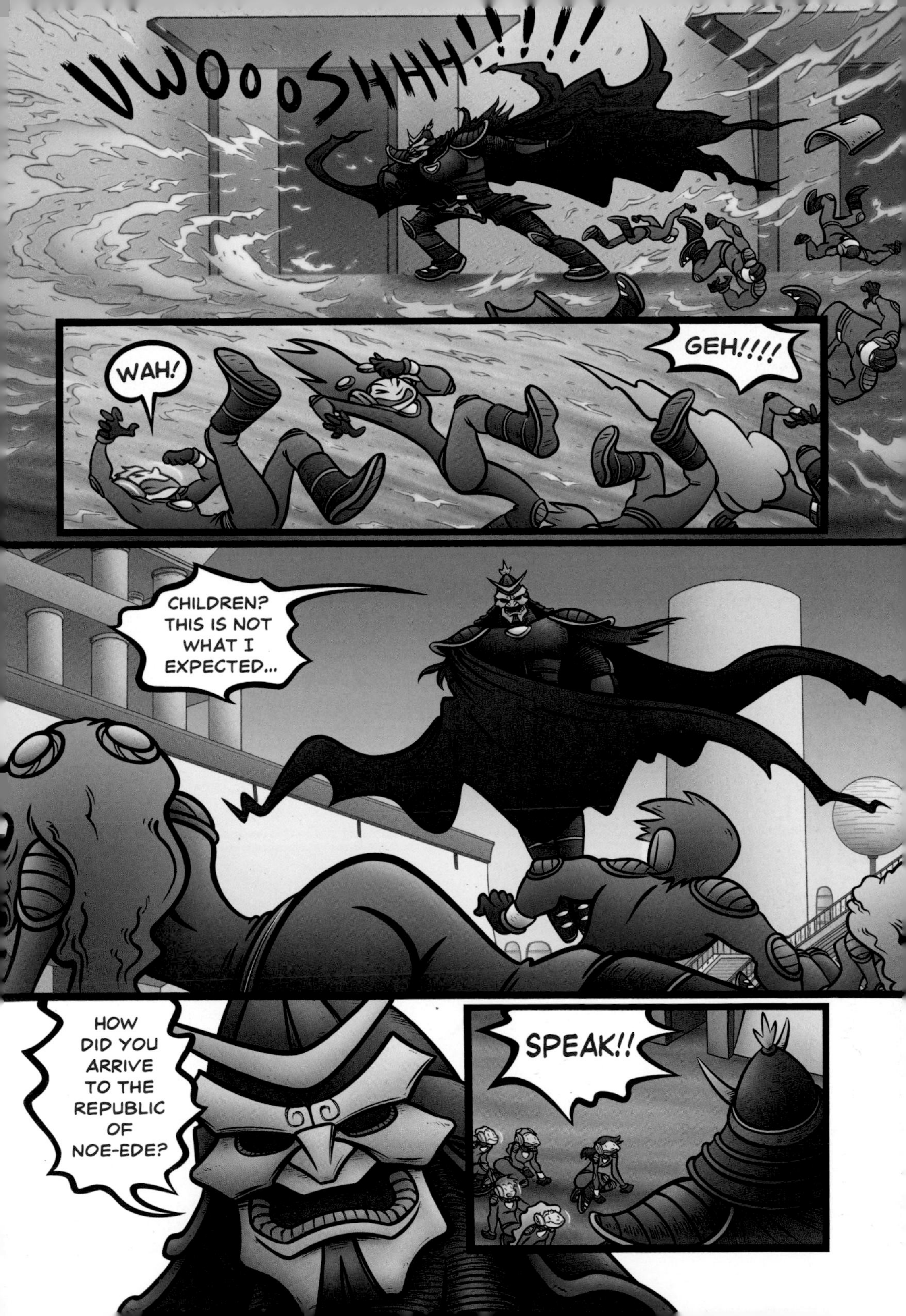
VWOOOSHHH!!!!!
WAH!
GEH!!!!
CHILDREN? THIS IS NOT WHAT I EXPECTED...
HOW DID YOU ARRIVE TO THE REPUBLIC OF NOE-EDE?
SPEAK!!

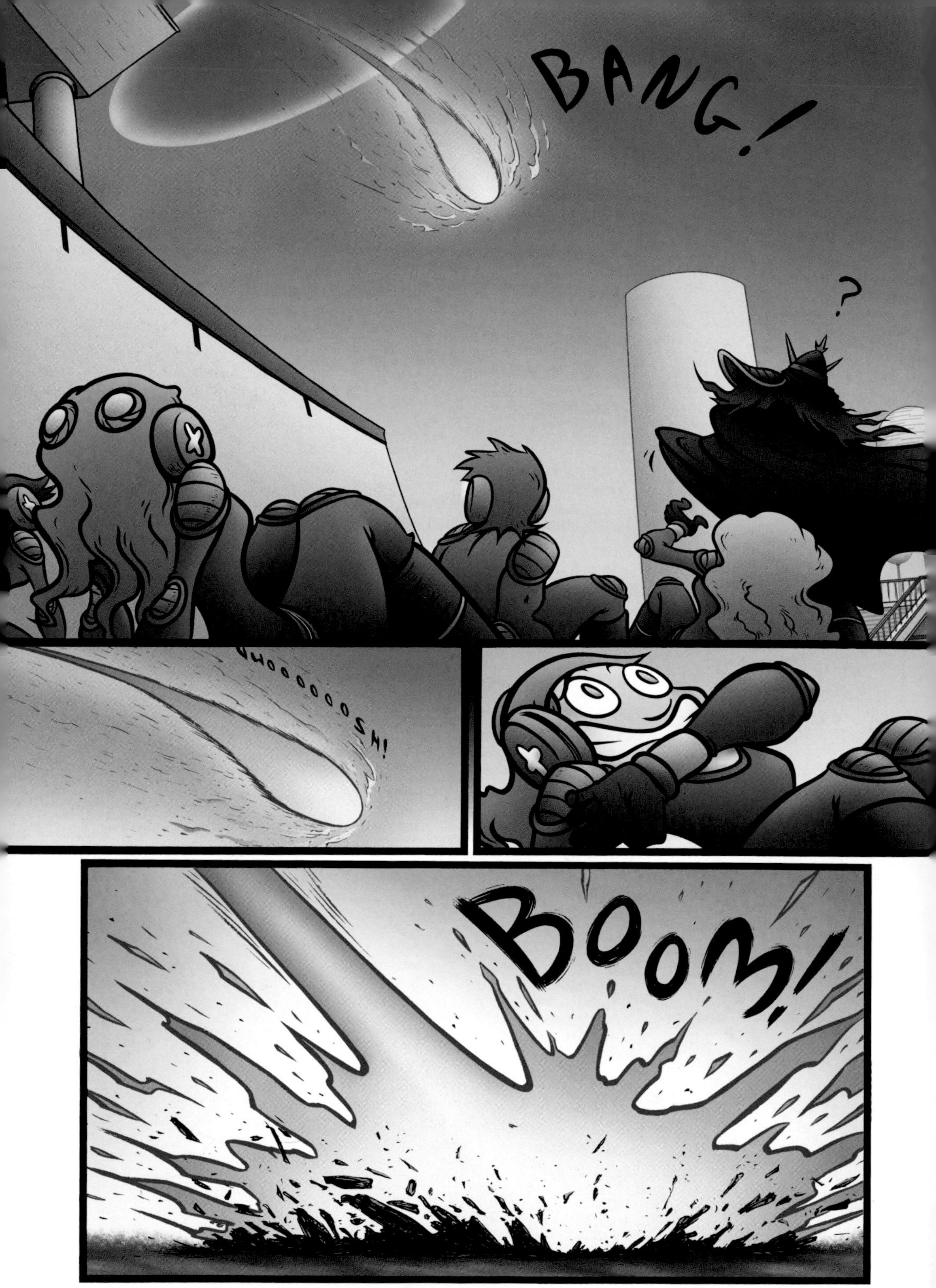
BANG!
?
WHOOOOOOOOOSH!
BOOM!

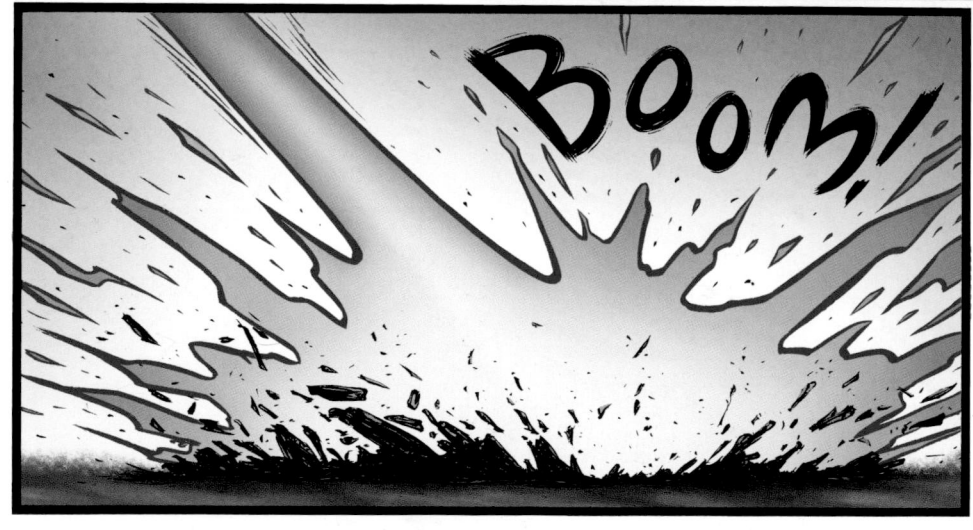

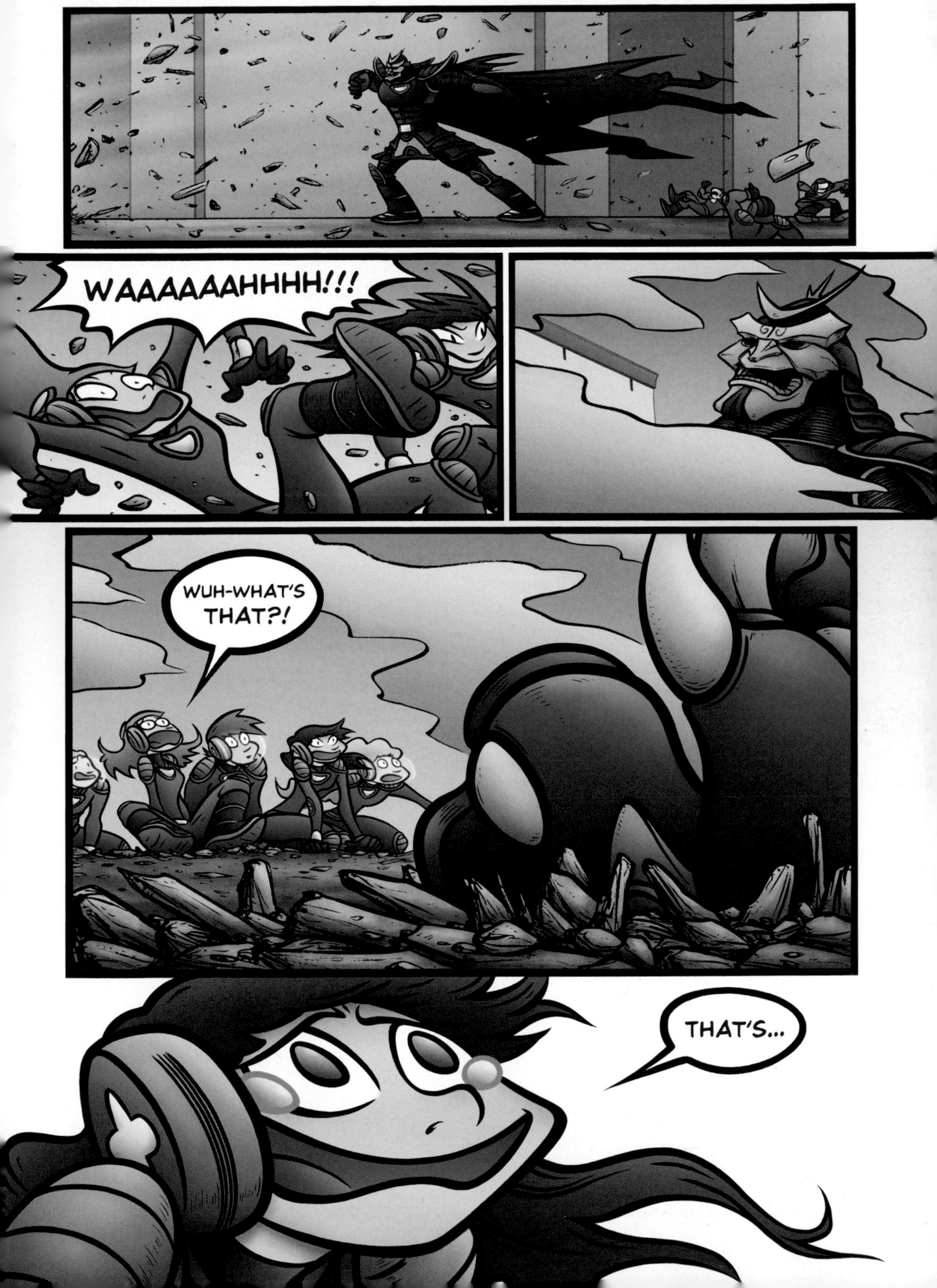
WAAAAAAHHHH!!!
WUH-WHAT'S THAT?!
THAT'S...

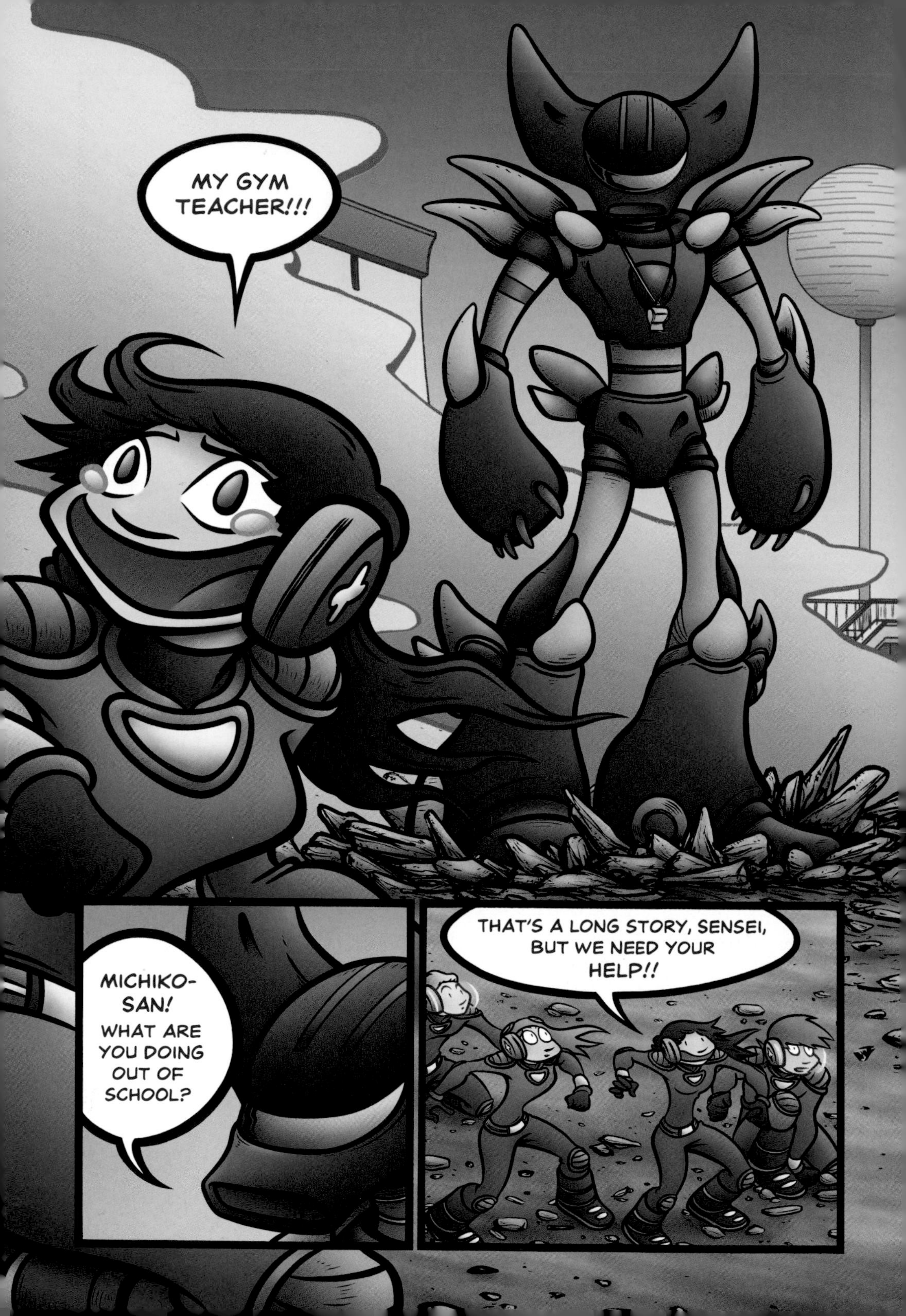
MY GYM TEACHER!!!
MICHIKO-SAN! WHAT ARE YOU DOING OUT OF SCHOOL?
THAT'S A LONG STORY, SENSEI, BUT WE NEED YOUR HELP!!

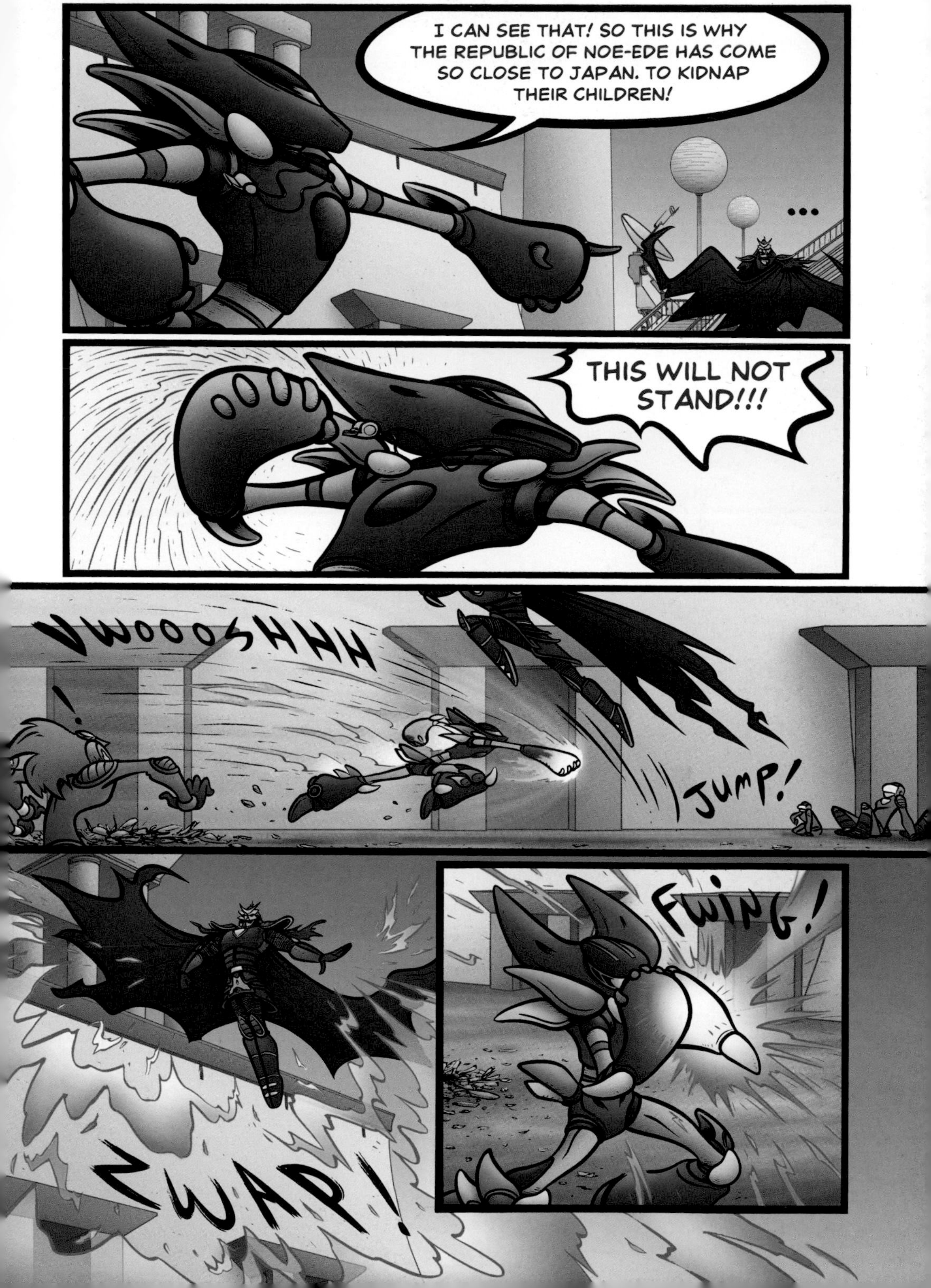
I CAN SEE THAT! SO THIS IS WHY THE REPUBLIC OF NOE-EDE HAS COME SO CLOSE TO JAPAN. TO KIDNAP THEIR CHILDREN!
...
THIS WILL NOT STAND!!!
VWOOOSHHH
!
JUMP!
ZWAP!
FWING!

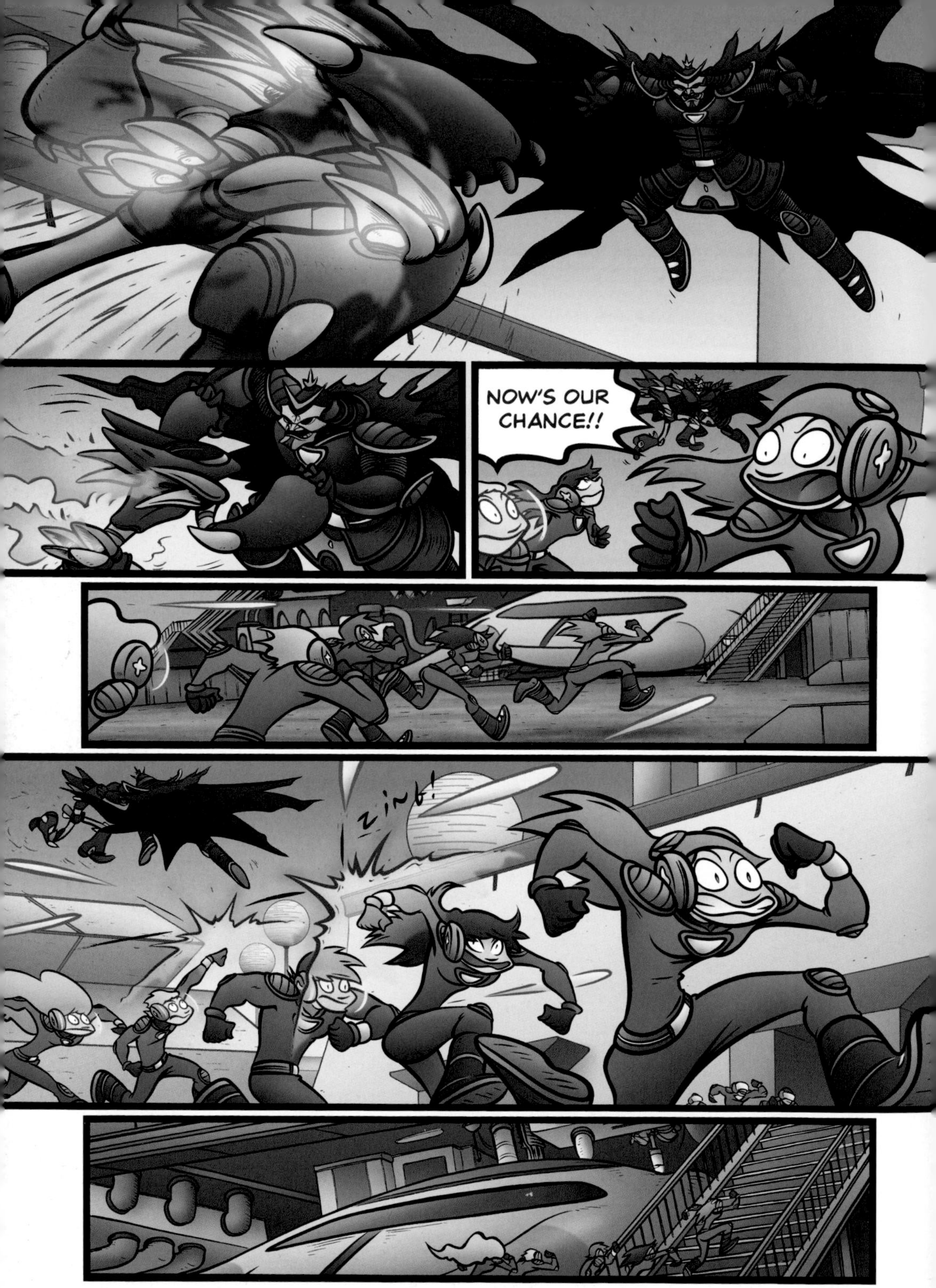
NOW'S OUR CHANCE!!
zink!

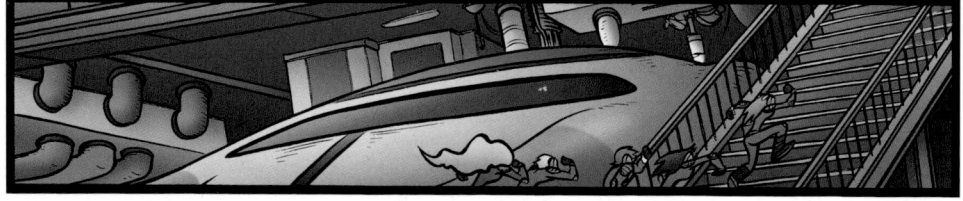

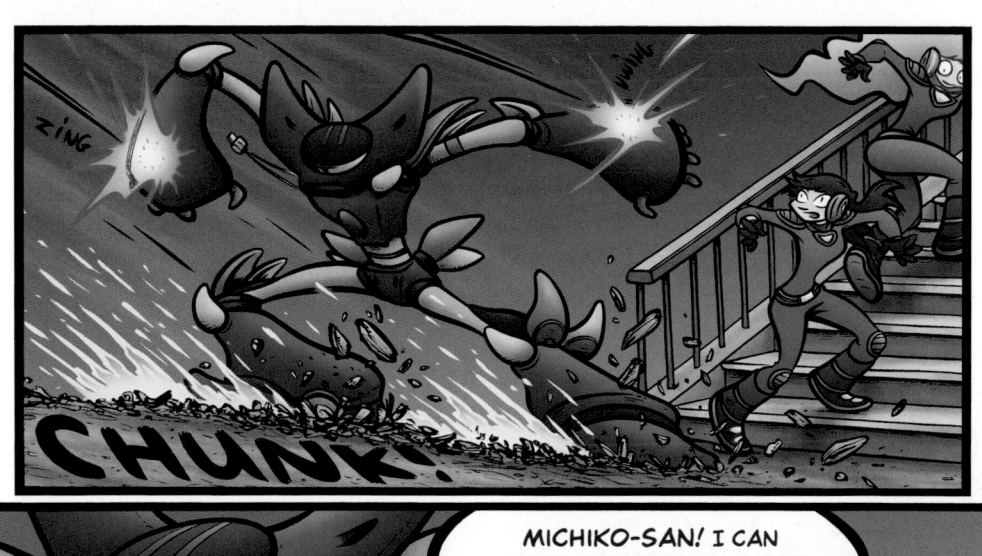

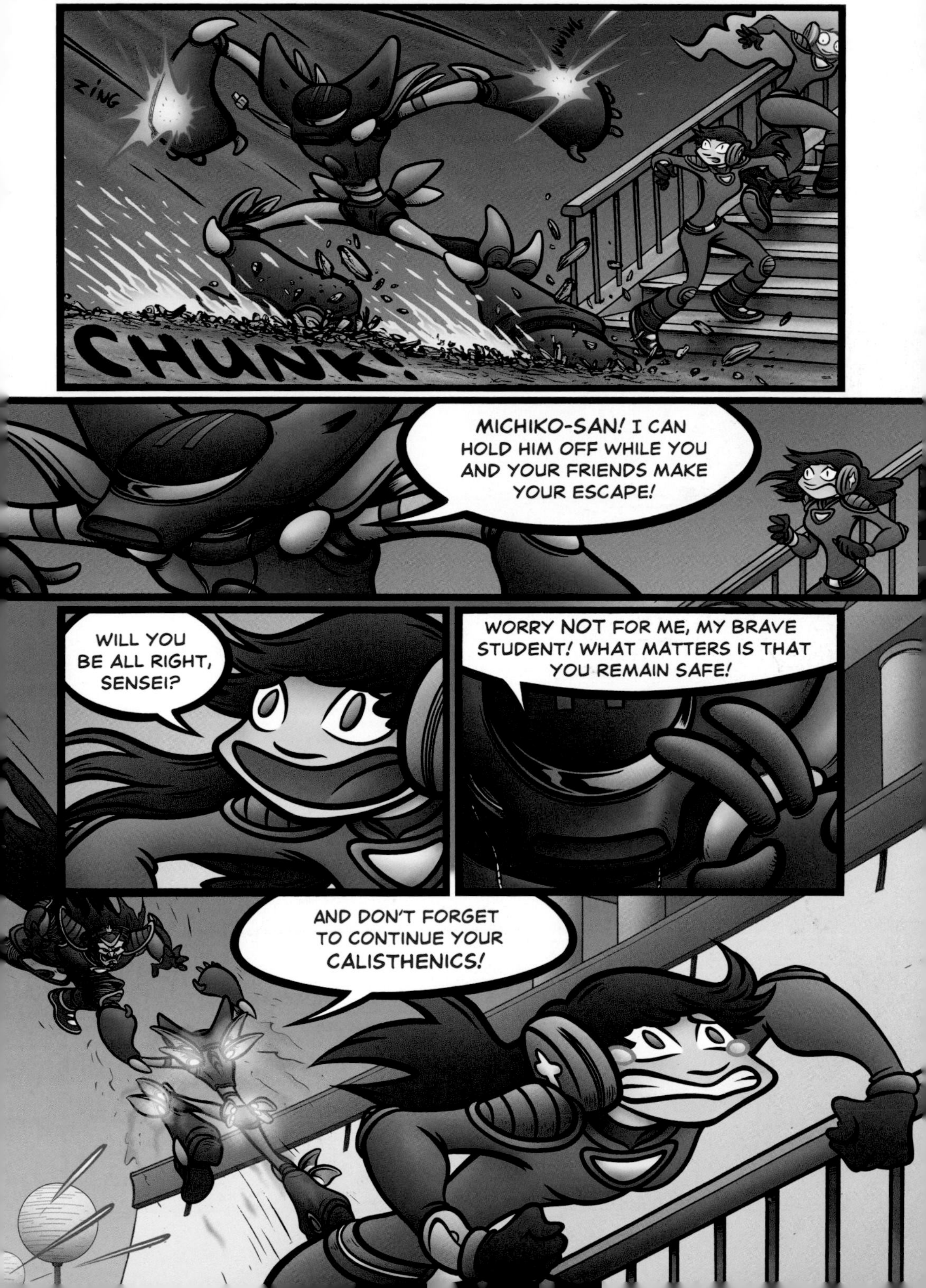
ZING
CHUNK!
MICHIKO-SAN! I CAN HOLD HIM OFF WHILE YOU AND YOUR FRIENDS MAKE YOUR ESCAPE!
WILL YOU BE ALL RIGHT, SENSEI?
WORRY NOT FOR ME, MY BRAVE STUDENT! WHAT MATTERS IS THAT YOU REMAIN SAFE!
AND DON'T FORGET TO CONTINUE YOUR CALISTHENICS!

UM, CAN YOU FLY THIS?

ACTUALLY, YEAH!

THANKS AGAIN, NIXON!

VWIP

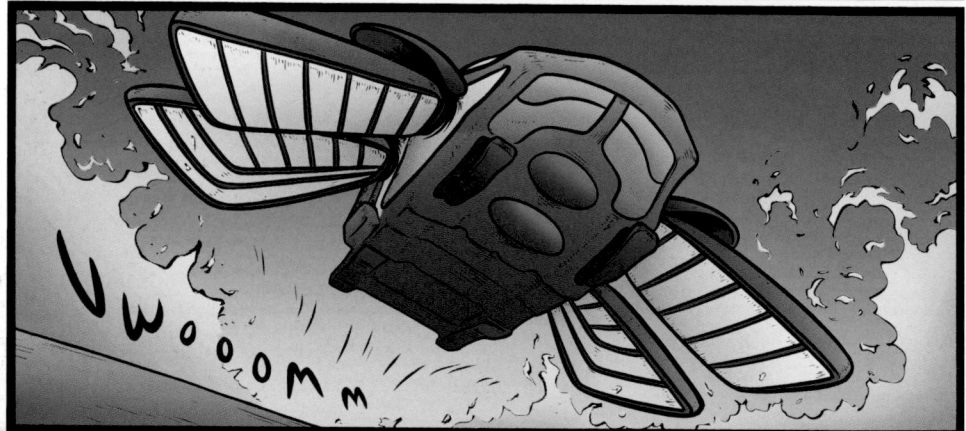

VWOOOMM

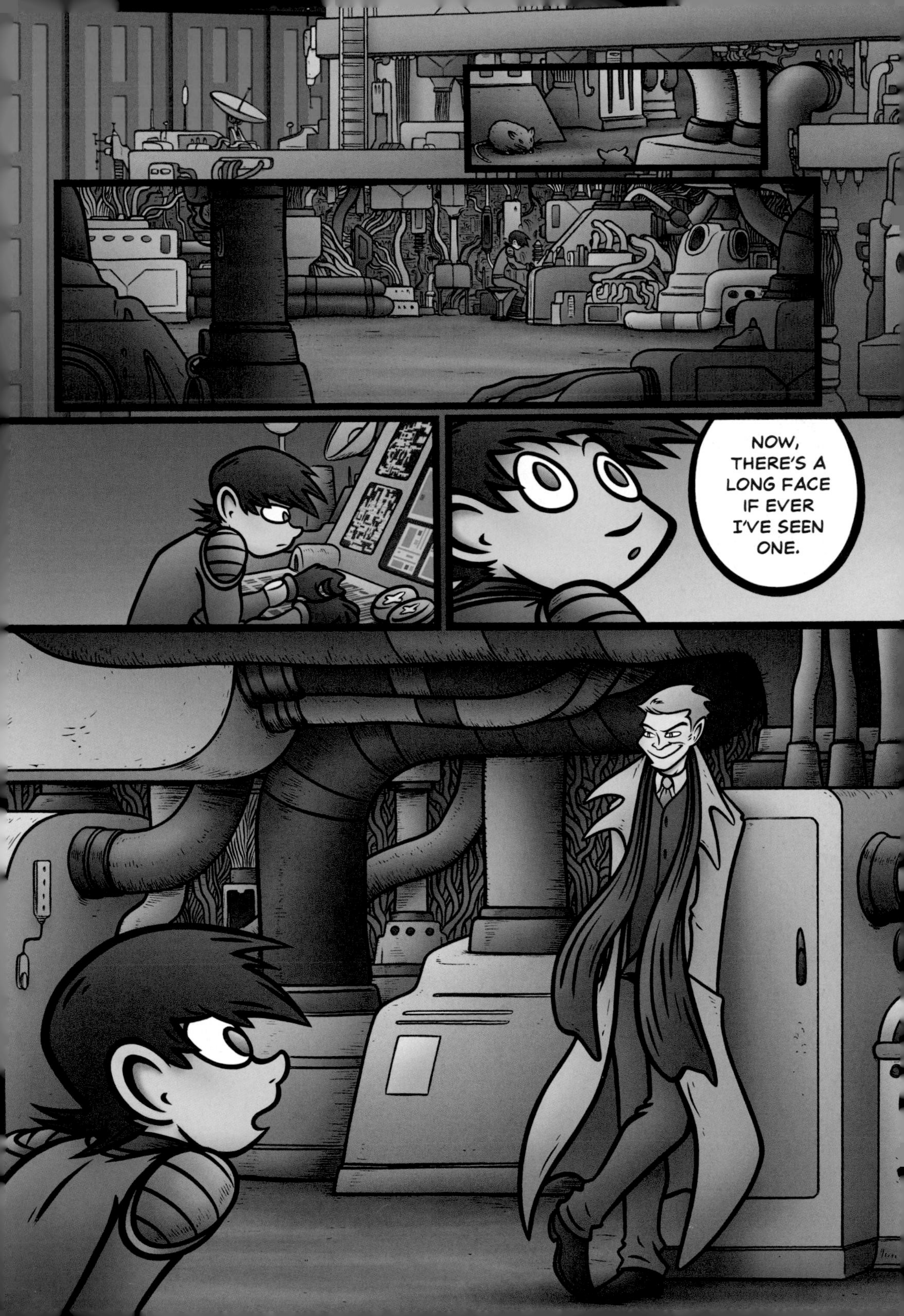
NOW, THERE'S A LONG FACE IF EVER I'VE SEEN ONE.

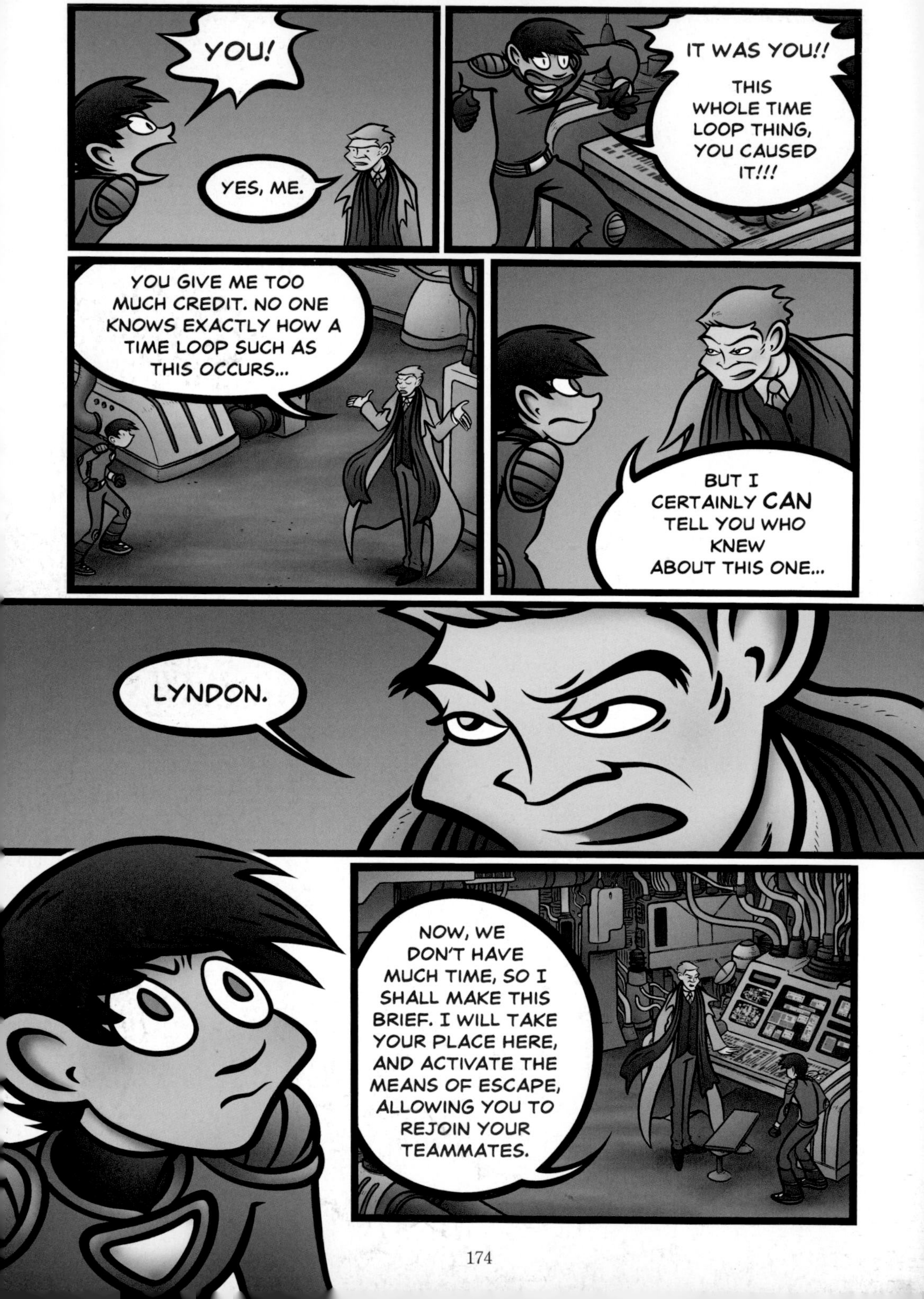
YOU!
YES, ME.
IT WAS YOU!!
THIS WHOLE TIME LOOP THING, YOU CAUSED IT!!!
YOU GIVE ME TOO MUCH CREDIT. NO ONE KNOWS EXACTLY HOW A TIME LOOP SUCH AS THIS OCCURS...
BUT I CERTAINLY **CAN** TELL YOU WHO KNEW ABOUT THIS ONE...
LYNDON.
NOW, WE DON'T HAVE MUCH TIME, SO I SHALL MAKE THIS BRIEF. I WILL TAKE YOUR PLACE HERE, AND ACTIVATE THE MEANS OF ESCAPE, ALLOWING YOU TO REJOIN YOUR TEAMMATES.

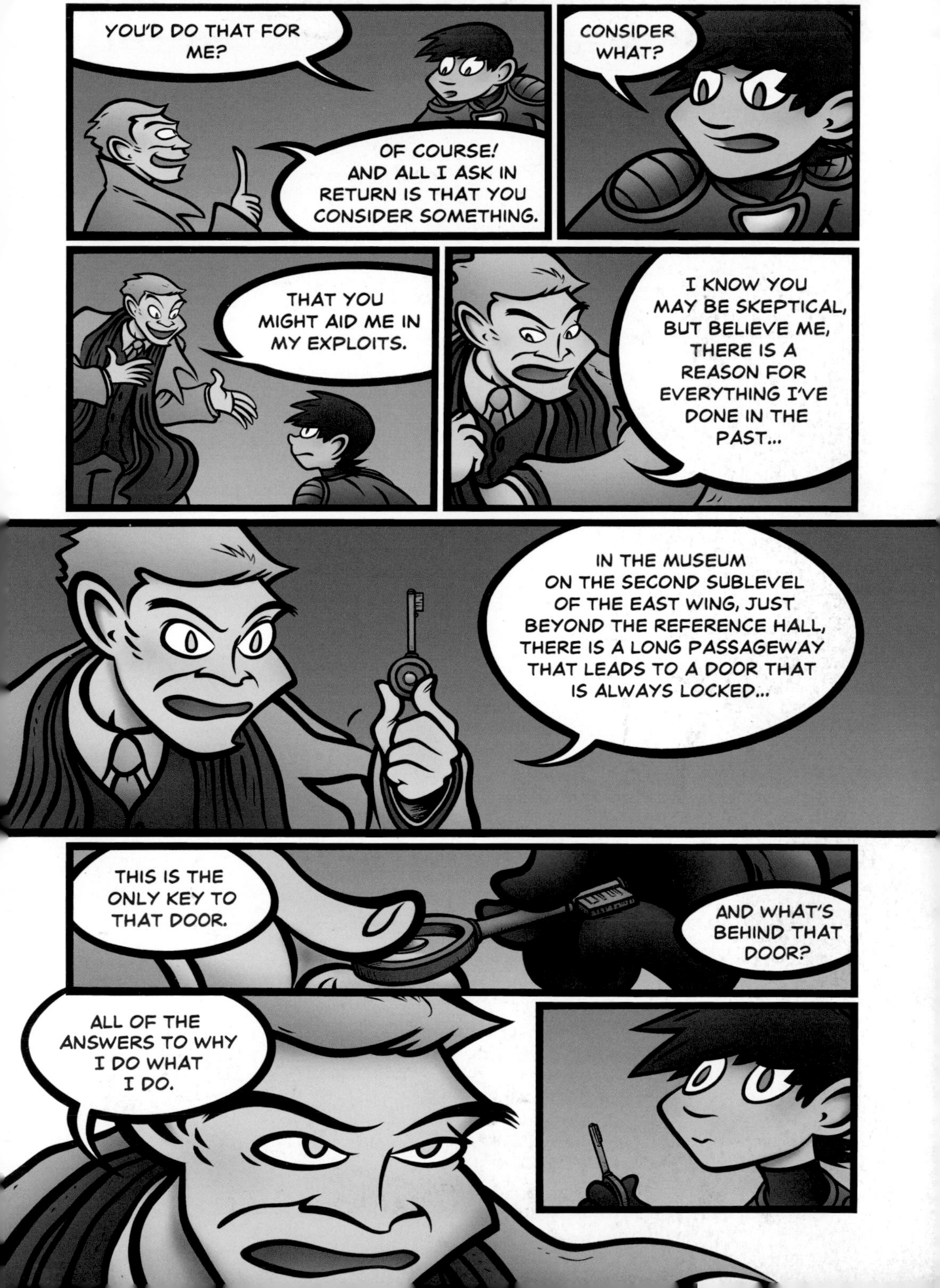
YOU'D DO THAT FOR ME?
OF COURSE! AND ALL I ASK IN RETURN IS THAT YOU CONSIDER SOMETHING.
CONSIDER WHAT?
THAT YOU MIGHT AID ME IN MY EXPLOITS.
I KNOW YOU MAY BE SKEPTICAL, BUT BELIEVE ME, THERE IS A REASON FOR EVERYTHING I'VE DONE IN THE PAST...
IN THE MUSEUM ON THE SECOND SUBLEVEL OF THE EAST WING, JUST BEYOND THE REFERENCE HALL, THERE IS A LONG PASSAGEWAY THAT LEADS TO A DOOR THAT IS ALWAYS LOCKED...
THIS IS THE ONLY KEY TO THAT DOOR.
AND WHAT'S BEHIND THAT DOOR?
ALL OF THE ANSWERS TO WHY I DO WHAT I DO.

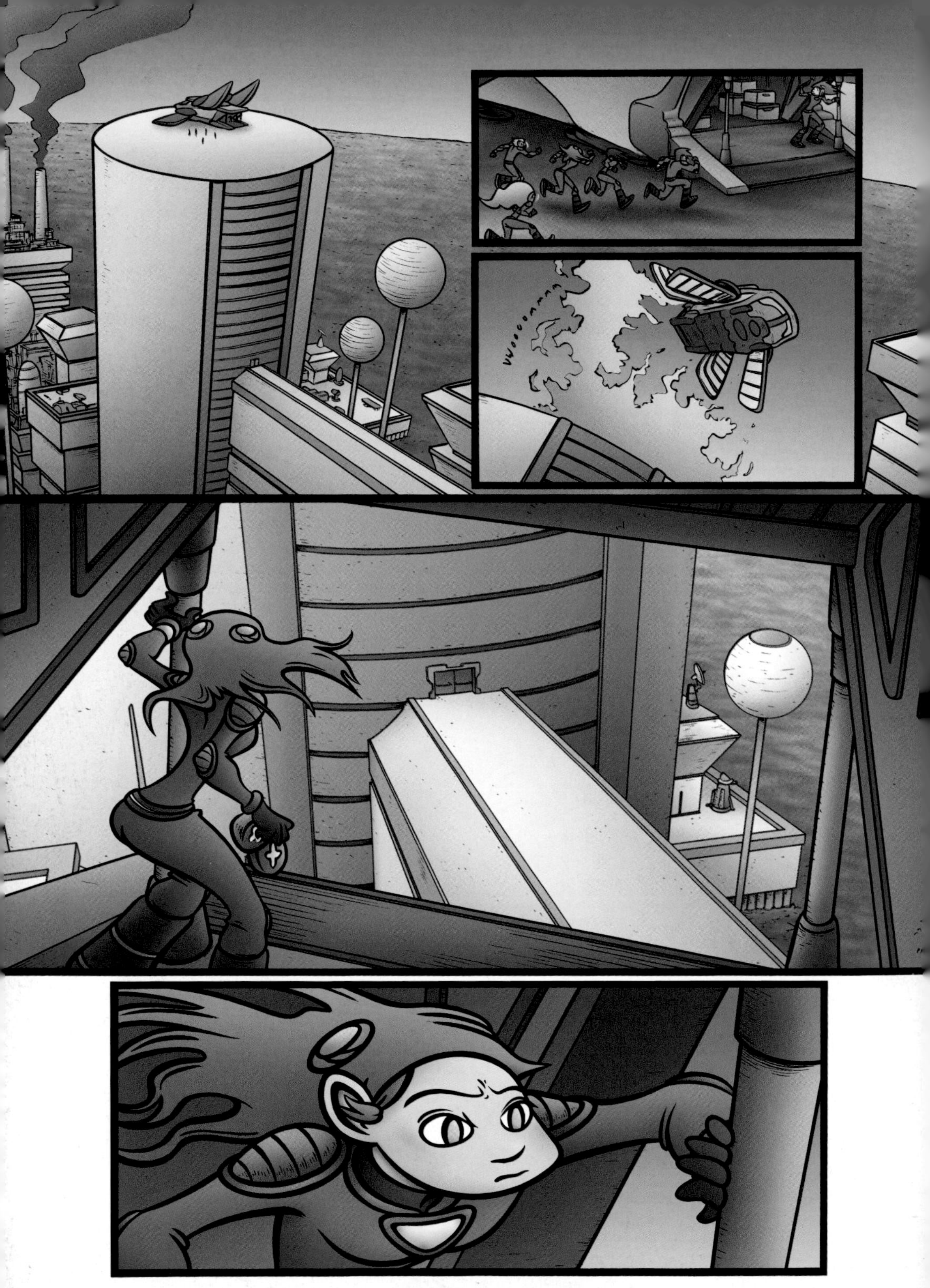
VWOOOOMMMM

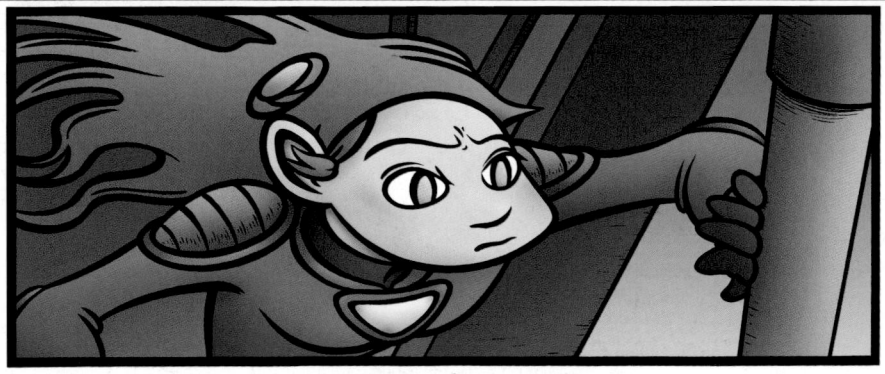

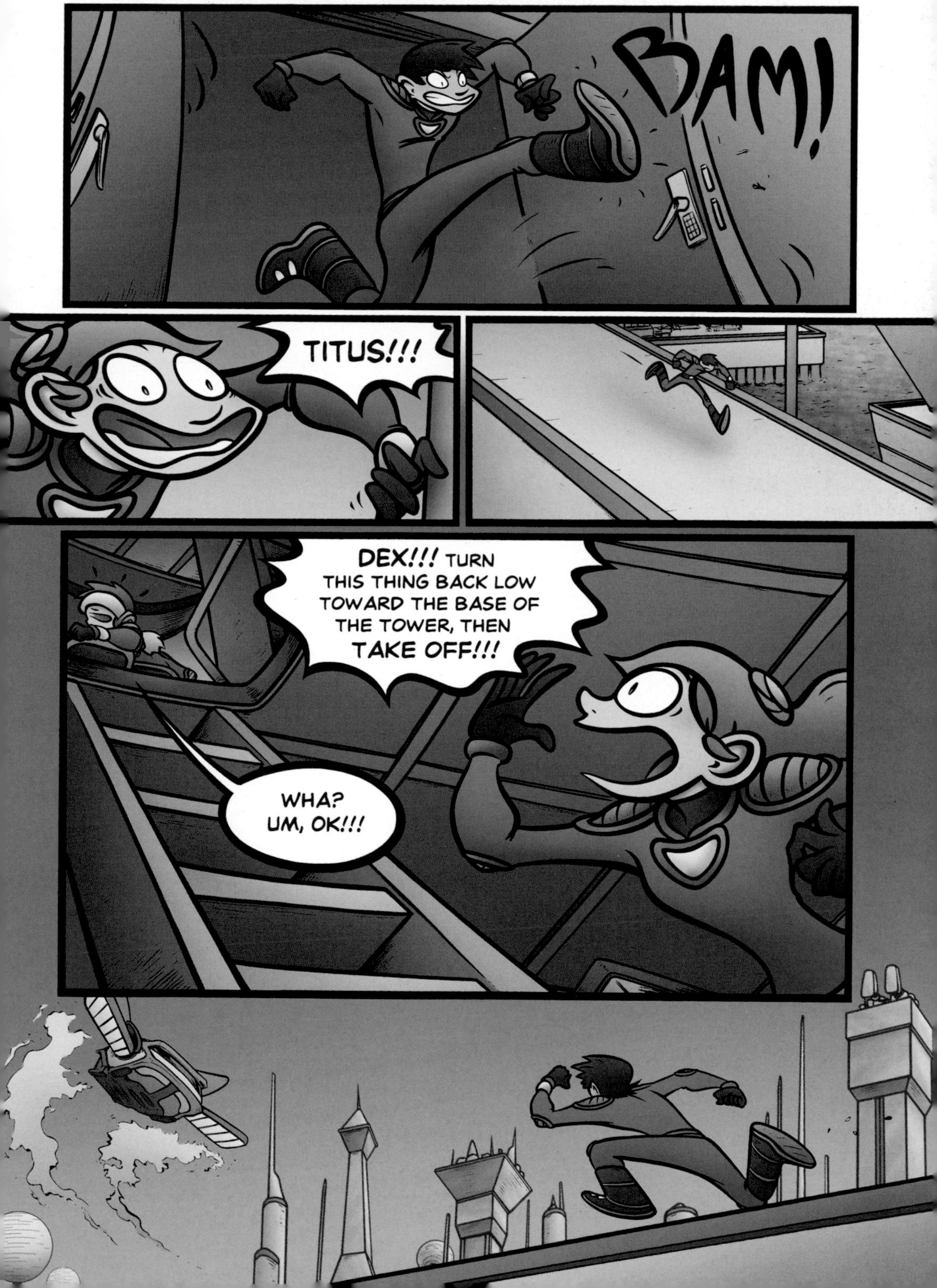
BAM!
TITUS!!!
DEX!!! TURN THIS THING BACK LOW TOWARD THE BASE OF THE TOWER, THEN TAKE OFF!!!
WHA? UM, OK!!!

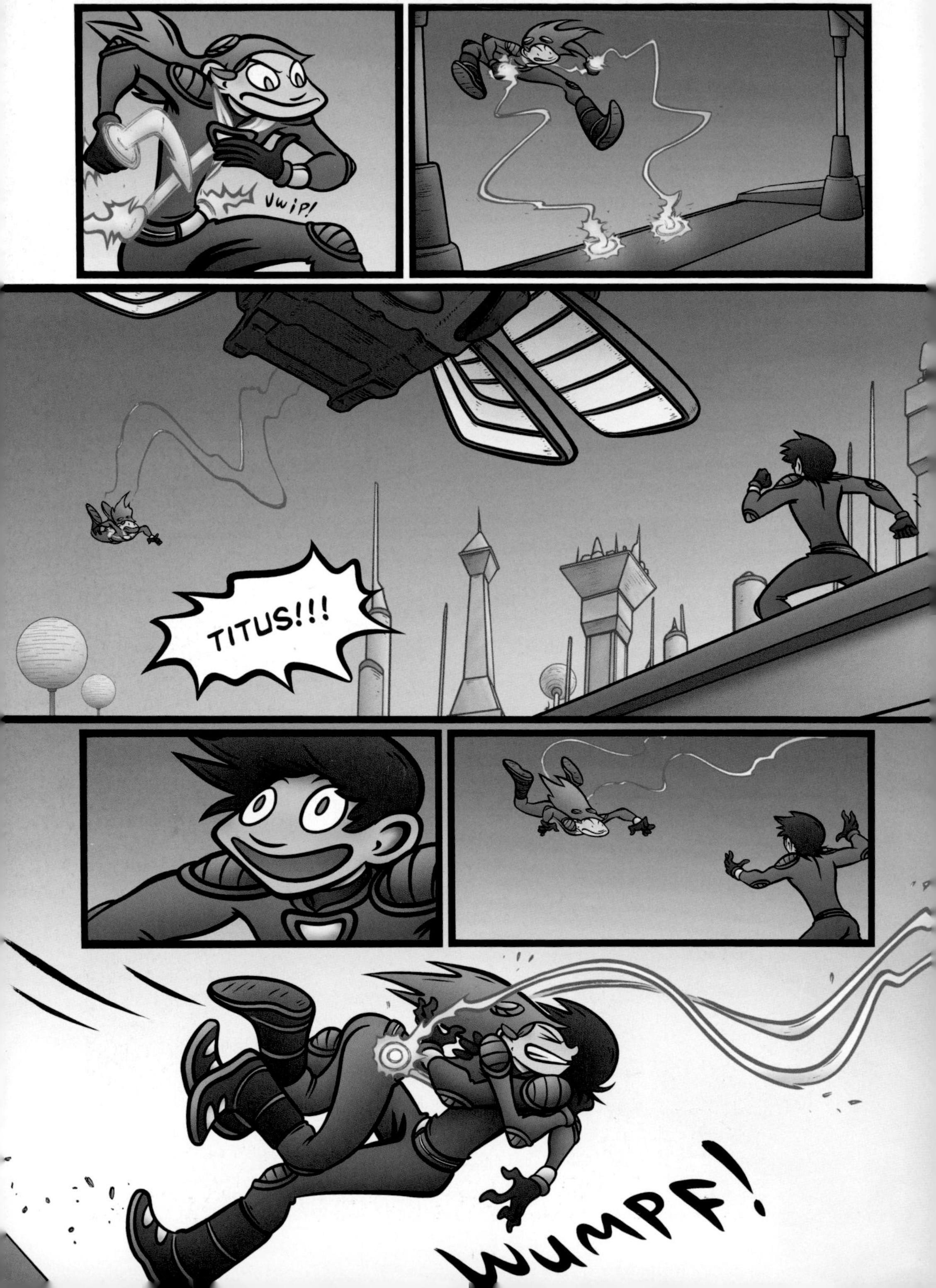

VWIP!
TITUS!!!
WUMPF!

UM...

VOOP

ZIIIIIIIIIIIIIIIIIIIIII!

CAREFUL!

WAH!!

CLUNK!

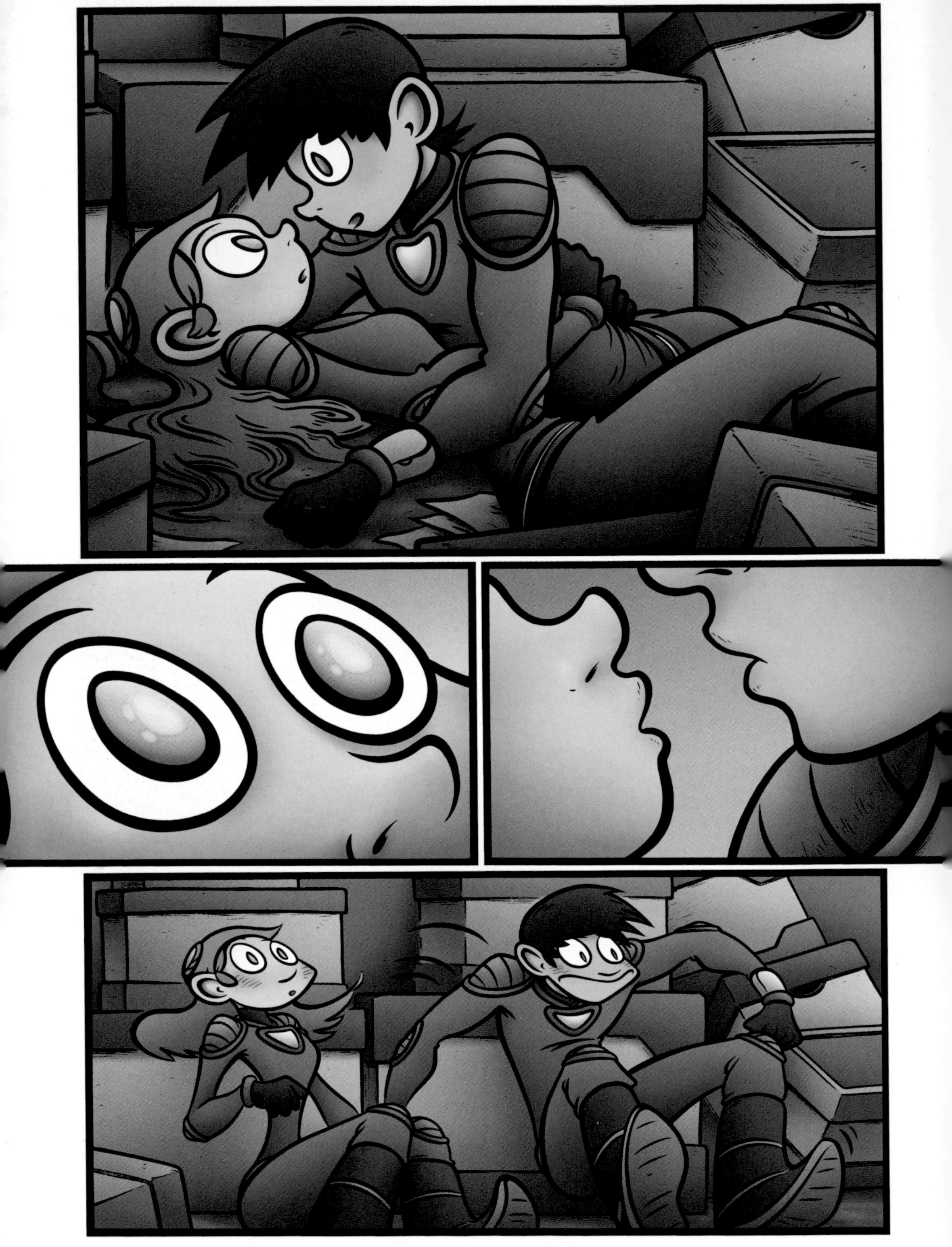

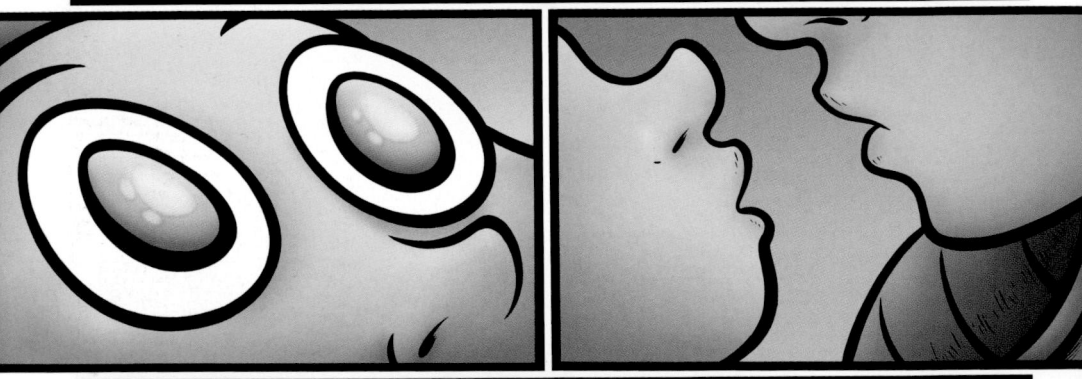

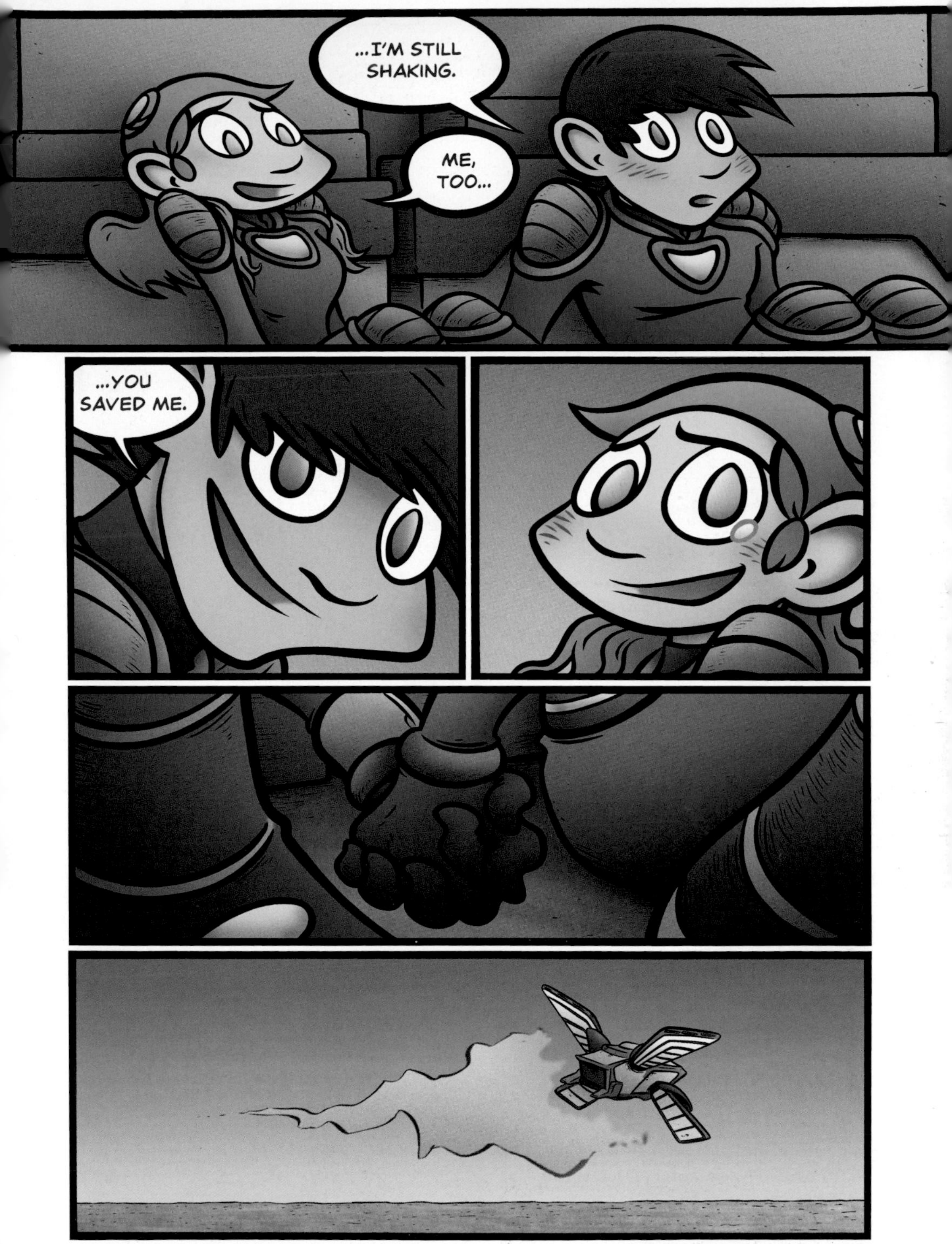
...I'M STILL SHAKING.
ME, TOO...
...YOU SAVED ME.

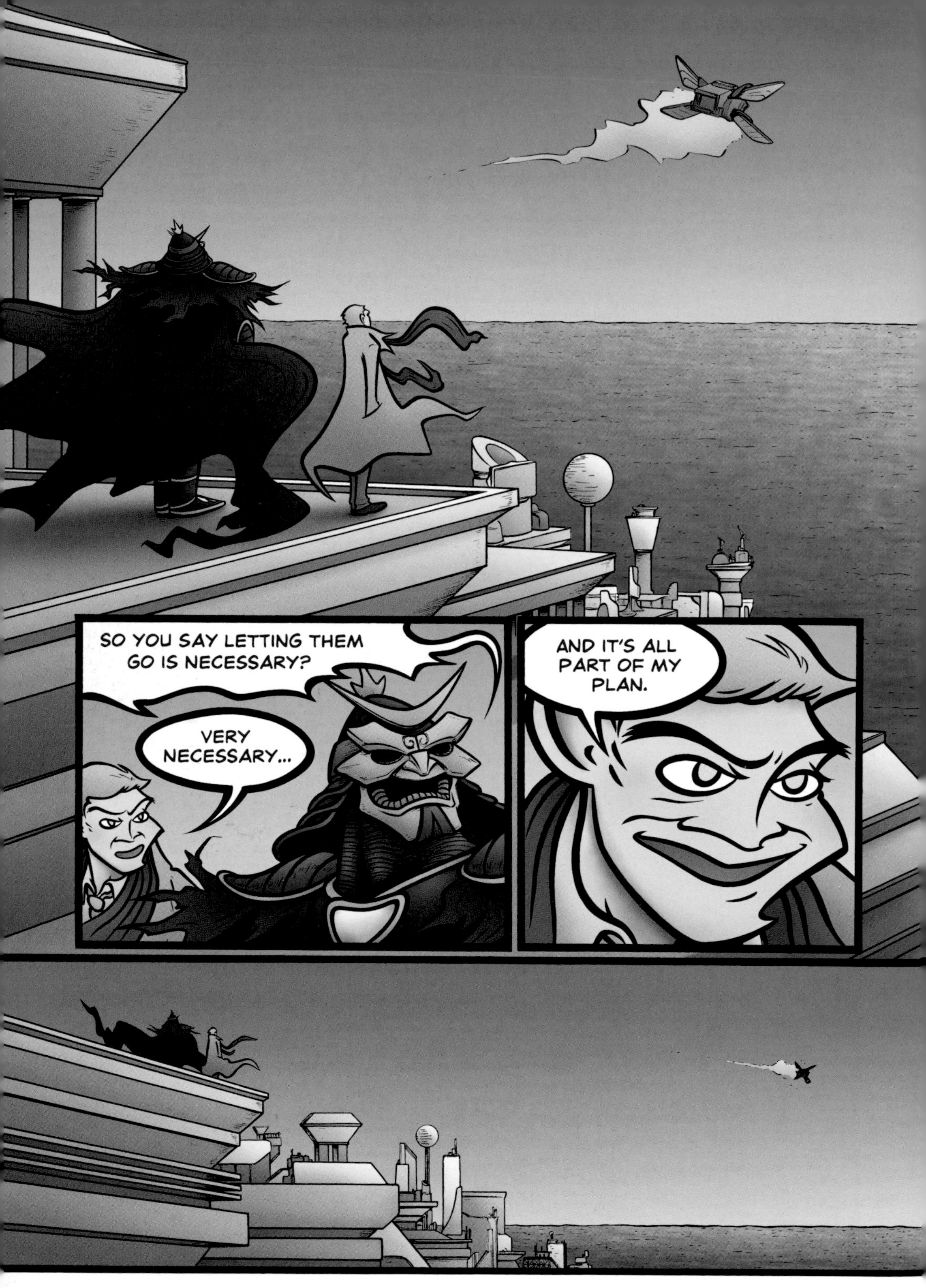
SO YOU SAY LETTING THEM GO IS NECESSARY?
VERY NECESSARY...
AND IT'S ALL PART OF MY PLAN.

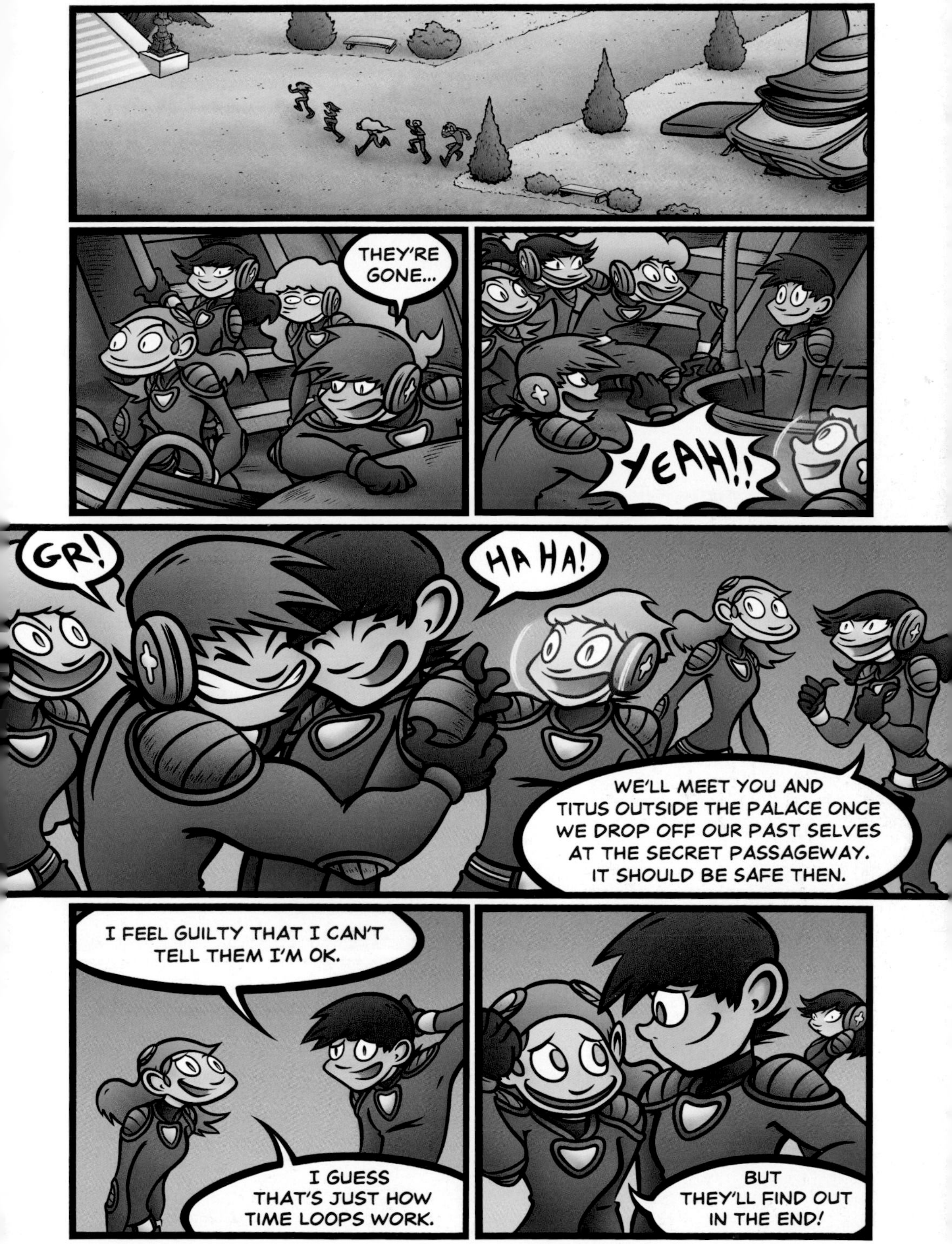
THEY'RE GONE...
YEAH!!
GR!
HA HA!
WE'LL MEET YOU AND TITUS OUTSIDE THE PALACE ONCE WE DROP OFF OUR PAST SELVES AT THE SECRET PASSAGEWAY. IT SHOULD BE SAFE THEN.
I FEEL GUILTY THAT I CAN'T TELL THEM I'M OK.
I GUESS THAT'S JUST HOW TIME LOOPS WORK.
BUT THEY'LL FIND OUT IN THE END!

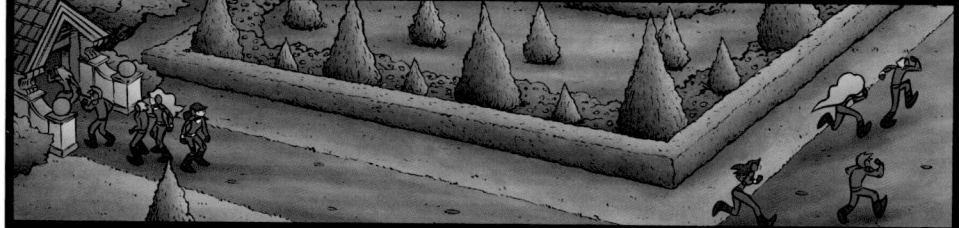

HUH?

THERE YOU ARE!

QUICKLY NOW, WE MUST LEAVE THIS TIME AT ONCE!!!

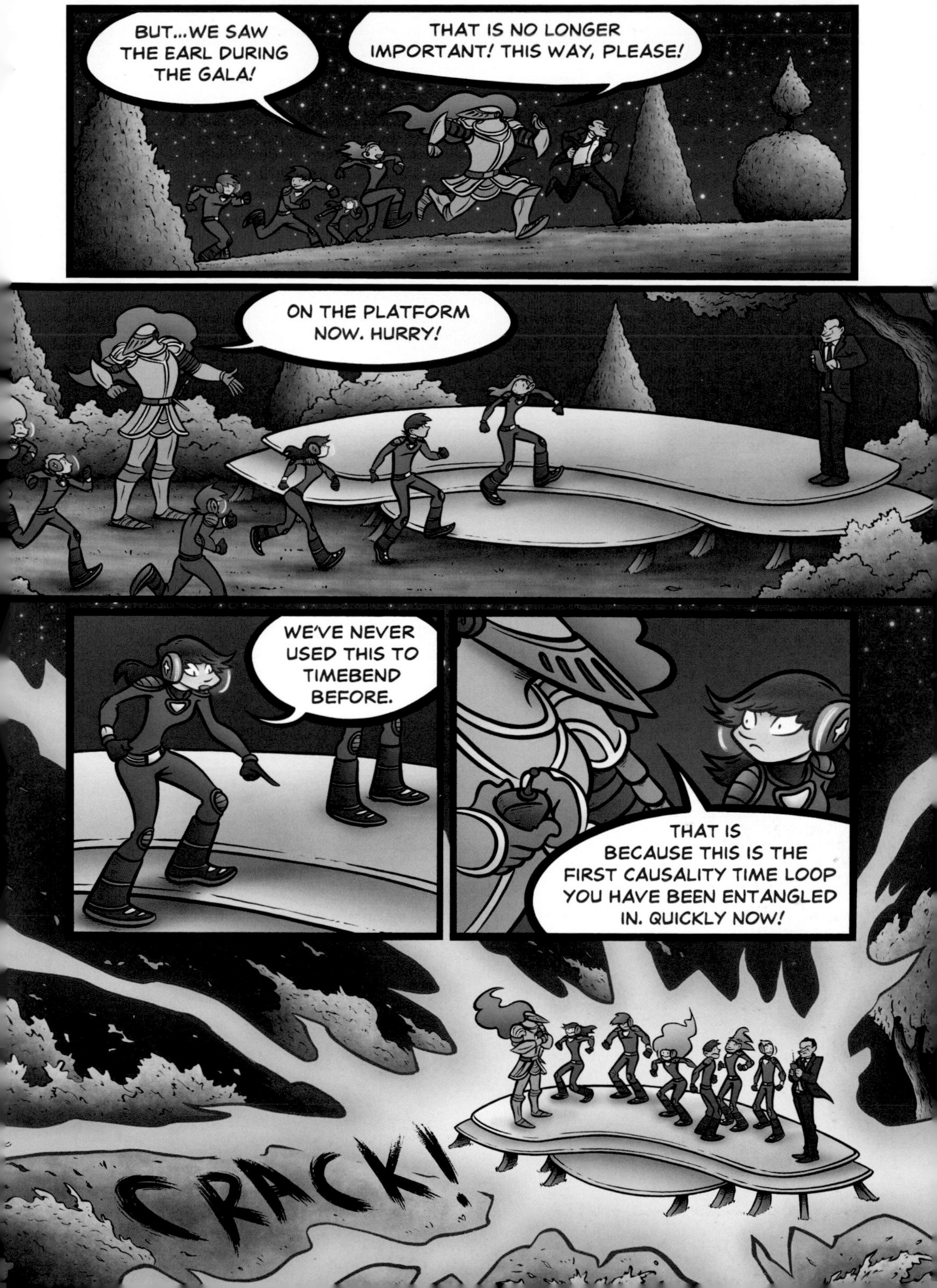
BUT...WE SAW THE EARL DURING THE GALA!
THAT IS NO LONGER IMPORTANT! THIS WAY, PLEASE!
ON THE PLATFORM NOW. HURRY!
WE'VE NEVER USED THIS TO TIMEBEND BEFORE.
THAT IS BECAUSE THIS IS THE FIRST CAUSALITY TIME LOOP YOU HAVE BEEN ENTANGLED IN. QUICKLY NOW!
CRACK!

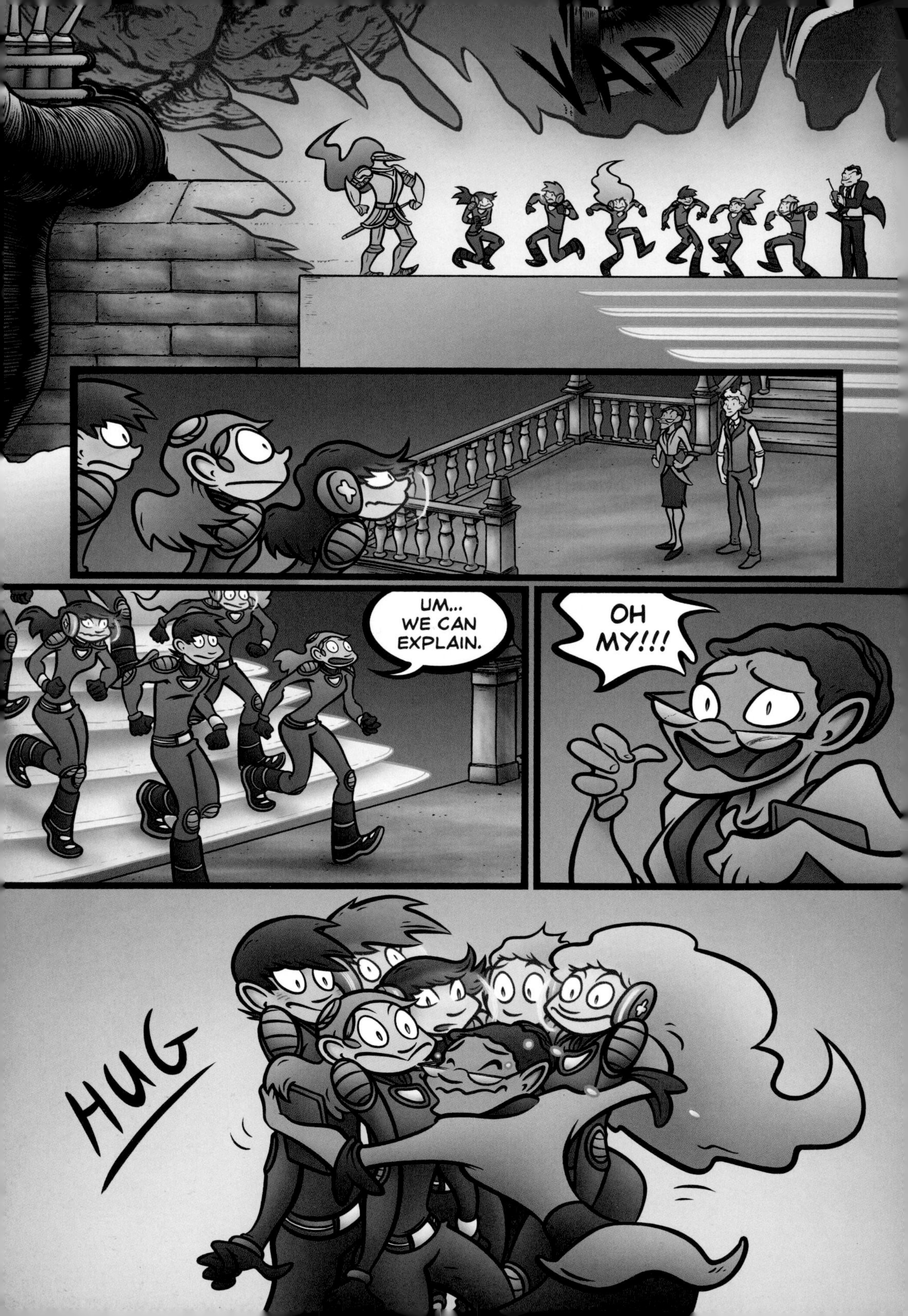
VAP
UM... WE CAN EXPLAIN.
OH MY!!!
HUG

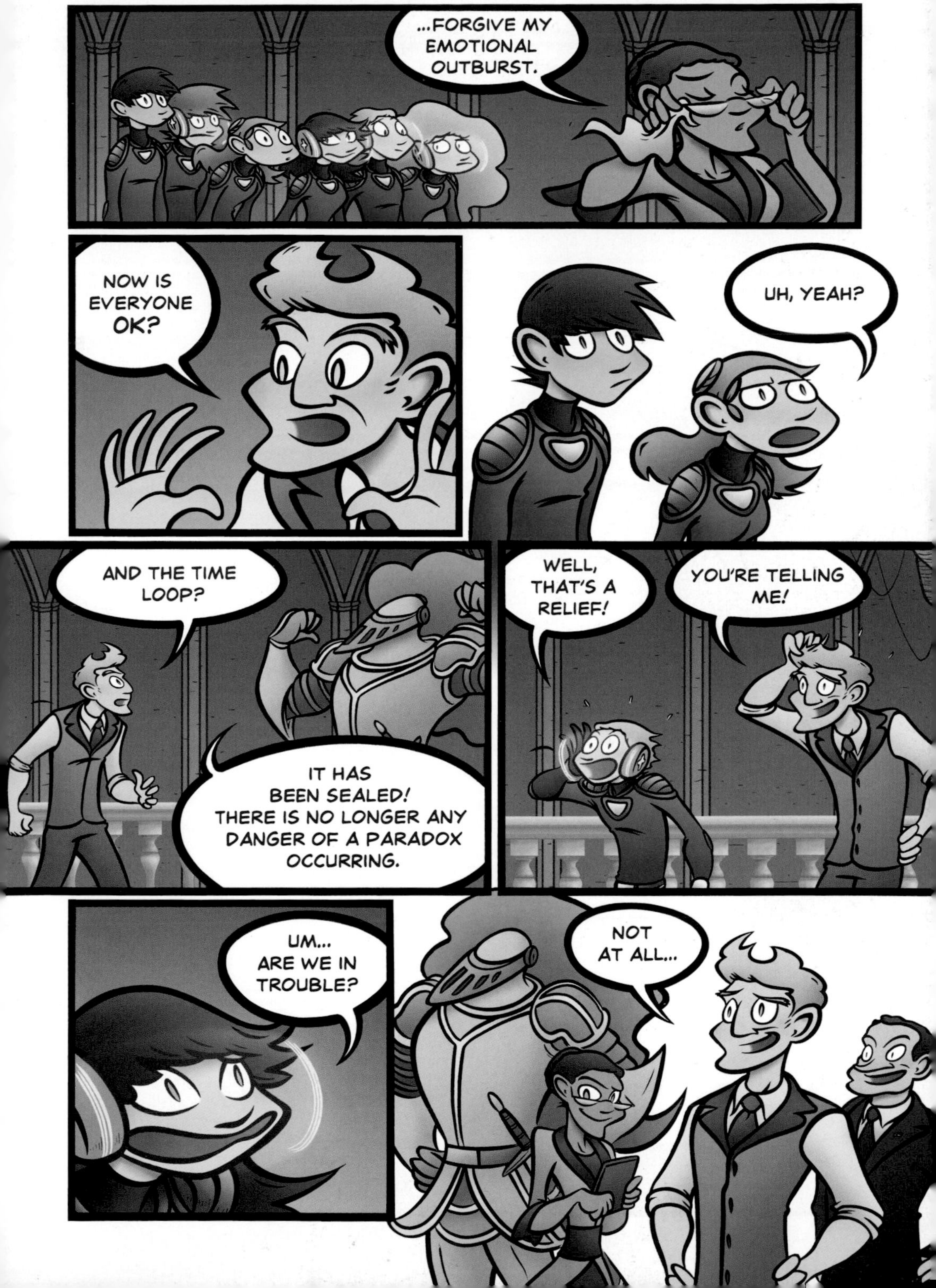
...FORGIVE MY EMOTIONAL OUTBURST.
NOW IS EVERYONE OK?
UH, YEAH?
AND THE TIME LOOP?
IT HAS BEEN SEALED! THERE IS NO LONGER ANY DANGER OF A PARADOX OCCURRING.
WELL, THAT'S A RELIEF!
YOU'RE TELLING ME!
UM... ARE WE IN TROUBLE?
NOT AT ALL...

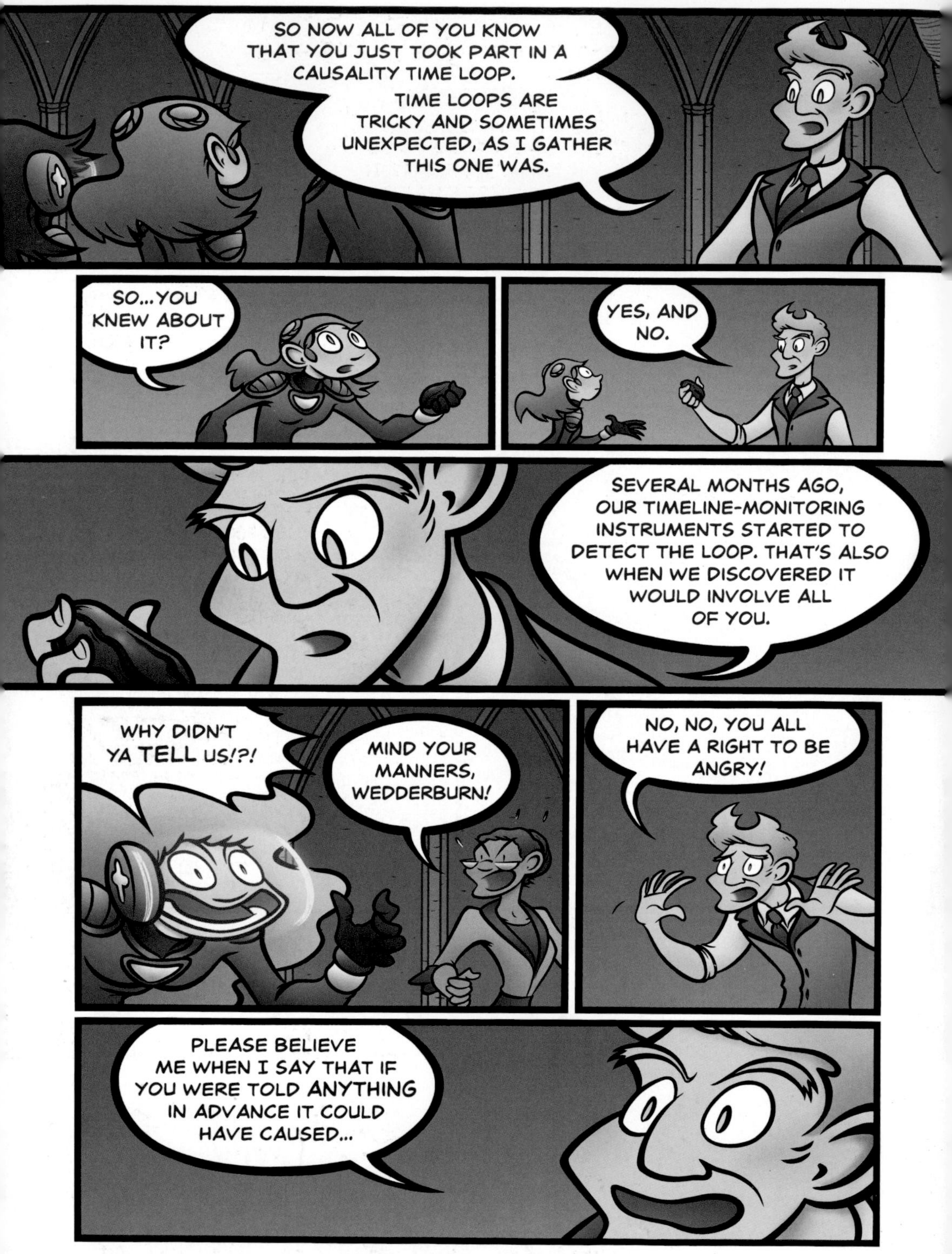
SO NOW ALL OF YOU KNOW THAT YOU JUST TOOK PART IN A CAUSALITY TIME LOOP.
TIME LOOPS ARE TRICKY AND SOMETIMES UNEXPECTED, AS I GATHER THIS ONE WAS.
SO...YOU KNEW ABOUT IT?
YES, AND NO.
SEVERAL MONTHS AGO, OUR TIMELINE-MONITORING INSTRUMENTS STARTED TO DETECT THE LOOP. THAT'S ALSO WHEN WE DISCOVERED IT WOULD INVOLVE ALL OF YOU.
WHY DIDN'T YA **TELL** US!?!
MIND YOUR MANNERS, WEDDERBURN!
NO, NO, YOU ALL HAVE A RIGHT TO BE ANGRY!
PLEASE BELIEVE ME WHEN I SAY THAT IF YOU WERE TOLD **ANYTHING** IN ADVANCE IT COULD HAVE CAUSED...

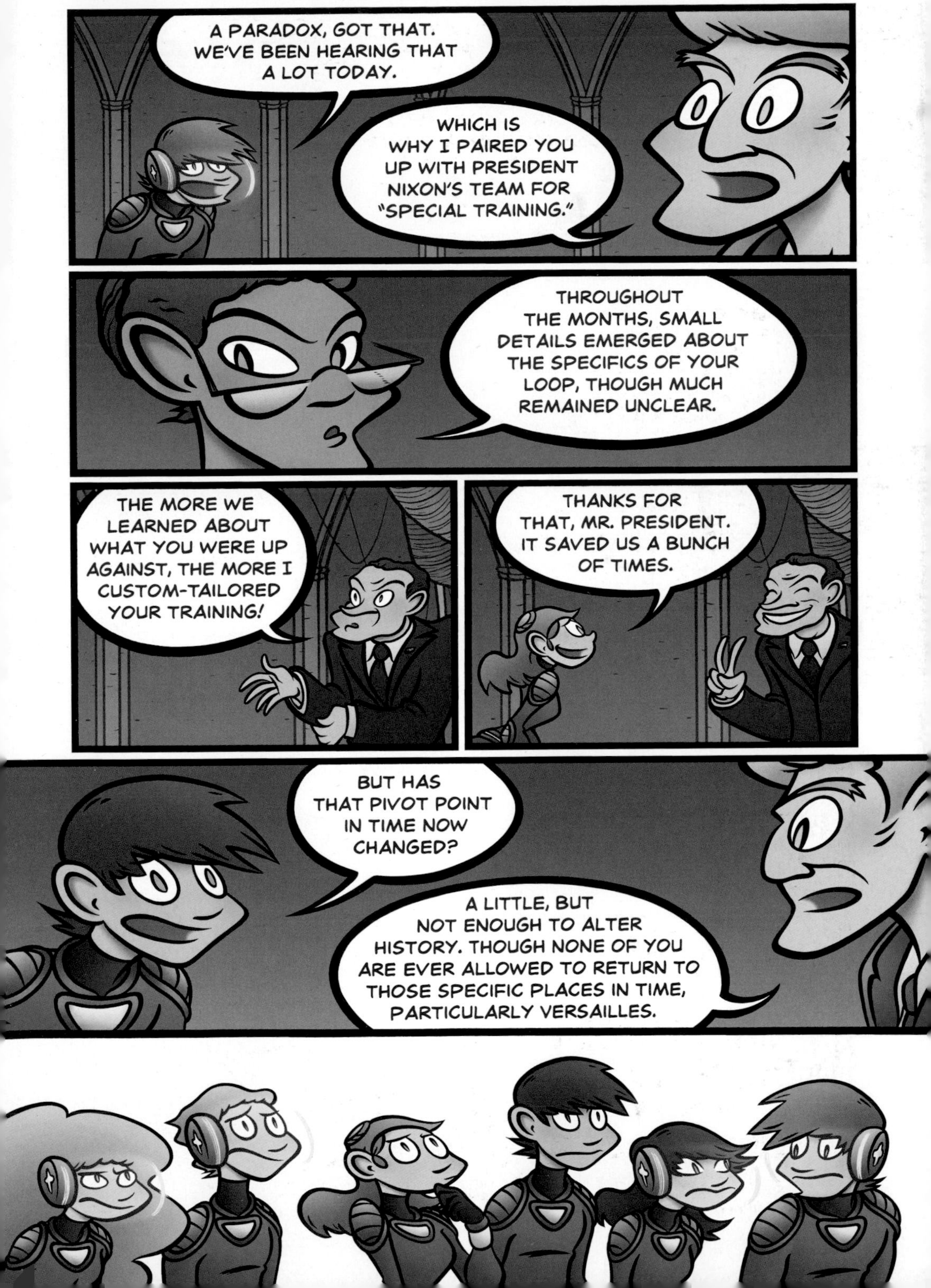
A PARADOX, GOT THAT. WE'VE BEEN HEARING THAT A LOT TODAY.
WHICH IS WHY I PAIRED YOU UP WITH PRESIDENT NIXON'S TEAM FOR "SPECIAL TRAINING."
THROUGHOUT THE MONTHS, SMALL DETAILS EMERGED ABOUT THE SPECIFICS OF YOUR LOOP, THOUGH MUCH REMAINED UNCLEAR.
THE MORE WE LEARNED ABOUT WHAT YOU WERE UP AGAINST, THE MORE I CUSTOM-TAILORED YOUR TRAINING!
THANKS FOR THAT, MR. PRESIDENT. IT SAVED US A BUNCH OF TIMES.
BUT HAS THAT PIVOT POINT IN TIME NOW CHANGED?
A LITTLE, BUT NOT ENOUGH TO ALTER HISTORY. THOUGH NONE OF YOU ARE EVER ALLOWED TO RETURN TO THOSE SPECIFIC PLACES IN TIME, PARTICULARLY VERSAILLES.

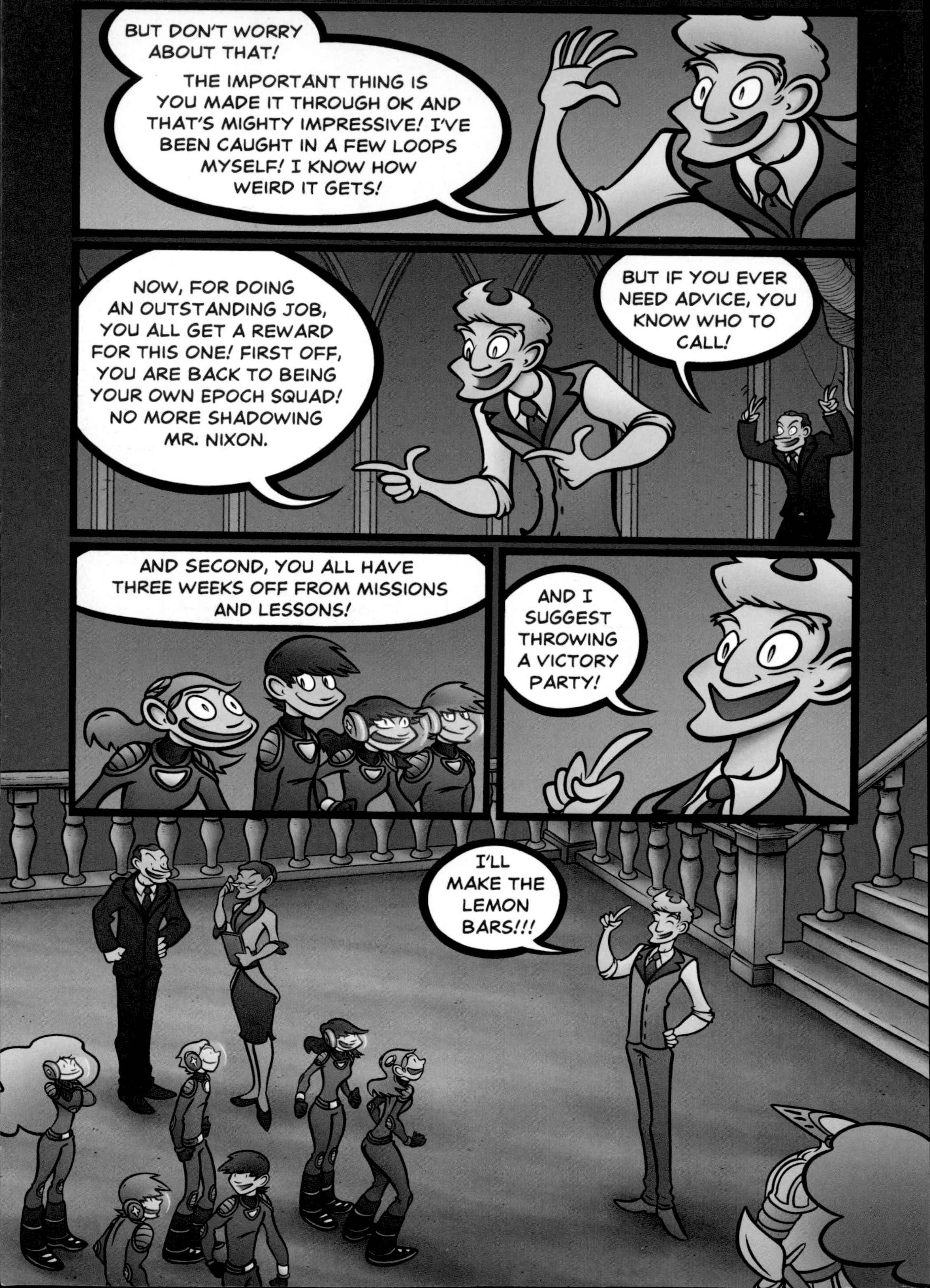
BUT DON'T WORRY ABOUT THAT!
THE IMPORTANT THING IS YOU MADE IT THROUGH OK AND THAT'S MIGHTY IMPRESSIVE! I'VE BEEN CAUGHT IN A FEW LOOPS MYSELF! I KNOW HOW WEIRD IT GETS!
NOW, FOR DOING AN OUTSTANDING JOB, YOU ALL GET A REWARD FOR THIS ONE! FIRST OFF, YOU ARE BACK TO BEING YOUR OWN EPOCH SQUAD! NO MORE SHADOWING MR. NIXON.
BUT IF YOU EVER NEED ADVICE, YOU KNOW WHO TO CALL!
AND SECOND, YOU ALL HAVE THREE WEEKS OFF FROM MISSIONS AND LESSONS!
AND I SUGGEST THROWING A VICTORY PARTY!
I'LL MAKE THE LEMON BARS!!!

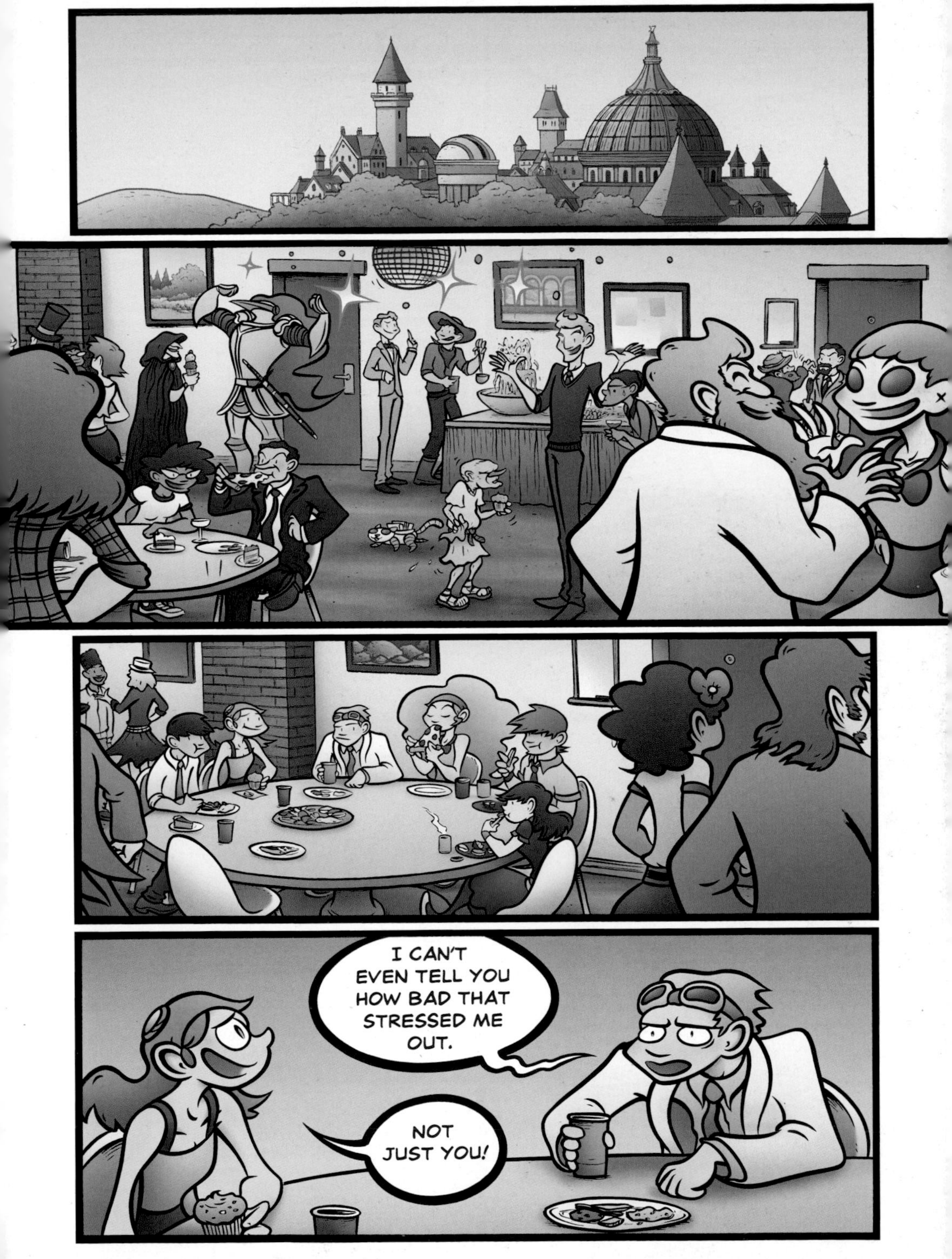
I CAN'T EVEN TELL YOU HOW BAD THAT STRESSED ME OUT.
NOT JUST YOU!

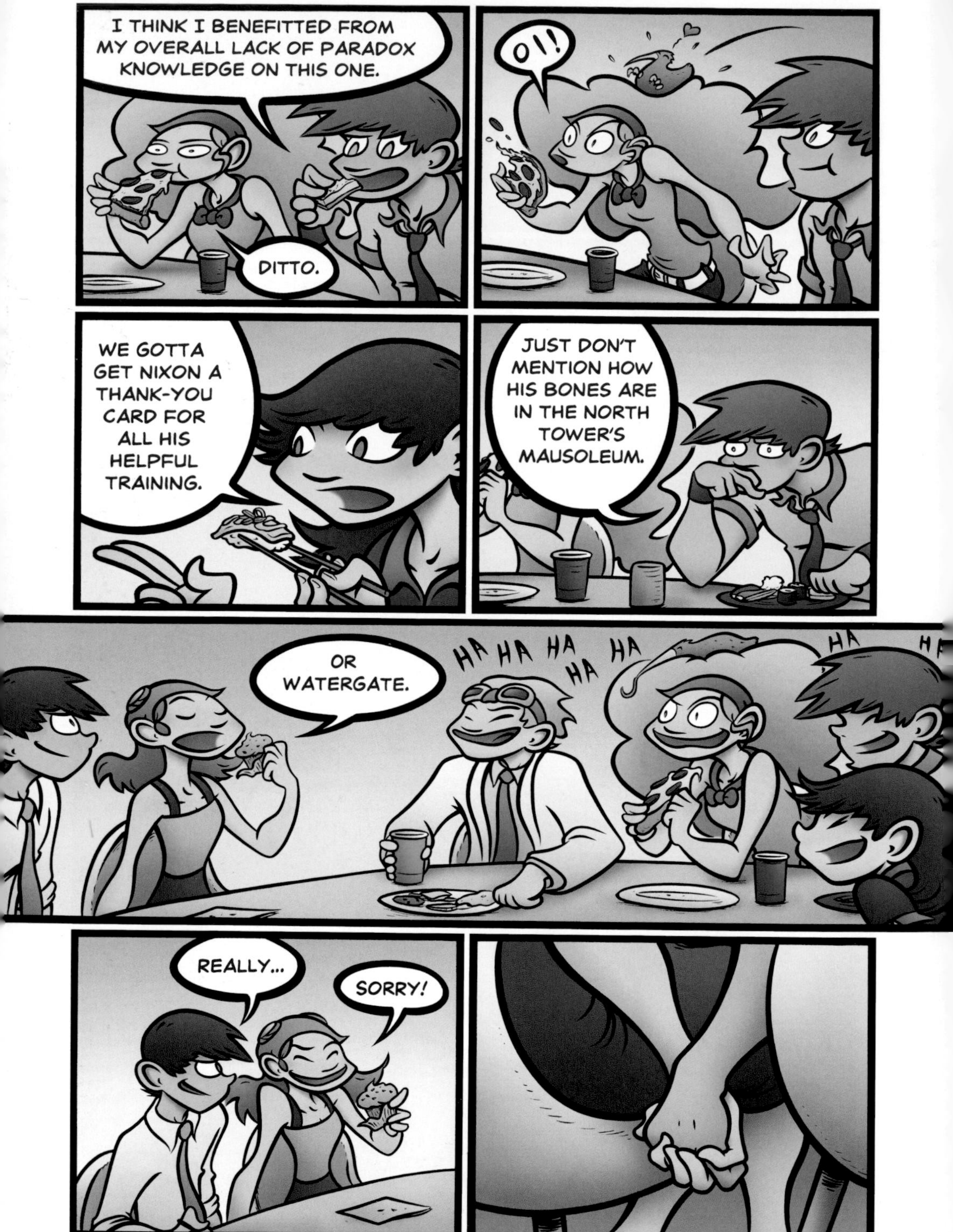
I THINK I BENEFITTED FROM MY OVERALL LACK OF PARADOX KNOWLEDGE ON THIS ONE.
DITTO.
OI!
WE GOTTA GET NIXON A THANK-YOU CARD FOR ALL HIS HELPFUL TRAINING.
JUST DON'T MENTION HOW HIS BONES ARE IN THE NORTH TOWER'S MAUSOLEUM.
OR WATERGATE.
HA HA HA HA HA HA
REALLY...
SORRY!

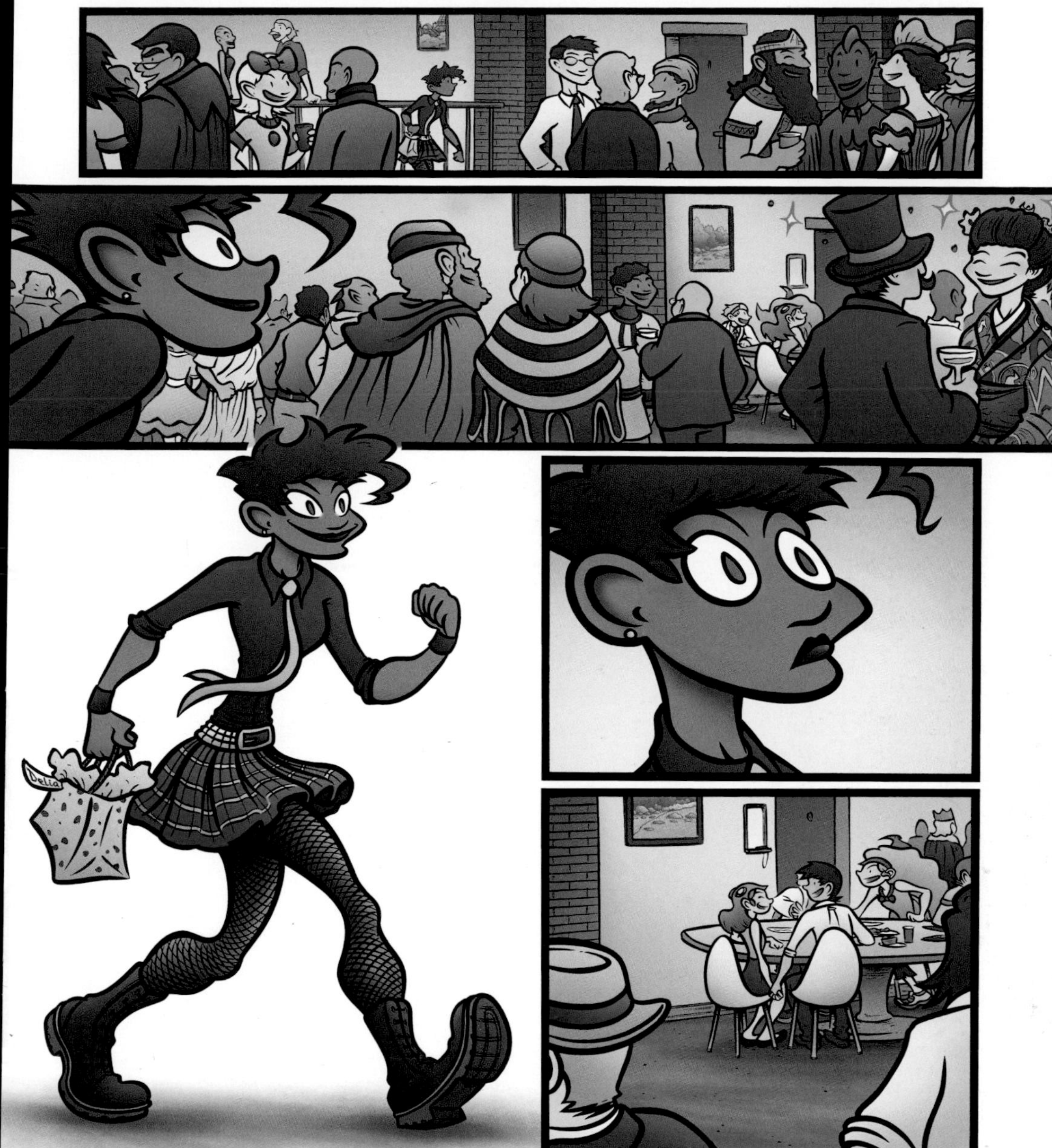
Delia

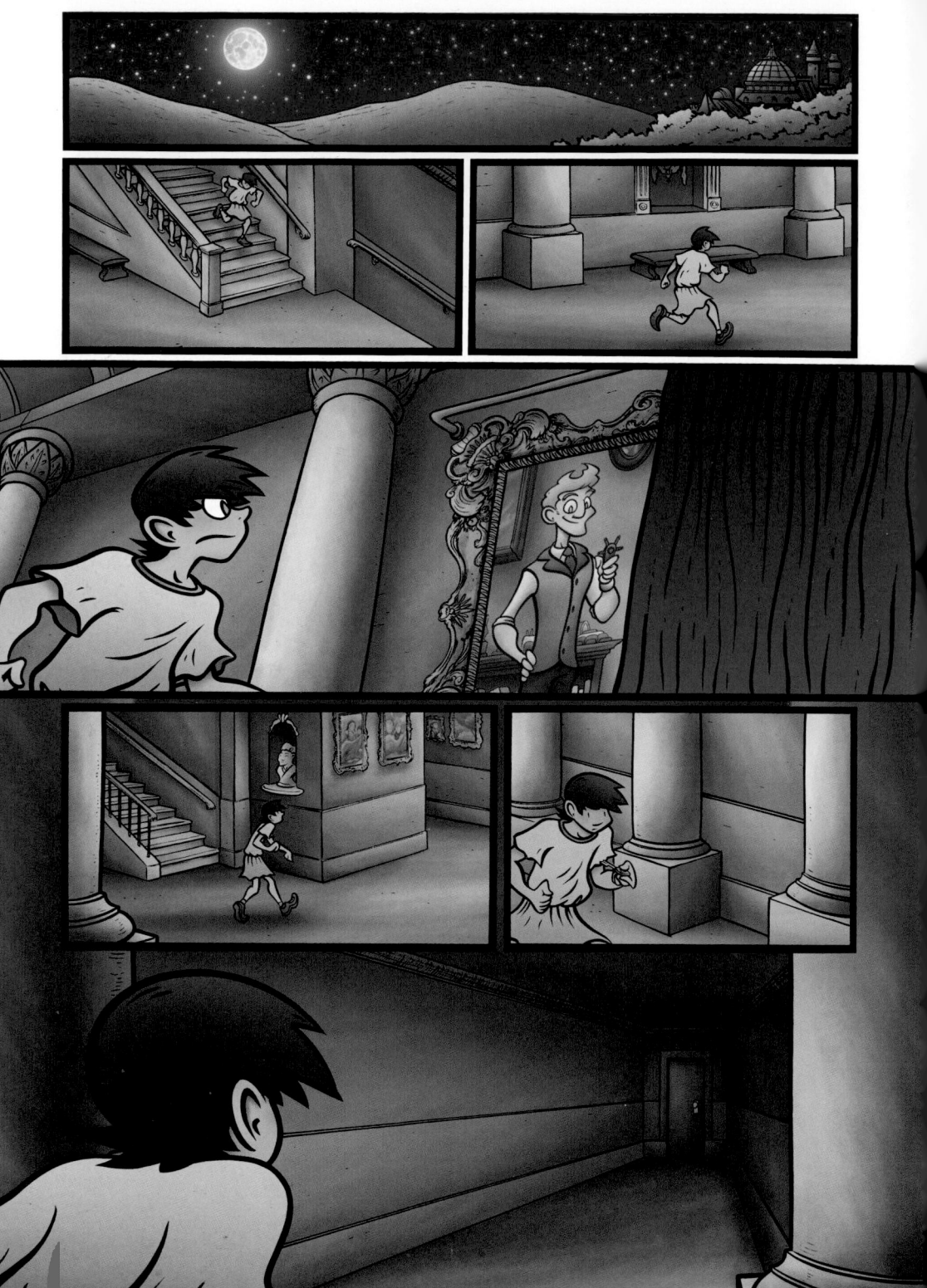

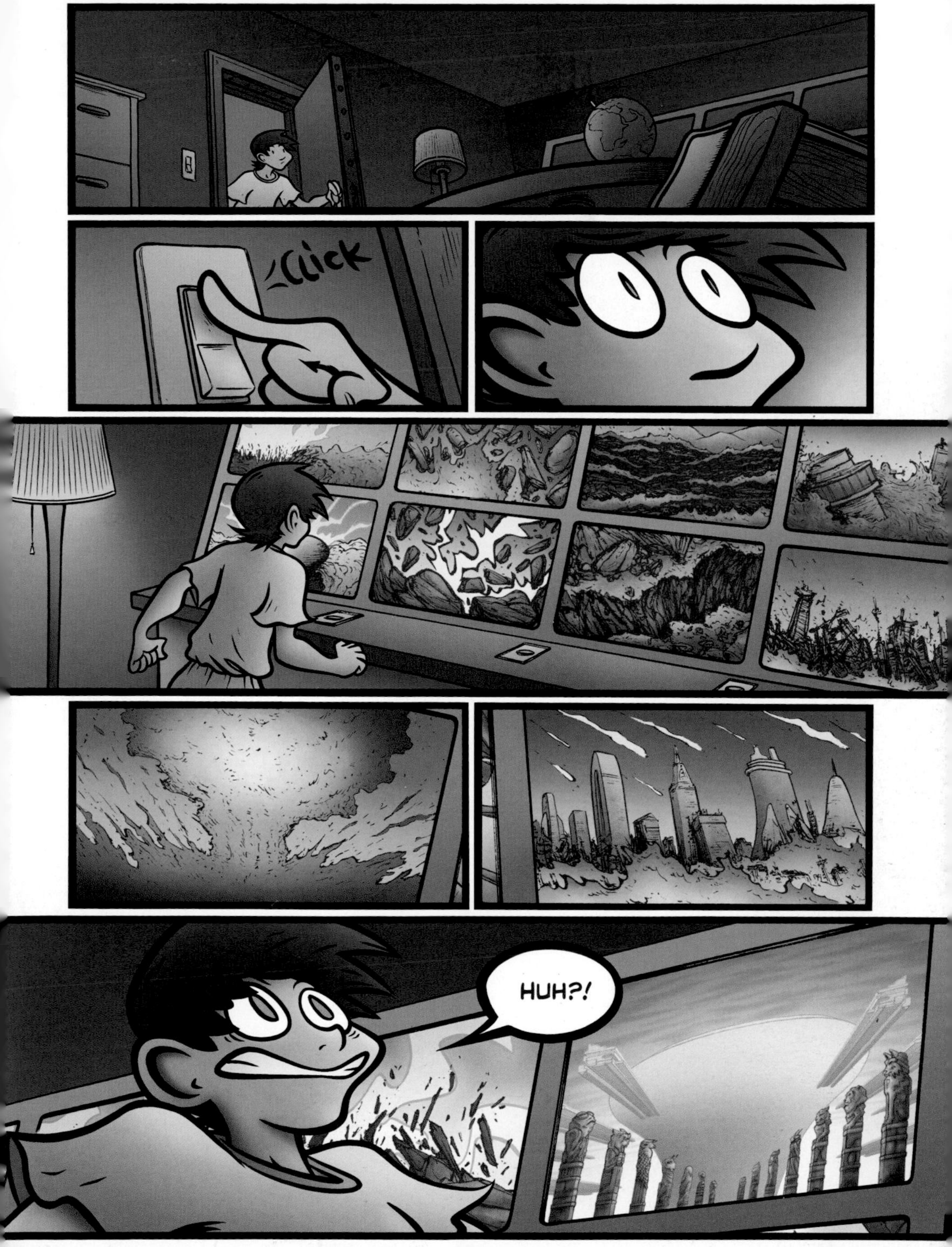
CLICK
HUH?!

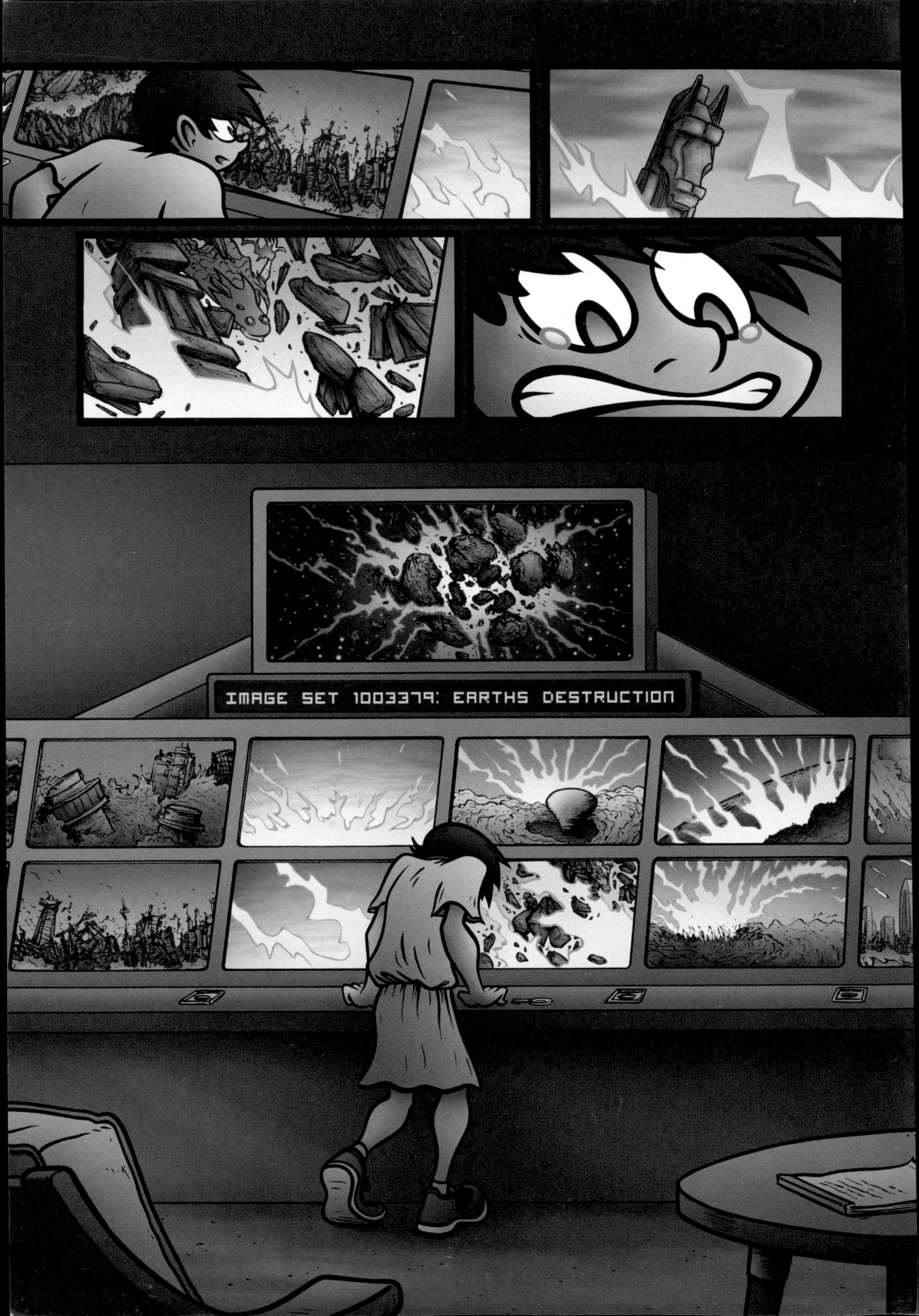
IMAGE SET 1003379: EARTHS DESTRUCTION

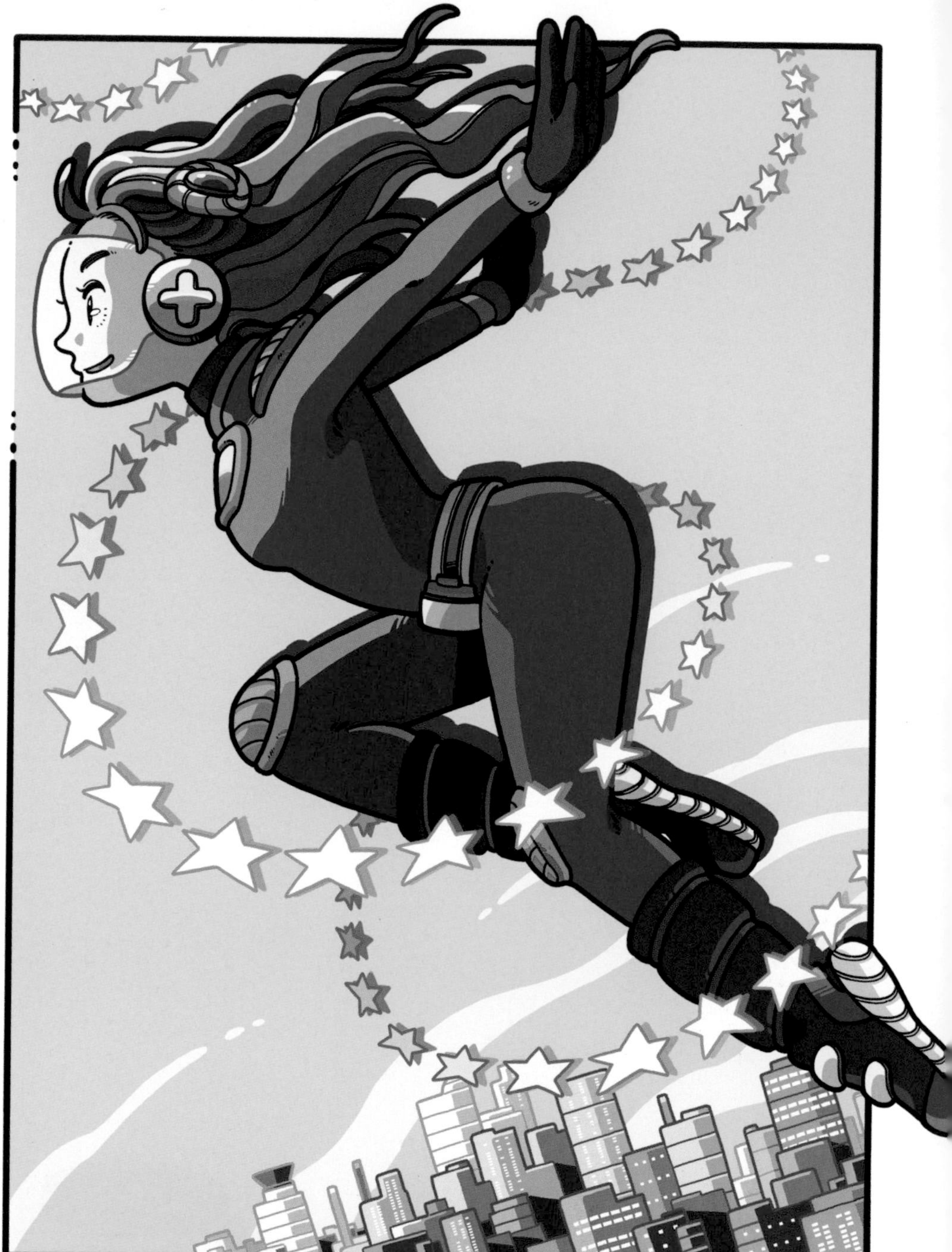

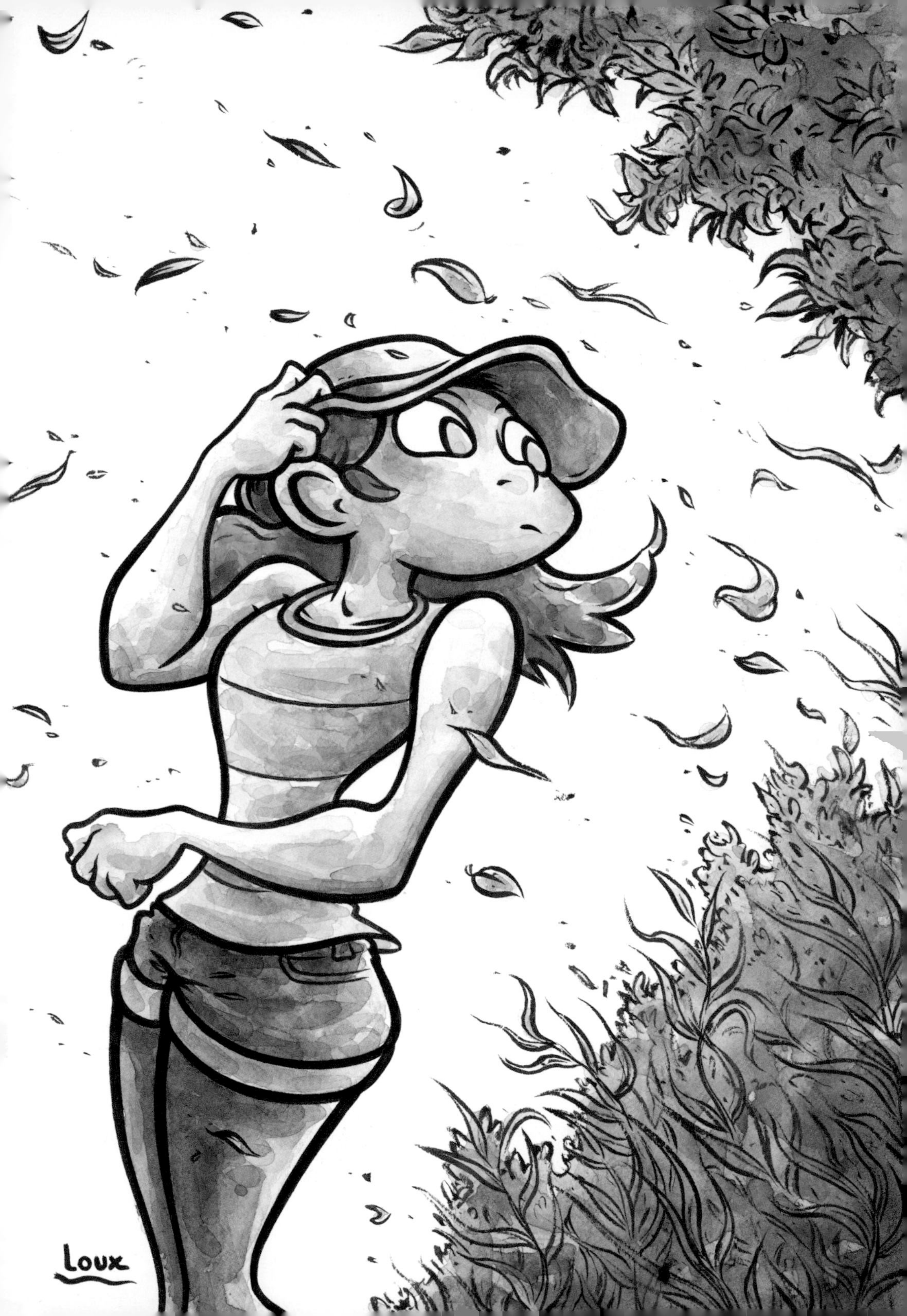
Loux

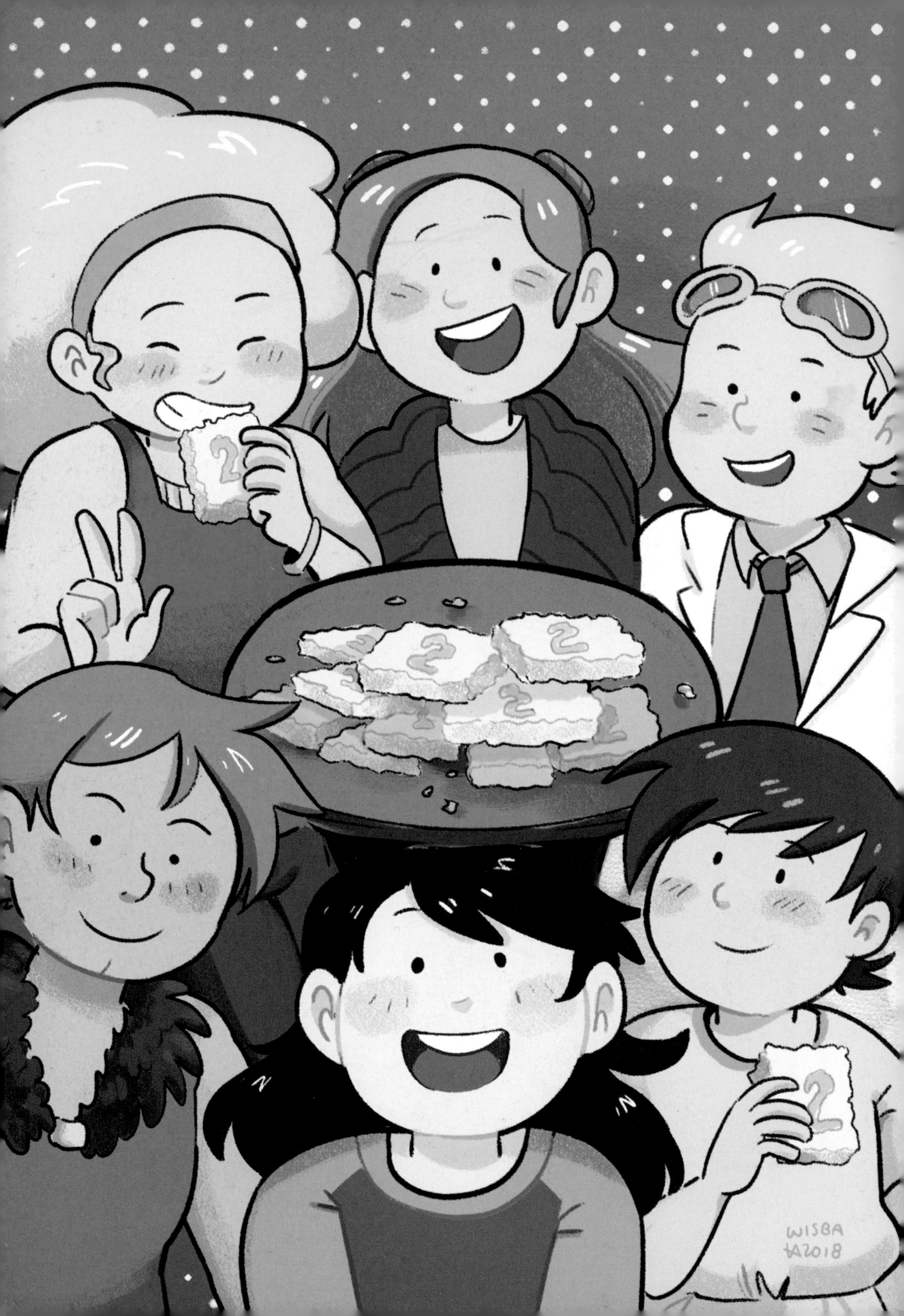
WISBA
TA2018

SPECIAL THANKS TO THOSE WHO HELPED MAKE THIS BOOK AND SERIES HAPPEN:

Abby Denson, Veronica Agarwal, Daniel Loux, Patsy Loux, Meiji Loux,
Brian Stone, Yuuko Koyama, Shawna Saycocie, Beth Parker,
Alexis Lambert, Alex Graudins, Gina Gagliano, Morgan Dubin,
Seth Fishman and the Gernert Company, and Mark Siegel and
every amazing person at First Second.

TIME MUSEUM PINUPS BY

Utomaru
dddddd.moo.jp

Matt Loux
mattloux.com

Veronica Agarwal
wisbafolio.com

Alex Graudins
toonyart.com

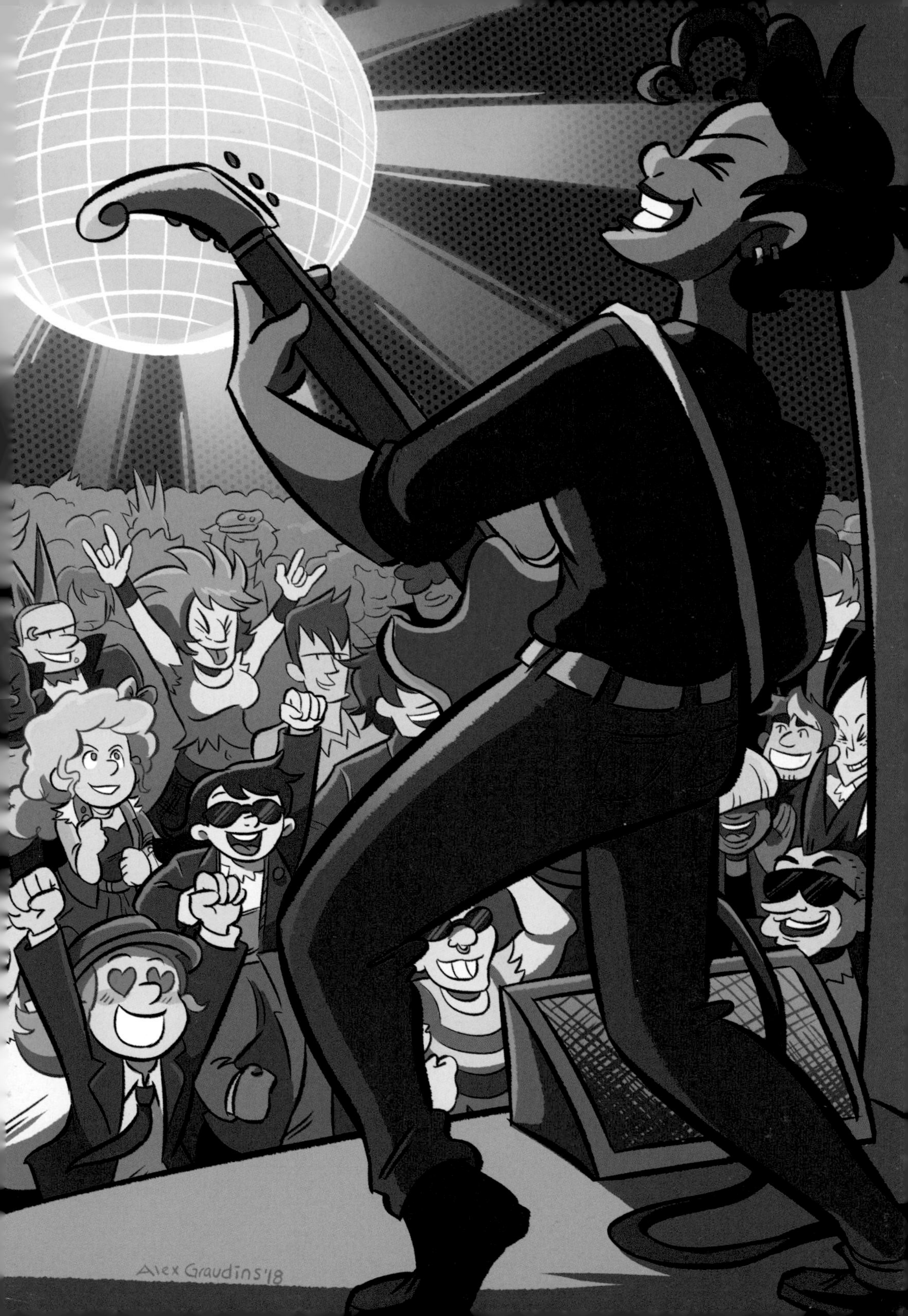
Alex Graudins '18